D1374275

TAMING CLINT WESTMORELAND

NEW YORK TIMES **BESTSELLING AUTHOR**
BRENDA JACKSON

Recycling programs
for this product may
not exist in your area.

ISBN-13: 978-1-335-40659-0

Taming Clint Westmoreland
First published in 2008. This edition published in 2022.
Copyright © 2008 by Brenda Streater Jackson

A Malibu Kind of Romance
First published in 2016. This edition published in 2022.
Copyright © 2016 by Synithia R. Williams

All rights reserved. No part of this book may be used or reproduced in
any manner whatsoever without written permission except in the case of
brief quotations embodied in critical articles and reviews.

This is a work of fiction. Names, characters, places and incidents
are either the product of the author's imagination or are used fictitiously.
Any resemblance to actual persons, living or dead, businesses,
companies, events or locales is entirely coincidental.

This edition published by arrangement with Harlequin Books S.A.

For questions and comments about the quality of this book,
please contact us at CustomerService@Harlequin.com.

Harlequin Enterprises ULC
22 Adelaide St. West, 41st Floor
Toronto, Ontario M5H 4E3, Canada
www.Harlequin.com

Printed in U.S.A.

CONTENTS

Brenda Jackson is a *New York Times* bestselling author of more than one hundred romance titles. Brenda lives in Jacksonville, Florida, and divides her time between family, writing and traveling. Email Brenda at authorbrendajackson@gmail.com or visit her on her website at brendajackson.net.

Books by Brenda Jackson

Harlequin Desire

The Westmoreland Legacy

The Rancher Returns
His Secret Son
An Honorable Seduction
His to Claim
Duty or Desire

Forged of Steele

Seduced by a Steele
Claimed by a Steele

Visit the Author Profile page at Harlequin.com for more titles.

TAMING CLINT WESTMORELAND

Brenda Jackson

ACKNOWLEDGMENTS

To Gerald Jackson, Sr., the love of my life.

To all my readers who have made the
Westmorelands a very special family in
their hearts. This book is for you!

To my Heavenly Father. How Great Thou Are.

Better a meal of vegetables where there is love than
a fattened calf with hatred.

—*Proverbs* 15:17

Chapter 1

Clint Westmoreland glanced around the airport and silently cursed. It was the middle of the day, he had a ton of work to do back at his ranch and here he stood waiting to meet a wife he hadn't known he'd had until a few days ago.

His chest tightened as he inwardly fumed, recalling the contents of the letter he'd received from the Texas State Bureau of Investigations. He'd learned from the letter that when he'd gotten married while working on an undercover sting operation five years ago as a Texas Ranger, the marriage had never been nullified by the agency. That meant that he and Alyssa Barkley, the woman who had been his female partner, were still legally married.

The thought of being married, legally or otherwise, sent a chill down his spine, and the sooner he and Alyssa could meet and get the marriage annulled the better. She

had received a similar letter and a few days ago they
had spoken on the phone. She, too, was upset about the
bureau's monumental screwup and had agreed to fly to
Austin to get the matter resolved immediately.

He glanced at his watch thinking time was being
wasted. It was the first of February and he had a shipment of wild horses due any day and needed to get things
ready at the ranch for their arrival.

When he had announced at his cousin Ian's wedding
last June that he would be leaving the Rangers after ten
years, his cousin Durango and his brother-in-law, McKinnon Quinn, had invited him to join their Montana-based,
million-dollar horse-breeding business. They wanted him
to expand their company into Texas. Clint would run the
Texas operations and become a partner in the business.
His main focus would be taming and training wild horses.

He had accepted their offer and hadn't regretted a day
of doing so. So to his way of thinking, at this moment he
had more important things he should be concentrating
on. Like making sure his horse-taming business stayed
successful.

He glanced at his watch again and then looked around
wondering if he would recognize Alyssa when he saw her.
It had been five years and the only thing he could recall
about her was that she'd been young, right out of college
with a degree in criminal justice. The two of them had
been together less than a week. That was all the time it
had taken to play the part of a young married couple who
desperately wanted to adopt a baby—illegally.

She had played the part of a despairing, wannabe
mother pretty convincingly. So much in fact that a sting
operation everyone had assumed would take a couple
of weeks to pull off had ended after the first week. Af-

terward, he had been sent on another assignment. From what he'd heard, she had turned in her resignation after deciding being a Texas Ranger wasn't what she wanted to devote her life to doing after all.

He had no idea what she'd done since then, as their phone conversation had been brief and he hadn't been inclined to even ask. He wanted the issue of their being married dealt with so they could both get on with their lives. She should be about twenty-seven now, he thought. On the phone, she'd said she was still single. Actually, he'd been surprised that she hadn't gotten married or something.

The sound of high heels clicking on the ceramic tile floor made him glance at the woman strolling in his direction. He blinked. If the woman was Alyssa, she had certainly gone through one hell of a transformation. Although she'd been far from a plain Jane before, there hadn't been anything about her to make him want to take a second look...until now.

He could definitely see her on the cover of some sexy magazine. And it was apparent that he wasn't the only person who thought so, judging by the blatant male attention she was getting. One man had the nerve to stop walking, stand in the middle of the walkway as if he were glued to the spot and openly stare at her.

Clint cut the spectator a fierce frown, which made the man quickly turn and continue walking. Then Clint felt angry with himself for momentarily losing his senses to play the part of a jealous husband, until he remembered that legally he *was* Alyssa's husband. So he had a right to get jealous if he wanted to...if that rationale at the moment made any damn sense, which it probably didn't.

He shook his head remembering how men used to have

the same reaction to his sister, Casey, and he hadn't liked
it then, either. For some reason he liked it even less now.

Alyssa was closer and the first thing he thought, besides the fact she was a looker, was that she certainly
knew how to wear a pair of jeans. Her hips swayed with
each step she took and impossible as it might seem, although he hadn't felt an attraction to her five years ago,
he was definitely feeling some strong vibes now.

He was so absorbed in checking her out that it hadn't
occurred to him just how close she was until she came
to a stop directly in front of him, up close and personal
and all in his space. Now he saw everything. The dark
eyes, long lashes, high cheekbones, full lips, head of curly
copper-colored hair and a gorgeous medium-brown face.

And he heard the sexy voice that went along with
those features when she spoke and said, "Hello, Clint.
I'm here."

She most certainly was!

He hasn't changed, Alyssa thought as she struggled
to keep up with his brisk stride as they walked together
out of the airport to the parking lot. At six-four he was
a lot taller than her five-eight height, and the black Stet-
son he wore on his head was still very much a part of
his wardrobe.

But she would admit that his face had matured in ways
that only a woman who had concentrated on it years before could notice. The first time they'd met she thought
he was more handsome than any man had a right to be,
and now at thirty-two he was even more so. Even then
she had concluded that the perfection of his features was
due to the cool, arrogant lines that underscored his eyes

and the dimples that set boldly in his cheeks—regardless of whether he smiled or not.

Then there were his chin and jaw that seemed to have been carved flawlessly, not to mention full lips that were, in her opinion, way too perfect to belong to any man. To say he hadn't made quite an impression on a fresh-out-of-college, twenty-two-year-old virgin was an understatement. The one thing she wouldn't forget was that she'd had one hell of a crush on him, just like so many other women who'd worked for the bureau.

"My truck is parked over there," he said.

His words intruded into her thoughts and she glanced up and met his gaze. "Are we going straight to the Rangers' headquarters?" she asked, trying not to make it so obvious that she was studying his lips.

Those lips were what had drawn her to him from the first. He'd been a man of few words, but his lips, whenever they had moved, had always been worth the wait. They demanded attention. And she would even go so far to say, demanded a plan of action that tempted you to taste them. Dreaming of kissing him had been something she'd done often.

Needless to say, she had been the envy of several female Rangers when she'd been the one chosen to work with him on that assignment. He was considered a private person and she seriously doubted that at the time he'd been aware of just how many women had lusted after him, or made him a constant participant in their fantasies.

"Yes, we can go straight there," he answered, breaking into the middle of her thoughts. "I figure it shouldn't take long to do what needs to be done. Hopefully no more than an hour," he said.

She was suddenly tempted to stop walking, place her

hand on his arm and lean up on tiptoes and go ahead and boldly steal a kiss. The very thought made her heart rate accelerate.

Inhaling, she tried concentrating on what he'd said. She, too, hoped that what needed to be done wouldn't take more than an hour. If she spent much more time with this man, Alyssa was certain she would lose her mind. Besides, she hadn't brought any luggage, just an overnight bag. After they took care of matters, she would check into a hotel for the night and fly back to Waco in the morning.

"So, how have you been, Alyssa?"

She glanced over at him. She knew he was trying to be cordial so she smiled accordingly, while thinking another thing he'd still retained over the years was that deep, sexy voice. "I've been doing fine, Clint. And you?"

"I can't complain."

She figured he couldn't if what she'd heard from the few friends she still had with the bureau was true. No longer a Ranger, Clint now operated a horse-breeding ranch on the outskirts of Austin on over three hundred acres of land. It was a ranch he had inherited from a close relative. And according to her sources, the horse-breeding business was doing quite well. Although she was curious as to why he had left the force, she really didn't feel comfortable enough with Clint to ask him about it. She would have sworn he'd make a career of it.

Deciding it was none of her business, she thought of something that was and said, "I can't believe the bureau would make such a mistake. The nerve of them sending that letter saying we're married."

They had reached his truck and he shrugged massive shoulders when he opened the truck door for her. "I couldn't believe it at first myself. I guess it's a good thing neither of us ever took a notion to marry."

She decided not to tell him that she *had* taken a notion a couple of years ago, and had come as close as the day of her wedding before finding out what a weasel she'd been engaged to. To this day Kevin Brady hadn't forgiven her for leaving him standing at the altar. But then she hadn't forgiven him for sleeping with her cousin Kim a week before the wedding.

From the corner of her eye she could tell that Clint was looking at her as she slid into the smooth leather seat and couldn't help wondering if he could see the heat that had risen in her cheeks denoting there was something she wasn't telling him.

"You look different than before," he said, as he casually leaned against the truck's open door.

She threw him a sharp glance at his comment and wondered if she should take what he'd said as a compliment or an insult. She decided to probe further and asked, "In what way?"

"Different."

A smile touched her cheeks. He was still a man of few words. "I am different," she admitted.

"In what way?"

She chuckled. Now he was the one asking that question. "I live my life the way I want and not the way others think that I should."

"Is that what you were doing five years ago?"

"Yes." And she figured he didn't need to know any more than that. He must have thought so, as well, because he closed the door and crossed in front of the truck to the driver's side without inquiring further.

"It will be lunchtime in a little while," he said after

easing onto the seat and closing the door shut. "Do you want to stop somewhere and grab a bite to eat before we meet with Hightower?"

Lester Hightower had been the senior captain in charge of field operations when they had done that undercover assignment five years ago. "No, I prefer that we meet with Hightower as soon as possible," she said.

He lifted a brow as he glanced over at her. "Maybe I spoke too soon earlier. If you hadn't taken a notion to get married before should I assume you might be considering such a move now?"

She stared over at him and he did something she hadn't expected. He smiled. And immediately she tried to ignore the heat that touched her body when the corners of his lips curved. "No, you can't assume that. I just don't like surprises and getting that letter was definitely a surprise."

He nodded as he broke eye contact to start the engine. "Yes, but it's one we shouldn't have a problem fixing."

"I hope you're right."

He glanced back over at her as he backed out of the parking space. "Of course I'm right. You'll see."

"What the hell do you mean we can't get the marriage annulled?" Clint all but roared. He could not have been more shocked with what Hightower had just said.

This was the first time, in all his twelve years of knowing the man, that Clint had raised his voice to his former boss. Of course, if he'd done such a thing while still a Ranger, he would have been reprimanded severely. But Hightower was no longer his superior, and Clint felt entitled to a straight answer from the man.

He glanced over at Alyssa. She had gotten out of her chair and was leaning against the closed door. He could

tell from her not-too-happy expression that she wanted
answers, as well. He frowned thinking he had known the
exact moment she had moved from the chair to stand by
the door. He had been listening to Hightower, but at the
same time he'd been very much aware of her. An uncomfortable sensation slid up his spine. He hadn't been this
fully aware of a woman in a long time.

"New procedures are in place, Westmoreland," Clint
heard Hightower say. "I don't like them nor do I understand them. And I agree the one in your particular situation doesn't make sense because proper procedures
weren't followed. But there's nothing else I can tell you.
We tried rectifying our mistake by immediately filing
for an annulment on your and Barkley's behalf, but since
so much time has passed and because the two of you no
longer work for the agency, the State is dragging their tail
in acknowledging that your marriage is not a real one."

"You're right, that doesn't make any sense," Alyssa
said sharply. "Clint and I have never lived under the same
roof. For heaven's sake, the marriage was never consummated, so that in itself should be grounds to grant an annulment."

"And under normal circumstances, it would be, but
the new person in charge of that department, a woman
by the name of Margaret Toner, thinks otherwise. From
what I understand, Toner has been married for over forty
years and takes the institution of marriage seriously. We
might not like it or understand her reasoning, but for now
we have to abide by it."

"Like hell!" Clint bit out, not believing what he was
hearing.

"Like hell or heaven, it doesn't matter," Hightower
said, throwing a document on the desk. "Thirty days.

Toner has agreed to grant an annulment to your and Barkley's marriage in thirty days."

Neither Clint nor Alyssa said anything for a long moment, both figuring it was best not to, otherwise they would say the wrong thing. Instead they decided to keep the anger they felt inside. But then finally, as if accepting the finality of their situation, Alyssa spoke. "I don't like it, Hightower, but if nothing can be done about it for thirty days, there's little Clint and I can do. It's been five years without me even knowing I was a married woman, so I guess another thirty days won't kill me," she said, glancing over at Clint.

He frowned. Although it wouldn't kill him, either, he didn't like it one damn bit. He enjoyed being a bachelor although unlike his brother, Cole, he'd never earned the reputation of being a ladies' man. But Alyssa was right, they had been married five years without either of them knowing it, so another thirty days would not make or break them. There was nothing in his life that would be changing.

"Fine," he all but snapped. "Like Alyssa, I'll deal with it for thirty more days."

"There's one more thing," Hightower hesitated a few moments before saying.

Clint's frown deepened. He had worked with the man long enough to detect something in his voice, something Clint figured he wouldn't like. Evidently, Alyssa picked up on it, as well, and moved away from the door to come and stand beside him.

"What other thing?" Clint asked.

Hightower shrugged massive shoulders nervously. "Not sure how the two of you are going to feel about it, but Toner wouldn't back down or change her mind about it."

"About what?" Clint asked in an agitated voice.

Hightower looked at him and then at Alyssa. "In order for the marriage to get annulled after the thirty days, there is something the two of you must do."

Clint felt his heart turn over. He felt another strange sensation slither up his spine. He knew, without a doubt, that he wouldn't like whatever Hightower was about to say. "And just what does Toner want us to do?" he asked, trying to keep his voice calm.

Hightower cleared his throat and then said, "She has mandated that during those thirty days the two of you live under the same roof."

Chapter 2

It didn't take much to figure out that Clint Westmoreland was one angry man, Alyssa thought, glancing over at him. They had left Hightower's office over twenty minutes ago, and now Clint was driving her to a place where she assumed they would grab a bite to eat. But he had yet to say one word to her. Not one. However, that didn't take into consideration the number of times he'd mumbled the word *damn* under his breath.

Sighing deeply, she decided to brave the icy waters and said, "Surely there's something we can do."

He speared her with a look that could probably freeze boiling water and his mouth was set in a grim line. However, to her his lips still looked as delectable as a slice of key lime pie. "You heard what he said, Alyssa. We can try to appeal, but if we're not successful we will still have to do the thirty days, which will only delay things," he said.

Do the thirty days. He'd made it sound like a jail sentence. And since he would have to share the same roof with her, she wasn't sure she particularly liked his attitude. She didn't like what Hightower had said any more than he did, but there was no reason to get rude about it.

"Look," she said. "I don't like this any more than you do, but if we can't change things then we need to do what Toner is requiring and—"

"The hell I will," he said almost in a growl when he looked back at her. He had pulled into the parking lot of a restaurant and had brought his truck to a stop. "I have more to do with my time for the next thirty days than entertain you."

She immediately saw red. "Entertain me? From saying that, I guess you're assuming if we do decide to live together for the next thirty days it will be here at your place."

He shrugged as if to ease the tension in his shoulders and said, "Of course."

She frowned. He sounded so sure and confident. She would take joy in bursting his bubble. "Wrong. I have no intention of staying here in Austin with you."

His eyes narrowed into slits as he continued to glare at her. "And just where do you assume you'll stay?"

She glared back. "It's not where I'll stay but where you'll stay. I'm returning to Waco and if you want to fulfill the terms of Toner's decree you will, too."

If she thought he was mad before then it was quite obvious he was madder now. "Look, lady. I have a ranch to run and I won't be doing it from Waco."

"You're not the only one who owns a business, Clint. I'm not going to drop everything that's going on in my life just to come out here to live with you."

"And neither will I drop everything I've got going on here to move to Waco, even temporarily. That's as stupid as stupid can get."

She had to agree with him there, but still that didn't solve their problem. According to Hightower, they needed to live under the same roof for thirty days, which meant that one of them had to compromise. But she didn't feel it should be her and evidently he didn't think it should be him, either. "Okay, you don't want to move to Waco and I don't want to move here, so what do you suggest we do to get that annulment?" she asked him.

He pulled his key out of the truck's ignition and said, "I don't know, but what I do know is that I think better on a full stomach." He opened the door to get out. "Right now I suggest that we get something to eat."

By the time the waitress had taken their order, Clint was convinced that somebody up there didn't like him. If they did, they would not have dumped Alyssa Barkley in his lap. The woman was too much of a tempting package and someone he didn't have time to deal with. The thought of her living under his roof, or for that matter, him living under hers, was too much too imagine. But he had been a Ranger long enough to know just how tangled red tape could get. Someone had screwed up. Otherwise they wouldn't still be married—at least on paper. As she'd told Hightower, the marriage hadn't even been consummated. It had been an assignment, nothing more.

"You're a triplet, right?"

He glanced at her over the rim of his glass. "Yes. How do you know that?"

She shrugged. "It was common knowledge among the

Rangers. I met your brother, Cole, once. He was nice. I also heard you have a sister."

"I do," he said, thinking about Casey, who had gotten married a few months ago. "If you go by order of birth, then I'm the oldest, then Cole and last Casey."

"Is Cole still a Texas Ranger?"

He figured she must feel a little more relaxed to be asking so many questions. "Yes, he is."

He didn't know her well enough to reveal that Cole's days with the Rangers were numbered. Like him, Cole planned to go out on early retirement; however, Cole hadn't decided what he'd do after leaving the force. Clint wasn't even sure if Cole planned to stay in Texas. His brother might take a notion to move to Montana like Casey had done to be near their father. The father the three of them thought was dead until a few years ago.

He took a sip of his coffee. In a way he knew what Alyssa was doing. She was trying to get his mind off the gigantic problem that was looming over their heads. But the bottom line was that they needed to talk about it and make some decisions. "Okay, Alyssa, getting back to our dilemma. What about you? Do you have any suggestions?"

She took a sip of her coffee and smiled before saying, "I guess I could go back to Waco and you remain here and forget we ever found out we were married and leave things as they are. As I said earlier, marriage isn't in my future anytime soon. What about yours?"

"Not in mine, either, but still, having a wife isn't something I can forget about," he said. *Several things could happen later to make him remember he was a married man.*

For example, what would happen if she decided, as

his wife, that she was entitled to half of everything he owned? His partnership with his cousin and brother-in-law was going extremely well. Not saying that she would, but he couldn't take any chances. He had bought out Casey's and Cole's shares of the ranch and now it was totally his. The last thing he would tolerate was a "wife" staking a claim on anything that had his name on it.

And then there was the other reason he wouldn't be able to forget he had a wife. She was too damn pretty. Her features were too striking and her body was too well-stacked. Even now sitting across from her at the table he could feel his temperature rise. Since he figured she hadn't gotten that way overnight, he wondered how he had missed noticing how good she looked five years ago. The only excuse he could come up with was that at the time he'd been too heavily involved with Chantelle and only had eyes for one woman. Too bad Chantelle hadn't had eyes for just one man.

"There has to be a way out of this," she said, interrupting his thoughts with a disgusted look on her face. Disgusted or otherwise, her frustration didn't downplay how full and firm her lips were, or how her eyes were so dark they reminded him of a raven's wing. He wondered if her copper-brown hair was her natural color and he felt a tug in his gut when he thought of the one way he could easily find out. He shifted in his seat. His jeans suddenly felt a little too tight, especially in the area of his zipper.

Evidently she was waiting for him to respond, because her dark eyes were staring at him. He leaned back in his chair. "There is a way. We just have to think of it."

Alyssa could feel Clint checking her out the same way she was checking him out, which only solidified her belief that living under the same roof with him wouldn't work. There was a strong sexual attraction between them, she could feel it. The thought that she drew his interest was something she couldn't ignore. Nor was it something for her to lose any sleep over. Plenty of women probably drew his attention. He was a man wasn't he? Hadn't Uncle Jessie explained after finding out what Kim and Kevin had done that when it came to women all men were weak? They often made decisions with the "wrong head." Of course, he couldn't come up with an excuse for Kim's behavior because she was his daughter.

"What sort of business do you own?"

She glanced up from studying the contents in her coffee cup to stare into Clint's cool, dark eyes. "I design Web sites."

"Oh."

She frowned. He'd said it as though he considered her profession of no importance. Granted it wasn't a mega-million-dollar operation like she'd heard he owned but it was hers; one she'd started a few years ago with all the money she had. She enjoyed her work and was proud of the way she'd built up her company. She had a very nice clientele who depended on her to keep their businesses in the forefront of the cyberspace market. Over the years she had won numerous awards for her Web site designs.

"For your information I own a very successful business," she said, glaring at him.

He glared back. "I don't recall saying you didn't."

No, he hadn't. But still, she really didn't care much for his attitude. "Look, Clint. You're agitated about this whole thing and so am I. I think the best thing for us to do is sleep on it. Maybe we'll have answers in the morning."

"Fine. I noticed you only brought an overnight bag," he said, leaning back in his chair.

"Yes. I thought that ending our marriage wouldn't take more than a day at the most. I planned to fly home in the morning."

"You're welcome to stay at my place tonight. I have plenty of room."

She appreciated the invitation but didn't think it was a good idea. "Thanks, but I prefer staying at a hotel."

"Suit yourself," he said, easing back up to the table when their waitress placed a plate full of food in front of him. Alyssa watched him dig in. He'd said he could think better on a full stomach, but was he really going to eat all that? She couldn't imagine him eating such hefty meals as the norm, especially since he had such a well-built body that was all muscle and no fat.

"Why are you staring at my plate?"

She shrugged. "That's a lot of food," she said when the waitress placed a sandwich and bowl of soup in front of her.

He laughed. "I'm still growing. Besides, I need all this to keep my strength up. What I do around the ranch is hard work."

"And what exactly do you do?"

He smiled over at her. "I'm a horse tamer. I have some of my men stationed out in Nevada. They capture wild horses then ship them to my ranch for me to tame. Once that's done, I ship them to Montana. My cousin and brother-in-law own a horse-breeding company. My sister works for them as a trainer."

"Sounds like a family affair."

"It is."

Alyssa intentionally kept her head lowered as she ate

her sandwich and soup. She didn't want to risk looking head-on into Clint's eyes again. Each time she did so made every cell in her body vibrate.

"I'm thinking of getting one of those."

She raised her head and gazed at him, trying not to zero in on his handsome features, while at the same time ignoring the sensations that flowed through her. "Getting one of what?"

"A Web site."

She lifted a brow. "You don't have one already?"

"No."

"Why not?"

"Why would I?"

"Mainly to promote your business."

"Don't have to. Durango and McKinnon are in charge of bringing in the customers. We have a private clientele."

"Oh. Who are Durango and McKinnon?"

He wiped his mouth with a napkin before answering. "Durango is my cousin and McKinnon is married to my sister, Casey. They are my partners and the ones who started the horse-breeding company. Now it has grown to include horse training and horse taming," he said.

She nodded. "If you did just fine without a Web site before, then why are you thinking about getting one now?"

He actually looked like he was tired of answering her questions. His tone indicated that he was only answering her in an attempt to be polite. "Because of the foundation I recently started."

"What foundation?"

"The Sid Roberts Foundation." And as if he was preparing for her next question, he said, "He was my uncle."

Her eyes widened. "Sid Roberts? The Sid Roberts? Was your uncle?" she asked incredulously.

"Yes," he responded, seemingly again with barely tolerant patience. And then as if he'd had enough of her questions he said, "Why don't you finish eating. Your soup is getting cold."

At least he had gotten her to stop talking, Clint thought, taking a sip of his coffee. Although he noticed what she was eating wasn't much. He'd thought Casey was the only person who considered soup and a sandwich a full-course meal.

Clint leaned back in his chair. The food was great and he was full, so now he could think. Yet he was far from having an answer to their problem. Part of him wanted to start the appeal process and see what would happen. But if the appeal failed, they would have to do the thirty days anyway.

"You didn't say why you are establishing a foundation for your uncle."

He glanced over at her. "Didn't I?" he asked tersely. He couldn't recall her being this chatty before. In fact, he remembered her as a mousy young woman who didn't seem to have the fortitude for her job as a Ranger. Although truth be told, he would be the first to give her an A for her acting abilities during their assignment together.

He couldn't help noticing how the sunlight shining through the window hit her hair at an angle that gave the copper strands a golden tint. He felt a sudden tingling sensation right smack in his gut. He didn't like the feeling. Since becoming partners with Durango and McKinnon nine months ago, he had placed his social life—and women—on hold.

"No, you didn't," she said, breaking into his thoughts and seemingly not the least put off by his cool tone.

He didn't say anything for a while and then asked, "What do you know about Sid Roberts?"

She smiled. "Only what's in the history books, as well as what my grandfather shared with me."

He lifted a brow. "Your grandfather?"

"Yes, he was a huge Sid Roberts fan and even claimed to being a part of the rodeo circuit with him at one time. I know Mr. Roberts was a legend in his day. First as a rodeo star then as a renowned horse trainer."

"Uncle Sid loved horses and passed that love on to me, my brother and sister. In my uncle's memory, we have dedicated over three thousand acres of land on the south ridge of my property as a reserve. A great number of the wild horses that are being shipped to me are being turned loose to roam free here."

"Why go to the trouble of relocating them here? Why not leave them in Nevada and let them run free there?"

He frowned. "Mainly because wild horses are taking up land that's now needed for public use. Legislation is being considered that will allow for so many of them to be destroyed each year. Many of these wild horses are getting slaughtered for pet food."

"That's awful," she murmured and he knew she was deliberately lowering her voice to keep out the anger she felt. It was the same with him every time he thought about it.

"Yes, it is. So I've established the foundation as a way to save as many of the wild horses as I can by bringing them here."

He felt they had gotten off track, and had put on the back burner the subject they really needed to be discussing. "So what are we going to do, Alyssa, about our marriage?"

She frowned. "You make it sound like a real one when it's not."

"Then tell that to Toner. And maybe it's time to accept that regardless of where we want to place the blame, legally we are man and wife."

Alyssa opened her mouth to deny what he said, but couldn't. He was right. They could sit and blame others but that wouldn't solve their problem. "Okay, you have a full stomach, what do you suggest?"

"You're not going to like it."

"Probably not if it's what I'm thinking."

He sighed deeply. "Do we have a choice?"

She knew they didn't but still… "There has to be another way."

"According to Hightower, there isn't. You heard him for yourself."

"I say let's fight it."

"And I say let's just do what we have to do and get it over with."

She nibbled on her bottom lip. "Fine, but there's still the issue of where we'll stay. Here or Waco." Each knew how the other felt on the subject. Alyssa knew she was being hard-nosed. To handle his business properly, he would have to be on his ranch, whereas she could operate just about anywhere, as long as she had her computer and server.

"Alyssa?"

She glanced up at him. "Yes?"

"I'm sure you prefer handling your business from Waco, but is there any reason you can't do it here if I help get things set up for you?" he asked, evidently thinking along the same lines as she had earlier.

She decided to be honest with him. "No."

"All right. Then will you?" he asked. "My ranch isn't all that bad. It's pretty nice actually. And with the hours I work, I'd barely be home most of the time so it will be as if you have the place to yourself. I won't be underfoot."

She tilted her head to study him. In other words they really wouldn't be under the same roof for thirty days—at least not all the time. In a way, she would prefer it that way. Being around Clint 24/7 would be too hard to handle. But she knew he was right. They had to do something and since it was easier for her to make the change why sweat it. That didn't mean she had to like it. At least the two of them were working together and doing what needed to be done to get their lives back on track and end what had been the agency's screwup and not theirs. But still…

"What about a steady girlfriend?" she decided to ask.

"Don't have one, steady or otherwise. Don't have the time."

She lifted a brow. *When did men stop making the time for women?* She thought they lived for intimacy.

"What about you?" he asked her. "Is there a steady man in your life?"

She thought about the occasional calls she got from Kevin as he tried to make a comeback, as if she didn't know that he and Kim were still messing around with each other. Kim took pleasure in making comments every once in a while to let her know she and Kevin were still seeing each other now and then. "No, like you, I don't have the time."

He nodded. "So, there's really nothing holding us back to do what we need to do to get the matter resolved," he said.

If only it were that simple, she wanted to say. Instead she said, "I need to sleep on it." She preferred not to make a decision right then.

"Okay. In that case would you mind doing your sleeping at the ranch?" Clint asked. "That way, you can check out the place to see if it will work for you."

She'd rather not stay at his ranch tonight but what he'd said made sense. She was used to living in the city. She wasn't sure how she would handle being out in such a rural setting. "Okay, Clint. I'll spend the night at your ranch and will give you my decision about things in the morning."

He tilted his head and looked at her. "I can't ask for any more than that."

Chapter 3

"Can you ride a horse?"

Alyssa glanced over at Clint. Sunlight streaming in through the windshield seemed to highlight his features. It had been bad enough sitting across from him at the diner trying to eat. Now they were back in the close quarters of his truck and everything male about him was out in the forefront again. She moved her gaze from his face to the strong, sturdy hands that were gripping the steering wheel, and then lower to his lap where the denim of his jeans stretched tight across muscular thighs.

"Alyssa?"

She nearly jumped when he said her name again, reminding her that she hadn't answered his question. "Yes and no."

He glanced over at her and frowned. "You either can or you can't."

"Not necessarily. There's another option—can and don't. Yes, I can ride a horse, but I choose not to."

He gave her a strange look. "Is there a reason why?"

"Yes. What if I say that horses don't like me?"

He gave a half laugh. "Then I'd say that if you feel that way it means you haven't developed your own personal technique of dealing with them. A horse can detect a lot from people. Whether you're too aggressive, too nice, sometimes both. A horse is the most easy-going animal that I know of."

"Yeah, you would say that since you tame them," she said, glancing out the truck window and thinking how beautiful the land was getting the farther they got away from the city.

"I'd say it even if I didn't tame them. If you stay at the ranch I guarantee you will develop a liking for horses."

"I never said I didn't like them, Clint. It's just I've been thrown off one too many times to suit my fancy. I know when to give in and quit."

He chuckled. "I don't. And if I stopped riding based on the number of times I've been thrown, I would have given up riding years ago. That's part of it. Learning to ride with the intent of staying on."

Alyssa heard what he was saying but it wouldn't change her mind. The truck had come to a stop and she glanced over at Clint. He was staring at her in a way that had her pulse racing, was making her feel breathless. A brazen image formed in her mind. "What?" she asked in a low voice.

It was as if that one single word made him realize that he'd been staring and when the truck began moving again, he muttered, "Nothing."

It was there on the tip of Alyssa's tongue to say yes,

it had been something and she had felt it, too, in the cozy space surrounding them. As she glanced back out the window, she thought that living on a ranch with him wouldn't be easy. The only good thing was that he'd said he would be gone most of the time. That was good to know for her peace of mind.

"Will your family have a problem with it?"

She glanced back over at him. He was staring straight ahead and she thought that was good. Every time he looked at her, sensations she hadn't felt in a long time, or ever, seemed to unleash inside of her. "A problem with what?" she asked, thinking she liked the sound of his voice a little too much.

"Living with me for a while at the ranch. That is if you decide to do it."

Alyssa sighed. There was no need to go into any details that certain members of her family wouldn't care if she left Waco for good. It was all too complicated to get into and too personal to explain. That was the only good thing about the thirty days. Time away from Waco was probably what she needed. Ruining her wedding day hadn't been enough for Kim. She was determined to sabotage any decent thing that came into Alyssa's life. "No, they wouldn't have a problem with it," she finally answered. "What about your folks?"

He glanced over at her and smiled and that single smile ignited a torch within her. She actually felt heat flowing through her body. "My family is fine with whatever I do. My brother, sister and I are extremely close but we know when to give each other space and when to mind our own business." He then chuckled and the sound raked across her skin in a sensuous sort of way.

"Okay, I admit when it came to Casey, Cole and I

never did mind our own business. We felt she was our responsibility, especially during her dating years. But now that she's married to McKinnon all is well," he added.

"Have they been married long?"

He shook his head. "Since the end of November. Cole and I couldn't ask for a better man for our sister."

Alyssa smiled. "That's a nice thing to say."

"It's the truth. Although we do sympathize with him most of the time. Casey can be pretty damn headstrong so McKinnon has his work cut out for him."

"So your immediate family consists of your brother and your sister?"

"We used to think that. My mother was Uncle Sid's sister and she came to live with him at the ranch when her husband was supposedly killed during a rodeo and she was left carrying triplets."

Alyssa slanted him a confused look. "*Supposedly* was killed?"

"Yes, that's the story she and Uncle Sid fabricated for everyone when in fact our father was very much alive. However, she felt she was doing him a favor by not telling him she was pregnant and disappearing. So Cole, Casey and I grew up believing our father was dead."

"When did you find out differently?"

"On Mom's deathbed. She wanted us to know the truth."

Alyssa immediately recalled her grandfather's deathbed confession. He'd revealed that he was her biological father and not her grandfather. It had been a confession that had changed her life forever, one that had caused jealousy within the family—a family that had never been close anyway. "What happened after that?"

He smiled over at her and she knew what he was thinking. She asked a lot of questions. Gramps would always tell her that, too. Thinking of the man whom for years she'd thought of as her grandfather sent a warm feeling through her.

"After that, Cole and I decided to find our father and develop a relationship with him. We knew it wouldn't be easy, considering we would be a surprise to him and the fact that we were grown men in our late twenties."

That hadn't been too long ago, she mused, considering he was thirty-two now. Probably around the same time she had been learning the truth about her own parentage. "Did you find him?"

He gave another chuckle, this one just as sensitive to her flesh as the other had been. "Yes, we found him, all right. And we found something else right along with him."

"What?"

"A slew of cousins we didn't know we had. Westmorelands from just about everywhere. We suddenly found ourselves part of a big family and it was a family that welcomed us with open arms. They've made us feel as if we were a part of them so quickly it was almost overwhelming."

Alyssa studied the sound of his voice and could tell that even now for him it was still overwhelming. He was blessed to be a part of such a loving and giving group. There, however, was one thing she'd noted. He hadn't mentioned how his sister had taken the revelation of the missing father.

"Your sister, how did she handle meeting her father for the first time?" she asked.

A part of her needed to know. She knew how she had handled it when she'd discovered that Isaac Barkley was her father and not her grandfather. A part of her had wished he would have told her sooner. That would have explained a lot of things and then the two of them would have been able to face the jealousy and hatred together. But he had died, leaving her all alone.

"It was harder for Casey to come around and accept things. She'd believed what Mom had told us all those years. She wasn't ready to meet a father who was very much alive. It took her a while to form a relationship with him, but that's all in the past now. In fact she moved to Montana to be close to him. She met McKinnon there and fell in love."

Alyssa sighed. A part of her wished she could find someone and fall in love but she knew that wouldn't be possible as long as Kimberly Barkley still existed on this earth. Kimberly was determined to destroy whatever bit of happiness came Alyssa's way.

"This is the entrance to the ranch, Alyssa."

Alyssa leaned forward and glanced out the windshield and side windows and caught her breath. What she saw all around her was spellbinding. Simply breathtaking. She had lived on a small ranch in Houston for the first thirteen years of her life and had loved it. Then one day, her mother had sent her away to live with her grandfather in the city. That was probably the one most decent thing her mother had ever done in her life.

"It's beautiful, Clint. How big is it?" Everywhere she looked she saw ranges, fields and meadows. She couldn't imagine waking up to this view every morning, every single day.

"If you include the reserve on the south ridge it's over fifty thousand acres. Uncle Sid was a ladies' man who never married and so he left the ranch to me, Cole and Casey."

Alyssa nodded. She didn't want to consider the possibility, didn't want to imagine how it would feel for once to not have to worry about Kim dropping in just make her life a living hell. The truck, she noticed, had stopped, and she lifted a brow as she glanced over at Clint.

He smiled. "I want to show you something."

He got out of the truck and she followed and he led her close to a cliff. "Look down there," he said, pointing.

And she did. It was then that she saw his ranch, sitting down in the valley below. It was huge, a monstrosity of a house that was surrounded by several barns and other buildings. There was a corral full of horses and she could barely see the figures of men below who were working with the horses. "It's absolutely stunning, Clint," she said, turning to him. It was then that she became aware of just how close they were standing, of the heat his closeness had generated and how the darkening of his eyes was beginning to stir a caress across her flesh.

She moved to take a step back and his hand reached out to her waist, to assist her, or so it seemed. But his hand stayed there and his touch burned her skin through the thin material of her blouse. Her gaze left his eyes and moved to his lips, the one part of him that had always fascinated her. The fullness of them made her imagine just how they would feel on hers. She thought they would be soft to the touch at first, but they would become demanding and hungry as soon as they connected with hers.

She wasn't a forward person, but one thing Gramps had always taught her was that sometimes, if it was something you really wanted, you just had to take the bull by the horns. Well, she intended to do just that.

He was bending his head toward her, or maybe she imagined that he was doing so. And just to be sure, she leaned forward and slid her hands over his chest. The first touch of his lips on hers sent pleasure points in her body on high alert and when she parted her lips on a sigh, he entered her mouth in one delicious sweep.

He tasted hot. He tasted like a man. And she settled into his kiss as if it was her right to do so. With their mouths locked together, their tongues tangled, stroked and slid everywhere. And then in a move she would have thought was impossible, he thrust his tongue deeper inside her mouth, causing her to instinctively latch on to it, suck it and stroke it some more. This was what you called total mouth concentration, the solicitation of participation and the promise of satisfaction. Everything was there in this kiss. And Clint Westmoreland was delivering in a way that made the quiet existence she had carved out for herself the last two years a waste of good time and energy.

The kiss was incredible, she thought, sinking deeper into it. She might have regrets later but now she needed this. Her entire body felt as if this was what she was supposed to be doing. And considering this was the first day she had seen him in over five years, the very thought of that was crazy and…

Clint abruptly broke off the kiss. He drew much-needed air into his lungs and fought the urgent pull in his loins. *How had he let this happen? Where was that control he was famous for? Where was his will to deny anything he thought might threaten his livelihood?*

He didn't say anything to Alyssa. He just stood there and stared at her while trying to get the rampant beating of his heart under control. Trying to fight the sensations overtaking him. She had been kissing him as passionately as he had been kissing her. At first her lack of kissing experience had surprised him, but she was a quick study. The moment his tongue came into play, she'd allowed hers to do the same, and without any hesitation.

"Okay, Clint, what was all that about?" she asked in a quiet tone.

She was staring at him while licking her lips. The intimate gesture made his stomach clench. "I think," he murmured, "that I should ask you the same thing. That wasn't a kiss taken, Alyssa, but one that was shared."

He waited for her to deny his words but she didn't. Instead she turned away from him and glanced back down to look at his ranch house. And before she could ask he said, "I'll promise to keep my desire under wraps for the next thirty days."

For a moment she didn't say anything, didn't make a move to even acknowledge that he had spoken. And then she looked back at him and at that moment a wave of desire, more intense than anything he'd ever encountered, raced through him.

"Can you?" she asked softly.

Holding her gaze, he was having a hard time keeping up. "Can I what?"

"Bottle your desire for thirty days." He watched as she inhaled deeply, drew herself up as if she was trying to take back control of the situation and he saw her eyes go from sensuous to serious. "I need to know before I make any decision about staying here with you."

He frowned. Was she afraid of him? He covered the distance separating them and came to a stop in front of her. Forcing her to look up at him, become the main focus of her attention. "Let me explain one thing about me, Alyssa," he said in a voice that he knew had her complete attention. "You don't have anything to fear if you stay here, least of all me. You set the boundaries and I will abide by them. I don't have a woman in my life right now, nor do I need one. What you see down there is my life. You are my wife in name only. I will remember that. I will respect that. But after the thirty days I expect you to go, just like I'm sure you'll want to leave. I don't have time for involvements. The only thing long-term in my life is this ranch and the running of it and the foundation. Those things are all I need. They are all I want."

At his blunt words she asked, "Then why did you kiss me?"

Clint saw her eyes were flashing and knew she was beginning to take what he was saying personally. "The reason *we* kissed each other," he said slowly, "is because of a number of things. Curiosity. Need. Desire. It was best that we took care of all three before we got to the ranch. Trust me, you won't become an itch that I'll be tempted to scratch."

Alyssa frowned, not sure she liked the way he'd said that. Had he found her kiss so lacking that he'd not be tempted to do it again? Kim had always said when it came to men she presented no appeal, or that she wouldn't recognize pleasure if it came up to her and bit her. Clint had certainly made a liar out of her cousin. Under his lips she had definitely recognized pleasure. She had actually drowned in it.

"Now," he said, interrupting her thoughts. "Do you want to go down to the ranch with me or would you prefer that I take you back into town?"

She glared at him. "I haven't made up my mind about anything."

"I didn't say you had. I just want you to have peace of mind in doing so."

Behind Clinton's terse words, she suspected he was low on tolerance. But then she'd come to that same conclusion earlier at the diner. She glanced down the valley at the ranch and then she glanced back at Clint. "I'm still staying at the ranch for the night."

"Then let's go. I've got plenty to do when I get there."

When they got back in the truck and he turned the ignition, she glanced out the window when the truck started moving. She had gotten her real taste of passion from the man who was her husband—at least on paper. And she had surrendered without thought or hesitation.

For some reason she sensed a wild streak in Clint, one that he probably didn't even know was there. A wildness she detected, one that had almost come out in their kiss. As far as she was concerned the man had desire bottled and it was fighting to become uncorked. If it ever broke free she didn't want to think of the consequences, the combustion or the fiery, hot passion.

And if that happened, was there a woman in this world who would be able to tame Clint Westmoreland? she wondered.

Chapter 4

Inviting Alyssa to spend the night at the ranch wasn't the smartest thing he'd ever done, Clint decided.

From the cliff the ranch house looked huge. But when you stood directly in front of it and got a close-up view, you got a clear picture of just how spacious it was. He hoped Alyssa would decide that in a house as large as his they could easily avoid each other for four short weeks.

The front door opened and Chester walked out. The man, who for years had been Clint's cook, housekeeper, and if there was need, ranch hand, was big. He stood at least six-four and weighed over two hundred and fifty pounds. At sixty-five he looked intimidating and mean as a bear. Once you got to know him, however, it didn't take long to see he was as soft and easygoing as a teddy bear.

Clint knew that Chester considered himself a surrogate father to the triplets. The old man was quick to brag that he'd helped Doc Shaw deliver the three. For that reason—in Clint's opinion—Chester lived under the false assumption that he knew what was best for them. He had been the one to convince Clint and Cole to find the father they hadn't known they had, and the one to talk Casey into building a relationship with their father.

And now with Casey happily married and living in Montana, Chester was on a bandwagon to get Clint and Cole to follow suit. He felt marriage should be in their future plans, the not-so-distant future. Chester claimed he wanted them to find the bliss he'd found in his own happy marriage of over thirty years. His beloved wife Ada died a few years ago. Even now everyone still missed the presence of the gentle and kind woman who had been the love of Chester's life.

Clint saw the way Chester was sizing Alyssa up. The old man was trying to see if she appeared sturdy enough to handle the roughness of a working ranch, and if she had enough brawn to handle Clint. According to Chester, the Golden Glade Ranch needed a mistress who was strong in both mind and body. Clint knew Chester believed Clint needed a woman who could take him on with fortitude.

He had told Chester that morning about the agency's mistake. Now he dreaded telling the old man he and Alyssa were being forced to live as man and wife for thirty days. Chester would somehow see such a thing as a sign that somebody up there was trying to tell Clint something. Clint easily recognized the calculating look in Chester's eyes and frowned.

"I know I've said it already, Clint, but your home is beautiful," Alyssa said.

Alyssa's words reclaimed Clint's attention. He moved

his gaze from Chester and back to her. The side of her face was highlighted by the sun. The soft glow of her features made him remember their kiss and how good she had tasted. Even now he wouldn't mind devouring her mouth again, relishing her taste once more. She glanced over at him and he felt a fierce tug in his stomach. He didn't like the feeling one damn bit.

Knowing she expected a response from him, he said, "Thanks. Let me introduce you to Chester and then I'll show you around."

As if impatient for an introduction, Chester came down the steps and went directly to Alyssa, offered her his hand and gave a half laugh and said, "Welcome to the Golden Glade. So you're Clint's wife. We're mighty glad to have you." Before she could respond he added, "And you're just what Clint needs around here."

And at that moment, Clint actually felt like slugging him.

The man's words drew Alyssa up short. It was true that she and Clint were legally married, but as far as she was concerned it was nothing more than a mistake on paper. A mistake that needed to be rectified. But a comment like that made her aware of the seriousness of their situation and just how quickly they needed to resolve the matter.

Not sure how to respond to Chester, Alyssa decided not to address his statement of their marital status and to accept his comment on the ranch by saying, "It's a beautiful ranch."

Clint had walked around the truck and appeared at her side. She glanced up at him and saw he was frowning at the older man. Evidently he hadn't appreciated the reminder of their situation, either.

"Thanks, and Clint is doing a fine job keeping it that way," Chester said. "But what I've told him numerous times is that what this ranch needs is a—"

"Alyssa, this is Chester. Cook and housekeeper," Clint said, smoothly interrupting whatever it was the older man had been about to say.

Not to be outdone the man merely nodded. "What this ranch needs is a woman's touch," he said as if he had not been interrupted.

Alyssa's thoughts began to whirl. *Why would Chester make such a comment? Didn't he know that her and Clint's marriage wasn't real?* She gave a quick glance at Clint but his features were unreadable. Deciding it wasn't her place to meddle in what was going on between Clint and one of his employees, she turned her attention back to Chester and said, "It's nice meeting you, Chester."

The man gave her a huge smile. "No, Alyssa, it is nice meeting *you*. Come on in and I'll show you around."

"No, I'll be showing Alyssa around," Clint said.

Both Alyssa and Chester turned to Clint. "I thought you had a lot of work to do," Chester said.

Alyssa had thought the very same thing and watched as Clint shrugged massive shoulders before he said, "What I have to do can wait."

Alyssa glanced back at Chester and for a quick second she could have sworn she'd seen a sparkle in the old man's eyes. "Suit yourself then," Chester said. "I need to start dinner, anyway." And then Alyssa watched as the older man gave her a final smile before going back into the house.

"I'll take you to the guest room you'll be using before giving you a tour," Clint said.

Alyssa turned in time to see Clint walk over to the

truck to get her overnight bag. She inclined her head as she continued to watch him. The man had such a sensuous walk, she thought.

As if he'd felt her eyes on him, he turned with a concerned look on his face. "Is everything all right, Alyssa?" he asked quietly.

She suddenly felt the need to hug her arms and protect herself from his intense gaze, but she didn't. Instead she appreciated his thoughtful consideration. No one had asked if everything was all right with her since her grandfather's death. "Yes, I'm fine. Thanks for asking," she said.

He only nodded before opening the truck door to pull out her bag. He then turned and walked back toward her. She knew that he was uncomfortable with the situation they had been placed in and he didn't like it any more than she did. But, they would work things out. She'd discovered five years ago that Clint Westmoreland was a man who could handle just about anything that came his way. She saw that strength in him and admired him for it.

"Come this way," he said. She noticed he had come to a stop directly in front of her. His closeness caused her to breathe unevenly and she swallowed deeply to get control of her emotions. It wasn't as if they hadn't spent time together before. While working that assignment five years ago, for one full week they'd been almost glued at the hip, trying to make their cover believable. They'd even shared a hotel room—although at night she would take the bed and he would crash on the sofa. But still they had shared close quarters and although she had been fully aware of him as a man, his presence hadn't affected her like it did now.

It seemed she was now more aware of the opposite

sex. Actually, in this case, she was more aware of Clint Westmoreland. She had been fascinated with him when they'd worked together, but now he took her breath away. And back then she had been so focused on doing a good job on her first assignment as a Ranger that everything else, including Clint, had been secondary. But that was not the case now. *How on earth would she survive under the same roof with this man for thirty days?*

He opened the door for her and then stood back for her to enter. Her stomach knotted and she felt her senses tingling. She had a feeling that once she walked over the threshold her life would never be the same.

Steeling himself, Clint watched as Alyssa entered his home. He couldn't recall the last time he had been so fully aware of a woman to the point that everything about her—even her scent was registering in his mind— seemed branded onto his brain cells.

If she decided to stay the thirty days, she would only be here for a short while, he reminded himself. He could handle that. His work days at the ranch were long and grueling. If he just kept his mind on the job at hand— running the ranch and keeping his uncle's legacy alive— he would be fine.

His thoughts shifted back to Alyssa as he watched her stand in the middle of his living room glancing around. She seemed in awe, incapable of speaking. Had she thought just because he spent most of his time outdoors that he didn't appreciate having nice things indoors?

"Everything is so beautiful," she said in a low voice when she began to speak.

He wasn't reluctant to agree and said thanks. "I hired

an interior decorator to do her thing throughout the house. Especially in the guest rooms."

She glanced over at him. "Do you get a lot of visitors?"

He chuckled. "Yes. The Westmoreland family is a rather large one and they love to visit. They like checking up on each other. I have a bunch of cousins who were close growing up. Like I said earlier, when they found out about me, Cole and Casey, they didn't hesitate in extending that closeness to us."

He glanced at his watch. "Come on and let me show you to your room so you can get settled in. I'll show you the rest of the house later."

A few moments later Alyssa's fingers trembled as she ran them across the richness of the guest room furniture. There had to be about ten or so guest rooms in this house. Clint had been quick to explain that his uncle loved to entertain and always had friends visiting.

The layout of the house actually suited the magnificent structure. Once you entered the front door you walked into this huge foyer that led into a huge living room. There was also an eat-in kitchen and dining room. The house had four wings that jutted off from the living room. North, south, east and west. Clint's bedroom was huge and was located on the north wing, and although he'd only given her a quick glimpse, she'd liked what she'd seen of it.

The beauty of every room in his home made her speechless. It seemed to be fitting for a king...and his queen, from the expensive furniture to the costly portraits that hung on the walls. He evidently was a man who liked nice things and who didn't mind paying his money for them.

Clint had left her alone to get settled and indicated he would be back in a few minutes. She knew he was trying not to crowd her, give her space and she appreciated that. She wondered at what point her heart would stop beating so wildly in her chest. When would the rapid flutter in her stomach cease?

She glanced over at the overnight bag. It contained her toiletries, fresh underwear, an extra-large T-shirt to sleep in and a pair or jeans and a top. If she decided to stay the thirty days she would have to return to Waco and pack more of her things. She supposed that her friends were wondering where she had gone. She hadn't mentioned her destination or the reason for her trip to anyone except her aunt Claudine. Aunt Claudine wouldn't tell anyone about her trip, Alyssa thought with a chuckle. Her sixty-year-old great-aunt would be tickled that for once she knew something that the other family members didn't.

Alyssa had already put away the few things she'd brought with her and was waiting for Clint when he knocked on the bedroom door. For some reason she felt restless and a call to Aunt Claudine hadn't helped when she was informed that Kim had already begun asking questions about her whereabouts.

When Clinton knocked again she quickly crossed the room, not wanting him to think she had taken a nap or something. She opened the door. He stood in the hallway, towering over her. "I told you that I'd be back. Are you ready for me to show you around?"

Looking up at him, his penetrating dark gaze seemed to hold her captive and she became aware of how even more fluttering was going on in her stomach. And it wasn't helping matters that she felt compelled to stare at his lips. Doing so reminded her of the kiss they had shared and how the moment his tongue had wrapped around hers an ache had begun within her. It was an ache that wouldn't go away.

At that moment she wasn't sure if going anywhere with him was a smart move. That and the fact that she seemed to be glued to the spot. But then she quickly decided that she wasn't about to let another man get to her again. Kevin had taught her a lesson she would never forget. She studied Clint's features again. They were still unreadable. "Clint..."

"Yes?"

He took a step closer, stepping into the room, and since she was glued to the spot she couldn't get her legs to move. She inclined her head back and looked up at him, thinking he was so tall, and much too handsome. She then saw the dark frown that creased his forehead. "What's wrong?" she asked. The words had come tumbling out before she could hold them in.

One of his broad shoulders lifted nonchalantly. "You tell me," he said.

She had said his name; however, because of the way he had been looking at her, the way that look had made blood rush through her veins, she had forgotten what she'd been about to say. She then remembered. "I was going to say that if you're busy I can just look around myself."

"I'm not busy, so let's go," he said.

She noticed right before he turned to step back into the hallway that the frown on his face had deepened, and she had a feeling that although he had invited her to stay for the night he still didn't like it one bit that she was there.

After giving Alyssa a tour of his home, he walked by her side down the steps to the outside. Her compliments had again pleased him, although he wasn't quite sure why they had. He'd never been one to place a lot of emphasis on what anyone thought of what he owned. He bought to satisfy his taste and not anyone else's.

"You said your sister moved to Montana. Does she come back to visit often?"

He glanced over at Alyssa as they walked down the stairs. She seemed to have gotten shorter and a quick look at her feet told him why. She had exchanged her three-inch high-heel shoes for a pair of flats. Smart move. A working ranch was no place for high heels. "Casey's been back once since she left and that was to get her wedding dress made. Mrs. Miller, a seamstress in town, always said she wanted to be the one who designed Casey's wedding dress if she ever got married," he said.

Her question quickly reminded him of something. "But she and McKinnon might be visiting within the next couple of weeks. Why?"

She shrugged her shoulders. "I was just wondering." And then she asked, "What about Cole?"

He glanced over at her again. "What about him?"

"Does he live here, too?"

"No, Cole has a place in town but most of the time he's on assignment somewhere." Clint had an idea why Alyssa asked about Casey and Cole and the chances that they would being paying a visit to the ranch anytime soon. "If you're concerned what my siblings will have to say about our situation if they happen to pop in then don't be. They won't ask questions."

At the uncertainty in her eyes, he went on to say, "And no, it's not because I usually let women stay over on occasion. It's just that my family respects my privacy. Besides, it's not like either of us has done anything wrong."

"So you plan to tell them the truth about who I am?"

"The part about you being my wife?"

"Yes."

He met her gaze. "I see no reason not to. Besides, Chester knows and if he knows then they know, or they will soon. He thinks I need a wife."

"Why does he think that?"

"He's afraid that like Uncle Sid, I'll get so involved with my horses that I won't take time out to build a personal life or have a family. He's determined not to let that happen. He would marry me off in a heartbeat if he could."

They said nothing for the next few moments, but as they continued to walk together around the ranch he was fully aware of the admiring glances Alyssa was getting from the men who worked for him. His mouth thinned; for some reason he was bothered by it.

"This is a huge place," she said, as if wanting to change the subject, which was okay with him.

"Yes, it is."

"Do you have a lot of men working for you?"

"Well over a hundred. And as I said earlier, Alyssa, if you decide to stay here, the chances of getting in each other's way are slim to none." As far as he was concerned life would be much easier, less complicated that way. The last thing he needed was for her or any woman to get under his skin.

"Ready to head back?" he asked and watched how she pushed a wayward curl back away from her face.

"Yes…and thanks for the tour."

As they walked back toward the ranch house—strolling quietly side by side—he wished like hell he could dismiss from his mind the memory of her taste that re-

mained on his tongue, and how even now, the memory of
his lips locked to hers was uncoiling sensations that were
running rampant throughout his body. His loins were on
fire just thinking about it. His body, in its own way, was
sending a reminder of just how long it had been since
he'd slept with a woman. It had been way too long and
today he was feeling it right down to the bone.

That wasn't good. He had told her that she wouldn't
become an itch that he couldn't scratch and he hoped like
hell that he didn't live to regret those words. He had to
remain calm, in control and more than anything he had
to remember that no matter how much desire was eating away at his senses, the last thing he needed in his
life was a wife.

Chapter 5

"I tell you, Alyssa, that girl is up to no good."

Alyssa tugged off her earring and switched her cell phone to the other ear. Claudine often said that about Kim, but in this case she was inclined to believe her great-aunt. She hadn't heard from Kim in months, at least not since her cousin's last attempt to sabotage one of the projects she'd been working on for a client.

It had cost Alyssa two weeks of production time and she had had to work every hour nonstop to meet the deadline date she'd been given. Of course, as usual, Kim had denied everything and there hadn't been any way Alyssa could prove her guilt.

"You're probably right, Aunt Claudine, but there's nothing that I can do. You know Kim, she's full of surprises." Usually those surprises cost Alyssa tremendously. Kim's bag of dirty tricks included everything from sabotaging important projects to sleeping with Alyssa's fiancé and then having a courier deliver the damaging photographs just moments before she was to leave her home for the church.

Her troubles with Kim started when Alyssa had arrived in the Barkleys' household to live with her grandfather and great-aunt. Her mother had never given Alyssa a reason for sending her away, but to this day Alyssa believed that Kate Harris had begun to notice her most recent lover's interest in her thirteen-year-old-daughter's developing body.

As Alyssa was growing up, her mother had never told her the identity of her father. In fact, Alyssa was very surprised to learn that she had a paternal grandfather. Right before her mother had put her on the plane for Waco, she had told Alyssa that she was the illegitimate daughter of Isaac Barkley's dead son, Todd. Todd had been killed in the line of duty as a Texas Ranger.

Alyssa had arrived in Waco feeling deserted and alone, but it didn't take long to see that the arrival of Grandpa Isaac and Aunt Claudine in her life was a blessing of the richest kind. They immediately made her feel wanted, loved and protected.

Unfortunately, her new relatives' acts of kindness didn't sit too well with her cousin Kim, who was the same age as Alyssa. Kim was the daughter of Grandpa Isaac's only other son, Jessie. Jessie's wife had died when Kim was six. From what Alyssa had been told, Jessie had felt guilty about driving his wife to commit suicide because of his unfaithful ways and had spoiled Kim rotten to ease his guilt. Kim was used to getting all the attention and hadn't liked it one bit when that attention shifted with Alyssa's arrival.

Alyssa couldn't remember a single time Kim had not been a thorn in her side. First, there had been all those devious pranks Kim had played so that Alyssa could get blamed. Fortunately, Grandpa Isaac had known what Kim was doing and had come to her defense. But instead of things getting better, the more Grandpa Isaac stood up for her, the worse Kim got.

Alyssa's teen years had been the hardest and if it hadn't been for her grandfather and great-aunt she doubted she would have gotten through them. And it didn't help matters that her mother never came to visit her, never bothered contacting her at all. Kim liked to claim that Alyssa was living off the Barkleys' charity and that there were some in the family who didn't believe that Todd Barkley had been her father anyway. That claim hadn't bothered Alyssa, because she could see that she favored her grandfather too much not to be his grandchild. Before he'd died everyone had found out that she had actually been his child. It had been a revelation that had shocked the entire family, especially when he had left her an equal share of everything. And in Kim's eyes, Alyssa's inheritance had been the ultimate betrayal.

"Alyssa…"

Her aunt pulled her thoughts back to the present. "Yes, Aunt Claudine?"

"Will staying with that man for a month be so bad? At least the marriage will be dissolved…if that's what you really want."

A smile touched Alyssa's lips. Her aunt was trying to play matchmaker again. "Of course that's what I want. It's what Clint and I both want. We don't know each other and like he said, we are victims of someone's mistake. I really don't think it's fair that we have to suffer because of it," Alyssa explained.

She heard her aunt chuckling. "I can't imagine having to suffer if I was to live under the same roof with a gorgeous man…and you did say he was gorgeous, didn't you?"

Yes, she had said that, and had meant it, as well. Clint's physical features were something she could not lie about. And that in itself was the kicker. Kevin had been a good-looking man but he couldn't hold a candle to Clint. She had never been this aware of a man in her life. "Yes, Auntie, he is a hunk."

"Then I suggest that you stay right there in Austin since your only other option is to bring him here to live. Can you imagine all the commotion that would cause? And it would give Kim another excuse to sharpen her claws and do some damage."

Alyssa had thought of that. She wanted to believe that Clint would not be the weakling that Kevin had been and that he would be able to resist Kim's charms. But usually all it took was for any man to set eyes on Kim and they were done for. Men would actually pause when she walked into a room. Too bad beauty was only skin deep, Alyssa thought.

"I'll ship you some things, Alyssa. Besides, a month away from this circus of a family will do you some good," Claudine said.

Funny, she had thought the same thing. "I have to think things through tonight and give Clint my decision in the morning. If I decide to stay I'll let you know."

"All right, I won't say anything to the others. Eleanor's daughter swears she saw Kim and Kevin together at some nightclub. Can you imagine the two of them see-

ing each other again after all they did to you? We heard
Kevin got a promotion with that company he works for.
That's probably why Kim is back in the picture. She's
determined to land a rich husband one way or the other."

In a perverse way Alyssa wished her cousin the best.
Even with all the low-down and underhanded things that
Kim had done, Alyssa couldn't find it in her heart to hate
her. She had tried when she'd gotten those photos of Kim
and Kevin in bed together, but now all she could do was
feel pity for them both. The thought that he and Kim were
seeing each other no longer bothered her. Any love she
might have had for him ended the day that should have
been her wedding day. If Kim was the type of woman
he preferred then more power to him.

She wondered just what type of woman Clint would
prefer. She could see a beautiful woman in his arms, in
his bed, giving birth to his babies. Alyssa was certain she
didn't fit the criteria for Clint's dream woman. She was
of average design and she didn't fit the "dream-woman"
mold. The only reason they were married now was because of someone's screwup. Even when they'd worked
together he hadn't given her a second thought, although
they had shared a hotel room for a week. Alyssa could
not forget sharing such close quarters with him, inhaling
his scent, breathing the same air, or sitting across a table
and sharing food with Clint Westmoreland.

That made her think of the meal they had shared less
than an hour ago. Chester had prepared a delicious meal,
but it had been just the two of them. She couldn't help
but notice that the older man, although still extremely
friendly, hadn't been as chatty as he'd been when she
had first arrived. Clint must have said something to him,
probably warning him not to put foolish ideas into her

head. Not that he could have. She was a realist, almost too much so at times—at least that's what Aunt Claudine claimed. Alyssa would be the first to admit that her dreams of forever after had gotten destroyed the moment she had seen those pictures on her wedding day. It would be hard, nearly impossible for anyone to make a believer out of her again.

She heard a noise outside her bedroom window and crossed the room to see what had caused it. The sun had set and dusk had settled in. One of the floodlights that was shining from the side of the house provided enough brightness for her to see Clint as he leaned against a post talking with two of his men.

It was hard not to take an assessment of Clint each and every time she saw him. From the window, she couldn't see every single detail, but she had a clear view of his thighs. He was standing with his legs braced apart and the muscles that filled his jeans were taut and firm. Just looking at him standing there in that sexy pose made her pulse race. She was actually feeling breathless. *This was her reaction to the man whom she was supposed to live with for thirty days?* She doubted she would be able to get through one day living with him let alone thirty. She was well aware from what he'd said earlier that day about his ability to control his desire if they decided to live together. He had basically given his word that he would abide by any boundaries that she set.

While she was thinking about what boundaries she would establish if she decided to stay, he turned toward the window as if somehow he'd felt her presence there. Their gazes locked. Held. And it seemed at that moment something, a tangible connection she could not define, passed between them. It was as if some understanding had been made, but for the life of her she didn't know what it was.

Dazed and more than a little confused, she took a step back on wobbly knees at the same time she dropped the curtain back in place to shield her from his view. She knew she had to rein in her uncontrollable imagination, urges and lust. If he could control his then she most certainly should be able to get a handle on hers. But she had to admit what she was experiencing was not something she encountered every day. She simply had never been the type of woman to get goggle-eyed over a man. But ever since she'd arrived in Austin, she had been doing that very thing.

Sighing deeply, she moved toward the bathroom hoping her new state of mind was something she got over real soon.

Clint frowned as he walked down the long hallway toward his bedroom. It was way past midnight. After taking care of the evening chores, he had hung around the bunkhouse and played a game of cards with some of his men.

He had stayed away from the house as long as he could, and now he was back inside. His mind wandered to what had happened earlier. He'd been standing out in the yard talking to a couple of his men until he happened to notice Alyssa staring at him from her bedroom window. He'd done the only thing he could do at the time, which was to stare back.

It seemed that against his will, his gaze had locked on hers. It was plain to see that Alyssa was getting to him and the brazen images of her that had been forming in his mind all day weren't helping. Hell, he may have bitten off more than he could chew in asking her to stay under his roof. If only there had been another way for them to end their marriage, he mused. Surely there was someone he could talk to about it.

His cousin Jared immediately came to mind. Jared was the attorney in the family. His specialty was the handling of divorce cases. Perhaps his cousin could give him some advice. He checked his watch. Jared was usually up late at night and Clint turned in the direction of his office, deciding to give his cousin a call.

He pushed open his office door and paused. There, sitting at his desk in front of his computer, was Alyssa. She hadn't heard him enter, and so he just stood for a moment and gazed at her. The soft lighting from the lamp, as well as the glow from the computer screen, seemed to beam on her, highlighting her features. Her hair was no longer hanging around her shoulders. She had pulled it up into a knot at the back of her neck.

Her full attention was on the computer screen and he watched her as she sat in front of it. Her head was tilted in such a way that showed off the slimness of her neck and her shoulders. She sat with perfect posture.

She seemed to be wearing an oversize T-shirt. On anyone else there probably would not have been a single provocative thing about her attire, but on Alyssa, just the part he saw was totally alluring. The way she was sitting made the shirt stretch tight across her chest, and he could plainly see the tips of her nipples. She wasn't wearing a bra. His fingers seemed to twitch and he knew he would love the feel of his fingers slowly stroking the budded tips.

His gaze moved to her face at the same time she parted her lips in a smile before she released a satisfied chuckle. Clint shifted his gaze from her lips to the computer screen to see what held her concentration. She was playing one of those games you downloaded off the Internet. *Alyssa.* She was busy trying to accomplish some goal and from the look of things, she was succeeding.

Deciding it was time to let her know that he was there, he stepped into the room. "Umm, that looks interesting. Can I play?"

She whirled in her seat and startled dark eyes seemed to clash with his as she stood abruptly. "I'm sorry. I should have asked to use your computer before—"

"You didn't have to ask, Alyssa," he said, interrupting her apology. "You are more than welcome to use it. Please sit back down and continue what you were doing. You seem to be having fun. What is it?"

She hesitated briefly before retaking her seat. Slowly her gaze slid from him to the computer screen. The one thing he had noticed when she stood was that the T-shirt was even more sensually appealing than he'd first thought. It barely covered her thighs and if that wasn't bad enough, it outlined her curves in a way that had blood racing through his veins.

"It's a game called Playing with Fire," she said softly and he had a feeling he was making her nervous. She glanced back over at him. "Have you ever played Atomic Bomberman before?"

He smiled, inwardly fighting the acute desire he felt at that moment. "No, I don't believe that I have," he said.

"Oh. Playing with Fire is sort of a flashy remake of Atomic Bomberman. The object of the game is to blow up your opponent before they blow you up," she explained.

Clint chuckled. "That sounds rather interesting. I take it you like playing games on the computer."

She shrugged. "Yes, it's a way for me to unwind.

Whenever I can't sleep I usually get up and play a game or two," she said.

He leaned against the closed door. "I see. Is there a reason you can't sleep?" Already his mind was thinking of his own version of Playing with Fire and the various ways it could be played. "Is the bed not comfortable?" Although he wished it wouldn't go there, his mind quickly thought of her in that huge bed alone.

"No, the bed is fine, really comfortable," she responded with what he denoted as a soft chuckle before adding, "It's just that I'm not used to sleeping in any bed but my own."

"I see."

She cleared her throat before standing again. "Well, I don't want to keep you out of your office," she uttered as she prepared to leave.

"You're not. I had come in to use the phone, but I can make the call from my bedroom just as easily. I'll leave you to your game." He paused a second then asked, "By the way, who's winning?"

He saw the smile that touched her lips, the sparkle that lit her eyes and the proud lifting of her chin. "I am, of course," she answered.

"Now why doesn't that surprise me? Good night, Alyssa," he said, returning her smile.

"Good night, Clint."

Clint turned and moved toward the door. When he felt the sudden rush of blood to his loins he muttered a curse under his breath and turned back around. Before Alyssa could blink he crossed the room and pulled her from the chair. The moment her body was pressed against his and her lips parted in a startled gasp, his mouth swept down on hers at an angle that called for deep penetration. He took hold of her tongue, wanting the taste of her again with a need that was hitting him all at once, and when she returned the kiss—their tongues participated in one hell of a heated duel—a disturbing acceptance entered his mind. He was not prone to giving in to sexual desires like this, he thought. He could get turned on just like the next guy, but never to this magnitude. His response to any woman had never been this strong, this intense, this mind-bogglingly obsessive. The more he tasted her, the more he wanted, and it wasn't helping matters that she felt perfectly right in his arms. Her softness felt so good against his hardness. *What the hell was wrong with him?*

He quickly decided he would have to figure out this change in him later, but not right now. Not when she'd wrapped her arms around his neck and pressed her body closer to his, and not when he could feel the tips of her breasts through the cotton of his shirt. His mind began imagining all sorts of things. He imagined how it would feel to have the tips of those breasts in his mouth, to toy with them using his tongue, or how he would love to spread her on his desk and take her there. Then there was the idea of him sitting in the chair and tugging her down in his lap and…

She suddenly broke the kiss and he watched as she backed away while forcing air into her lungs. He was doing likewise. He was breathing like he had just run a marathon, but each time he inhaled, her scent filled his nostrils. It was a scent that was getting him aroused all over again.

She lifted her head to look at him and that's when he noticed the knot in her hair had come undone and it was flowing wildly around her shoulders, making her look even sexier than before.

"Was that supposed to be a good-night kiss?" Her voice was soft and breathy.

That hadn't been what he'd expected her to say. Actually, he had expected her to dress him down in the worst possible way. *Was it possible that she was admitting that she had wanted the kiss as much as he had?* She didn't seem to be placing the blame entirely on him, although he had been the one to make the first move.

He leaned back against the door as his gaze went to her mouth. "Yes, it was a good-night kiss," he said. "Want another one?"

"No. I doubt if I could handle it," she responded, shaking her head.

A smile touched his lips. Again her comment had surprised him. "Sure you can. Do you want me to prove it to you?"

"No, thank you."

He chuckled softly. "In that case, I'll let you get back to your game." Without giving her a chance to say anything else, he opened the door and quickly walked out of the room, closing the door behind him.

He paused for a second thinking it was obvious that they had the hots for each other. If she remained under his roof there was no way he would be able to keep his hands off her. He wondered if the kisses they'd shared would be a determining factor in whether she stayed or went back to Waco. Would living together be too much of a temptation? Thirty days was a long time.

She'd said she wasn't used to sleeping in any bed other than her own. In a way he had been glad to hear that. On the other hand, he figured she had to know that if she remained at the Golden Glade, at the rate they were going, she would eventually share his.

As he made his way toward his bedroom, thinking about the explosive chemistry between them began to annoy the hell out of him. He was a man known to have a multitude of control. In the past when lust consumed his body he had a way of dealing with it. Any available and willing woman would do. But he had a feeling that his usual solution would not work this time. His body wanted only one woman and that wasn't good.

Alyssa released a deep breath the moment Clint closed the door behind him. It was simply amazing that one man could have that kind of effect on her. Every single time she saw him, every time he kissed her the result was the same—passion. *When would the attraction she had for him wear off? What if it never did?*

Maybe she needed to rethink her decision to remain at Clint's ranch for the thirty days. It was a decision she hadn't yet told him she'd made, only because she had mentioned that she would need to sleep on it. And she had, which was the main reason she was up now. Once the decision had been made she couldn't get her body to go back to sleep. It had become restless and for the first time ever, fiercely aroused.

And for him to find her in his office wearing only a large T-shirt was embarrassing. But the house had been quiet for a long while and she figured everyone had gone to bed for the night. His bedroom was in a different wing and so she had assumed the coast was clear. She thought that she could sneak into his office for a while and not be noticed. But he had noticed. And so she made a new promise—no more late-night game-playing on the computer for her.

She inhaled deeply. In the morning she would tell him

of her decision to stay. She would also tell him that her decision came with stipulations. He'd said earlier that day, after their first kiss, that he was able to control his desire for her. If kissing her the way he did was his desire under control, she didn't want to think how the kiss would be with those same desires unleashed.

Chapter 6

Alyssa's heart immediately began beating harder when she walked into the kitchen the next morning to find Clint seated at the table. Although it appeared he was just starting in on breakfast, she knew he was there waiting on her. His expression indicated that he wanted to know her decision.

She glanced around the large kitchen, trying to ignore the pulse that was erratically thumping in her throat. It was a sin and shame that Clint looked so good this early in the morning. He was staring at her with those dark, piercing eyes of his, and the way the sunlight captured the well-defined planes of his face made him appear hauntingly handsome. Alyssa found his good looks quite disturbing, given the fact she was trying to resist her attraction to him.

Seeing him only reminded her of her behavior with

him last night in his office. He had once again kissed her mindless, engulfing her with a degree of passion she thought was possible only in those romance novels Aunt Claudine read. Alyssa had gone to bed dreaming about him, their kiss and the things she wanted to do with him beyond a kiss. She had awakened mortified that such thoughts had entered her mind. She would need to take steps to make sure her dreams never became a reality.

For her own sake and well-being, she had reached the conclusion that setting ground rules with Clint would be the only way they would survive living under the same roof. Otherwise, she was setting herself up for many tiring days and disturbing nights, Alyssa realized.

"Where's Chester?" she asked.

Clint leaned back in his chair. "He's off on Wednesdays. At least, he takes off after breakfast and then returns at dinnertime. It's the day he's at the children's hospital being Snuggles the Clown."

Alyssa lifted a brow. "Snuggles the Clown?"

"He spends his day in the children's ward making the kids laugh. He's been doing it for over twenty years now and he's a big hit. That's how he and Uncle Sid met. Chester used to be a rodeo clown," Clint said.

At first Alyssa couldn't picture Chester as a clown, but then as she thought about it, she changed her mind. He had a friendly air about him and would probably be someone who loved kids. She didn't know any clowns and found the thought of him being one fascinating. "You have to love kids to do something like that," she said.

"He does. It was unfortunate that he and Ada never had any of their own."

"Was Ada his wife?"

"Yes. They were married over thirty years. She died

six years ago from an acute case of pneumonia," Clint explained.

"That's sad," she said quietly.

"It was. He took her death pretty hard. They had a very strong marriage."

A very strong marriage. Alyssa wondered if that meant the same thing as the two of them were deeply in love. "So he's been working at the ranch a long time?"

"Yes, Chester's been working here since before I was born," Clint said.

Alyssa could hear something in Clint's voice that went beyond mere likeness of Chester. It was easy to tell that Clint considered Chester more than just a housekeeper and a cook. He considered the man an intricate part of his family. While giving her a tour of the outside of the house, he had introduced her to several of the men who worked for him. Some of them were older and full of experience in the taming of the horses. The younger ones were learning the ropes, but everyone, as Clint had been quick to point out, played an important part in the running of his operation. The men had been friendly and respectful and when he had introduced her as nothing more than a good friend, it was apparent they had accepted his word.

"You'd better dig in while the food is warm," Clint said.

Taking his statement to mean he was tired of answering her questions, she walked over to the stove to fix her plate and pour a cup of coffee, feeling Clint's gaze on her with every move she made.

"I'm glad you know to do that," he said.

She turned and looked at him, bewildered. "Do what?"

"Fix your own food."

At her confused look he said, "A lot of women wouldn't. They would expect to be waited on hand and foot."

Alyssa turned back around to scoop eggs onto her plate wondering if he'd ever met Kim. Her cousin would definitely be one of those type of women. Uncle Jessie still called Kim his princess and she took it literally. "Well, I'm not one of them," she said when she came to the table to sit down. "I'm used to fending for myself."

She had barely taken her seat when Clinton folded his arms across his chest and asked, "Okay, what have you decided?"

Instead of answering him, she stared down into the dark liquid of her coffee for a moment before glancing up at him. "Do you have to know this minute?"

"Any reason you can't tell me this minute?" he countered, with a little irritation in his voice.

She set her cup down knowing the last thing they needed was to get agitated with each other. Besides, he was right. There wasn't a reason she couldn't tell him now. "No, I guess not."

She didn't say anything for a few moments and then met his gaze. "Before I commit to anything, I want you to agree to something," she said.

He lifted a dark brow. "Agree to what?"

"Agree that you won't try to get me into your bed."

He smiled. "My bed?"

"Or any bed in this house." She thought it best to clarify. "And to be more specific, I want your word that you won't try to seduce me into bed with you."

He laughed softly and held her gaze for a long moment. "Define *seduce*," he said.

Alyssa was aware that he was toying with her, but she was more determined than ever to make sure he understood her position. "You're a man, Clint. You know very well what seduction entails," she said.

His smile deepened. "And you think I'd do something like that?"

She didn't hesitate in answering. "Yes. I'm certain of it. In less than twenty-four hours we've kissed twice, which leads me to believe you would try seducing me."

He stared at her for a moment, eyed her reflectively and then said, "You're right. I would in a heartbeat." And then he asked, "And we've kissed twice, you say?"

Like he didn't know it. "Yes," she said, now very annoyed.

"Want to go for three?" he murmured in a voice that was so husky that it sent shivers through her body.

She eyed him sternly. "I'm serious, Clint."

"So am I."

She stared into his deep, penetrating gaze. Yes, he was serious. He was dead serious. The very thought that he wanted to kiss her again, tangle his tongue with hers and taste her, made the breath she was breathing get caught in her throat. *Had he just admitted that he enjoyed kissing her?* Well, she could admit that she enjoyed kissing him, as well. There was something devastatingly mind-blowing about the feel of him thrusting his tongue deep into her mouth, moving it around, latching on to hers and...

"Anything else you want from me?"

She shot him a cool look. "Maybe I'd better add kissing to the mix. I think it's a good idea if we refrain from doing it," she said.

"That can't happen," he said. She noticed that his lips curved into an easy smile.

His response had been quick and decisive. Alyssa tried

remaining calm. She felt a rush of blood that gushed through her veins. "Why can't it happen?"

"Because we enjoy kissing too much. The best thing to do is to stay in control when we do kiss. Personally, I don't see anything wrong with us kissing. It's merely a friendly form of greeting," he said.

Yeah. Right. It was a form of greeting that she could do without. Especially because kissing Clint Westmoreland made her want to indulge in other things. Things that were better left alone.

"Like I said, Alyssa," he said, interrupting her thoughts. "The key is self-control. As much as I want you and as much as kissing you places temptation in my path, I promise I won't take our attraction to the next level. I have too much work to do around here to get involved with a woman—in any way," he said.

She admired his iron-clad control…if he really had it. He sounded so confident, so sure of himself, she would love to test his endurance level to see what it could or could not withstand.

"But I have to admit you bring something to the table a lot of women haven't," he said.

She glanced over at him and her pulse jumped at the way he was looking at her.

"And what might that be?" she asked softly.

"Although it's only on paper, you're my wife. Perhaps it is because I've seen things from a male perspective, but it's as if knowing you're bound to me is opening up desires and urges that I usually don't have. The fact that we are married makes me crave things."

She frowned. *In other words, having a woman under his roof was making him horny,* Alyssa quickly surmised. "Then I need to add another condition to my visit. That from a female perspective, whatever desires are opening up for you, I suggest that you take your time and close them. I may not have all the self-control you claim to have, but I have no interest in getting involved with a man—in any way. Besides, if I were to get involved with a man it would have to be serious. I'm not into casual relationships where the only goal is relieving sexual frustrations," she said.

He was silent for a moment as he stared at her, and for a fraction of a second she thought she saw a challenging glint in his gaze. And then he said, "I won't try getting you into my bed…or yours…but I won't promise to keep my mouth to myself. I can't see us denying ourselves that one bit of indulgence."

"Why? When it won't lead anywhere?"

He inclined his head. His gaze locked with hers. "I desire you. Kissing you is a way to work you out of my system. I believe the same could be said for you, as well. At the end of the thirty days I suspect you will be ready to leave as much as I'll be ready for you to leave," he said.

Alyssa held his gaze and read what she saw in his eyes. He really believed that and she would go even further to say he was counting on it.

"Because we would have kissed each other out of our systems by then?" she asked, needing to be sure she understood his logic in all of this.

"Yes," he replied evenly.

"And you think you're that elusive and wild at heart."

He lifted a brow. "Wild at heart?"

"Yes. You don't think there's a woman who exists who's capable of capturing your heart," she said.

"I know there's not."

He had said the words with such venom that she was forced to ask. "Have you ever been in love, Clint?"

She could tell by the look that appeared in his eyes that her question surprised him. She saw the way his shoulders tightened, the firm grip he held on his coffee cup and knew she had waded in turbulent waters.

For a while she thought he wasn't going to respond, but then he did.

"No," he said.

For some reason she didn't believe him. Not that she thought he was lying to her, but she figured that the love he might have had for someone had been so effectively destroyed that it was hard to recall when that emotion had ever gripped his heart. It had been that way for her after she'd discovered what Kevin had done. It was as if her love had gotten obliterated with that one single act of unfaithfulness. She couldn't help wondering about the woman who had crushed Clint's heart.

"Are you satisfied with our agreement?"

Alyssa dragged in a deep breath. The issue of them kissing hadn't been fully resolved to her liking, but the way she saw it, he was not a man to force himself on anyone. If she resisted his kisses enough times, he would find some other game to amuse himself. "Yes, I'm satisfied," she said.

"So, are you agreeing to remain here for thirty days, live under the same roof with me?"

Intimate images flooded her mind. She forced them out. His home was humongous. His bedroom was on one side of the house and hers on the other. Chances were there would be days when their paths wouldn't even cross. "Yes, I'm agreeing to do just that," she said.

He nodded. "I'll call Hightower and let him know.

By the way, what about more clothes for you? You only
brought an overnight bag," Clint said.

"I spoke with my aunt yesterday and she told me if I
decided to stay she would send me some things."

"Your aunt is the only family you have?"

She might as well be, she wanted to say.

"No, I have an uncle and several cousins," she said
instead. "My mother sent me to live with my grandfather and Aunt Claudine when I was thirteen. Over the
years Aunt Claudine has become a surrogate mother to
me," she added.

"And your grandfather?"

A pain settled in her heart. She wanted to correct him
so badly.

"My grandfather died four years ago," she said softly.

"That was about the same time I lost my mother," he
said, looking down at the coffee in his cup. She could
hear the sadness in his voice. He glanced up and at that
moment an emotion passed between them—a deep understanding of how it felt to lose someone you truly cared
about.

"Were you close to her?" she asked.

"Yes. Casey, Cole and I were her world and she was
ours. She and Uncle Sid, along with Chester and the other
old-timers on the ranch were our family. What about your
mother? You said she sent you to live with your grandfather and aunt when you were thirteen. Do the two of
you still keep in touch?"

In a way Alyssa wished he would have asked her anything but that. That her mother could so easily send her
away and not stay in touch was still a pain that would
occasionally slither through her heart.

"No. I haven't seen or heard from my mother since the day she sent me away," she said.

Deciding she didn't want to subject herself to any more of his inquiries about her family, she stood. "I need to make a few calls. In addition to contacting my aunt, I need to make sure I have everything I need to continue my business while I'm here. That means I will need to use your computer a lot," she said.

"I don't have a problem with that."

Alyssa nodded. "Okay. I'm sure you have a lot to do today, as well," she said, picking up her plate and cup and carrying both over to the sink. "And since today is Chester's day off, I'll take care of the dishes as soon as I've made those calls."

With nothing else to say, Alyssa walked out of the kitchen.

Clint continued to sit at the table. From the moment he had gotten the letter from the bureau advising him of his marriage to Alyssa, he had simply assumed that getting out of the marriage would be easy—a piece of cake. He had miscalculated on a number of things. First, the bureau being so hard-nosed over such a blatant mistake and second, his attraction to the woman who was legally his wife. Now, he was fully committed to go to extraordinary restrictions to keep his hands off of her. In other words, to stay out of her bed and to make sure she stayed out of his.

Neither would be easy.

That was what made the thought of the next thirty days so disconcerting. A part of him wanted to rebel. *Why not have sex with her?* After all it was just sex, no big deal. They were mature adults who evidently had healthy appetites with no desire to get caught up in anything other than the moment. Right? Wrong.

He couldn't help but recall her words about not being one to indulge in casual affairs, which gave him a glimpse into her character. While engaging her in conversation, he had taken in everything she'd said—even some things she hadn't said, especially about her family.

The Texas Ranger in him could detect when someone was withholding information. He hadn't wanted to pry, but she'd deliberately omitted mentioning a few things. Such as why her mother had given her up at thirteen and had never once come back to see her. And when she had mentioned her cousins he hadn't heard that deep sense of love and warmth he'd felt whenever he spoke of his. Granted, he didn't expect every family to be like the Westmorelands, but still he would think there was a closeness there. He had heard the deep love and affection in her voice when she had spoken of her grandfather and aunt.

And then he could very well be reading more into it than was there. It could be that she was a private person and hadn't felt the need or wasn't stirred by any desire to tell him any more than she had. Wife or no wife, it wasn't "expose your soul to Clint" day.

He rubbed his hand down his face. Why did he even care? he wondered. What was there about Alyssa that made him want to dig deeper and unravel her inner being, layer by layer? With that thought in mind, he was about to get up from the table when his cell phone went off. He stood to pull it off the attachment on his belt. "Hello," he said.

"So what's this I hear about you having a wife?"

He couldn't help but smile when he sat back down.

He could envision his sister with her long black lashes lifting in a way that said she had every right to know everything she asked him.

"I see Chester's loose lips have been flapping again," he muttered, thinking he needed to have a talk with the old man. Of course, Clint knew that all the talk in the world wouldn't do any good with Chester.

"He knew I had a right to know," Casey Westmoreland Quinn said in a serious tone. "So tell me about her."

He sighed. Since she hadn't asked what happened to make him have a wife in the first place, he could only assume that Chester had covered that information with her already. "What do you want to know?"

"Everything. What's her name? Where is she from? How old is she? Is she someone that you used to work with who I've met already? And so on and so forth."

Clint frowned. Alyssa reminded him of Casey with her endless questions.

"Her name is Alyssa Barkley. She's from Waco and she's twenty-seven. And no, you've never met her. She became a Ranger right out of college and then left not long after that assignment we did together. She was only with the Rangers for a year," he said.

"So you didn't make a good impression on her then, did you?"

"I wasn't trying to. I was all into Chantelle at the time," he said.

"Please don't mention her name," Casey said in feigned terror.

Clint chuckled. Casey and Chantelle had never gotten along from day one. His sister had warned him about her but he wouldn't listen. Now he wished he had. But at the time he had been thinking with the lower part of his body and not his brain. Chantelle caught the attention of any man within one hundred feet. But then so did Alyssa. However, it had taken only a few moments spent with Alyssa to know she and Chantelle were very different.

Alyssa wasn't all into herself. She didn't think she was responsible for the sun rising and setting each day. Chantelle had thought she was all that, and like a testosterone-packed fool, he had played right into her hands without considering the consequences.

"So what have the two of you decided to do since the bureau won't annul your marriage?"

Casey's question reeled his thoughts back in. "Do what they want and live together for thirty days," he said.

"That's asking a lot of the two of you. Maybe you ought to seek out the advice of an attorney," Casey said.

"We thought of that, but in the end it might only delay things," he said, and his conversation with Jared last night had only confirmed his suspicions. "Alyssa thinks it will work since she's able to do her job from anywhere. She's a Web site designer."

"Um, maybe you can get her to design the Web site for Uncle Sid's foundation that we're setting up," Casey suggested.

"I mentioned it to her briefly, and you're right. It might be something she can do while she's here if she has the time."

"She'll be at the ranch when McKinnon and I visit in a few weeks," Casey said as if thinking out loud. "I'm looking forward to meeting her."

Casey's intonation immediately sent up red flags. He knew his sister. After that Chantelle fiasco she had gotten a little overprotective where he was concerned. He found it rather amusing although not necessary. "Don't forget who's the oldest, Casey," he decided to remind her.

Over the phone line he heard her unladylike snort. "But only by a mere fourteen minutes. I would have been the oldest if it wasn't for Cole holding me back."

Clint laughed. That's the reason Casey liked telling everyone for her being the last born. She had gotten that tale from Chester, who had convinced her she was in position to be born first. "Whatever. Look, Case, I have a lot of work to do around here today. I'm expecting another shipment of horses," he said.

"Wonderful. McKinnon and I will talk with you later to let you know the exact day we'll be arriving."

Moments later Clint ended the call with Casey thinking that she was usually a good judge of character. He wondered what she would think of Alyssa.

Chapter 7

Alyssa glanced around Clint's office thinking how the one in her home was a lot smaller. She loved her small apartment. It was just the right size for her. All she needed was a kitchen, bedroom, bath and working space. She had considered the living and dining rooms as a bonus.

She studied the different pictures on the wall and recognized the one of Sid Roberts. Another showed a woman with three little ones—about the age of five or six—at her side. She knew that it was a picture of Clint, his mother and two siblings. There was another framed photograph of his mother alone. She was beautiful and Alyssa could easily see Clint's resemblance to her; the likeness seemed very strong. She thought that Clint favored his mother until she saw yet another photograph of a man she immediately decided had to be Clint's father. Any resemblance she'd attributed to his mother dimmed when she compared the image of Clint she had in her mind to the picture of his father. Clint had his father's domineering features. Both Clint and Cole, whose looks were nearly identical, had inherited their father's forehead, chiseled jaw and matching dark eyes. They had also inherited their dad's sexy lips, the lips that she loved to look at on Clint. The father, whom Clint said he'd only met a few years ago, definitely was a good-looking man. Alyssa quickly formed the opinion that Casey, although she had her father's eyes, had inherited more of her mother's features.

Alyssa tensed when she heard her cell phone ring. She had recently gotten a new number and hoped that Kim hadn't gotten hold of it. Flipping the phone open, she smiled when she saw it was her aunt calling. "Yes, Aunt Claudine?"

"Just wanted you to know that I got those boxes shipped off like I said I would. You should get them in a few days."

"Thank you. I appreciate your going to the trouble," Alyssa said.

"No trouble. Kim dropped by this morning trying to sweet-talk me into telling where you were. I didn't tell her a thing. Actually, I told her you were off seeing a client."

"Thanks, I appreciate it," Alyssa said.

"Jessie also called asking about you, but I figured Kim put him up to it."

Alyssa had to assume the same thing. Her uncle rarely sought her out these days.

"And how are things with you and your cowboy?"

Alyssa chuckled. "He isn't my cowboy, but things are going just fine." At least she hoped they were. She hadn't seen him since breakfast that morning. She knew he had returned for lunch because she had heard him when he'd ridden up on his horse. She had glanced out the window—being careful not to be been seen this time—and watched as Clint dismounted and walked with his horse toward the stables. The way the jeans hugged his body nearly took her breath away.

"I'm glad to hear it. Well, I've got to go. Eleanor is dropping by later and we're going to attend a church function together later."

"Okay, Aunt Claudine, and thanks for everything," Alyssa said.

"You're welcome."

Alyssa hung up the phone thinking how appreciative she was of her aunt.

"How are things going?"

She turned to see Clint standing in the doorway.

"They're going fine. My aunt is shipping some boxes to me and I'm hoping to get them in a few days," Alyssa said.

Opening her mouth and getting words out had been a real challenge, especially with the way he was looking at her. Heat was beginning to slither through her body from the intensity of his gaze. He stood leaning in the doorway and she could feel her control begin to unravel. Whether she liked it or not, desire seemed to grip her each and every time she saw him.

"In the meantime," he said, interrupting her thoughts, "I figured you might need some additional clothing so I placed a few items of clothes on your bed."

She lifted a brow. "Clothes?"

"Yes."

"Women's clothes?" There was a suspicious note in her voice which she wished wasn't there. She further wished he wouldn't pick up on it.

"Yes, women's clothes. You and Casey are about the same size so I took the liberty of borrowing some of her things for you. When she left for Montana she wasn't certain she would be staying so she left some of her things here," Clint said.

Alyssa felt relief that the clothes belonged to his sister and not some other woman. She was mature enough to know that Clint had probably dated a slew of women over the years. Some had probably stayed at the ranch. That was his business. And what he did after the thirty days were up and their marriage was annulled was also his business. *So why did the thought that his business could include other women bother her?*

And then there was the thought that he had been in her bedroom. Granted, this was his house, the one he'd grown up in as a child, which meant that he probably knew the location of every room blindfolded. But the idea that he had been in the room where she'd slept last night, had gotten close to the bed, made every nerve in her body tingle.

"Thanks for being so thoughtful," she managed to say as she stood.

"No problem."

When it became obvious that he had no intention of leaving—he just stood in that same spot staring at her—she raised a brow.

"Is there something else?"

"Yes, there is," he said.

She felt the lump in her throat. She didn't want to ask but felt compelled to do so anyway.

"And what is that?"

"Chester wanted to know if you would be joining us

for dinner," Clint said, clearly uncomfortable with extending the invitation to her.

Alyssa released another deep sigh as she studied his expression. That hadn't been what she expected him to say and she felt a touch of unwanted disappointment. It had been her idea that they agree on how far they would take their attraction, so why was she feeling so edgy?

"Alyssa?"

"Yes?"

"Will you be joining us?"

She wondered if he really wanted her to.

"And how do you feel about me joining you for dinner, Clint?" she asked quietly.

He rubbed his chin as he continued to look at her. She watched as his gaze slowly scanned her body from head to toe. He smiled slightly and then said, "We're having meat loaf. I'd much rather look at you across the table than down at a plate of meat loaf." He added, "Chester usually burns it. He says it's supposed to taste better that way."

She couldn't help her smile. "Does it? Taste better that way?"

"Not really," he said, looking thoughtful. "But then the only taste I seem to enjoy lately is yours."

His words singed fire through her body with the force of a blowtorch. A woman could only take so much flirting with a man like Clint. She watched as he slowly moved away from the door to walk toward her. And as if her feet had a mind of their own, they moved, and she found herself coming from around the desk to meet him. He came to a stop right in front of her and his eyes stared into hers.

"This is crazy. You know that, don't you?" As he asked

her that question, he leaned forward and circled her waist with his arm. The heat of his words warmed her lips.

"Yes. Real crazy," she heard herself mumbling in response.

"I'm going to be real pissed about it later," he said, catching her bottom lip between his teeth for a gentle nip. "But right now, at this minute, I have to taste you again."

And then as if to prove his point, when she tilted her head up to him he reached out and gently took hold of a section of her hair and tenderly pulled her mouth closer to his, locking it in place. He was determined to take the kiss deeper. Make it even more intimate.

She didn't think that was possible until she felt the tip of his tongue coaxing hers to participate. Hers gave in and together they explored every sensitive area of her mouth. Her senses went on full alert and she became a turbulent mass of longing. In all her twenty-seven years, it had taken a trip to Austin to discover what it meant to be kissed senseless.

The kiss seemed to go on nonstop and Alyssa felt herself being passionately consumed with a need that was making her feel weak. It just didn't seem possible that within days of seeing Clint again after five years, she could be this attracted to him.

He pulled back and ended the kiss, but not before gently nipping at her bottom lip as if she was a tasty morsel he just had to have. And then he took his fingertip and traced it across her wet and swollen lips. "You did want my kiss, didn't you?"

She didn't answer immediately, and then she decided to be totally honest with him. "Yes, I wanted it. But—"

He quickly swooped down and captured her mouth with his again, and she hungrily opened her mouth beneath his. Yes, she had wanted it and he was making sure she was getting it.

This time when he pulled back he placed a finger against her lips to make sure she didn't utter a single word.

"No buts, Alyssa. I know my limitations. I'm aware of the terms that I agreed to. The only person who can renege on them is you," he said.

Arousal was shining in his eyes and she could feel his erection pressed hard against her stomach. "And if you ever decide to do so," he added in a husky tone, "you're fully aware of where my bedroom is located. You are more than welcome to join me there at any time."

"Are you sure Alyssa will be joining you for dinner?"

Clint first glanced at the clock on the stove before meeting Chester's gaze. "That's what she said, but who knows, she might have changed her mind."

Chester stood leaning against the counter and held a spatula in his hand. He narrowed his eyes at Clint as he placed his arms across his chest. "What did you do to her?"

Clint rolled his eyes. "I didn't do anything to her. I merely told her that—"

"Sorry I'm late," Alyssa said as she rushed into the kitchen.

Both men's gazes shifted to Alyssa. Clint's gaze went from her to Chester's accusing glare. *If you didn't do anything to her then why are her lips all swollen?* the old man's expression seemed to say.

Instead of cowering under Chester's glare, Clint stood and returned his gaze to Alyssa. "No harm done. Besides, you are worth the wait," Clint said.

And he meant it. She was wearing one of Casey's outfits that he'd placed on the bed for her. Funny thing was, he never remembered Casey looking that good in the sundress.

"Thank you," Alyssa said.

She crossed the room to take her place at the dining room table—space usually reserved for the lady of the house. Clint wondered if she knew that. He sat down as she began easily conversing with Chester, asking how his day had been at the hospital. While setting everything on the table, Chester told her of how one of the kids had been afraid of him and how he had finally won the child over by doing magic tricks.

"Will the two of you need anything else before I go?"

"Where are you going?"

"I'm going to the bunkhouse to feed the ranch hands," the older man said and smiled.

"Oh," Alyssa said. "No, I won't need anything else."

"Neither will I," Clint tacked on, more than ready for Chester to leave the two of them alone. He had heard the catch in her voice letting him know that the thought of being alone with him made her nervous. She should be nervous, Clint thought. Whether she knew it or not, she was driving him crazy. If the outfit she was wearing wasn't bad enough, her scent was definitely getting to him, almost drugging his senses, eating away at his control. The sundress had spaghetti straps and revealed soft, creamy flesh on her arms and shoulders. It was skin he ached to feel, touch and taste. He would love to trace his tongue along her arm and work his way up to her shoulders and—

"Clint, Chester is saying something to you," Alyssa was saying.

He blinked at her words and then sent a sharp glance in Chester's direction. The old geezer had the nerve to smile as if he knew where Clint's thoughts had been.

"What?" Clint probably asked the question more roughly than he should have, but at that moment, he really felt like he was losing it.

The older man's smile widened when he said, "I was trying to get your attention to remind you that I won't be here in the morning. Snuggles the Clown is doing another performance at the hospital."

"I remember," Clint said shortly.

"Oh, by the way, Alyssa offered to do breakfast for the men in the morning," Chester said, undeterred by Clint's sour expression or gruff tone.

Clint shifted his gaze from Chester to Alyssa. "You did?"

"Yes. It's the least I can do around here," Alyssa said.

Clint frowned. "That's a lot of food to prepare. Nobody said you had to do anything around here," he said.

"I know, but everyone around here has chores. Fixing breakfast tomorrow will help me to feel useful," she replied.

"What about the work you were doing on the computer for that client?" Clint was not sure he liked the idea of her in his kitchen performing domestic tasks. There hadn't been a woman in his kitchen since Ada died.

"I'm almost done and on deadline," Alyssa said, smiling proudly.

Clint leaned back in his chair. "Well, let me know when you're ready to take on another customer. I was serious when I mentioned I needed a Web site for the Sid Roberts Foundation."

She lifted a brow. "And you want me to do it?"

"Only if you have the time. The next time you're in my office take a look in the side drawer on your right. There's a folder with information about the foundation in there. If you decide to do it, we can sit down and discuss it when I get back," he said.

"Get back? Are you going someplace?"

He heard the catch in her voice again. "I'm not going off the property so I'll still be safe in saying we were together for the thirty days, but I'll be spending a couple of nights under the stars on the south ridge. The horses arrived today and the ones I've decided not to train I'll be setting free on that designated land that's governed by the foundation," Clint said.

"And how long will you be away from the ranch?"

He shrugged. "It usually takes a couple of days."

"Oh," Alyssa said.

"Well, folks, I'll be leaving," Chester said. Clint shot the older man a glance. He'd forgotten he was still in the room. He had been too focused on Alyssa and that wasn't good.

"So, did you get a lot accomplished today?" Clint asked as he loaded his plate with food.

Alyssa watched him and was again amazed at the amount of food he consumed. "Yes, I put in a lot of time doing that Web site. It's for a teachers' union in Alabama."

He nodded. "How do you get your clients?"

"Word of mouth mostly. One satisfied client will tell another. But I'm also listed in all the search engines and that helps," she said.

"I take it that you're good at what you do," Clint said.

She glanced up and met his gaze. She hoped they were

still talking about the same thing. "Yes, I'm good. I believe in satisfying my customers and I rarely get complaints. If you need references then I can—"

"No, I don't need references."

Conversation between them ceased again, which was fine with her since he seemed keen on eating his meal. She wondered if he still thought the taste of the meat loaf had nothing on her. It was hard to tell since he seemed to be enjoying every bite of it. But then whenever he kissed her it appeared that he tried to gobble her up, as well.

"Is something wrong?"

She blinked. "No. Why?"

"You're staring. You have a tendency to do that a lot when we eat together. Is there a reason why?"

Alyssa shifted in her seat. There was no way she could tell him that she found watching him eat fascinating… and a total turn on. He seemed to appreciate every piece he put into his mouth. And the way he would take his time to chew it, methodically getting all he could from each bite, let her know he would make love to her the same way. Given the chance, Clint would savor her in the same way that he ate. Goose bumps formed on her arms at the thought of it.

"No reason," she said after pausing for a moment to gather her thoughts. "It's just that I'm totally in awe of how much you eat."

He lifted a brow. "And I'm in awe as to how little you eat. You remind me of Casey. She eats like a bird, as well," he said.

She heard the fondness in his voice for his sibling. "I appreciate your sharing her clothes with me. I hope she won't mind," she said.

"She won't," he said, effectively closing discussion on the subject. "Will you be using the computer later?"

"No," she said, shaking her head. "I'm through for the day. I thought I might look through that folder you were telling me about on your uncle's foundation. Why?"

"Because I need to use it to log in the information on the horses we got in today," he said. He glanced at his watch as he pushed his plate aside. It was clean. "I play cards with the men on Wednesday night so I'll be leaving the house again after logging in that information. And I won't be back until way after midnight," he said with a smile. "I'm telling you this just in case you want to play another game on the computer later. I promise not to interrupt you this time."

"This is your house, Clint. You have free rein of any place in it."

He cocked his head and looked at her. "Even your bedroom?"

The glint in his eyes indicated that he was teasing her. At least she hoped he was.

"No. According to our agreement bedrooms are off-limits," she said.

"Um, that really doesn't bother me. The bedroom is one of the places I least like for making love," he said slyly.

She suddenly felt like she was under the influence of some sort of drug. Sensations were surging through her, touching all parts of her body, but especially the area between her thighs.

"What is your favorite place?" she couldn't help asking.

Alyssa stared as he put his glass of lemonade down.

His gaze was intent on holding hers. She tried fighting it but she was being pulled into his sensuous web.

He smiled and that smile, like his words, touched her all over. It added kerosene to her already blazing fire. "Before the thirty days are up," he said in a deep, throaty voice, as his gaze held hers, "I intend to show you."

An hour or so later Alyssa stood at her bedroom window and watched as Clint walked across the yard to the bunkhouse, which meant his office was empty again. She needed to think and wanted a quiet place to do so. His office was the perfect place.

The man was getting to her in a big way and he was doing so with a degree of confident arrogance that astounded her. He wasn't pushy or demanding. He wasn't even using manipulating tactics. He was merely being his own sexy self.

Before the thirty days are up, I intend to show you.

Those words were still ringing in her ears, still causing an ache in parts of her body that aches had never invaded before. The area between her thighs was actually throbbing. Clint had basically assured her that he would make love to her at some point before she left his ranch. Such a statement was bold, bigheaded…and heaven help her, probably true.

She inhaled sharply. *How could she of all people, someone who rebuffed men's sexual advances with mediocre kindness, even contemplate such a thing happening?* She was not only contemplating it, Alyssa was actually anticipating it.

She shook her head to clear it, needing to focus mainly on the facts. Clint Westmoreland was the sexiest man she had ever seen in clothes, so naturally a part of her—the feminine part—couldn't help wondering what he looked like without clothes. That kind of curiosity was new for her.

Then there was the way Clint carried himself. He had a self-assured nature that was very attractive. And lastly, she couldn't downplay the fact that since meeting him, she experienced an all-consuming desire that had invaded her entire body. It wasn't in her normal routine to lust after a man but she was definitely lusting after Clint Westmoreland.

She turned away from the window, her mind stricken by what she was thinking, her body shaken by what it needed. The couple of times she had made love with Kevin, it hadn't done anything for her. She hadn't felt the earth shake and she hadn't experienced the feeling of coming out of her skin. In fact, she had been inwardly counting the minutes when it would be over. Was it possible an experience with Clint would be just the opposite? Would it be one she wouldn't want to end? Such thoughts made her draw in a shaky breath.

As she crossed the room and slipped between the cool covers of the bed, she had a feeling that sleep wouldn't come easily for her tonight, especially since the aches in her body wouldn't go away.

By the time she finally closed her eyes, she was convinced that dreaming about all the things Clint could do to her wasn't sufficient. She wanted to experience the real thing.

Chapter 8

The next morning Alyssa entered the kitchen to find Clint already sitting at the table drinking coffee. She frowned. She had hoped to get up before him and have breakfast started.

"Chester said he usually doesn't start cooking until around five o'clock. You're up early," she said, glancing at him while going straight to the sink to wash her hands.

A smile touched the corners of his lips as he shrugged one broad shoulder. "I thought I'd have a cup of coffee while watching you work," he said.

She raised her chin defiantly. "You don't think I can handle things?" Alyssa asked in an accusing tone.

"Oh, trust me. I believe you can handle things. Chester wouldn't let you in his kitchen if he thought otherwise. I just wanted to watch you do it and offer my help if you need it," he said.

"Thanks."

"Don't mention it."

A short while later Alyssa wondered if she'd been too quick to give Clint her thanks. Each time she moved around the kitchen she felt his eyes on her and had a feeling his intense stares had nothing to do with her culinary skills. She was dressed in another of the outfits belonging to his sister. This one was a pair of jeans and a top. He'd been right. She and Casey were about the same size and so far everything she'd tried on fit perfectly.

She turned around from the stove to tell him that everything was ready and her gaze collided with his. She saw something flicker in the dark depths of his eyes and that fiery light sent a burning sensation through her middle. She swallowed the lump in her throat. "Everything is ready."

Then, following Chester's instructions, she called the foreman at the bunkhouse to let him know the meal was ready to be picked up. She had prepared enough food to feed at least fifty people and was grateful for all those times she had helped Aunt Claudine and the other older ladies at church prepare meals for the homeless.

She hung up the phone only to find Clint standing only inches away from her and her pulse rate escalated. He was the epitome of handsome and radiated a sex appeal she couldn't deal with this early in the morning.

"You did an outstanding job," he said, and the sound of his voice only added to her discomfort. Alyssa began to feel a tingling sensation all over.

She tried playing off the feeling. "Save your compliment until after you've tasted it," she tried saying lightly.

He smiled. "Don't have to. I watched you. You definitely know your way around the kitchen."

She chuckled. "Thanks to Aunt Claudine, I would have to agree. I helped her out with feeding the homeless at least once a week. I never thought doing so would come in handy one day," she said heartily. "It felt good doing it. Chester has everything so well organized. This kitchen is a cook's dream."

"And you, Alyssa Barkley, are a man's dream," he said in a low voice.

He leaned forward and she knew he was going to kiss her. Just then she heard the sound of footsteps on the back porch. She took a step back.

"The guys are coming for the food," she said softly.

"So I hear," he said silkily and took a step back, as well. He glanced at his watch. "It's time for me to go, anyway."

"You're not going to stay and eat breakfast?" she asked quickly, before she could stop herself. Alyssa prayed he hadn't heard the disappointment in her voice.

"I'm going to eat with the men in the bunkhouse before leaving." And then before she could blink, he had recovered the steps and placed a tender kiss on her lips. "I'll see you in a couple of days."

Alyssa nodded, thinking she could definitely use two days without him hovering about. She would have two full days to get her head screwed back on right.

That first day Alyssa was still convinced that distance was just what she needed from Clint. She was glad he would be away from the ranch. Once her boxes had arrived, she'd taken the time to unpack. Her aunt had sent her everything she needed, from an adequate supply of clothes for the chilly days of February yet to come, to a sufficient supply of underwear.

By the second day Alyssa found herself glancing out the window wondering if perhaps Clint would return a day early—even though she tried to convince herself that she really didn't want him to. She enjoyed her talks with Chester and a few of the ranch hands who had remained behind.

On the third day, Alyssa paced the floor in his office when she couldn't sit still long enough to work at the computer. And every time she heard a commotion outside the window she found herself racing toward it to see if it was Clint returning. By late evening after sharing dinner with Chester, she found herself standing on the front porch staring out into the distance. She was reminded of a woman standing on the shore waiting for her man to return from the sea. The comparison struck her. For the first time since coming to Austin, she began to realize that her emotions were getting too deep. It was becoming obvious to Alyssa that she was developing feelings for Clint.

She sighed deeply, knowing it didn't make sense. They had been reunited just days ago. The only excuse she could come up with was that Clint Westmoreland—with his arrogant confidence and untamed sensuality—was more virile than Kevin could ever hope to be. She hadn't been involved with a man since that fateful day—her wedding day.

Finding out Kevin had been unfaithful had been a blow, but what had been even more of a shocker was the very idea that he felt they should forget what he'd done and move on. She couldn't move on. Instead she had sought to protect her heart from further damage the only way she knew how—avoid any personal dealings with men. She had responded in just the way Kim had counted on.

Alyssa had long ago accepted that her cousin didn't want her to be happy and didn't want Alyssa to have a man in her life. The thought of Alyssa having a man who loved her, who wanted to give her his world and his babies was something Kim was determined to prevent.

She knew Aunt Claudine was right when she would say that she needed to move on and not give Kim the victory. But she hadn't met a man worthy of such a task… until now.

Clint Westmoreland made her want to take a chance on living again in a way she had denied herself for almost two years. And even if it was only for the time she stayed on his ranch, she knew that she wouldn't have to worry about Kim being around to sabotage her relationship with Clint. Alyssa was smart enough to know that any relationship that she developed with him wouldn't last. At the end of the thirty days he would want her gone, off his ranch and out of his life.

In the past, Alyssa had avoided casual relationships, but for some reason she didn't see the time that she would spend with Clint as a casual fling. It would be more than that. Indulging in pleasure seemed a fitting term for their relationship. She considered her feelings for Clint a reawakening. If she had an affair with him, it would be a way to rebuild her self-esteem and regain her confidence as a woman. It would also be a way to enjoy life before returning to the mundane existence she'd carved out for herself in Waco.

"Nice night, isn't it?"

Alyssa was pulled out of her reverie when Chester walked out onto the porch. She was discovering each and every day just how much she liked the older man. He was loyal to Clint and his siblings to a fault and she liked that. It reminded her so much of how her relationship with her grandfather had been and the relationship she shared with her aunt now.

"It is a nice night," she said simply. She knew he was perceptive enough to figure out why she was outside standing on the porch in the dark and his next statement proved it.

"Sometimes it takes longer than the two days to set free the horses. Some of them can get real frisky when they are taken out of their element. I bet the reason Clint hasn't returned yet is because he's had his hands full."

Alyssa sensed that Chester was telling her that Clint hadn't been staying away from the ranch just to avoid her. *How had Chester known that was exactly what she had been thinking?*

Alyssa smiled as she pulled the jacket she was wearing more tightly around her shoulders. February was proving to be a colder month than January.

"Clint said that your grandfather used to be a bronco rider," Chester said.

"Yes, he was. In fact that's how he met Sid Roberts. It was an experience he took pride in telling me about while growing up."

"You were close to him," Chester said.

"Yes, he was the most special person in my life."

Less than an hour later when getting ready for bed, Alyssa remembered those words and knew in her heart that Clint was becoming a special person to her, as well.

Clint almost weakened as he gazed down at a sleeping Alyssa. A stream of light from a lamppost poured into her window and illuminated her features. He wasn't sure what she was wearing under the bedspread because her body was completely covered, but she looked incredibly sexy.

Okay, he had broken their agreement and had come into her bedroom. He'd done so because Chester had told him that she had stood outside on the porch that night waiting for him to return.

At first Clint hadn't wanted to believe it, but then a part of him realized that the possibility existed that she had indeed missed him…like he had missed her. Clint stiffened at the thought that he could miss any woman, but whether he liked it or not, he had. And she had constantly invaded his dreams since she'd come to the ranch. He didn't like that, either.

How could she get to him so deep and so quickly? He'd had other women since Chantelle, but none of them had made a lasting impression. None of them had even come close. But Alyssa was making more than a lasting impression. She was carving a niche right under his skin and it got deeper and deeper each and every time he saw her.

He studied Alyssa when she made a sound in her sleep. A lock of her hair had fallen onto her face. He leaned down and brushed the tendril back, careful not to wake her. He sighed knowing he had no right to be there, but also knowing that he would not have been able to sleep a wink if he had not looked in on her. He also knew his presence in her bedroom was about more than that. It was about wanting to be close to Alyssa.

He hated knowing how much he had wanted to see her and be with her. Clint fervently hoped that by the morning he would have regained control of the situation. He had to get whatever emotions he was battling in check and start putting her at a distance.

He frowned as he turned to leave the room and contemplated his plan of action with difficulty. It would mean more days spent away from the ranch. That had been his plan in the beginning. *Then why did the thought of following through with his original strategy leave such a bitter taste in his mouth?*

Upon awaking the next morning, Alyssa heard a group of men talking not far from her bedroom window. She got out of her bed and slipped into her robe before crossing the floor to the window and glancing out. Her heart nearly stopped beating. The three men she saw were among those who had left the ranch with Clint, which could only mean he had returned, as well. She couldn't help the smile that covered her lips as she headed for the bathroom.

Less than thirty minutes later she was dressed and eager to get down to breakfast before Clint left for the day. She felt a burning desire to see him, come face-to-face with him and get all into his space. She looked at herself one last time in the mirror before she left the room. She didn't look bad in her jeans and shirt, she thought with a smile. She also wore the new boots she had purchased the day before yesterday when she'd caught a ride into town with Chester. Alyssa felt like a bona fide cowgirl.

She breathed in deeply and with shaking hands she reached to open her bedroom door. Alyssa hoped that by the time she made it to the kitchen her heart would no longer be beating so wildly in her chest. It would be a struggle to keep it together knowing Clint was back and they would be once again breathing the same air.

She opened the door to step out into the hallway and her heart caught. Standing there, leaning against the opposite wall as if he'd been waiting for her, was Clint. Alyssa was speechless. And before she could open her mouth to utter a single word, he moved from the spot, pulled her into his arms and kissed her, devouring her mouth with an urgency that astounded her.

Alyssa sagged against him and wrapped her arms around his neck as his mouth and tongue continued plundering hers. She didn't think about struggling to keep herself together or trying to gain any semblance of control of the situation. The only thing she could think about was that he was back. He was here. And he was taking her mouth with a hunger that meant he had missed her to the same degree she had missed him. That thought made her giddy.

Everything was forgotten. How she had intended to protect her heart from further damage, and how she had decided at some point during the night to retreat back into her hands-off strategy. All her concentration was on the intense arousal overtaking her belly as she kissed Clint with the same fervor and passion that he was kissing her.

And then when he finally released her mouth, he didn't let go of her lips. He took the tip of his tongue and outlined a sensuous path from one corner to the other, over and over again. Alyssa heard herself groan. She actually felt her panties get wet. Clint had the ability to reach down, deep inside of her, to a place no man had gone for two years. He was stirring up a need, one as intense as anything she had ever encountered.

"I've got to go," Clint whispered against her moist lips. The deep, raspy tone of his voice knocked down the last reserve of strength she was trying to hold on to.

"Breakfast?" she asked. The only word she could get her lips to form.

"I've already eaten. I need to be on that back pasture. I'll be gone all day and wanted to see you before I left. I wanted to taste you."

His words made every single cell in her body multiply with excitement. Then, as if the kiss they'd just shared would not be enough to sustain him through the day, he took hold of her mouth with lightning speed once more. She returned the kiss. She hadn't been aware that she was so starved for such male interaction until now, but not interaction from just any male. She wanted it only from Clint.

When he finally released her mouth she knew her lips would be swollen again. Anyone seeing her would know why, but at the moment she didn't care.

"I have to go," he said again, and as if fighting the urge to take her into his arms yet again, he stepped back. He stared at her for a long moment before reaching out and gently touching her swollen lips with his fingertips. "I promised myself last night that I wouldn't do this," he said in a low, throaty voice. "But I can't seem to help it. You, Alyssa Barkley, are more of a temptation than I counted on you being."

Without giving her a chance to say anything he turned and she watched him walk away.

"Hey, boss, are you okay?" one of Clint's men inquired some hours later as he was saddling one of the horses.

Clint glanced up at Walter Pockets, frowned and said gruffly, "I'm fine. Why do you ask?"

The man, who had only been working for him a couple of years, hesitated. "Well, because you're putting the saddle on backward," he said.

"Damn," Clint said and quickly removed the saddle. He placed it on the horse's back correctly, grateful that only Pockets had seen him make such a blunder. "My mind was elsewhere," he said. He knew that was a lame excuse. He would be the first to get on his men if they were to let their minds wander while performing even a menial task. Working on a ranch required focus. And yet, he was not focused at all today.

"I can ride out and check on things if you want me to," Pockets said.

Clint thought about the man's offer. It was almost lunchtime already. He had pretty much decided to stay out on the range and eat with his men, but now he was thinking differently. Kissing Alyssa had not gotten her out of his system. Instead it seemed that each time their lips connected she was getting even more embedded under his skin. Yet he could no more seize an opportunity to kiss her than he could stop breathing.

"Thanks, Pockets," he finally heard himself say. "I'd appreciate it if you would. I've got a matter up at the house I need to take care of." That was saying it as honestly as he could.

Less than thirty minutes later he was walking into the kitchen. Chester glanced up from stirring a pot with a surprised look on his face. "I didn't expect you back until late tonight."

Clint shrugged. "I finished early. Where's Alyssa? Is she in my office?"

"No, she asked if she could borrow the truck to go into town. She said she was going to take a shower, so I guess she's in her bedroom getting dressed."

The thought of a naked Alyssa standing under a spray of water got him even more unfocused and aroused and he was grateful to be standing behind the kitchen table. Wondering why Alyssa needed to go into town, Clint headed toward his office.

"Maybe you ought to think about going with her," he heard Chester say. Clint drew up short and turned around.

"Why should I think about doing something like that?"

Chester smiled. "Because you could help her with all those bags and boxes she plans to bring back."

Clint frowned. "What bags and boxes?"

"From shopping. I figure she's going into town to do some shopping," Chester said.

Clint folded his arms over his chest. "Why in the hell would I want to accompany any woman shopping?"

Chester chuckled. "That would give you a chance to spend time with her under the pretense of being helpful. And don't insult my intelligence by asking why I think you'd want to spend time with her, Clint. I saw her lips at breakfast."

Clint's frowned deepened. "And?"

"And I think you need to go easy on them," the older man said with a sly chuckle.

Clint honestly didn't think he could. Instead of telling that to Chester he turned and walked out of the kitchen.

"Where are the keys to the truck, Chester?" Alyssa asked, glancing around. She could have sworn when Chester had given them to her earlier she had placed them on the top of the breakfast bar.

"Clint has them," Chester said.

She whirled around with a surprised look on her face. "Clint?"

"Yep," Chester answered without looking up from stirring the pot on the stove.

"Oh. I thought he was going to be gone all day," Alyssa said.

The older man did manage to smile. "Yeah, I thought so, too, but I guess he had a change in plans."

"Does that mean he needs to use the truck?"

"No," Chester said, chuckling. "I think it means that he's going into town with you."

Alyssa swallowed the lump in her throat. "Are you sure?"

"Positive. In fact he's waiting outside for you," Chester said.

Alyssa knew she looked startled, but Chester wouldn't know because he didn't seem to be paying attention to her. He was focused on his cooking.

"Well, I guess I'll see you in an hour or so," she said, glancing at her watch.

"Don't count on it," Chester said.

"Excuse me?" she responded, not sure she had heard Chester correctly.

"Nothing," the older man said.

Alyssa eyed Chester in confusion, certain that he had said something. However, instead of questioning him further, on wobbly legs she headed toward the living room to leave. *Why would Clint want to accompany her into town? Had he gotten a call from Hightower? Surely he would have told her if he had.*

She stopped short of opening the door, needing to pull herself together. This would be the first time she saw him since their morning kiss. It was a kiss from which she still hadn't fully recovered. And she had assumed that since he would be away from the ranch all day and she wouldn't see him again until tomorrow at the earliest, that she would have time to compose her senses.

Taking a deep breath, she opened the door and saw Clint standing in the yard. He was leaning against his truck and her stomach became filled with butterflies when she realized that he was waiting for her.

She was careful walking down the steps, trying not to trip. She was amazingly aware of the appraisal he was giving her with his dark, intense eyes. He was looking her up and down, from the top of her head to the toes of her booted feet.

She decided to return the favor and check him out, as well. She saw that he'd taken the time to shower and change, too. He looked good enough to eat leaning against the truck in a pair of jeans and a blue chambray shirt. His legs were crossed at his booted ankles and he wore a black cowboy hat on his head. He was the epitome of sexy, the essence of what she definitely considered a fine man and the personification of everything male.

As she walked up to him she saw desire in his eyes and she took a misstep. He reached out and caught her arm and brought her closer to him. The front of their bodies touched and his lips were mere inches from hers.

"Are you okay?" he asked in a low, husky tone.

She wanted to tell him that no, she wasn't okay, and she wouldn't fully recuperate until she left his ranch for good. In the meantime, for the first time in her life she was beginning to think about all the things she could get into while she was there. And when she left, she would have solid, red-hot memories to hold on to during the night while lying in her bed alone. "Yes, I'm fine," she finally managed to say.

In response, as quick as a cricket, he swiped his tongue

across her lips just seconds before releasing her. She blinked, not sure he'd done it until she felt the wetness he had left behind.

"Ready to go?" he asked in a husky voice, transferring his hold from her arm to her hand. The feel of his touch had her heart thudding in her chest.

"Yes, I am," she said.

He opened the truck door for her and she slid inside. He stood there a moment and she wondered if he was going to kiss her again. He leaned closer but instead of kissing her he snapped the seat belt into place around her hips.

"Thanks," she barely managed to get out.

He smiled. "No problem." And then he straightened and closed the door.

With almost stiff fingers she clutched her purse as she watched him walk around the front of the truck to get inside while whistling a tune she wasn't familiar with. Then he was buckling up his own seat belt and starting the engine. "Where to?" he looked over and asked her.

Her eyebrow arched. He definitely seemed to be in a good mood. "You're taking time away from your busy schedule to be my personal chauffeur," she said as a grin touched lips that were still warm and wet from his kiss.

He grinned back. "I guess you could say that. When I heard you were going to do some shopping in town I decided that now was a good time to get that new belt that I need."

"Oh." But that didn't explain why he was back at the ranch when he had mentioned that morning he would be gone all day. Alyssa decided it really didn't matter why he had altered his plans. He had and she was glad about it.

"So where to first?" he asked her again.

"What about the Highland Mall?" she asked. That particular mall had been her favorite when she lived in Austin as a Ranger.

"The Highland Mall it is."

She settled back in her seat, anticipating how the rest of the day would pan out.

Chapter 9

It was late afternoon before Clint and Alyssa returned to the ranch. In addition to shopping, Clint had suggested they see a movie. He could tell that Alyssa had been surprised by his suggestion. There were ten movies showing and they had narrowed their selections down to two. They couldn't decide which of the two to see, so they ended up viewing both.

Clint had enjoyed Alyssa's company immensely. He'd discovered several new facets of her character. For instance, Alyssa loved Mexican food and she was thrilled about her work as a Web designer. During the course of the day, she'd explained the process of setting up a Web site and how each design was tailored to the individual needs of each client. She'd also gone into detail about search engines and how invaluable they were to anyone who frequented the Internet.

They ate lunch at the mall food court and he had enjoyed watching her eat every single bite of her meal. In fact, he had gotten turned on just from watching her eat. *Was that crazy or what?*

And another thing that was crazy was that he had enjoyed being with her while she shopped. In his opinion, she was a smart shopper. He had definitely learned a lot today about working a clearance rack.

"So where do you want these bags and boxes?" he asked as he followed her into the house.

"You can carry them into my bedroom."

He glanced over at her and grinned. "Is that an invitation?"

She shook her head and grinned back. "You may enter my bedroom this time, but only to deliver my packages, Clint."

As they walked together down the wide hallway that turned off into the wing where she was staying, a part of him regretted his decision to make sure the guest room she used was so far from his bedroom.

"Did I tell you how nice you look today?" he asked softly as they neared her bedroom.

She glanced over at him. "Thank you."

He could tell his compliment had caught her off guard. When they reached the bedroom, he stood back while she led him in. "You can place everything on the bed."

"Sure," he said. He had come into the bedroom last night while she had slept and the memory of seeing her so relaxed and at peace sent sensations of desire spiraling through him now.

After placing the items on the bed, he turned and saw her watching him. And there it was again. He had felt it all day around her—the spark, sizzle and steam that seemed to emanate between them. He knew she was aware of it, too.

"I believe this one is yours," she said, retrieving a single bag from the bed and offering it to him.

"My belt," he said and chuckled.

He took the bag and then gently pulled her to him. He saw the flicker of passion in the depths of her eyes. "I always say I'm not going to kiss you and end up doing it anyway," he said.

"Why?"

A smile touched his expression. "I've told you why. Do you want me to remind you?"

"Yes, why not?" she teased.

He leaned into her, let her feel the evidence of his desire that was pressed hard against her. He spread the palms of his hands at the center of her back, bringing her closer to the fit of him. "Should I say more?" he asked in a voice that sounded deeper to his own ears.

She held his gaze. "Yes, say more," she said daringly.

He leaned over and licked her cheek with the tip of his tongue. "I like tasting you and one of these days, Alyssa, I plan on tasting you all over."

He heard her sharp intake of breath. He was being blunt, but he was also being truthful. Things couldn't continue between them at the rate they were going. They hadn't made it to their second week together and already things were almost sizzling out of control. Hadn't Chester just today hinted that he should go easy on her lips? As if he ever really could.

"Remember our agreement," she said in a quiet voice.

"I remember it," he said, still holding her close. "Do you?"

She tilted her head up and looked at him. "Yes, I do."

"You're the one who initiated this, Alyssa, and you're the only one who can finish it. I will adhere to our agreement as long as you want me to," he said.

"B-but what about all these insinuations you're making?" she whispered accusingly.

He smiled, thinking about all he had said. "What about them?"

She studied his features and then evidently decided he wasn't serious. "You're teasing me," she said.

"No," he said. "I'm not teasing. I'm dead serious."

As if tired of what she perceived as his game-playing, she lifted her chin and said, "You can't have it both ways, Clint."

He laughed although his features were without humor. "Sweetheart, when I finally have you, I plan on having it in ways I've only recently dreamed of." And as if to prove his point, his thighs moved at the same time he pressed gently in the curve of her back to bring her closer to him.

He then leaned down and placed a gentle kiss on her lips and felt himself harden even more. "I'll see you at dinner."

"I'm skipping dinner tonight," Alyssa replied.

"Not because of me, I hope," he said in a low tone.

"No," she said tightly. "Because of me."

Alyssa stretched out on the bed. It was nearly midnight. She had taken a shower and changed into one of many oversize T-shirts she enjoyed sleeping in.

Good to her word, she had skipped dinner because she needed to be away from Clint. She had called her aunt earlier and they had chatted awhile. Luckily, Aunt Claudine hadn't asked her anything about Clint and Alyssa had had no reason to bring him up.

Chester had knocked on her door earlier to make sure she really didn't want anything to eat and had even offered to serve dinner to her in her room if she preferred. She had assured him she was fine and she wasn't hungry. She figured Chester thought the reason she was missing dinner was because of a tiff she'd had with Clint, which wasn't the truth. She just needed distance from him right now. He had the tendency to prevent her from thinking straight. He would say things with such conceit that he rattled her confidence. He seemed so sure of her when she wasn't sure of herself, she thought.

Her cell phone rang and she frowned wondering who would be calling her at this hour. Aunt Claudine was usually in bed by nine. She sat up and reached for the phone. Her frown deepened when she saw the caller indicated Kim was on the line. She wondered how Kim had gotten her number. There was no way Aunt Claudine would have given it to her.

"Yes?" She decided it was time to stop avoiding her cousin.

"Well, well, for a moment I thought you had dropped off the face of the earth," Kim said.

Alyssa rolled her eyes. "What do you want, Kim?"

"Where are you?"

"It doesn't matter to you. What do you want?"

"Everyone is wondering where you are. You just took off without telling anyone," Kim said smartly.

"I did tell someone," Alyssa replied.

"Yeah, we figured Aunt Claudine knew where you are but she isn't talking. All she's saying is that you left town to go visit a client."

"Whatever," Alyssa said, sidestepping Kim's attempts to get more information.

"Really, Alyssa, don't you think it's time for me and you to sit down and have a little chat? I'm sick and tired of you blaming me because you can't keep a man. It's not my fault that they end up finding you inadequate and prefer me to you," Kim said.

"Look, Kim, I have to go."

"And you're not going to tell me where you are?"

"No."

"Suit yourself."

"I will. Goodbye and please don't call back." Alyssa then hung up the phone.

Inhaling deeply, she swung her legs off the bed as she fought back the anger she felt. Overconfident people were wearing on her nerves, although she had to admit that Kim was very different from Clint. She couldn't imagine Clint ever deliberately hurting anyone. Deciding she needed to work off some of her negative energy, she decided to slip into Clint's office to play a game on his computer.

It was late and chances were he was in bed asleep by now. At least she hoped so. She opened her bedroom door and, as expected, the entire house was quiet. She appreciated the night-lights that lined the hallway as she made her way from her wing toward the one where Clint's office was located. As far as she knew, they were the only ones living in the main house. Chester lived a few miles away in a house on land Sid Roberts had willed to him.

Alyssa slowly opened the office door and found the room empty. She quickly moved across the room to Clint's desk. Kim's words had put her on edge. She was still fuming while waiting for the computer to boot up.

She turned when a knock sounded on the door. She

went still when Clint walked in. Closing the door behind him, he leaned against it.

Alyssa tried not to let her focus linger on his dark eyes, but when she moved her gaze to his strong jawline and kissable lips she realized she was in trouble looking there, too. She returned her gaze to his.

"I thought you were asleep," she said when she finally found her voice.

A smile touched the corners of his lips. "As you can see I'm very much awake."

Yes, she could definitely see that. She could also see in his nonchalant stance against the door just how perfectly his jeans fit his body, and with his chambray shirt open past the throat, she got a glimpse of his hairy, muscular chest. But what really caught her attention was the area below the belt. Not only was Clint very much awake, he was very much aroused, as well.

The thought that he wanted her was enough of a reason for her heart to pound and her pulse to drum. If that wasn't bad enough, her lips began tingling from remembered kisses. She already had a number of them tucked away in her memory bank.

She swallowed deeply as desire began to thrum through her and felt her body automatically respond to his. "Is there a reason why you're here?" she asked, hearing the slight quiver in her voice.

"Yes," he said in an arrogant tone as he moved away from the door and slowly strolled toward her.

From the glow of light off the computer screen she was conscious of every single thing about him, including the dark pupils in his eyes and the faint growth of stubble on his chin.

When he reached the edge of the desk he placed his

hands palms down as he leaned closer and brought his face mere inches from hers.

"Tonight," he whispered against her lips, "I want to teach you another version of Playing with Fire."

Alyssa slowly backed away. She then tilted her head and looked up at him. "You agreed," she reminded him in an accusing voice, one she could barely force past her lips.

"I agreed not to seduce you into my bed, Alyssa," he said. He momentarily released her gaze to glance around the room. "There's not one bed in here," he said.

She tilted her head a half inch higher. "You don't need a bed to do what you want to do. You've said so yourself," she said defiantly.

He smiled. "Yes, I did say that and it's true," he said in a husky voice. "To make love to you I don't need a bed. But you'll have to be willing, Alyssa. I would never force myself on you."

She believed him. But she also knew it wouldn't take much coercing on his part right now. He had become her weakness.

"I won't do anything you don't want me to do. Come play with me," he said throatily. "Trust me," he added as he offered her his hand.

The look in his eyes stirred her in a way she would not have thought possible and without realizing she was doing so, she began leaning toward him. And when she reached out and placed her hand in his, she knew she had literally sealed her fate.

Clint Westmoreland was demanding more of her than she had ever shared with any man. She was taking a risk, opening her heart up in a way she had never done with

Kevin. And as she continued to gaze into the turbulent darkness of his eyes she suddenly knew why. Not only did she trust him, she had fallen in love with him, as well.

She was not going to waste her time wondering how it happened, or why it had happened. She was willing to accept that it had happened...just as she was willing to accept it would be a one-sided love affair that would lead nowhere. At the end of the thirty days she would be leaving. But at this very moment, she had tonight and wanted to take full advantage of it.

"I do trust you, Clint," she finally said softly. "Teach me how to play your game."

Chapter 10

Still holding her hand in his, Clint moved around the desk to gently pull her up from her seat and into his arms. He knew she had to see the desire flaring in his eyes, had to know from his aroused state just how much he wanted her. And he did want her and had from the first, when he'd seen her at the airport.

Leaning slightly, he took the liberty to place his open hands over her bottom, bringing her closer to him, and groaned through clenched teeth when he felt her softness come to rest against his hardness. Desire ripped into him, adding to the heat that was already there.

"Alyssa." He moaned her name just moments before covering her mouth with his, devouring with an intensity that shook him to the core. He'd become familiar with her taste, the very essence of her flavor, and each time his mouth was reacquainted with it, one part of him wanted to savor it slowly, while the other part wanted to devour her whole.

He was too far gone to savor yet he refused to be rushed. He wanted to make their passion something she would enjoy. That way she would let him make love to her again…and again…and again.

In his mind, nothing about their relationship had changed. They were just taking things to the next level. They were adults and they would be able to handle it. They would make no promises, just pleasure. In thirty days, their marriage would be annulled and Alyssa would leave. His life would continue just the way it had before getting that fateful letter from the bureau. For some reason the thought of Alyssa leaving made him feel uneasy.

She pushed against his chest so he could release her mouth and when he saw her lips he understood why. Already they looked thoroughly kissed. "Don't know just how much of that I can handle," she whispered, trying to catch her breath.

He knew he could kiss her in other ways and was anxious to explore those options with her. In his mind, the game of playing with fire was basically doing just that, and he was curious to see just how much heat she could handle.

"Come with me," he said as he led her over to the sofa. He sat down and then pulled her down in his lap. Immediately, he brushed a feathery kiss on the top of her head. When he saw her trying to pull the T-shirt she was wearing down to cover her exposed thighs, he stilled her hands.

"Don't," he whispered.

He reached out his hand to stroke her flesh there, liking the feel of her soft skin. From that first day he had enjoyed looking at her legs. But lately she had covered them up with jeans. The jeans she wore always emphasized her womanly curves, so he'd had no reason to complain, until now.

In fact, when it came to Alyssa, he was unable to find fault with anything. The only thing that gave him reason to pause was her unwillingness to discuss her family at any great length. He had tried getting her to talk about them while they were at the mall, but she hadn't had a lot to say. He couldn't help but wonder what they thought of her living with him for thirty days. Had she told them the full story like he had told his siblings? he wondered.

Cole had called earlier tonight from Mexico where he'd been for the past month on assignment. Like with Casey, Chester hadn't wasted any time sharing the news. It didn't come as a surprise that Cole had thought the situation rather amusing. Cole said he was glad it was Clint caught in that predicament and not him. Cole had claimed that he was too much of a ladies' man to be tied down to just one woman. The first question his brother had asked was if Alyssa was pretty. Clint had assured him that she was.

"Are you sure you don't want to keep her around?" Cole had asked.

Clint's response had been quick and resounding. "I'm positive. At the end of the thirty days she's out of here."

"Clint?"

The sound of Alyssa's voice pulled him from his reverie. He realized his hand had moved higher on her thigh. He smiled when he answered her. "Yes?"

"What are you going to do to me?" she whispered, tilting her head back to look at him.

In an amazingly calm voice, he said, "I'm going to introduce you to another version of Playing with Fire, but the object of the game will remain the same. My goal is to blow you up and, baby, I'm about to make you explode all over the place."

He murmured the words against her lips and felt them quiver beneath his. He then shifted her position in his lap to remove her T-shirt and wasn't surprised to find her completely naked underneath her nightclothes. She said she trusted him; now he would see just how much.

He stood with her in his arms and then laid her back on the sofa, fully open to his view. His gaze slid over her, lingering on her breasts, the gold ring in her navel, her womanly core and her long, beautiful legs.

"You are beautiful," he whispered, barely able to get the words out. Entranced, fascinated and totally captivated, he slowly dropped down to his knees in front of her, needing to touch her, taste her all over.

He reached out and his fingers immediately went to her breasts, cupping them in his hands before leaning closer to let the tip of his tongue taste the curve of her throat. Then he pulled back and watched his fingertips swirl around a budded nipple, feeling it pucker beneath his touch.

A soft moan escaped her lips and he saw she had closed her eyes, was biting on her lower lip. Little did she know he hadn't even gotten started.

"How does my touch feel, Alyssa?" he asked in a low voice as he continued drawing circles around her nipples with his fingertips.

"Good," she murmured in a voice so low he could barely hear her.

"Do you like it?"

"Yes," she responded and it seemed her words had been an effort. She refused to open her eyes to look at him.

He then slowly moved his hands, lowering them to her stomach, skimming the taut skin there. She felt soft to the touch and he smiled at the ring in her navel.

He eased his hand between her open thighs and heard her sharp intake of breath when he nudged her thighs even farther apart, wanting to touch and explore her everywhere. His fingers dipped inside of her. She was wet, drenched, and her scent consumed him totally.

Fighting the urge to taste her, he removed his hand from her and let his fingers travel downward past her knees and then to her beautiful feet. There wasn't a part of her he wanted left untouched.

"Now for the taste test," he whispered, determined to taste Alyssa's first orgasm on his lips.

She opened her eyes and stared at him. "I don't think I can handle much more."

He smiled. "You can. Trust me."

She nodded and he leaned forward and captured her nipples in his mouth. And things started from there. Never had he wanted to taste a woman so badly, and he went about showing her how much. She looked so sensual and sexy that intense emotions tore into him as he moved his mouth lower to the area he craved.

She let out another deep groan the moment he lowered his head between her legs, and when the tip of his tongue touched her she nearly came off the sofa. But he had no intentions of letting her go. He pulled back only long enough to shift her body to place her legs over his shoulders. He was filled with a primitive sexual energy that was consuming him. He intended to transfer that energy to her in this very intimate way.

He tightened his hold on her hips and lowered his mouth to her and immediately found his mark, capturing her womanly core, locking his mouth to it. She tasted sweet. She released a litany of moans and arched her back and he greedily began tormenting her with his tongue.

Her body was on fire, he could feel it. She was on the verge of exploding. He could feel that, as well. His grip tightened on her hips when she let out a scream and he continued to hungrily stroke her with his tongue, enjoying the way she was pushing her body against his mouth.

God, she was responsive, completely filled with passion, a fantasy come true. And when she couldn't take any more and blew up, when an explosion racked her body, he continued to give her a hard kiss. He felt his own loins about to burst and fought back for control. This was her time. His time would come later.

Tonight was for her.

When the last quake left her body, he pulled her into his arms and kissed her. He would give her time to recover and then he intended to perform the process all over again.

Sitting across the room at his desk, Clint's gaze encompassed Alyssa, who was knocked out on his sofa. He smiled, thinking that too much passion could definitely do that to a person. Deciding he wanted to let her sleep but didn't want to leave her alone, he decided to pass the time browsing the Internet.

First he checked out the Web site that advertised her company and was impressed with what he saw and the listing of references. Her clients consisted of both corporations and a mom who was using the site to organize a carpooling network.

Deciding to use one of those search engines she had told him about at lunch, he was able to locate several foundations that had a similar goal as the Sid Roberts Foundation—saving wild horses. One such organization was located in Arizona. Reaching for a pen, he jotted the information down. He would contact the organization the next day.

Then with nothing else to do, he decided to search Alyssa's name. Perhaps such a search would list other Web sites that she'd done or was associated with.

In addition to bringing up several sites that her name was linked to, he was also given a list of news articles in which her name appeared. One was an article about an award she had received for Web design. A semblance of pride touched him at her accomplishment.

Then his gaze sharpened when it came across another article. It was one that announced her marriage engagement. Clint instantly felt a sharp pain that was similar to a swift kick in his abdomen. Alyssa hadn't told him she'd been engaged.

He flipped to another article and his breath caught at the headlines that read Attorney Kevin Brady Weds Alyssa Barkley.

Clint's shoulders stiffened but he managed to force them to lean forward in his chair as he read the article that was dated two years ago. "In the presence of over five hundred guests, prominent Waco attorney Kevin Brady wed local Web designer Alyssa Barkley." There was also a picture of a beautiful Alyssa in a wedding gown.

Clint flipped off that particular screen, angered beyond belief at the thought that there was a possibility he had just made love to someone else's wife. During their very first conversations the day she'd arrived in Austin,

Alyssa had told him she was not married. Yet the article indicated that she had been married. Even if she had gotten a divorce, she should have told him about it. This changed everything, Clint thought angrily.

Stunned, he stood and moved away from the computer, feeling let down and used. Taking the chair on the other side of the sofa, he decided not to wake her. So he waited until she finally awakened a half hour later. He watched as she slowly opened her eyes, saw him sitting in the chair and smiled at him. He could tell by her expression that she was confused by his refusal to return her smile.

"Clint?" she asked, pulling her naked body up into a sitting position. "What's wrong?"

He didn't say anything as he tried to ignore her nudity before she reached for her T-shirt and pulled it over her head. Then in a voice tinged with the anger he was trying to hold in check, he asked, "Why didn't you tell me you had gotten married, Alyssa?"

Chapter 11

Alyssa went stiff. From Clint's expression she knew he mistook the gesture for guilt. A part of her immediately wondered if it mattered what he thought since he had been quick to think the worst of her, to believe she could be married to someone and willingly participate in what they had shared tonight. Her anger flared. *Just what type of woman did he think she was?*

But then she knew what he thought did matter. What he had done tonight, not once but twice, had been intense, passionate and an unselfish giving of himself. "I asked you a question, Alyssa," Clint said in the same hard voice.

Reining her anger back in and holding his gaze, she shook her head. "I'm not married, Clint."

"But you were," he said.

It wasn't a question, it was an accusation. She wondered where he had gotten his information. It would seem like the handiwork of Kim, but she knew that couldn't be the case.

"Alyssa," he said.

Apparently she wasn't answering quickly enough to suit him. The details of the humiliating day of her wedding were something she didn't like remembering, much less talking about. Having all those people at the church know the reason she hadn't gone through with the wedding—that she had been unable to satisfy her future husband to the point where already he'd gone out seeking the attentions of others—had been a degrading experience for her.

Knowing Clint was waiting for a response, she lifted her chin and tilted her head and slanted him a look.

"I've never been married, Clint," she said.

She saw his anger die down somewhat, but she also saw the confused look in the depths of his dark eyes.

"Then explain that picture and this article on Internet," he said.

So that was where he'd gotten his misinformation, she thought. With as much dignity as she could muster, Alyssa sat up straight on the sofa.

"The wedding was supposed to take place, but it didn't and it was too late to pull the article scheduled to run in the newspaper. To be honest, I didn't even think about calling the papers to stop the announcement from printing the next day. I had other things on my mind," Alyssa said.

Like how my cousin could hate me so much to do such a thing, and how my fiancé, the man I thought I loved, could allow her to use him to accomplish such a hateful act, she thought.

"You're saying that you called things off on your wedding day?"

She heard the incredulous tone of his voice as if such a thing was paramount to the burning of the flag. "Yes, that's what I'm saying," she said.

She knew that statement wouldn't suffice. He needed to know more. So she began talking and remembering that dreadful day. Her feelings of shame and embarrassment hadn't lessened with time.

"I was home that day getting ready to leave for the church when a courier delivered a package for me. It contained pictures of my soon-to-be husband in bed with someone I knew. The pictures arrived just in time to ruin what should have been the happiest day of my life," Alyssa said.

She watched Clinton's fury return, but this time it wasn't directed at her.

"Are you saying that while engaged to you your fiancé was sleeping around? And with someone you knew and that the person deliberately wanted to hurt you?"

She nodded. "Yes, and the pictures were very explicit. Kevin didn't even really apologize. He said he felt his behavior was something I should be able to forgive him for. He said I should get over it because it just happened that one time and meant nothing."

"Bullshit," Clint said.

Alyssa tried not to smile. "Yes, that's what I said."

"And the woman involved?"

"She accomplished her goal, which was to hurt me and embarrass me. She wanted to prove that there was nothing that I considered mine that she couldn't have," Alyssa said.

He frowned. "She doesn't sound like a very nice person."

She thought that over for a moment. "In my opinion, she's not."

The room got quiet and Alyssa was very much aware of him staring at her, so she tried looking at everything else in the room but him. She wondered what he was thinking. Did he agree with some of the others who'd pitied her because they felt she hadn't been able to hold on to her man, keep him from wandering?

She heard Clint move and when she glanced over in his direction she was startled to find him standing in front of her. She lifted confused eyes to his. When he reached out his hand to her, she took it and he gently pulled her to her feet and off the sofa. Instantly, his arms went around her waist and he pulled her tighter to him.

"I just made a mistake in accusing you of something when I should have checked out the facts first," he said, in a low, husky tone. "I'm sorry and I can assure you that it won't happen again," he said, holding her gaze with his.

"And I'm glad you didn't marry that guy because if you would have married him, you wouldn't be here with me now." A few moments later he added while placing his palm against her cheek, "Besides, he didn't deserve you."

That's the same thing her aunt had said that day. Over the years, Claudine had just about convinced Alyssa that it was true. Touched by what he'd said, Alyssa tilted her head back and slanted a small smile at him. "Thank you for saying that," she said.

"Don't thank me, sweetheart, because it's true. Any man who screws around on a woman like you can't be operating with a full deck."

Alyssa shrugged. "You haven't seen the other woman," she said.

"Don't have to. Beauty is only skin deep and a real man knows that. I'm not the kind to get taken in by just a pretty face," Clint said and he smiled down at her. "Although I would be the first to admit that you do have a pretty face," he added in a husky voice. "Come on. Let me walk you to your room."

She drew in a deep breath thinking how quick and easy it had been to fall in love with Clint. Even now, when she knew he didn't feel the same way, she loved him so deeply it made her ache. It also made her want to express her love in the only way she knew how, and with the time limit they had, the only way she could.

"We didn't finish the game," she said softly, remembering the two orgasms he had given her and how she had passed out before returning the favor.

He reached out and gently caressed her bottom lip. "No, we didn't, but you've had enough for one night. We'll play again at another time. Trust me."

She did and it suddenly occurred to her at that moment just how much.

Alyssa woke up the next morning overwhelmed that in just one night things had changed between her and Clint. There was no doubt in her mind that he still expected them to annul the marriage and for her to return to Waco at the end of the thirty days. But then, she thought, smiling, there was also no doubt in her mind that he wanted her the way a man wanted a woman. He had proven as much last night.

She glanced over at the clock and quickly sat up as her heart jumped in her chest. It was just before eight in the morning. Clint was an early riser. On most mornings he was up and out before six. She wondered if she had already missed him.

She slid out of bed and moved quickly to the bathroom to take a shower, remembering his hands and mouth on every part of her body. Moments later in the shower and under the spray of warm water, she glanced down and saw the marks of passion his mouth had made on her skin. Most of them, like the ones on her stomach and thighs, could be easily covered by her clothes, but the ones on her neck were blatantly visible. They would be hard to hide. At the moment she didn't care.

A short while later she'd finished dressing. She'd decided to wear a new pair of jeans she had purchased the day before and a top she had picked up while at the mall. Sighing deeply, she left the bedroom, hoping Clint was still around and hadn't left the ranch for the day.

"Is there any reason your eyes are glued to that door?" Chester asked, chuckling. Clint didn't answer. "Hey, give her a while. She'll be coming through that door at any minute. Unless your wife has a reason to sleep late this morning," Chester teased.

Your wife.

Clint felt his stomach roll into a knot. It was only when he was conversing with Chester that Clint remembered that legally Alyssa was his wife. As his spouse, she was as deeply embedded as any woman could get in his life.

"*Does* she have a reason to sleep late, Clint?"

Chester's question broke into his thoughts. He didn't bother glancing over in Chester's direction because he had no intention answering the old man. Yes, Alyssa had plenty of reasons to sleep late this morning and all of them involved what they had done in his office last night. He got hard just thinking about their "game" and was grateful he was sitting down and away from Chester's prying eyes. The old man saw way too much to suit Clint.

"Clint, you're not answering my question."

Clint's gaze remained glued to the door that separated the kitchen from the dining room. "And I don't intend to, Chester. Don't you have work around here to do?"

"Don't you?"

Clint frowned. He did have plenty of work to do and he was getting behind in it if the truth was known. But he needed to see Alyssa. All through the night he thought about what she had shared with him about her unfaithful fiancé and her horrible wedding day. Her revelations had nagged at him to the point where he'd been unable to sleep.

He then recalled how he had found out about Chantelle's infidelity. When she believed his future aspirations did not include anything else other than being a Texas Ranger, Chantelle had sought out greener pastures and had married a banker.

Clint knew all about betrayals. He knew how it felt to believe you were in love with someone and believe that person loved you back only to have that love tarnished with treachery.

Somewhere in the house he heard a door close and the sound snapped him out of his thoughts. He glanced over at Chester. "Don't you have the men to feed?"

Chester chuckled. "I've fed them already, but if that's a way of asking me to get lost, then I'll take the hint," he said, wiping off his hands with a kitchen towel. "Lucky for you I can come back and clean this stove later." The older man smiled over at Clint before grabbing his hat off the rack and turning toward the back door.

Before reaching it Chester turned around. "Have you given any thought to attending the annual benefit for the children's hospital I was telling you about? This year it will be held at the governor's mansion. Important people from all over Texas will be there. I reminded Casey about it. The function will happen during her visit, and she and McKinnon have agreed to go.

"And I even took the liberty to contact some of your cousins. Most of them said they would fly in to attend. Wasn't that real nice of them?"

Chester paused only long enough to add, "I haven't gotten a firm commitment from Cole or you, though." He chuckled. "At least this year you won't have a problem getting a date since you have a wife."

Clint shot Chester a glare before the man turned around to open the back door. Chester was barely out of the door when Clint stood up, immediately dismissing what Chester had said from his mind. The man was becoming a smart-ass in his old age.

Clint heard steps and felt his stomach clench in anticipation. He was eager to see Alyssa. Ready. Eager. Waiting. The kitchen door swung open and then she was there. Smiling at him. And she looked so damn good in a pair of jeans, shirt and cowboy boots. Her thick, copper-brown hair flowed around her shoulders, framing her gorgeous face. She looked prettier than anything or anyone he had seen in a long time.

"Good morning, Clint," she said.

Without responding, he walked around the table and pulled her into his arms and whispered, "Good morning, Alyssa." He leaned down and captured her lips, needing to taste her again, to have her in his arms, to be consumed by her very essence. He didn't understand what was happening to him and at the moment, he didn't want to analyze his feelings or scrutinize his actions. The only thing he wanted to do was what he was now doing, exploring Alyssa's mouth with a hunger that astounded him.

He finally raised his head and gazed down at her moist lips, and when she whispered his name he leaned down again for another taste as pleasure tore through him. It was the kind of pleasure that licked at his heels, filled him with a warm rush and had certain parts of his body aching for relief.

This time when he pulled back again he placed a finger against her lips. "I love kissing you," he whispered.

She smiled sweetly. "I figured as much, especially after last night."

He smiled. "Come on, let's feed you. Chester kept your breakfast warm."

"And yours?"

"I've already eaten, but I'll join you at the table and drink another cup of coffee while you eat."

"All right," Alyssa said.

He took her hand and led her to the table thinking that he could definitely get used to her presence in his home.

She melted a little bit inside each and every time Clint glanced her way. A couple of times he had looked at his watch. She knew he had work around the ranch to do, but he was putting his work aside for her. But she didn't want to keep him from doing his job.

"I got a chance to read all that information about the foundation and the reason for it," she said, to break the comfortable silence between them.

He took a sip of his coffee as his intense gaze still held hers. "Did you?"

"Yes. And I got some wonderful ideas for the site that I would like to share with you. That is if you were really serious about my doing a web design for it," she said.

"Yes, I'm serious. I've even spoken to Casey about it," Clint assured her.

She raised a brow. "You have?"

He chuckled. "Yes. I'm president and executive director of the board that consists of my brother and sister. We've hired several others to work with us who are just as determined as we are to relocate as many horses as we can. We also want to educate the public to the plight of the wild horses," Clint said.

She nodded. "I guess all three of you love horses."

He grinned. "With a passion, and speaking of horses, I want you to have all your work done by three o'clock today."

She lifted a brow. "Why?"

"Because you and I are going riding," he said.

She frowned. "If you recall, I told you I'd rather not get on a horse," Alyssa said.

"I recall, but riding a horse is just like riding a bike. If you take a fall you get back on and try again."

"Even if you break your arm in the fall?"

"Yes, even if you broke your arm. How old were you when it happened?"

"Ten," she said.

"Ten? Then it's definitely about time we do something about conquering your fear about riding. So, do we have a date at three?"

"Yes, we have a date," she said with a smile.

Chapter 12

Alyssa took a deep breath as she stepped out on the front porch. Like the day before, Clint was in the yard waiting for her. This time he wasn't leaning against his truck. Today he was sitting on the back of what Alyssa perceived as the largest horse she'd ever seen. The big black stallion was beautiful, although he looked very mean.

"He won't bite," Clint said.

She glanced up at Clint, not at all certain. "Are you sure about that?"

"Positive. I wouldn't let anything harm a hair on your head. I thought I'd start you off easy. Today you'll ride with me. Royal can handle the both of us."

"Royal?"

"Yes. He was the first stallion we brought from Nevada last year. He was very wild and unruly," he explained.

She grinned. "And of course you tamed him."

"I did. And he's been my horse ever since," Clint added with pride.

She looked at the fierce-looking animal and then back at Clint. "Evidently you're good at what you do."

"I'm not perfect. I make my share of mistakes, but thanks," he said. "Now come closer so I can lift you up."

Ignoring the way the horse was looking at her, she went closer so that Clint could hoist her up onto the horse's back. He effortlessly pulled her up to sit behind him. She gripped her arms tightly around his waist.

He glanced over his shoulder at her. "Ready?"

"As much as I'll ever be. And you promise I won't fall off?"

He smiled. "I promise," he said.

Satisfied with his answer, she rested her chest against his back. "Then, yes, I'm ready," she said, trying to sound brave.

And she held on as Clint trotted for a few moments around the yard. And then when they reached the wide, open plain, he took off and she held on to him for dear life.

Clint liked the feel of Alyssa holding on to him as they continued their ride. He knew where he was taking her. Clint had a special spot on his ranch and he wanted to share it with Alyssa.

"You okay back there?" he asked her. She hadn't said much since they had left the ranch.

Instead of answering right away, she tightened her arms around him and snuggled even closer. He could feel the hardened tips of her breasts against his back. He could tell she wasn't wearing a bra and it felt good. And the way her thighs were squeezing him as she tried to grip the horse's sides turned him on.

"Yes, I'm fine," she finally said. "Where are we going?"

"You'll see," he said over his shoulder. "We'll be there in a minute."

As if satisfied with his response, she continued to hold on and together they rode against the wind.

It didn't take them long to get to the south-ridge pasture and he brought Royal to a stop near a thicket of oak trees. Dismounting, he took the horse's reins and securely tied them to a tree. He then glanced up at Alyssa, who was sitting demurely on the animal's back, and thought she looked totally incredible. Thick desire flowed through his bloodstream as he looked at her.

He walked back over to the horse and lifted his arms to help her dismount. The moment their bodies touched, fire blazed his loins and more than anything, he wanted to kiss her right there, under the beautiful blue sky.

And so he did.

He took her mouth with a hunger that always astounded him, and when she offered him her tongue, he greedily devoured her. The sounds of her moans ignited his cells. She continued to kiss him back and every stroke of her tongue was sure, refined and totally into what she was doing.

He pulled back. It was either that or else be tempted to take the kiss all the way. He hadn't brought her here for that. He had wanted to show her something, share something with her. "Come here," he said, grabbing hold of her hand and leading her toward the edge that looked down into a valley.

She followed his gaze and he knew she saw what he

was seeing. Down in the valley there were thousands of wild horses running free. "Clint, this is truly magnificent," she said.

He glanced over at her, continued to hold her hand. "That night while you slept and I was on the computer, I looked up several other foundations that are similar to the one we started for Uncle Sid. Others have made it their business to save the horses, too."

A sound below caught their attention and they glanced down to see two horses that seemed to be at war with each other. "Stallions constantly struggle for dominance of their herd," Clint explained as they watched what was happening below. Two stallions were fighting it out, rearing up, biting and kicking each other. "Stallions go about gathering breeding mares into a band that they consider theirs," Clint said.

He chuckled. "Sort of like a harem, so to speak. And then they have the job of defending their band from other stallions who try to steal their mares. That's when there's fighting. The stallions are merely trying to hold on to what they consider theirs."

"So a herd only consists of a stallion and their mares?" Alyssa asked, seemingly fascinated by the information he was sharing.

"Eventually," Clint responded. "Once the mares give birth then the young foals stay with the band. However, once those young foals grow up and become young stallions they are chased away from the herd by the leader of the pack."

"What happens to them? The young stallions?"

"Usually young stallions gather together in their own herd—a bachelor band," he said and smiled. "They are fine until horniness sets in and then they go out looking for an available mare—which usually is in a band belonging to another stallion, and that's when more fighting takes place," he said.

"I understand horniness can be just plain awful," Alyssa said, smiling up at Clint.

"Yes," he agreed, returning her smile, knowing she was trying to tempt him. It was working. He pulled her to him, wanting her to feel just how much he desired her. "How about another game of Playing with Fire in my office later tonight?" he asked throatily.

She smiled up at him. "I wouldn't miss it."

When they returned to the ranch they were met by one of Clint's men, who said one of the wranglers had been thrown and was being rushed to the emergency room. Clint immediately went into action. Telling Alyssa that he would call her later, he got into his truck and took off.

While waiting for him to return, Alyssa tried to do some work. She made notes on the proposal she would present to Clint and his siblings on the Web site design for the foundation.

Hours later, she stood and stretched her body. It was almost nine in the evening and Clint still hadn't returned. Nor had he called. Chester had assured her the young man had only broken a few bones and should be okay. Alyssa truly hoped he would be.

She almost jumped when she heard the sound of her cell phone ringing. Picking it up, she smiled when she saw it was her aunt Claudine. She was glad it wasn't Kim calling to harass her again. Her cousin hadn't bothered calling her back after that night.

"Aunt Claudine? How are you?"

She hadn't spoken to her aunt in a couple days so they

spent the next hour or so catching up. When they finally ended their call, Alyssa decided to take a long and leisurely bubble bath.

A short while later after slipping into a T-shirt, she couldn't help but recall the words Clint had spoken to her a week or so before.

I know the terms of the agreement and the only person who can renege on them is you. And if you ever decide to do so, you're fully aware of where my bedroom is located. You are more than welcome to join me there at any time.

He had issued the invitation and now she intended to accept it. Walking out of her bedroom, she headed down the long hallway that led to the wing where Clint's personal domain was located.

When he came home tonight she would there, waiting for him.

Clint entered his house thinking hospital chairs were murder on a person's body. But at least Frankie would be okay. The kid was tough. He had a broken rib and collarbone to prove it. While at the hospital when he'd been trying so hard not to worry about Frankie, he allowed his mind to think about Alyssa. Clint hoped she hadn't been waiting for him in his office as he had asked her. He glanced at the large shopping bag that he was carrying. A display at one of the hospital's gift shops had reminded him that tomorrow was Valentine's Day. It seemed like years since he had purchased a card or candy for a woman, but tonight he had bought something for Alyssa.

Deciding the first thing he needed to do was take a shower, he entered his bedroom. The moment he opened the door, he picked up Alyssa's scent. A small table lamp provided a faint glow in the room and he quickly scanned the area. His breath caught in his chest when he saw Alyssa curled up in his bed.

He placed the gift bag in a chair and then went into the bathroom and closed the door to take a shower. She needed as much sleep as she could get now, because he fully intended to keep her awake for the rest of the night.

Alyssa was dreaming. Clint was in bed with her, caressing her stomach with his fingertips at the same time he was kissing her awake. But she refused to wake up for fear her fantasy dream would end.

"Alyssa."

She heard his voice and smiled dreamily at the way he said her name. Dreams could seem so real at times, she thought....

"Wake up, sweetheart. I want you."

And then she realized it wasn't a dream. Alyssa felt Clint's very real, hot breath caress the words against her lips. She forced her eyes open and found his eyes holding hers. She was immediately pulled into their dark depths.

"You're home," she whispered sleepily.

"Yes, I'm home," he said.

And then he was kissing her with an intensity that shook her to the core, made her wet between the legs, filling her with a physical hunger that was just as intense as it had been the previous night. She became warm and tingly all over and she felt she was under some sort of sensual torture.

And then he pulled back from her lips and began using his tongue like he had last night—causing tiny little quivers to invade her body every place it traveled. First, he caressed her in the hollow of her collarbone, and then lower to her breasts. When he moved his mouth even lower, she gritted her teeth, refusing to scream out like she had last night. The effort was useless. When the tip of his tongue began greedily lapping the essence of her femininity, she lifted her hips off the mattress at the same time his name was ripped from her throat.

"Clint!"

And then she felt her thighs being nudged farther apart as he settled the weight of his body between them, and just seconds before her body exploded into a shattering climax, he entered her in one deep thrust.

She screamed again and arched her body as he continued to thrust powerfully into her, without any signs of letting up. Each stroke was with relentless precision that suddenly brought her to another climax. It was as if he couldn't get enough of her and the greedier he became, the more shamelessly she welcomed him, encouraging him to penetrate deeper.

Her nails raked his back and she bit him several times on the shoulder, but he refused to let up. A primitive need was driving him. The same need that was taking over her.

And then he shouted her name at the same time she felt the sensational buildup of his body coming apart on top of her. Together they shuddered as pleasure ripped through her in a way she felt all the way to her bones.

And while the last of the tremors vibrated through their bodies, he pulled her closer into his arms and kissed her tenderly. She knew how it felt to be consumed in passion, gripped in the clutches of desire and then to glory in the aftermath of fulfillment. The experience was simply priceless and she knew in her heart she would only be able to reach that level of satisfaction with him.

* * *

It was close to nine the next morning before Alyssa came awake to find she had spent the night in Clint's bed. A smile touched her lips when she remembered their night together. It was as if a searing need had taken over them and they had filled that need the only way they knew how. Sensations flooded her just thinking about it. Luckily for her, he'd been prepared and had used a condom. Birth control had been the last thing on her mind. They had made love several times, all through the night, and each time she reached an orgasm, he had been right there with her.

She lay on her back a moment thinking Clint would have had breakfast already and left the ranch, which meant she wouldn't get the chance to see him until later. She had a number of things to do today to stay busy. She slid out of bed thinking it was time to return to her own room when she noticed the huge red gift bag sitting on Clint's dresser with her name on it. She quickly crossed the room and pulled off the card.

Her heart caught at the single question on the card.

Will you be my Valentine?
—Clint

It then occurred to her that today was Valentine's Day. It had been years since she'd had a reason to remember it or for someone to give her a gift. Even while she'd been dating Kevin he hadn't bothered to acknowledge the day. His excuse was that he didn't need a designated day to give her something. Kevin had claimed the day was nothing more than a day for businesses to make money off gullible consumers.

She smiled. If Clint was a gullible consumer then she appreciated it because it really made her day knowing he had thought of her. She then looked into the bag and her smile widened when she saw among the tissue paper a box of chocolate candy and an oversize T-shirt. She chuckled when she read the wording on the shirt—I Like Playing with Fire.

She knew the shirt was a private joke between them.

She turned her attention back to her Valentine's Day card and smiled. She would definitely be Clint's Valentine, she thought. And set her mind to work on ways to make him hers.

It was almost ten that night before Clint returned to the ranch. He and his men had spent the majority of the day away from the ranch and he was glad to be back. He figured Alyssa would be asleep now and wondered if like last night she would be in his bed.

He also wondered if she had liked the gift he had left her. Conflicting emotions were running through him. She had been an itch he thought he would never be tempted to scratch. Now he was tempted beyond reason.

He opened the door to his bedroom and his gaze went to the empty bed. Immediately, he felt a sense of disappointment. Then his heart skipped a beat when he saw the note on his pillow. He quickly crossed the room. He picked it up and read the words Alyssa had scrawled on the paper.

Yes, I will be your Valentine.
Come to me. I am waiting.
—Alyssa

Clint had no idea how long he stood there, glued to the spot, rereading her message. And then with an insatiable thirst he knew that only she could quench, he quickly headed for the bathroom, already tugging his shirt out of his jeans. He would take a shower and then he would go to Alyssa, determined not to keep her waiting any longer than he had to.

Alyssa heard the soft knock on her bedroom door and her pulse began to race. She glanced around the room, hoping the lit candles weren't overkill, but she liked candles. She thought the lush vanilla fragrance that filled the air was nice. She hoped Clint thought so, as well.

She then glanced down at herself. Clint had seen her in enough T-shirts so she decided tonight would be different. She had borrowed the truck and gone into town and purchased this particular outfit to stir things up a bit. Not that she thought it took much to arouse Clint. He seemed capable of that feat just from looking at her at times, she thought with a smile. Alyssa wanted this night to be special.

She made it to the door on shaky legs and inhaled deeply before turning the handle. There he stood in the doorway and when desire flared in his eyes when he looked at her, she smiled knowing her outfit would be a big hit. They would definitely be playing with fire to-night.

My God, Clint thought as he stood there staring at Alyssa. She was wrapped up like a gift, in bright red wrapping paper with a huge white bow. How in the hell had she managed it?

As if reading his thoughts she said, "It wasn't all that

difficult getting into it. But the only way it comes off is for you to *unwrap* me. Now that might be the hard part."

Not in his book, he quickly thought. *Unwrapping* her would be easy, especially taking off the big white bow which covered the essence of her femininity. Now that would definitely be a treat and not a challenge.

He swiftly entered the room, closing the door behind him. It was then and only then that he allowed his gaze to shift from her just long enough to glance around. He saw the lit candles and heard the soft music playing in the background. His gaze then returned to her.

He reached out, closed his hands around her waist, found the start of the ribbon and began pulling, watching before his eyes as she unwrapped. By the time he was able to pull off the bow, his body was hard and thick. He parted her thighs the minute the last piece of wrapping dropped to the floor.

The bed was not far away, but he doubted he would make it that far. Instead he went to the zipper of his jeans and took out his aroused member. Like last night he was prepared and had already put on a condom, not willing to take any chances. He knew to what degree he wanted her.

He lifted her onto him and entered her in one smooth thrust. It had been years since he'd made love to a woman in a standing position, but tonight he had no choice. He wanted Alyssa now.

He backed her against the wall as she wrapped her legs around him and tilted her hips for deeper penetration. And with another deep thrust he planted himself inside her to the hilt.

"You're some gift, sweetheart," he whispered as he began moving in and out of her. And moments later when he felt her come apart in his arms he followed her over the edge and they clung together, drowning in the waves of ecstasy as he murmured her name breathlessly. She clung to him and it took all he could do to continue to stand upright.

"Now for the bed," he said a moment later when he felt himself getting hard all over again. Every nerve in his body, every cell, seemed branded by her touch, the essence of her being. His senses suddenly became filled with an emotion he refused to accept. And as he crossed the room to the bed, he knew they were counting down the days together. These precious moments were meant to be savored.

Chapter 13

The days passed so quickly that a part of Alyssa wished there was some way she could slow things down. But then she looked forward to each night that she spent in Clint's arms. Neither of them spoke about the short time they had left, although they were both aware that in less than a week their days together would end.

Everyone was looking forward to Clint's sister and her husband's visit. Chester was already preparing what he knew to be Casey's favorite foods.

"You're going to like Casey," Chester had said to Alyssa one day while she helped him prepare lunch for the men. "I'm glad she has McKinnon. He has definitely made her happy."

Chester seemed so sure of what he said that Alyssa couldn't help but be happy for Casey. She would be able to spend the rest of her life with the man she loved.

Alyssa knew that she wasn't to be so lucky. But at least she would have plenty of memories to sustain her.

She smiled. Clint had already warned her not to even think about not sharing his bed during his sister's visit. She knew Cole and some of Clint's cousins and their wives would also be visiting. Even Clint's father and stepmother were coming. They all were coming to attend the charity ball that would be held in the governor's mansion that weekend. To say the house would be filled to capacity was an understatement.

She knew that Cole and Casey already knew why she was there, but she couldn't help wondering how many of Clint's other relatives knew the reason for her presence. *Had he talked to them about it? Did his father know she and Clint were married?* She tried not to consider their circumstances as an embarrassing situation any longer. Besides, a part of her didn't want to worry about what other people thought about her relationship with Clint. Why should they hide their love affair? she wondered. They were lovers. She couldn't help but shake her head at the absurdity of it all. They were a married couple who were also lovers.

And on top of everything else, they were becoming close friends. Good to his word, Clint took her riding every day and now she no longer feared riding on a horse alone…as long as Clint was close by.

She glanced at the folder on the desk as she sat in Clint's office. The proposal she had worked up for the foundation was complete and ready to present to Clint and his siblings when they arrived.

If they liked her proposal and accepted it, she and Clint would still be in contact with each other, at least until she had the site up and running. After the site was operational, she would be available to maintain it. It was a service she offered to all her clients. She didn't relish the thought of having a continuing business relationship with Clint after their marriage was annulled. It would open her up for heartbreak if Clint decided to begin to date again.

She closed her eyes, not wanting to think of such a thing happening, although she knew that eventually it would. Clint was too good-looking a man not to have a permanent lady in his life. But then, according to Clint, his uncle Sid had died a carefree bachelor, although Chester was convinced Sid had an offspring out there somewhere. He recalled a woman once writing Sid telling him she had given birth to his son, but stating she didn't want or need anything from him. She'd merely felt it was the right thing to do to let him know. However, she hadn't provided a return address, which eliminated the chance of Sid finding out if the claim was true, or establishing a relationship with his child.

"Alyssa?"

At the sound of her name she immediately came out of her reverie and discovered the sound was coming from the intercom system. It was Clint. She stood and quickly crossed the room to the box on the wall and pressed a button. "Yes?"

"Where are you?"

She smiled. "In your office. Why?"

"I'm in the living room. I want you to come out and meet my sister and brother-in-law," Clint said.

A lump suddenly formed in Alyssa's throat. She was definitely nervous about meeting Clint's family, but knew she couldn't hide out forever.

"I'm on my way."

* * *

In less than a day Alyssa was convinced she totally liked Casey Westmoreland Quinn. And her husband, McKinnon, in addition to being knockout gorgeous, was a very kind person. Alyssa thought the two made a beautiful couple and it was very easy to see they were very much in love.

"You and I need to go shopping," Casey exclaimed to her the following morning at breakfast.

Alyssa's lips spread into a smile as she took a sip of her coffee. "We do?"

"Yes. You mentioned you don't have anything to wear to the charity ball this weekend and neither do I. Besides," Casey added as a grin spread across her lips, "that way I get to spend time with you without Clint hovering about. He seems to think I'm going to reveal some deep, dark, embarrassing secret about him from our childhood. He's really overprotective where you're concerned. I guess I should thank my lucky stars that the two of you are already married."

Alyssa frowned. Surely Casey knew her and Clint's marriage wasn't going to last forever. In fact they were merely biding time waiting until the day came where they could end it. Alyssa's thoughts were interrupted when Casey's cell phone went off.

"Excuse me, Alyssa, while I get this."

Alyssa stood from the table to refill her coffee while Casey answered the phone. Clint and McKinnon had left the ranch early that morning and weren't expected to return until dinnertime. Clint was eager to show McKinnon the most recent pack of wild horses that had been shipped from Nevada.

"Great! That was Spencer," Casey informed her, after

she had finished the call. "He and Chardonnay just arrived and are at the airport. They should be arriving at the ranch within the hour."

Alyssa raised a brow. "Chardonnay?"

Casey smiled. "Yes, that's her name. Her family owned a winery in California and she was named after her grandfather's favorite wine."

"Oh."

"So we might as well wait and take Chardonnay with us," Casey said.

Alyssa then decided to ask, "Do you know who else is coming?"

"Shopping with us?"

Alyssa shook her head, grinning. "No, coming to the ranch to attend the charity ball this weekend," she said.

Casey looked confused. "Didn't Clint tell you?"

"Not really. He mentioned some of his family was coming, but he didn't say exactly who. I'm sure he mentioned it to Chester for him to get the guest rooms prepared, though," Alyssa said.

Casey frowned. "Never mind if he did mention it to Chester. You're the mistress of the ranch and he should have specifically told you. You shouldn't be hearing it secondhand. Men can be so fruity at times," Casey said.

From what Casey had just said, it was apparent she wasn't aware of the circumstances surrounding her and Clint's marriage. "It's not that Clint's fruity," Alyssa said, coming to his defense. "It's just that he doesn't consider me as the mistress of this ranch."

Casey raised a brow. "And why not?"

Alyssa sighed. If Clint hadn't informed his sister of anything, she wasn't sure it was her place to do so. She hesitated to find the proper words, couldn't find them, shrugged and then said, "Because he just doesn't."

Casey stared at her as if trying to figure out what she meant and then a smile touched her lips. "Oh, you're talking about that business with the thirty days and how the two of you have to live under the same roof and all of that?"

Alyssa nodded. *So Clint had told her.* "Yes."

Casey chuckled before taking a sip of her coffee. "I wouldn't worry about that if I were you. Trust me, Clint plans to keep you," Casey said.

Alyssa shook her head. "No, he doesn't," Alyssa argued.

Casey laughed. "Yes, he does and what's so sad is that besides being fruity, some men are also slow. Clint is one of the slow ones. Chances are he hasn't even realized what he plans to do with you yet, poor thing."

Alyssa stared at Casey, wondering how she could make such an assumption. The only excuse she could come up with was that since Casey was happily married and in love she thought everyone should be the same way. Alyssa decided not to argue, and to let Casey continue to think whatever she wanted to believe. But Alyssa was fully aware of the real deal surrounding her marriage to Clint and that at the end of thirty days he expected her packed and ready to leave.

Two nights later Alyssa lay in Clint's arms after thoroughly being made love to. The sound of his even breathing let her know he had gone to sleep, but she was wide-awake…and thinking.

All of Clint's relatives who were attending tomorrow

night's ball had arrived and she found all of them to be extremely nice and friendly. The house was full and without it being verbally expressed, Clint looked to her to be his hostess and instinctively she had taken on the role. When he introduced her, he simply said she was Alyssa. He didn't give her last name or what role she played in his life. She could only assume the masses thought she was his live-in lover since she wasn't wearing a wedding ring and it was obvious they shared the same bed. But what was confusing was that when the relatives talked among each other in her presence and his, she was referred to as Clint's wife and he did nothing to correct them.

She guessed in a way it didn't matter what they thought since all of them would be leaving on Monday. And then she would leave less than a week later.

Less than a week.

Boy, how time flies when you're having fun, she thought. And she was having fun. Returning to Waco didn't have the appeal it once did. She had bonded with Chester and the men who worked for Clint, and she thought he had a very special family. They were so different from hers. Even his father, Corey, and stepmother, Abby, were absolutely wonderful. She could feel the closeness and the love among everyone. Those were two things that her family lacked.

"Alyssa."

Clint had whispered her name in his sleep and she snuggled closer to him. She would miss this. Going to bed with him every night and waking up to his lovemaking each and every morning. But as someone once said, all good things must one day come to an end. Over the week she would prepare for the heartbreak she would encounter the moment Clint drove her away from the ranch to the airport. To prepare for that day she needed to start distancing herself from him and she would do so once his family left and it was just the two of them again. It would be for the best.

Alyssa glanced around the huge ballroom filled with people. Chester had been right. Everyone important from all over Texas was attending the charity benefit to give their financial support to the children's hospital. It was even rumored that the President and First Lady would be making an appearance.

She had to admit that she was rendered speechless when they arrived and Clint introduced her to the host and hostess as his wife. Alyssa figured the reason he had done so was to not cause her any embarrassment later. So far no one had questioned his sudden acquisition of a wife. And a few times when one or two people referred to her as Mrs. Westmoreland, she had to stop from stating that wasn't her name.

Another thing she noticed was that the Westmorelands seemed to run in a pack. All of them were standing together in one spot and it was obvious they were a family. All the men in the family resembled one another in their facial features, height and sex appeal. And the Westmoreland women—sisters, cousins and wives—were all beautiful. They made stunning couples. There were Clint's cousin Jared with his wife, Dana; his cousin Storm with his wife, Jayla; his cousin Spencer and his wife, Chardonnay; his cousin Dare and his wife, Shelly; his cousin Thorn and his wife, Tara; and his cousin Ian and his wife, Brooke.

The group also included Clint's brother Cole, who didn't bother to bring a date; his cousin Reggie, who hadn't brought a date, either; Casey and McKinnon; and Clint's father and stepmother, Corey and Abby Westmoreland. Such an imposing group, she thought, and several times Thorn, who was nationally known for the motorcycles he built and raced, was approached by several people wanting his autograph.

"Did I tell you how beautiful you look tonight?"

Alyssa glanced up at the tall, handsome man who hadn't left her side all evening. She smiled up at him. "Yes, you told me. Thank you," she said.

And if he hadn't, his gaze had said it all when she had walked out of the bathroom after getting dressed. Casey, who had once owned a clothing store, had been instrumental in helping her select a dress, a short, black, clingy number that Casey claimed would hit her brother between the eyes when he saw it. Alyssa wasn't sure whether Clint had gotten hit between the eyes, but it was evident he liked seeing her in the dress. And if she was reading his mind correctly, he was counting the hours until he would get the chance to take it off of her.

"Well, well, look who's here. I can't believe my eyes. What are you doing here, Alyssa?"

Dread settled in the pit of Alyssa's stomach at the sound of that voice. She turned and tried to retain her composure when she not only saw Kim but also Kevin. She shook her head, shocked, not believing they were here tonight, of all places, and together. Kim was plastered to Kevin's side as if she wanted to make it obvious that tonight they were a couple.

Alyssa found her voice to speak. "Kim, Kevin, how are you? It's nice seeing the both of you and I'm here for the same reason you are, to support the children's hospital."

"Like you can afford to do that," Kim said with an obvious sneer, not caring who standing around her was listening. "Aunt Claudine claims you left Waco to go work for a client, but I figure you're still licking your wounds because I took Kevin away from you."

Alyssa knew Kim was deliberately trying to embarrass her in front of everyone and a part of Alyssa wished at that moment she was anywhere but there. Having all her personal business exposed to everyone, especially the Westmorelands, was humiliating.

But then she happened to notice that Clint had moved closer to her side, had placed a protective arm around her waist. And out of the corner of her eye she saw the other Westmorelands closing ranks around her, as well.

"Please introduce me to your friends, Alyssa," Clint said.

Only someone as up close, intimate and personal to Clint as she was would detect the edgy steel in his voice. She glanced up at him. He hadn't taken his gaze off Kim and Kevin, and the look in his eyes matched the tone she had heard in his voice.

She cleared her throat. "Clint, this is Kevin and Kim. Kim and I are cousins. Kevin and Kim, this is Clint Westmoreland," Alyssa said.

It was only then that Clint shifted his gaze back to her and she was aware that already he had figured things out. Kevin was her former fiancé and Kim was the woman who had deliberately slept with him to ruin her wedding day. Kim was also Alyssa's cousin.

Kim, who appreciated a good-looking man when she saw one, smiled sweetly at Clint. "So, you're that client she ran off to work for," she said in a smooth, silky voice as her flirty gaze raked him from head to toe.

Clint smiled at Kim, although anyone knowing him could see the smile didn't quite reach his eyes. "No, I'm not Alyssa's client," he said in a clear and firm voice. "I'm Alyssa's husband."

Chapter 14

Alyssa thought for as long as she lived she would never forget the shocked look that appeared on Kim's face with Clint's statement. Kim was dumbstruck. Kevin had also seemed to lose his voice, but had quickly regained it. While Kevin stood there babbling, trying to apologize for Kim's rudeness, Clint had taken Alyssa's hand in his, and he, as well as the other Westmorelands, had walked away leaving Kim and Kevin looking like fools. In the end, the embarrassment had been theirs.

They had returned home a few hours ago. Neither Clint nor any of the other Westmorelands had brought up the incident with Kim and Kevin. Alyssa guessed that before the night was over Clint would talk to her about the ugly scene and the party.

She was already in bed, but Clint, his brother and cousins were engaged in a card game. Although she was

tired and sleepy, she was determined to stay awake and
talk to him. He deserved to know the entire story as to
why Kim disliked her so.... Not that it was an excuse for
her cousin's behavior.

Later, Alyssa glanced toward the bedroom door. It
opened and Clint walked in. He had removed his jacket
and tie, and the two top buttons of his shirt were open.
He closed the door behind him and stood leaning against
it and stared at her. She knew she owed him an apology.
In trying to embarrass her, Kim and Kevin had probably embarrassed him, as well. He hadn't deserved it, just
like he didn't deserve the predicament that had placed
her here, messing up his life as he knew it.

He didn't say anything. He just continued to stare at
her. He hadn't seemed upset with her during the course
of the evening but she couldn't help wondering if he'd
only held his temper in check around his family, and if
now, since they were alone, he would let her know how
he really felt.

"Why didn't you tell me the full story?" he finally
asked.

Alyssa sighed. There was no need to pretend she didn't
understand what he was asking. "At the time I didn't
think there was a need, Clint," she said, hoping he understood. "Besides, whenever you spoke of your relatives I
could feel the love and warmth all of you shared. It's not
that way in my family."

He then moved and came closer to the bed and sat on
the edge. "Kim really has issues, doesn't she?"

Alyssa thought that was a nice way of putting it. "Yes.
She'd always been the center of attention and when I arrived on the scene it didn't sit well with her. And later

when I found out my grandfather was actually my father, then she—"

"Whoa. Back up," he said, interrupting. "What do you mean your grandfather was actually your father?"

Alyssa knew that he deserved to know everything. "On his deathbed, the man who I thought was my grandfather confessed to being my father. Before then I'd always thought I was the illegitimate daughter of his dead son, the one who had been a Texas Ranger and had died in the line of duty."

She paused before continuing. "From what I understand, my grandmother died years ago and my grandfather was a widower who had raised two sons, Todd and Kim's father, Jessie. When Todd was killed, Grandpa was really torn up about it and went out drinking to drown in his sorrows. That's the night he had an affair with my mother. She was working as a waitress at the bar. She told him she had gotten pregnant and he provided for my care. When she sent me to live with him, a decision was made to let everyone think I was Todd's illegitimate daughter. The only person who knew the truth other than Grandpa was Aunt Claudine."

Clint nodded. "What was the reason that your mother gave you up?"

Alyssa sighed again before answering. "Because she found out that her new boyfriend was trying to come on to me."

She saw Clint's face harden at that statement. "And you haven't seen or heard from her since?" he asked.

"No. And according to Aunt Claudine, she never wrote or asked how I was doing. She no longer cared," Alyssa said sadly.

The pain she felt whenever she remembered her mother's denial came back, and she didn't realize tears were in her eyes until Clint reached out and took his fingertip and wiped one away. "This has been one heck of a night for you," he said softly. "Go on and get some rest."

She nodded, still unable to decipher his mood or feelings on what she had told him. Without removing his clothes he stretched out on the bed beside her and held her in his arms. And he stayed there with her until she went to sleep.

Alyssa woke the next morning in bed alone. She couldn't help wondering what the Westmorelands thought of her. Nor could she help wondering what Clint thought of her, as well. This was the first morning, since they'd begun sleeping together, that he hadn't woken her with lovemaking.

That thought remained on her mind while she showered and got dressed. When she opened the door to the hall, Clint was standing against the wall waiting for her. He was dressed in a pair of jeans and a chambray shirt. As usual, he looked great.

"Good morning," he said, smiling at her.

It was a smile that made her insides feel somewhat jittery.

"Good morning, Clint," she said, searching his expression in an attempt to decipher his mood.

"I know you haven't eaten breakfast yet, but I was wondering if you would go riding with me this morning. I promise not to keep you out long."

"Sure," she said and shrugged.

They walked together through the house. The place seemed rather quiet, especially for a house full of guests. It was after eight in the morning. She had discovered over the past few days that the Westmorelands were early risers.

"Where's everyone?"

"Sleeping in late, I guess," Clint said.

"Oh."

When they walked outside she saw two horses were saddled and ready for them. Clint helped her mount Sunshine, the docile mare he had given her to ride, and then he mounted Royal. She glanced over at him.

"Where are we going?"

"To the south ridge," he said mysteriously.

She nodded. They hadn't ridden on that part of his property in a while. Thanks to Clint she felt comfortable riding and appreciated the slow pace he set for them. They rode in silence, enjoying the beautiful morning.

They had been riding for a while when Clint finally brought the horses to a stop. "This is a nice place to stop," he said, glancing over at her.

For what? she couldn't help wondering. *Was he going to ask her to leave the ranch? Had he figured out that the best way to end their farce of a marriage and quickly was to forget the annulment and file for a quick divorce instead?*

She watched as Clint dismounted from Royal and tied him to a tree before coming back to help her off of Sunshine. He tied Sunshine to a tree, as well.

"Come on," Clint said, reaching for her hand. "Let's take a walk so we can talk."

She pulled her hand back. "Talking isn't necessary. I know what you want."

His brows drew together. "Do you?"

"Yes, I do," she said.

"And what do you think I want?" he asked, leaning against an oak tree.

She glanced around instead of looking at him and then she brought her gaze back to his.

"You want to skip the annulment and go straight to a divorce," Alyssa said.

Clint could only stare at her. What she had said was so far from the truth it was pitiful. What had happened last night at the ball had been an eye-opener for him. When Kim had said those insulting remarks his protective instincts had kicked in. He had immediately wanted to shield her from any kind of hurt, harm or danger.

Something else had also kicked in. His heart. He realized at that moment how much he cared for her. He loved her. And he wanted to always be by her side to protect her from the Kims and Kevins of the world. For him it wasn't a matter of lust, as he had first assumed. He realized now that his feelings for Alyssa were a matter of love. He couldn't imagine her leaving him or the ranch next week. He had no intentions of letting her go and the sooner she knew it the better.

"There will be no divorce, Alyssa. And there won't be an annulment," he said as he took a step toward her.

"What are you saying?"

A smile touched his lips and he reached into his back pocket and pulled out a small box and opened it. There was a beautiful wedding ring in the box.

"I'm saying that what I want is to marry you all over again. Make it truly right this time. Since the laws of Texas declare we're already man and wife, let's make it real. Let's renew our vows," he said.

He then got down on one knee and glanced up at her.

"Alyssa, will you continue to be my wife, till death us do part?"

Alyssa was shocked speechless. Tears flooded her eyes. She shook her head and tried wiping the tears away with her hand—the one Clint wasn't slipping the ring onto.

"But—but you can't want to stay married to me. You don't love me," she said.

Satisfied the ring was a perfect fit, Clint stood and smiled at her.

"Now that's where you're wrong. I do love you. I think I fell in love with you the first time we played our own special game," he said.

"Oh, Clint," she said, smiling through her tears.

He pulled her into his arms and murmured against her ear, "Is that a yes?"

She pulled back and smiled up at him. "That's definitely a yes! Oh, Clint, I will marry you again," she said.

"Thank you, sweetheart," he said. And then he was lowering his mouth to hers while pulling her closer into his arms. The kiss was long, deep and passionate. Clint knew that it wasn't enough, but he broke the kiss off anyway. He knew there was something else he had to tell her.

"You know when we left the ranch and you asked where everyone was?" he asked her.

She nodded. "You told me they were probably sleeping in," she said.

"I lied."

Alyssa lifted a brow. "They aren't sleeping in?"

"No."

A confused looked touched her features. "Where are they?"

"In the barn getting things ready."

He could tell by her expression that now she was really confused so he decided to explain things. "I told everyone last night that I planned to ask you to marry me today. Abby suggested that while we had everyone here, we might as well renew our vows today. We can always have a reception for the rest of the family later, preferably on my father's mountain in Montana when the weather gets warm," he said.

Alyssa truly didn't know what to say at first.

"Your family is doing that for me?"

Clint smiled. "They are doing it for us. They know how much I love you. I think they realized it before I did because all of them, with the exception of Cole and Reggie, have been there, done that. They know what it is like to fall in love with your heart even when your mind is still in denial," he said.

He leaned down and kissed her again and when she wrapped her arms around his neck and returned the kiss, he knew that when they married this time around, it would be forever.

Epilogue

"You tricked me," Alyssa said.

She looked at herself in the full-length mirror before turning around and giving Casey an all-accusing look.

Casey laughed. "I did not. I just know my brother and figured he would get around to popping the question sooner or later. I just thought you should be prepared when he did. Like I said, he's slow. And since we were going shopping that day, I figured you might as well purchase a second dress just in case."

Alyssa shook her head. She had tried on several outfits for the ball and Casey had convinced her to buy the two she liked the best instead of just one. Now it seemed the second outfit, a beautiful off-white tea-length gown, would be the one she would marry Clint in. She had to admit that it was simply perfect.

"You look beautiful, Alyssa," Aunt Claudine said from across the room.

"Thanks, Aunt Claudine," Alyssa said lovingly to her aunt.

Her aunt's arrival had been another surprise the Westmorelands had sprung on her. They had contacted Claudine the night before and made arrangements for the older woman to fly in for today's festivities.

Alyssa still couldn't believe what the Westmorelands had accomplished in a single night. When she had been in her bedroom wondering how they felt about her after that embarrassing fiasco with Kim and Kevin, they'd huddled together somewhere with Clint and planned the ceremony for today. They were determined to make her one of them. And in her heart, she knew her marriage today would be more than just a renewing of her and Clint's vows. The marriage ceremony would affirm her love for Clint, but it would also proclaim her membership in the Westmoreland clan.

Tara Westmoreland glanced at her watch. "It's about time for you to make an entrance," she said, smiling. "The last thing you want to do is to keep a Westmoreland man waiting on his wedding day."

Alyssa smiled as she glanced around at all the women in the room. Westmoreland women, all of them, except for her aunt. "Thanks for everything. I already feel blessed having all of you in my life," Alyssa said. She had a feeling they knew what she meant.

"There're a few more where we came from," Shelly Westmoreland spoke up. "And they're all dying to meet you and send their love and regrets that they can't be here. We plan to have a reception on Corey's Mountain. With the exception of Delaney and Casey, we ladies became Westmorelands through marriage. What we discovered is a sisterhood that's very special and we welcome you with love."

Tears filled Alyssa's eyes. She was finally getting a family who would love her as much as she loved them.

Thirty minutes later, Alyssa was walking across the span of the room to where Clint, dressed in a dark suit, was standing beside his brother and father. She had asked Chester to give her away and he had truly seemed honored to do so. Casey was her matron of honor.

When she reached Clint, he smiled as he took her hand in his. She smiled back and together they faced the minister. Alyssa knew this was a new beginning for her and she would have a lot to tell her grandkids one day about how she was able to tame the wild and elusive heart of Clint Westmoreland.

* * * * *

Synithia Williams has loved romance novels since reading her first one at the age of thirteen. It was only natural that she would one day write her own romances. When she isn't writing, Synithia works on water quality issues in the Midlands of South Carolina while taking care of her supportive husband and two sons. You can learn more about Synithia by visiting her website, synithiawilliams.com.

Books by Synithia Williams

Harlequin Kimani Romance

A New York Kind of Love
A Malibu Kind of Romance
Full Court Seduction
Overtime for Love
Guarding His Heart
His Pick for Passion

HQN

Forbidden Promises
Scandalous Secrets
Careless Whispers

Visit the Author Profile page at Harlequin.com for more titles.

A MALIBU KIND
OF ROMANCE

Synithia Williams

To my parents, Lisa and Sam,
thank you for always supporting my dreams.

Chapter 1

Dante Wilson stared at the supermodel twins dancing together at his post-concert party in Vegas and had one thought: he loved his life! What wasn't there to love? He was one of the world's bestselling artists, his family ran a music dynasty, he'd finished a sold-out world tour and he was pretty sure he'd be going home with one or both of the twins. He leaned back against the plush leather sofa, took a sip of the champagne in his hand and grinned.

The Vegas strip was a colorful backdrop outside the window of the penthouse suite, which was filled with celebrities, their entourages and musicians—all there to help him celebrate. The guy to Dante's right, basketball star Jacobe Jenkins, pulled his long designer-jean-clad legs in and leaned forward, resting his elbows on his knees. "I know what you're thinking."

Dante shifted in his seat. He'd lost his dress shirt earlier while dancing, and wore only a white T-shirt and black slacks. "If you're assuming my thoughts have something to do with the twins, then you're right."

Jacobe chuckled. "I should have bet money on that. You go through more women than any other guy I know. And I'm surrounded by professional basketball players all day."

"Perks of the job," Dante said. "But after tonight I'm slowing down with the female distractions. Tonight's about releasing some steam after the tour before getting back into the studio. Though I love partying, I'm going to have to do less of this for a while." He waved his hand to indicate the energetic crowd.

"Damn, Dante," Jacobe said, once again stretching out his legs. "You just got back in the country, and you're going back to the studio."

"To stay on top of my game, I can never really take a break. Plus, I'm excited to get back to Malibu and get to work on the music I want to do."

Jacobe raised a brow. "That classical stuff?"

Dante shook his head. "It's not classical stuff. It's a fusion of hip-hop, jazz and rock *with* classical influence. Wait until you hear it—you'll dig it."

Jacobe gave Dante a skeptical look before he turned to watch one of the many beauties at the party walking by. Jacobe's skepticism didn't deter Dante's confidence in his next move. Not much anyway. Dante had built a solid career using the Wilson family legacy and his own talent. He could sing, play several different instruments and dance. After seventeen years doing the music his family and their label wanted him to do, Dante was ready to do his own thing.

Not that he regretted seventeen years of pop stardom.

Show business was in his family's blood—starting with his great-grandfather, who'd performed on the Chitlin' Circuit in the 1950s, to his grandfather, who'd started his own record label in the 1970s. Then to Dante's father, who with a smooth baritone singing voice, hit songs and a shrewd business sense, turned that label into one of the country's most successful. The biggest names in music signed with W. M. Records.

Dante was fiercely proud of his family's legacy. But pride didn't diminish a growing frustration with the pressure to keep doing the same type of music that everyone else was doing.

"Are you sure the music you're doing will be successful?" Jacobe asked.

Dante shrugged. "I can't say one hundred percent, but I know there's an audience. The group I'm working with, Strings A Flame, they've got a following. If I sign them to W. M. Records and record an album with them, then that's all it'll take."

"You're pretty confident in your pull," Jacobe said, turning away from the woman he'd been watching.

"I've been around for nearly twenty years. I'm allowed to be confident in my staying power. I know the market isn't as big—that's why I'm opening a nightclub. I'll debut the music there, see how the fans react, then go from there."

"You've got it all planned out."

"Always," he said with a confidence that he couldn't allow to waiver. The only hitch in his perfect plan was his dad. Otis Wilson wanted hip-hop and R&B right now, the more commercial the better. He'd originally brushed off Dante's plans to sign S.A.F. and hadn't shown any interest in backing an album. He needed the nightclub to be successful to convince his dad otherwise.

Jacobe looked at Dante. "What do you know about opening a nightclub?"

"Nothing. I'm partnering with Raymond, but we may still need someone to come in and handle the day-to-day." Dante pointed to Raymond, who was walking over to where he and Jacobe were sitting.

Raymond was an up-and-coming star in the R&B world with two hit albums in the past five years. He had enough popularity to make some people think Raymond's future in the Rock and Roll Hall of Fame was set, but Dante had seen enough artists crash and burn to know two hit albums didn't mean a thing. However, the kid was smart and had invested his money in other ventures outside the entertainment industry, including a nightclub called Masquerade in Atlanta that he and another rapper opened a few years ago. It was now the hottest spot in the city. When Raymond mentioned opening a place on the West Coast, Dante immediately brought up his idea. Raymond had agreed after listening to some of the music Dante and S.A.F. had put together.

"Dante," Raymond said with a grin on his face. He held out his hand and gave Dante a fist bump before doing the same with Jacobe.

"This party is where it's at," Raymond said.

"I told you the best way to celebrate the end of a tour is with a party in Vegas," Dante said as he and Raymond slapped hands again.

The song changed, and the same twin models who'd had Dante's attention before gyrated to the music. Dante sipped the champagne in his hand and grinned at the women, who both blew kisses his way.

"Most definitely the way to end a tour," Raymond said, grinning. "Did you tell Jacobe about our plans for the club?"

"I was just telling him about that."

Raymond nodded and grinned. "It's going to be hot, right?"

Jacobe lifted his chin in agreement. "Nothing Dante has done thus far has failed. I don't see why this would. Even though I'm still trying to imagine the music. I keep imagining symphonies with rapping when I think about it."

"I'll send you one of our songs. That'll help," Dante said, still not bothered. Jacobe was a die-hard classic hip-hop fan, and he had a hard time with any other variation in the genre.

Dante looked at Raymond. "It wouldn't hurt to find another partner to come in and help oversee the details of the development," he said. "W. M. Records has a firm it's used for the other nightclubs the label has invested in, but I don't want to use them. They'll go to my dad for his influence, and he'll turn the place into another carbon copy of an LA club. That's not what I'm going for."

Raymond snapped his finger. "I've got someone in mind."

"Really? Who?"

"You ever heard of Julie Dominick?"

Dante ran through the females he may have heard about but came up empty. "Should I know her?"

"She's the woman that handled the development of Masquerade."

Dante's brows rose. "Really?"

"That's my girl, Julie. She negotiated the deal to land that prime location in Buckhead and kept other investors from snagging it up. She oversaw the entire operation, from acquisition to construction, and did a damn good job."

Jacobe chuckled. "What, is she paying you to be her public relations person?"

Raymond shook his head. "Nah, I just wanted you to know the type of work she can do. We should consider her."

"Working her magic in Atlanta isn't the same as working her magic in California," Dante said. "I'd rather go with someone who knows the ins and outs on this side of the country."

"I know Julie—she can do it." Confidence and affection filled Raymond's voice.

Dante's eyes narrowed. "How do you know her? This isn't some old girlfriend you're trying to give the hookup to?"

"Nah, not like that. Julie and I are cool. We met in college, and she's been my homegirl ever since. She got me started in music actually, promoting my music and getting me gigs in and around Atlanta. Now she's started her own development firm, and I want to help her out."

"Is that all? No guy I know just helps out a female for no reason."

Raymond rubbed his jaw and lifted a shoulder. "I wouldn't mind if Julie and I became more than friends one day."

"I figured."

"But it's not like that. Julie is the kind of woman you make your number one chick. We've talked about finally getting together if both of us were single when we turned thirty. That's only a few years away. Who knows—this may bring us together."

A sexy woman in a skimpy red dress walked past. Raymond and Jacobe both went slack jawed and watched her walk by with more than a little interest. Raymond, ever bold, reached out and took her hand, then pulled her against his side. The woman giggled, wrapping her arms around Raymond's neck.

Dante chuckled and shook his head. "You're ready to settle down, huh?"

Raymond wiggled his brows. "I said a few years off. Come on—look up Julie. She's opened some other spots on the East Coast. We can at least meet with her and then decide."

Dante's cell phone vibrated in his pocket. He pulled it out to find a picture of his father, in his best blue pinstripe suit sitting behind his desk at W. M. Records, on the screen. "I'll think about meeting her. Excuse me, fellas." He stood and punched the button to answer the call.

Dante put the phone to his ear. "Dad, hold on a minute."

He walked away from the main area of the party and into the suite's master bedroom, which was, thankfully, empty. "You still there?"

"Sounds like one hell of a party." Otis Wilson's deep baritone, which was the hallmark of his career, came through the phone.

"You know I like to celebrate the end of a tour in style."

Otis laughed. "I don't blame you. Man, if you could have seen the parties we had back in the day."

"I heard the stories. You guys partied too hard for me."

"That's the truth," Otis said, his voice laced with nostalgia. "What are you doing after you leave Vegas?"

Dante fought not to sigh. He'd told his dad during the

entire concert tour what he planned to do. "I'm going to Malibu to look into opening my club."

"You're still on that? Come on, Dante—why are you wasting your time?"

"It's not wasting time. I've spent seventeen years doing what the market told me to do. Now I want to pursue my own things."

"Dante, you can dabble in that classical–hip-hop fusion mess on the side, but the money is in mainstream music. I just left a meeting with Antwan, and he's interested in doing a joint album with you." Antwan was the biggest name in hip-hop, and the fact that he was unhappy with his label was no secret. Ever since that news had gone public, Otis had let Dante know he would try to recruit Antwan to W. M. Records. Hard.

"Having Raymond on your concert tour gave you a boost with the younger generation. If you do an album with Antwan, then follow it with your own R&B, you'll sell even more."

The same song Otis had sung since Dante announced his tour. Otis always followed the money, which normally meant following the mainstream trends.

"I've sold enough that I trust being able to try something new. I'll consider a collaboration with Antwan after the club is up and going."

"You put out that crappy music and your name will be nothing. We can't afford the hit. Not after what your sister pulled last year."

Dante pinched the bridge of his nose. His sister had a strong pop music career, but, for some reason, she'd tried to go hard-core hip-hop the previous year. The only thing hard about her album was how hard it hit the bottom of the charts.

"What Star tried and what I'm trying are not the same."

"Dante, I need you to do the album with Antwan." The urgency of Otis's tone was unexpected.

Dante frowned. "What's going on?"

"The thing with your sister was just the icing on the cake. We've got artists that are considering not resigning, and sales are down. We need Antwan to breathe new life into W. M. Records and another set of hit albums to rebuild confidence with our current artists."

"How bad are sales?"

"I didn't want to get into this, but we've gone down about five percent the past two years. I wouldn't worry, we've had down years before, but if we lose some artists and can't sign a big name, then we may be talking double-digit losses. They haven't crucified us in the business news yet. But another year with profit losses, and they will."

"Damn," Dante grunted and ran a hand over his forehead. He sat back on the bed while his dad's revelation took root in his brain. The Wilson legacy, and the success of W. M. Records, was what he'd lived for and built his career on. If they had multiple years of losses, even small ones, pretty soon the speculators would begin to spread rumors that things weren't going well at W. M. Records. Artists would jump ship. Sales would dwindle. Best case, they'd take several years to rebuild. Worst case, they would fold or have to consider a merger with another label just to stay afloat.

"Go ahead and open the club," Otis said. "You mentioned that Raymond wants to put his name on it. Fine, that'll help. But before you turn it into some hippie hangout, think about doing the album with Antwan, and maybe booking some of our commercial artists there instead."

Dante hated the idea of his dream becoming something else, but he also hated the idea of his family's legacy suffering. "I'll think about it."

"Good."

They talked for a few more minutes. Afterward, Dante tossed his phone on the bed. The fate of W. M. Records and the good argument Otis had for Dante to continue making the music that sold swirled in his brain. He'd never considered that what happened to Star could happen to him, but with the state of affairs at W. M. Records, it was a real concern. As much as he wanted to try his hand at new, different music, he honestly loved his lifestyle and the perks of being famous. One bad album wouldn't ruin him, but it could take him from being one of the most celebrated men in the music industry to a laughingstock.

Dante swore and rubbed his temples. *Damn.* He really didn't want to think about that.

There was a knock on the door before it opened. The two models he'd watched dance before peaked their heads in. Their grins promised a welcome distraction from his shaky confidence—something he'd never felt before. Smiling, Dante waved the women in. Tomorrow he'd worry about what to do with his music career. Tonight his music was still popular and so was he. Time to get back to relaxing after another successful tour and worry about reality later.

Chapter 2

Julie Dominick hung up the phone on her desk and jumped up from the leather chair. Her red high heels tapped on the tile floor as she rushed across the hall to the office of her business partner, Evette Dean. She gave two swift knocks on Evette's open door before hurrying in.

"You'll never guess who I just talked to," Julie said in a rush.

Evette slowly turned away from her wide-screen monitor and raised a brow—her natural response whenever Julie came to her bouncing in excitement. Evette's light brown hair was twisted in the usual no-nonsense bun at the back of her head, and her polka-dot tan blouse and matching black pencil skirt were flawless, as always. If not for the spark in Evette's dark eyes, Julie would think she hadn't garnered her friend's interest.

"Then you better tell me."

Julie stood before Evette's neatly arranged desk. "Raymond just called."

Evette's raised brows lowered into a frown. The spark of interest was gone. She waved a hand and turned back to her monitor. "I thought you were talking about someone."

Julie reached over and placed a hand over Evette's hands, which were already typing away on the keyboard. "You will never guess what he wanted."

Evette sighed and turned back to Julie. "What did he want?"

"He's opening a nightclub, and he wants us to manage the development."

The interest returned full force. Evette sat forward, her eyes wide. "Are you serious?"

"There are two things I don't play around with, and that's business and money."

"That's great! When, where, what type of club?"

Julie waved her hands back and forth to stop the flow of questions. "He's finished the concert tour, and now he's in Malibu, California. He wants someplace upscale but with a casual vibe where they can host live performances. He's already bought the location and needs another partner to help oversee the day-to-day operations."

"When are you going?" Evette's voice indicated that Julie should be packing instead of talking.

Julie took a deep breath and fell into the leather chair across from Evette's glass-top desk. "I'm not sure if I'm going."

Evette's excitement morphed into confusion. Not surprising. Out of the two of them, Julie was definitely the one who didn't hesitate when the time came to make bold decisions. "You're not sure?" Evette asked. "When have you ever not been sure about doing something this big?"

More times than Julie would ever admit. Faking confidence after walking away from Nexon-Jones, a powerhouse in the nightclub and restaurant development world, to start her own firm was proof of that.

Some thought she was crazy for leaving Nexon-Jones, where she was on the fast track to being one of their most promising agents. The decision had been easy after her boss had asked her to get a little more *comfortable* with a potential client. Julie walked and started Dominant Development. A bold name for a bold move. Go hard or go home.

The bold move worked enough to get Evette to walk away with her, and their combined determination had led to Dominant Development's name being behind the openings of nightclubs around the southeast with more than a few celebrities tied to them. Having one of R&B's newest stars as a best friend didn't hurt either. Raymond had helped her get her first nightclub opened at the start of his career and later had introduced her to his celebrity friends. This was the first time he'd brought up opening a new place with her.

"We need to fix the situation in Miami," Julie said.

"All the more reason to go," Evette countered. "If you do this, everyone will forget about the failure of the Miami club."

Julie winched. "We don't say failure. We say setback."

A big setback in the case of their small firm. They had started strong, opening successful nightclubs in Atlanta, Charlotte and Nashville. The name Dominant Development was garnering respect until the Miami nightclub. Crash-and-burn failure was an understatement. The place hadn't stayed open for six months before fights between rival gangs and rumors of drug trafficking shut it down. Julie had been leery of working with the newly rich rapper who had wanted the club, but the guy was at the top of the charts at the time, and she'd fallen back on her *go all in or go home* rule. Regardless of how well her other nightclubs were doing, the disaster that was the Miami club is what people were talking about now.

"Setback, failure, call it what you want. We need another big opening," Evette said.

"Yes, but we also just landed two new clients, and those projects are going to take a lot of effort. We are on the verge of needing one more agent."

Evette raised her pointer and middle fingers. "Two."

"Fine, we need two more people to handle the workload. It's not a good time for me to hop on a plane and fly across the country to open a new nightclub."

Evette took a deep breath, which meant she was trying hard to think about Julie's arguments instead of just blowing her off. "I hear what you're saying, but I think this is the perfect time. If you open a nightclub associated with Raymond, and it's successful, it will wash away the mess that was Miami and get us in the playing field on the West Coast. The jerks at Nexon-Jones will lose their minds. Isn't this why you started this place?"

No truer words were spoken. After leaving Nexon-Jones, Raymond had introduced her to rapper Antwan Harmon, who went by just Antwan. Her attraction to Antwan was immediate; she'd fallen for his swagger and intensity, and was even a little thrilled by his street appeal. When he'd stopped talking with Nexon-Jones about opening a club in Atlanta and trusted her to open the place instead, she'd fallen in love. She'd stolen a major client from her former employer and found the man she'd spend the rest of her life with. The former thought had worked out, the latter not so much. Opening night, she'd found out she was just one of many women in love with Antwan.

Her heartbreak was coupled with the knowledge that her former boss started spreading the word that she'd only landed Antwan's account because she was sleeping with him. She'd also heard that some blamed her for making the decision about the Miami club because of her "relationship" with the client. Now she made sure to keep a very wide distance between her and any person she worked for.

"I'd feel guilty if I left you alone in the midst of this."

"Girl, quit being crazy. We've already narrowed down the agents we want to interview. I'll handle bringing on the new agents."

"I wanted to be involved."

"Why? You don't trust my judgment?" Evette asked without any indication that she believed the statement.

"Of course I do," Julie said with sincerity. She trusted Evette more than anyone. "If this pans out, I'll be out there for several months, at least until the club is opened."

"You can come back once or twice a month if it gets really crazy back here. Let go of some of that control freak, and go get us more business. Besides, isn't the point of having a famous friend so he can help you out?"

"Says who?"

"Says me. Let your friendship with Raymond be useful for once."

Julie chuckled and leaned back in the chair. "I don't know why you dislike him so much. Raymond has been a great friend. He helped me out when I was turning into a poor, sad basket case. He taught me how to—"

"Guard your heart," Evette finished with a hand wave. "I know. You and those crazy dating rules."

"They aren't crazy. I got caught up in that relationship with Antwan and thought there was more to us than there was. You remember how pathetic I was. If it weren't for Raymond schooling me on the way men think, I would've fallen for more pitiful lines and believed I was in a relationship with a guy when I was actually a booty call."

"Raymond's so-called education—" Evette made air quotes with her fingers "—has given you a convenient excuse to keep men at arm's length."

"I date." Julie shrugged. "Guys love me. Unfortunately, they love me for all the wrong reasons."

The few celebrity men she met were just as conceited and into playing games as Antwan. She preferred dating men outside the entertainment industry. Sadly, the few she had dated either played the same games or thought she was a good route to meeting famous people.

"Guys love trying to break through the wall you've surrounded yourself with. You're a challenge."

"Which is ten times better than being an easy conquest."

"I still think Raymond's education is just a way for him to keep you single."

This time Julie waved away Evette's words. "We're just friends, Evette. For the hundredth time, Raymond only gives advice on men when I ask for it, and he's spot-on every time. He's not keeping me single—the lack of available men is keeping me single."

Evette grunted. "I can't argue with that. Anyway, back to my original point. If Raymond wants you to oversee opening his nightclub—regardless of how busy we are here—I think you should go. At least see what his plans are and make sure it's worth our time."

"There's one more little thing."

"What's that?"

Julie studied her perfectly polished nails. "He's opening the place with Dante Wilson." Her voice was blasé when she knew this news would shatter any sense of calm Evette had.

Evette slapped her desk with both hands, her eyes as wide as saucers. "Dante Wilson?" Julie nodded. "*The* Dante Wilson? Mr. I Can Sing, Dance and Play a Dozen Instruments Dante Wilson? Dante Wilson of W. M. Records, whose parents, grandparents and great-grandparents were music legends?"

Julie chuckled. "The one and same."

Evette pointed at Julie. "You're getting on that plane, today, and you're checking out this lead. Why didn't you say that first?"

"Because I didn't want it to sway your decision. This is huge, but if you had any hesitation about handling the two new accounts, hiring new staff and our current projects while I was on the West Coast, I would have said no."

Evette took another deep breath. "Julie, I appreciate you thinking of me, seriously, but if you are not in Malibu by the end of the week, I swear I'm going to strangle you." Her calm tone gave way to excitement by the end of the sentence.

Julie grinned and stood. "No need for violence. I'll go back to my office and finally click Submit."

"On what?"

"The purchase of the plane ticket I started buying before coming in here."

Chapter 3

Julie sat in the backseat of the car Raymond had waiting for her at the airport and reviewed the list of reputable contractors in and around Malibu, California. Paying attention to the details instead of taking in the beautiful sights along the Pacific Coast Highway was proving difficult for her. Between the awe-inspiring mountains and sparkling sea, she really wished she was there for pleasure instead of business. But business was the reason she'd left Evette in Atlanta, so she tore her eyes away from the views and scanned contractor websites.

Picking contractors before actually being vetted as Raymond and Dante's final partner was presumptuous. Raymond basically wanted her to come and talk about possibly working with them. She'd mainly gotten her jobs by acting as if she already had them. The tactic hadn't failed her yet.

Later, when the car pulled down one of the gated entrances that she assumed blocked the way to the homes of Hollywood's rich and famous, her stomach churned like the waves against the bluffs she'd admired on the drive up. She was actually about to meet Dante Wilson. Thanks to her friendship with Raymond and her work opening popular nightclubs, she wasn't easily starstruck. However, she'd listened to and loved Dante's music for most of her life. From her preteens through her bad breakup with Antwan, the guy always had a song on the radio rotation that seemed to fit the mood of her life.

She'd dressed nicely for her flight. Albeit her black trousers, white cowl-neck blouse and tailored red blazer were travel worn, she still looked casual but professional. While the driver announced their arrival at the gate, Julie pulled out her compact to double-check her makeup and smooth her hand down the back of her stylish pixie cut.

The gates opened, and the driver maneuvered the car down the long drive and parked in front of a huge stone villa. She would have been impressed by the house and its magnificent views if not for the obvious signs of a party going on. She frowned in confusion when the driver opened the door, where she was greeted by music coming from the back, along with laughter and voices. Three women in skimpy bikinis and two men in board shorts stood out front. Another car pulled up, and the group got in.

She glanced at the driver. "Are we at the right place?"

"Yes, ma'am. This is Dante Wilson's residence."

Julie nodded, then turned back to the sounds of revelry coming from the villa. She crossed the stone-tiled entrance to the front door. Julie rang the doorbell, unsure if the chime would even be heard over the sounds of the party. Hell, did she even need to ring the bell?

A guy wearing blue-and-red swim trunks opened the door. "Hey, come on in," he said, waving her inside.

Julie thanked him, entered the home and immediately felt overdressed. Men in swim trunks and women in bathing suits filled the house. The main area, with tan stone walls, dark walnut floors, modern furnishings and expensive decorations, was completely open to the outside, where a crystal-blue infinity pool overlooked the ocean. Even more people in bathing suits milled around the expansive outdoor living space.

"Are you here for the party?" the guy asked.

"Umm, I'm meeting with Raymond," she said.

"Oh, come on—he's out by the pool."

Julie followed him through the crowd out to the pool. "He's there." He pointed.

Raymond was in the middle of the pool, playing water polo with several bikini-clad women. Of course he would be. Julie rolled her eyes, but she smiled despite her disappointment that he wasn't prepared for a real meeting. Raymond would never change. They'd met freshmen year in college at a party. Though she'd flirted with him, she'd turned down his attempts to get her in bed. She'd never felt that way about Raymond. Eventually, their flirty relationship had become a close friendship by the time they graduated and Raymond's music career kicked off. She knew if there was a party to attend or a good-looking woman to get with, Raymond was there.

Still, as she stood by the pool, sweltering in a blazer while everyone else was clad in swimwear, a strong pull of annoyance that Raymond hadn't mentioned she would be walking into a pool party and not a business meeting swept through her. She really hoped he wasn't wasting her time. She loved Raymond like a brother, but she wouldn't hesitate to wring his neck if he pulled her away from Atlanta over a whim of his.

"Hey, Raymond," she called. Her voice, and the annoyance in it, carried above the music and female laughter.

Raymond turned away from the game to look her way. His grin widened. "Julie!" he exclaimed with slight surprise.

She worked very hard not to roll her eyes again. The volleyball hit him in the side of the head, and a chorus of chuckles came up from the various women in the pool.

Raymond shook his head and blinked several times. "I'm coming out now." He swam to the edge of the pool and pulled himself out of the water. Every woman in the pool eyed his muscular body with desire and enthusiasm—chiseled muscles beneath smooth tan skin, a pretty-boy face with green eyes to boot. Julie understood their admiration, though she didn't share their desire.

He took a few steps to her and tried to hug her. Julie jumped back and held up a hand. "No way, you're soaking wet."

Raymond's eyes flashed with mischief that Julie knew all too well. "I'm serious, Raymond—this is a new blazer, and you can't mess it up with a chlorine-filled hug."

He chuckled and edged closer. "I haven't seen you in ages, and you won't hug me because of a jacket."

Julie took a step back. "No, I won't hug you, but I do feel like punching you."

That stopped his movement. "What did I do this time?"

Julie raised a brow and looked around. "Ray, I thought

we were meeting to discuss business. Instead you're having a party."

"Oh, that," he said with a shrug. "We can still talk." He waved over a woman lounging nearby. The beauty stood and brought him a towel. "Thanks, baby." Raymond slapped her behind as she walked away, then wiped the excess water from his face.

"You know, I'd rather talk when you're not in the middle of an orgy. I'll check into the hotel, and we can meet up tomorrow."

She'd booked the hotel suite for a month with plans to extend that or possibly rent someplace if it seemed the club opening would take a long time. If it fell through, she would make Raymond pay any hotel cancellation fees.

"No! Sorry, Julie, this party just kind of happened."

Julie doubted that. There were too many people here for the party to *kind of* happen, but she kept that thought to herself. "All the more reason to wait until we can really talk about things."

"Seriously, we can. Dante is here. I told him you were coming today."

Julie glanced around at the people present. She recognized some celebrities and reality stars, but Dante wasn't in the mix.

"He's inside," Raymond said. "Come on. At least say hello, since you got all dressed to impress, and then stay and relax for a while."

"Raymond, I'm here on business, not to relax."

"Not all business is handled in a boardroom, Julie. Chill out for a second and come meet Dante."

He took her hand and gently tugged her toward the door. Julie twisted her lip but let him lead her. Honestly, she shouldn't be surprised that Raymond asked her to meet him to discuss business at the same time Dante "accidentally" threw a party. His fun personality and spontaneity were part of the persona that had turned him into a star.

"How was your flight? Did the driver get to the airport on time? I gave him your arrival and told him to be there on time." Raymond fired off the questions.

Julie answered those and the half-dozen others Raymond threw her way as they walked through the crowded living area toward the back of the house. His questions reminded her of their college days when he always worried about her walking across campus at night by herself. His concern for her welfare was why she'd eventually viewed him as a brother. His concern grew after her breakup with Antwan. She knew Raymond blamed himself for introducing her to the guy, and she believed that was why he was so forthcoming with her about all the sleazy ways men thought and the tricks they pulled.

In the back of the house, the sounds of the party were replaced by the sound of piano music along with Dante's smooth tenor singing.

"Let me hold you in my arms. Let me comfort you all night long. Let me be the man to kiss away your fears."

Julie's heart ached as the words took her back to the time after the Antwan breakup when she'd listened to this song and yearned for a guy to be all those things. She'd listened to the song repeatedly. She hated herself for moping so much over a man who didn't deserve it, and hearing Dante sing stirred up the longing she'd thought was long gone.

She and Raymond stopped at the open door of the room where the music came from. A large grand piano stood in the center of what she could see was a music room with other instruments, framed albums and pictures of the Wilson family lining the walls. Dante sat behind the piano; four women in colorful bikinis surrounded him like beautiful birds. She hadn't listened to the song in ages. His voice swept her up in thoughts of how nice having a man actually kiss away her fears would be.

She'd known Dante was handsome and that he could sing, but to witness his talent and his beauty up close and personal took her breath away.

His eyes were closed, and the flash of his perfect white teeth gleamed between lips that made her think of marathon rounds of kissing, touching and sexing. His head swayed gently back and forth to the sound of the music. His curly dark hair was tapered at the sides and thicker on the top. A dusting of hair covered his square jaw. Julie's gaze slid over wide shoulders in a white shirt unbuttoned just enough to give a glimpse of a smooth muscled chest and warm brown skin. As if she were still standing beneath the sun, Julie's body burned. Her nipples hardened, and a slow, sultry heat that matched the smoldering sound of Dante's voice slid through her body.

Julie shifted from one foot to the other. This was not good. She could not be attracted to him. She tried to ignore her primal response, but the concentration of heat between her thighs continued in a mocking *sucks for you* kind of way.

The music stopped, and no one spoke until the last note drifted away. Dante opened his eyes, and the ladies clapped and squealed their praise. His lips spread in a wide-open grin. His sexy dark eyes sparkled with a look that made a woman want to forget every lesson about acting like a lady. A sound, part whimper, part suppressed giggle, rang in her ear; a second later, she realized she'd made the sound.

Raymond shifted beside her. Dante looked up, his dark gaze connecting with hers so hard she gasped out the little bit of air that remained in her chest. *Oh, hell, I'm screwed.*

"Raymond," Dante said, his very interested eyes still on Julie, "please introduce your beautiful friend."

Chapter 4

Dante's smile widened as the woman with Raymond snapped her mouth closed and lifted her chin. He didn't miss the blatant desire burning in her wonderful light brown eyes before she'd hidden the emotion behind a professional mask. His gaze slowly traced over her body, and his abdomen tightened with anticipation. Forgetting the beauties who'd dragged him to the music room, and the fun he'd planned to have with them, Dante stood and crossed the room.

He took in more of her appearance the closer he got. He liked everything he saw: short, stylish hair highlighted blond, the bangs just long enough to brush arched brows; clear, direct amber eyes; and a full, sensuous mouth. Her black pants didn't hug her curves, but the material didn't hide her shapely figure either. The red blazer brought attention to her waist and the scooped neckline of her shirt drew his eyes to her sexy cleavage. Sexy cherry-red heels brought her to almost his height.

"Dante," Raymond said. "This is Julie Dominick."

Dante held out his hand. "Julie Dominick." He said her name slowly, enjoying the sound. "It's very nice to meet you."

He took her hand and kissed the back, catching a whiff of her perfume. The warm scent brought to mind dark rooms and Julie sliding across satin sheets beneath him.

"It's a pleasure meeting you, Dante," she said, and she didn't pull her hand away. "Out of all your songs, that is my favorite."

Her gaze was straightforward—no batting lashes or shy glances. He liked that immediately. She was a woman who wasn't hesitant. Despite her directness, that hot spark from when their eyes first met was nowhere to be seen. He wanted the spark back.

"I'd be happy to sing it for you anytime you'd like."

Her smile tipped up at the corners, and she slowly slid her hand out of his. The gentle glide of her slim fingers sent shivers down his arm. "Raymond didn't tell me you were having a party. I expected a business meeting."

She'd ignored his obvious flirtation, which meant she was going to try to ignore what he'd noticed and felt between them. He should do the same, but direct and beautiful women were his weakness.

"A friend came over, and before we knew it there was a houseful of people. The whole party happened on a whim."

"Hmm, is opening your club also due to a whim?" She looked from Dante to Raymond. He heard the insinuation that they were wasting her time. Dante grinned. Direct, beautiful and bold. Ballsy for a woman trying to go into business with him. He liked her even more, even if he didn't like the assumption that he wasn't serious about opening the club.

"I promise you, I'm very serious about the opening of my club. I'd like to debut new artists under my own label there. My family wouldn't support these artists at venues owned and managed by W. M. Records."

Her brows rose. He'd surprised her.

"Then I'll do everything I can to make sure this place opens smoothly."

Raymond smiled at them both. "I'm telling you, Dante, Julie is the right person for the job."

His body was definitely on board with Julie handling this project, but his brain interjected. This was important to him for multiple reasons; he couldn't just go with the decision the head below his belt was trying to get him to make.

"We'll see. I'm talking to a few other developers."

The corner of her inviting lips lifted, and her head tilted to the side. "Talk to them all you want. I know I'm the right person. In the next few days, you'll know it, too."

Dante added "confident" to the things about Julie Dominick that were making ignoring the head below his belt harder.

One of the women from the piano came over. "Are you ready to sing for us again?" she asked with a bright smile.

Julie stepped back. "I mentioned to Raymond that I can come back tomorrow to discuss business. I'm more than happy to do that."

Raymond placed a hand on her arm. "Don't leave, Julie."

Dante zeroed in on Raymond's hands on Julie, so familiar, without a bit of hesitation or awkwardness between them. Raymond said nothing was going on between him and Julie, but he'd also said she was the woman he could consider settling down with later, which meant Dante should pull back. No matter how his body reacted to her, he shouldn't step on Raymond's toes that way.

"Stay," Dante said. "Change and join the party."

She shook her head. "I'm not prepared for a pool party."

Raymond chuckled. "You can't tell me you came to Malibu and didn't bring a swimsuit. Get the thing out, and come sit by the pool. I know this is a business trip, but you can have a few minutes to enjoy yourself."

She glanced at Dante, and he nodded. He may not step on Raymond's toes, but that didn't mean he didn't want her to stick around so he could see her in a bathing suit. Maybe the desire caused by that thought showed in his expression because the spark he'd witnessed earlier made a brief appearance in Julie's eyes. It was quickly hidden when she turned to Raymond. "Fine. I'll change and join you."

Raymond dragged Julie away to get her bags and showed her where to change. Dante would have preferred to do that himself, but she was Raymond's friend. Better for Dante to keep his distance.

He sang another song for the ladies in the music room but wasn't really into having fun with them anymore, so he ushered them back to the pool. They kept him company, and he listened to them talk about inconsequential things. Each one tried to gain his attention and figure out who he'd spend the rest of the day with. It was a question he'd been debating before Julie walked through the door and broke his thoughts, scattering them like balls on a pool table.

The source of the scattering came out onto the patio, Raymond with her. Dante took a sip of beer that stuck in his throat. He coughed and sat up in his chair. Julie in a business suit was a man's fantasy; Julie in a bathing suit was a man's erotic dream. The red one-piece suit was plastered to full breasts and a flat stomach. It rose high on her hips; no sarong or wrap hid the perfection of her thighs and legs. Confident with a capital *C*. She'd switched the heels for a pair of red sandals. Dante took another gulp of his beer to stop his groan of appreciation from escaping.

She and Raymond settled into chairs across the pool. They talked and laughed, looking every bit the close friends Raymond said they were. She glanced around the space. Her gaze stopped several times as she took in the various people. When she stopped on him, a small smile lifted her lips and made his heart jump before she continued her perusal. What did that smile mean? Did she feel the same knocked-out-of-breath feeling when their eyes met, or was she just smiling at a potential business partner she had to acknowledge? He couldn't say she was looking only for him because she seemed to check out everyone there.

He ran a hand over his face. *What the hell?* When did he become the guy obsessing over what a woman was thinking? Julie's closeness with Raymond meant he had to keep his hands to himself. If she did get the job, getting involved with her might cloud his judgment about the club. He should ignore her.

A woman that Raymond had hooked up with came over to him and Julie. Raymond introduced her. Julie smiled and held out her hand. Dante noted her friendly and jealous-free greeting. The woman clung to Raymond's side. After a few minutes of talking, Julie waved Raymond and the woman away. They strolled toward the door. Julie watched them, but there was no hint of regret, anger or disappointment on her face. *Okay, maybe they are just friends.*

Her eyes lifted and met his. Dante's heart danced behind his rib cage. Again, she gave him a small smile, then looked away. He was up and out of the chair in an instant.

"I'll have to tell Raymond to never leave a beautiful woman alone at a party," he said as he sat next to her. "Someone else may slip in."

Her smile was good-natured, not flirtatious. "Actually, I was waiting for him to leave. He has a way of unintentionally blocking. Now I'm free to talk with whomever I want."

Dante liked the sound of that. "Really?"

"Yeah."

"Anyone here you're interested in having a conversation with?"

Her smile made him hot all over. "Actually, there is a guy I wouldn't mind talking to."

Dante's grin widened. He slid his arm across the back of the chair and moved closer. "I'd love to know who."

She looked over his shoulder, then used her head to indicate behind Dante. "Him. The guy in the green trunks."

Dante frowned and glanced around. Carlos, the drummer they'd had to call in on the last leg of the tour after Dante's original drummer got sick, stood on the other side of the pool. There was something about Carlos that Dante didn't really like, but he'd chalked his feelings up to his dislike of unexpected changes. Carlos played well and hadn't caused any problems on tour, so Dante ignored his weird feelings toward the guy.

"Him?"

"You sound surprised," she said, and he swore amusement filled her voice.

"I thought you might be interested in someone else."

"Really, who?"

There was definite humor in her amber eyes.

"I thought you'd want to spend more time with Raymond."

She shook her head, then crossed her long and shapely legs. "Oh. Not really. Ray and I have plenty of time to catch up while I'm working with you two."

Spoken as if she already had the job. "Him leaving with another woman didn't bother you?"

Her eyes sparkled with amusement and she waved a hand. "That. No. I've known Ray way too long to get upset when he ditches me for another female."

"Did it used to bother you?"

She shook her head. "No. Ray is cool, but I know him too well to fall for him."

"That's good to know."

"Why? Did you think my relationship with him would compromise my ability to do the job?"

"I just like to be sure."

"You can be sure. I don't mix business with pleasure, and I never date partners."

He leaned in and stared into her beautiful eyes. "I'm sure exceptions can be made."

Her smirk was cute, and the twist of her full lips made him want to kiss her. "Ray and I are not worth an exception."

Dante rubbed his chin. "What if I'm the exception?"

A spark flashed in the depths of her eyes. She shifted, then looked away. When she looked back at him, the spark was gone, all interest hidden.

"I'll admit I used to drool over your posters in my music magazines when I was a teen. You once occupied a fair amount of space in my fantasies, but that was fifteen years ago. Girlish fantasies gave way to adult responsibilities."

He leaned forward until only a few inches separated them. "Forget the girlish fantasies. I want to be a part of your very grown-up thoughts."

She held his gaze for what felt like hours. Despite the neutral expression on her face, he noticed her quick inhale. The rhythm of excitement he got when pursuing a new woman quickened his pulse.

Her brows rose, and her head tilted to the side. "Have brunch with me tomorrow. I'll tell you about my grown-up thoughts." There was no flirtation in her voice; she sounded almost businesslike, but the humor remained in her eyes.

Dante wasn't sure what that meant, but he wasn't about to deny a chance to be with her tomorrow. "I know a place."

She shook her head. "I've already looked up local restaurants, and I'd like to go to Geoffrey's. I'll meet you there at nine."

This woman knew what she wanted, meaning she was going to be damn difficult to resist. "I'll be there."

Her devilish smile made him feel as if he were missing something. "It's a date." She stood and walked away.

Dante watched the sexy sway of her hips, his body hardening with each one of her assertive steps. His desire was quickly doused when she crossed over to speak with Carlos.

What the...? Women didn't typically leave him to talk to another man. For the first time, he'd been thrown off by a woman.

Julie shifted her position next to Carlos, and her gaze flitted to Dante for a second. Dante grinned and leaned back in the chair. Her quick look got him back on balance. Julie Dominick may play impartial toward him, but she was interested. He couldn't step to Raymond's girl like that, but he damn sure was going to enjoy the heat sizzling between them.

Chapter 5

Julie casually sipped ice water and stared out at the magnificent ocean view from the patio at Geoffrey's Malibu. Immediately after booking her trip, she'd looked into places that would work for relaxed business meetings and that offered superb food. As she looked over the brunch menu, she was pleased with her choice.

After putting down the water, she pulled out her tablet and navigated to the website of the contractor she was considering hiring for the club. The sun was hot, and she wore a sleeveless beige blouse with a tan pencil skirt, so she wasn't sweltering like yesterday. She leaned forward to get more shade from the white umbrella over the table to see the screen better. She'd gotten a list of reputable contractors from the coworkers who didn't hate her for her abrupt exit from Nexon-Jones. She'd narrowed her choices down to three firms, and, depending on their availability, along with Dante's and Raymond's schedules, she hoped to have one secured by the end of the week.

"She's right here, Mr. Wilson." The host's voice came from behind Julie.

She glanced up from the tablet to where the young man indicated to her. Dante smiled and thanked the host, looking every bit the sex symbol that he was in a fitted dark gray T-shirt, white pants and dark shoes. Julie swallowed hard and sucked in a breath. The man had thrown her off yesterday. She'd assumed Dante would be charming, flirtatious even, but when he'd indicated that he should be the exception to her no-mixing-business-and-pleasure rule, her mind became slushy.

How badly she'd wanted to take him up on that offer was almost embarrassing. Getting involved with a guy in the entertainment industry, and a business partner at that, went against many of the rules that prevented her from being played by a man.

"Good afternoon," she said with what she envisioned to be a professional, I'm-not-drooling-internally smile.

"You're early." He pulled out a chair and sat down.

"I'm typically early when I have a meeting."

He raised a brow and placed his forearms on the table. The breeze brought over the scent of the sea and his enticing cologne. Dante leaned closer to her. "Meeting. I thought this was a date?"

She had left him with that impression, and she had to admit, there were plenty of things worse than going on a date with him. Too bad for him. She wasn't here to have a fling with Dante or jeopardize her reputation.

But she would flirt. Flirting went a lot further and got her a lot more than being an ice-cold superbitch. From what she knew about men, flirting was just another tactic they used to throw a woman off her game.

"This isn't a date," she said with a smile.

"You promised to give a little insight on your very adult thoughts."

The way he said "adult thoughts" had her imagining all types of adult things—things that involved him, naked and smiling.

Julie leaned back in her chair. "Are you sure you're ready to hear them?"

"Oh, I'm very sure."

"I'm glad to hear that. Because I've thought about this all morning." She leaned forward.

Excitement entered his eyes. "You have?"

"All night, honestly. I can't get the thoughts out of my mind."

"Sometimes talking about things helps, or having a helping hand." His warm hand covered hers. The touch nearly made her forget this was supposed to be harmless flirting.

"Are you willing to help?"

"In any way possible."

"I thought you would be." She glanced down at his long fingers casually brushing the back of her hand. Each light stroke was like a dose of steroids to her pumped-up hormones. "You've got nice hands."

"They're willing to help you in any way."

The muscles of her thighs clenched. Julie pulled her hand away. *Time to remember this is supposed to be harmless flirting.* "Good, because I'm meeting with a contractor that I'm considering hiring to help with the renovation of the building you've picked out for the club. I'd like to get your opinion."

His smile froze for a second before his brows drew together. "Excuse me?"

"I've narrowed the choices down to three, and, of course, I won't pick one without discussing the details with you and Raymond first. I'm glad you're so willing to help."

"So that's why you invited me here?"

"Of course. Why else would I?" She tried to look innocent but knew he had to see the humor in her expression. She was having a hard time not chuckling at his confusion.

Julie quickly turned and nearly sagged with relief when she saw the hostess bringing the contractor to their table. She stood and held out her hand to the man beside the hostess.

"Orlando Salvatore," she said.

Orlando nodded and took her hand. He was tall with wavy dark hair, gleaming straight teeth and a body honed from working in construction. His white shirt and dark brown pants accentuated broad shoulders and strong legs.

"And you must be Julie Dominick." His handshake was firm but not too tight.

"I am. Thank you for meeting me this morning."

"No problem at all. I'd love to work on this project."

Julie grinned, then held out her hand to Dante, who watched her with slightly narrowed eyes. "He needs no introduction, but this is Dante Wilson. Obviously, he'll be involved with choosing the contractor for the job."

"Of course," Orlando said. "It's very nice to meet you, Mr. Wilson. I'm a big fan."

Dante slowly stood and shook Orlando's hand. "Flattery will get you everywhere."

Orlando grinned. "I only speak the truth."

Julie sat, and then Orlando and Dante followed suit. Julie ignored Dante's direct gaze on her. Outwardly, anyway. Inside, her body was a ball of nerves. She hoped to impress Dante with her proactive approach to handling the development of the nightclub. It was the reason she'd invited him here this morning. *Go hard or go home.*

"I've been looking at your website, Orlando," Julie said. "I'm impressed with the jobs you've handled. I see that you've also been chosen to open a nightclub in LA. Will you be able to handle another job?"

She didn't like small talk and preferred going directly into any concerns. She trusted the recommendation she'd gotten from her former coworker, but she couldn't forget he still worked for Nexon-Jones.

Orlando handled her direct question easily and went right into the number of crews he had working for him and how he scheduled his workload. He answered all Julie's questions easily and impressively while they waited on their food. Dante perked up and stopped glaring at her long enough to ask Orlando some of his own questions. From the interest and satisfaction that flashed on Dante's face, she guessed he was also impressed by Orlando.

By the end of the meal, her questions were done. After a few minutes of small talk, Julie wrapped up the meeting.

"Thank you again for meeting with me, Orlando," Julie said. "I'll be in touch before the end of the week."

She stood and so did the men. Orlando shook Dante's hand, then hers. When she would have pulled back, he held on. "The pleasure was all mine. I hope to hear from you soon, regardless of the outcome."

Orlando's smile and the flirtatious tone were clear.

Julie returned his smile with one of her own and nodded. "I'll be sure to give you a call."

"Do that," Orlando said before leaving.

Dante looked at Orlando's retreating back and then at Julie. "What was that?"

"What was what?" Julie sat back down.

Dante sat and motioned his head in Orlando's direction. "That?"

"That was me thinking I've found our contractor. Didn't you like him?"

"He was all right."

"All right? Did you look at the work he's done, all on time? That's big when it comes to contractors. Of course, I'm going to check his references."

"You're ready to hire him already?"

"He was my top choice, but we've got another interview later today."

His brows rose. "We do?"

"Yeah." She checked her watch. "I agreed to meet her for a late lunch. Are you available?"

"Her?"

Julie raised a brow. "Do you have a problem with a woman?"

He raised his hands. "Not at all. At least this time you won't spend the meeting grinning and giggling over the guy."

"I don't giggle."

"Yes, you do." He quirked a brow. "It would be cute. If you were giggling over me."

She laughed. "Still want me to make you my exception to the no-business-and-pleasure-mixing rule?"

"I'd like to know if you were considering it."

She eyed him from head to toe. "I've already considered it."

"And?"

"And you're talented, sexy and very smug. I'm not interested."

Dante rubbed his jaw. "If you would have let this be a real date, I think you would be. I envisioned this morning going a lot differently."

"What did you envision?"

"Brunch, sightseeing, maybe a kiss."

She glanced at his lips, imagined them on hers and was hit with a wave of longing, which she quickly pushed aside. "I'm here to work. I promise—I will not be kissing you."

"I believe that not only will we kiss but that you'll initiate it." He looked so arrogant and sure of himself that, for a second, her heart trembled, and she believed he might be right.

Chapter 6

Dante met up with Raymond at the end of the week at a jazz club in Los Angeles. When he wasn't on tour or working on an album, Dante preferred the laid-back atmosphere of his villa in Malibu over the constant hustle of LA, unless there was a party worth attending. Tonight there was a huge party planned after Jacobe's basketball game. Dante never refused a chance to party.

He found Raymond in the club's VIP section, watching a lovely and curvy woman singing onstage. They'd agreed to meet here before going to the game and then the party. After sitting in an interview with another contractor and Julie that morning, and after she'd made it obvious, yet again, that she wasn't giving him any play, Dante was more than ready to spend the night partying.

Dante strolled over and sat next to Raymond. "What's up with your girl?"

Raymond raised a brow. "Who?"

"Julie."

Raymond grinned and sipped on the drink in his hand. "Nothing, she's just trying to do a good job."

"When did we officially make her a partner?"

Raymond chuckled. "We didn't. Julie always tackles a job like she's got it. By the time she's finished putting the pieces together, people wonder why they wouldn't partner with her."

Dante was in that exact predicament. She had pulled together the best contractors in the area and drilled them on their ability to perform. After seeing her in action, he wondered why he should look for anyone else.

"She knows her stuff. I thought we were meeting for brunch the other day, and she's setting up interviews with potential contractors."

Raymond frowned. "You met her for brunch? When?"

"Tuesday. I thought you knew?"

"I knew she was checking out some contractors but not that she was meeting with you to do that."

Dante leaned back on the black couch and spread his arms across the back. "I thought she had agreed to a date."

Raymond sat up straight and put his drink on the table. "You asked her on a date?"

"After you left her at the pool to hang out with that other woman, I didn't think you'd have a problem."

"Why didn't you tell me you *thought* you were going out with her? I told you about us."

Dante raised a hand. "Hold up. Us—what us? She was at the party for a second, and you walked away with another woman."

Raymond slid forward on the chair and tugged on his

black leather pants before holding out his hands. "That woman from the party doesn't mean anything. Julie is the one. The one I'm going to settle down with. After I finish, you know." Raymond popped his collar. "Enjoying myself."

"What makes you think she's going to want to settle down with you after you finish sleeping with half of the female population?"

"Because of the pact we made in college. If we're both single, then we'll get together."

"So you think she's just going to sit around being single waiting on that day to come?"

"She has so far," Raymond said smugly. "Julie hasn't gotten serious about any guy since getting her heart broken a few years back. I was the guy who helped her get through that. We would have hooked up then, but, you know, my career was just starting. She said she didn't want to hold me back or make me keep promises. So we agreed to be friends."

"Why does that make you so sure she's waiting for the day you two can finally be together?"

Raymond grinned and sat back in his chair. He crossed one ankle over the opposite knee, the epitome of someone used to getting his way. "Whenever I need her, she's there. Don't get me wrong—I'm there for her, too. We're cool. She doesn't bug me about the women I date, but she still calls me when she's having trouble figuring out a man she's with. I give her advice."

Dante's eyes narrowed. "What type of advice?"

"I tell her rules that men date by. Then she ends up calling a dude on his crap, breaks things off and lets me know that, yet again, I helped her out."

"You're sabotaging her relationships."

Raymond shook his head. "No. I tell her what men think. Julie's smart enough to figure out the rest. Every once in a while she meets a decent fellow, and I tell her that. In the end, she breaks up with them." Raymond smiled. "Now you understand?"

"Understand what?"

"She's breaking up with ratchet dudes and good dudes. She's waiting on us."

"I see that you're keeping her waiting in the wings. Besides, I don't think she sees things the same way you're seeing them. She says she's not interested in you."

"What's she supposed to say? 'I'm waiting for the day that Raymond and I can finally be together'?"

Dante knew no woman would admit to holding a torch for one guy for years, but he didn't believe that was the case with Julie. He'd watched her and Raymond. Granted, it was just one time, but he could tell a lot about what a woman was thinking by watching her. Julie had been happy to see her friend but also annoyed there was a party going on instead of a business meeting. She hadn't watched Raymond with any sense of longing, and no tell-tale signs of desire or attraction popped up when they were together. If anything, Dante figured Julie had listened to Raymond's advice enough to know he was trying to keep her waiting in the wings. Maybe she was doing the same with Raymond, letting him think there was a chance one day so that she could still rely on her friend when she needed him.

Or maybe you don't want to believe she's really not interested in you.

"I take it that you're telling me this because you want me to stay away from Julie," Dante said.

"I'd prefer it if you would. I really like Julie, and while

I don't think she'll fall for you, it would be weird later when she and I get together for you two to have history."

"Do you really like her, or are you just trying to hold on to her?"

The smug look left Raymond's face. "I do really like her. She's beautiful, hardworking and confident. I've only seen Julie cry once in the years I've known her. *Once.* You know how often women like to throw around tears. I've had a crush on her for years, have wanted to get with her just as long, but the timing is never right. If we would have hooked up back when she was hurt, it would have worked for a while but not long."

"Why not?"

"You know how life is on the road. Before I blew up, I could count on one hand the number of women I'd slept with. I hit that same number in one night after my single hit number one. I want Julie, but I don't want to hurt her either." Raymond picked up his drink and turned to the stage.

Dante frowned and also watched the woman performing. If it wasn't for the earnestness in Raymond's tone, Dante would have called bull. Instead he understood Raymond's logic. Life as a celebrity was nothing but constant temptation. He'd had girls and, at times, grown women throwing panties at him when he was only thirteen. One of the reasons he hadn't settled down was because of that. He didn't rule out *maybe* getting married one day. If he could find what his parents had that made them stay together despite the enticements. He just hadn't found the woman who got him feeling that way yet. He was sure that the love he sang about existed, and that he'd know it when he found it.

"I'll respect your wishes," Dante said, the words burning his tongue. Raymond was his boy, and he wouldn't do that to his boy.

"Thanks, man," Raymond said.

The woman onstage stopped singing. She looked at Raymond, who grinned and waved her over.

"Did you invite Julie to the game and after-party tonight?" Dante asked. If Raymond knew he would one day marry her, Dante figured he would be trying to spend as much time with her as possible.

"Nah, I told her I'd give her a call tomorrow. She said she was tired after the meetings today."

"You two could just hang out."

Raymond smiled at the singer walking over. "I've got another woman meeting me at the party. Besides, she mentioned Carlos called to ask her to dinner. I think she's going out with him."

Jealousy and anger flared up in Dante. "And you don't care?"

Raymond shook his head. He stood as the singer entered the VIP area. "We ain't together yet. Carlos is just another date, and definitely no threat to me. He won't mean anything." Raymond ran his hand up the arm of the singer and gave her a seductive smile. "You want to come back to my place?"

The woman grinned. "Of course."

Dante shook his head. Was this dude serious? "Raymond, what about the game?"

Raymond waved Dante's words off. "I'll be at the after-party."

"Do you even know where he's taking her?" Dante asked.

Raymond paused in the middle of taking the woman out of the VIP. "Who?"

"Carlos," Dante bit out, trying hard to hide his frustration with Raymond. "What if this guy is crazy?"

Raymond smirked and looked at Dante. "Julie can handle herself. Even if I were concerned, they're going to that new sunset restaurant on the PCH. There will be so many people there, nothing can go wrong."

Raymond put his arm around the woman and led her toward the door. Dante watched them, his jaw clenched. He'd listened to Raymond spout off about wanting to be with Julie. Maybe Raymond even believed some of his own bull. However, Dante was absolutely certain about one thing. Despite how much Raymond had gotten it into his head that he and Julie belonged together, they didn't. Dante doubted Julie wanted Raymond, and he damn sure knew that if Raymond really wanted to be with Julie one day, he wouldn't be asking another woman back to his LA condo before meeting up with a different woman at the after-party when his future soul mate was in town. In town *and* going out with someone else.

No, if Raymond really wanted Julie, he would be marching his happy ass right down the Pacific Coast Highway straight to the place his woman was at and breaking up any would-be romantic notions that this wannabe playa Carlos had gotten into his head.

Dante stood and went to the door with purposeful strides. If she were his woman, that's exactly what he would do.

Chapter 7

Carlos asking her out, after they'd only had a brief conversation at the party, was completely unexpected. With Raymond busy for the night, she had no real reason not to accept his date. When Carlos mentioned visiting Sunsetters, a new restaurant and bar overlooking the ocean rumored to have the best seafood in the area, she'd readily accepted.

After devouring the delicious shrimp tortellini, Julie and Carlos ordered the gianduja chocolate soufflé to share for dessert, and Julie finished her pineapple mojito while they waited. The sun set over the ocean, bathing the late evening in oranges and reds, while a warm breeze caressed them in the outdoor seating area. The relaxing sounds of the waves hitting below the bar blended in with the lively conversation of the crowd.

The buzz from inside the restaurant increased. Carlos stopped talking, and they both glanced to the door.

"What's going on?" She lifted her head to try to see through the crowd to the excitement but couldn't see who or what it was.

"Since opening there have been several celebrities who've popped in. They always like to try the new places."

Julie nodded. "More than likely." She glanced at Carlos. "I guess our service will go down now."

He fiddled with a button on his white golf shirt—something she'd realized was a nervous habit of his. "That's not necessarily a bad thing. The longer we sit here, the more time I get to spend enjoying your company."

Carlos blatantly admired her neck and shoulders, exposed by the turquoise halter top she wore, before lowering his hand to hers on the table. He was attractive, and Julie was enjoying herself, but his hand on hers didn't ignite any of the sparks the same touch had when Dante did it.

Carlos was subtle, but his intentions were clear. He'd be willing to take their date as far as she'd let him. So far she was only willing to go as far as a good-night kiss.

"It has been a fun night."

The buzz from inside the restaurant came out onto the deck. Julie turned just as the crowd parted and a hostess ushered Dante toward the bar. She'd spent a lot of time with him this week interviewing contractors, so she really shouldn't feel so breathless to see him again. That didn't stop the air from rushing from her lungs when his dark eyes met hers from beneath the rim of his black fedora. His clothes were casual, red shorts that brushed the knee and a black button-up shirt. A diamond earring sparkled in his ear, and the glint of a platinum chain, tasteful, not big and bulky like other artists wore, peeked from his open collar.

Dante stopped following the hostess and strolled over to their table.

"Julie, funny finding you here," he said. Then he glanced at Carlos. "With Carlos."

Julie raised her chin. He didn't sound like he was surprised to see her there at all.

Carlos held out his hand. "Good to see you again."

"Same here," Dante said. Again, the tone of his voice didn't jibe with his words. She got the distinct impression that Dante didn't think seeing Carlos again was good. "I thought you were heading to the East Coast for a gig."

Carlos shook his head. "The gig fell through. Though I normally hate losing a job, losing this one opens the door to other possibilities," he said with a warm smile at Julie.

Julie returned his smile, but the movement felt brittle. She drummed her fingers on the table, suddenly annoyed about Dante being there. She had been enjoying her time with Carlos and the slight attraction she felt toward him. Then *he* had to walk in and, with just a look, turn her insides as soft and gooey as the soufflé she'd ordered— a look, a smile and way too much sex appeal to be fair.

"What brings you here?" she asked.

Dante leaned his hand on the back of her side of the booth. The breeze chose that second to conspire against her and wrapped her in the masculine scent of his cologne. "I was hoping to run into someone. A person I'd like to spend a lot more time with, but she keeps avoiding being alone with me."

Intense dark eyes zeroed in on her, and the melodic tenor of his voice sang to her soul. *You'll initiate the kiss.* Words spoken with the confidence of a man who had years of experience with women not hesitating to be alone with him after only knowing him a week. She wanted to kiss him. Thought about kissing him several times while they interviewed contractors, which is why she'd clung to her rule to never show a guy how much he rattled her. If she gave Dante the upper hand, he'd have her mind twisted in knots over him in less than an hour.

"I hope the person you're looking for shows up," she said.

"She already has," he said. "Enjoy your date, but call me later." The sentence wasn't a question. It was a clear and definite command. Cocking a brow, Dante nodded to Carlos and then casually strolled back to the hostess, who took him to the bar.

Julie's mouth fell open. Had he just tried to stake a claim on her in the middle of her date? She had no quick comeback—a first for her. She had rules and maneuvers for the sly games men played. Straightforward and blatant moves of possession weren't something she was used to.

"I guess I have some competition for your affections," Carlos said in a good-natured tone, but his fingers toyed with the button of his shirt.

Julie snapped her mouth shut and looked away from Dante. "I'm sorry, what?"

Carlos gave a knowing smile. "Dante is interested in you."

She pulled her thoughts together and sat up straighter. "Interested or not, I don't date business partners. He's just being persistent because I made that rule very clear. He's only interested because I'm not falling at his feet. Men like him enjoy the chase, but the chase is all they're interested in."

"You make attraction sound so matter-of-fact. You don't think he'd want you if you made his pursuit easier?"

She shrugged. "I doubt it. Most women would die to

be with Dante Wilson, whether or not falling for him was considered unprofessional. I'm one of the rare women who won't—therefore, he's interested. That's the way guys are. They're intrigued by women who are different. We women get sucked into the thrill of being chased and let our guards down, only to have the guy grow tired of the novelty after he's gotten to know you better. Then we're left in love and heartbroken, while he moves on to once again chase some-one else. It's a cruel but never-ending cycle."

Carlos flinched, then took a sip of his drink. "Ouch, you have a bitter view of our sex."

This wasn't the first time a man had called her bit-ter, and the claim didn't bother Julie. When faced with the truth, most guys preferred attributing the truth to a woman's bitterness. "I'm not bitter, just realistic."

He leaned on the table and took her hand between his. "And what's my interest in you?"

"I think you are attracted to me and want to start a casual dating thing while I'm in town."

His grin would be considered dangerous to her heart, if Dante hadn't already threatened it. "Oh, really?"

"Really, with the ultimate goal of getting me into bed. I'm going to let you know now that I'm very selective about the men I sleep with, so don't get your hopes up."

"Double ouch," Carlos said, but his grin remained. "You are different."

Julie shrugged. "Aren't we all?"

Laughter came from the bar. Julie glanced that way to the small crowd of people who now surrounded Dante. Carlos squeezed her hand, and she tore her gaze away from Dante.

"I like *your* different."

The waiter returned with their dessert, and she quickly

pulled away from Carlos's grasp. She didn't like what she saw in his eyes. Desire, genuine interest, but also some type of calculation. He was probably choosing the best tactic to get her into bed. She liked Carlos all right, but she wouldn't play with his emotions by pretending like she wanted to take him to bed. She could practically hear Evette sucking her teeth before saying, "See, there you go pushing a good man away again." Maybe she was, but the truth was she was only in California until the club opened. After that, she had no interest in pursuing a long-term relationship.

They ate the delicious soufflé, and Carlos made her laugh with his interesting stories about working with various recording artists. As much as she tried to focus on the rest of her date, her attention kept diverting to Dante. And while he gave a good show of enjoying the crowd of people hanging on to his every word, she caught several of the glances he threw her way. To make things worse, every time she was distracted, noticing Dante notice her, Carlos noticed them both pretending not to look at the other.

Dante stayed for only thirty minutes, long enough to order a drink, take a few pictures with fans and delight the crowd. He paid his tab and left, a smug smirk on his face as he waved goodbye to her and Carlos. The smugness annoyed her more than him showing up. Of course, he would know his arrival would distract her from her date. He was throwing her off her game, and she didn't like it.

The interest in Carlos's eyes had slowly morphed into defeat with every glance she'd tried to sneak Dante's way. Julie checked the time, ready to end the ruined date. "I really should get back now. I've got a long day ahead."

Carlos nodded and signaled for the waiter. "You can bring the check now."

The waiter shook his head and smiled. "No need. Dante took care of it already, along with the tip. You two have a good night."

Julie's jaw dropped. Carlos tried to grin, but the smile was flat. "I guess Dante just upped the ante."

Julie snapped her mouth shut and gritted her teeth. "I'm so sorry, Carlos. That was uncalled for."

He shrugged. "Hey, he's a man used to getting what he wants. Looks like he really wants you."

His attempt to sound unbothered was ruined by the annoyance in his voice. She couldn't blame him; there wasn't a man she knew who would accept another guy swooping in and covering the costs of his date. Dante's my-cock's-bigger-than-yours move was bold and uncalled for.

Go hard or go home.

Julie fumed as they left the restaurant. Dante may not want to accept that she was serious about nothing happening between them, but that wasn't her problem. He was just another smug, arrogant celebrity who thought he could buy anything he wanted, including her affections. Well, the man had better get his mind right. She would make absolutely sure he understood that you didn't play games with Julie Dominick.

Julie swerved the rental car to the gate blocking the way to Dante's house. She wanted to plow right through the wrought iron blockage, drive straight to the front of his house and bang on his door. Instead she lowered the driver's window and smashed the button on the call box with her finger.

"Hello, Julie." His sexy tenor filtered through the machine.

Damn him and her body for the tremble that went through her. "How did you know I was calling?"

"Smile for the camera."

Julie glared at the box, then the security camera affixed to the top of the gate.

"Did you come by to thank me for dinner?"

Trembles forgotten, anger shot through her. "Not at all. We need to talk."

"Come on in," he said. A buzzing sound filled the air before the gate opened.

Julie gritted her teeth and entered the property. The sun had set, but the view of his home in the dark was just as spectacular as during the day. Lights led the way down the long drive, nestled in tropical plants. More lights shone directly onto the stone villa, giving the place a warm and welcoming feel. The beauty of the place nearly took her breath away. Nearly. She was still too angry to appreciate his wealth. After jumping out of the car, she slammed the door and marched to the large wooden door.

Before she could bang out her anger with her fist, it swung open. He'd changed into loose black lounging pants, which flowed around his long legs in dark waves. A sleeveless white T-shirt clung to every muscle of his torso. Julie licked her lips and fought to breathe normally. He seemed to constantly snatch the air from her lungs.

"Hello, Julie," he said again, stepping back and holding the door open.

"You've got some nerve, Dante." She didn't cross the threshold. Wouldn't go into the house. Couldn't, when he looked like he was ready to jump into bed, and everything from his eyes, scent and smile invited her to jump in with him.

"Really? Why?"

"How dare you pay for dinner?"

"I dare because I wanted to."

"What would make you want to do something so smug, arrogant and rude? You should have seen the look on Carlos's face."

He smirked and shrugged before leaning against the door. "I almost stuck around just so I could see the look on his face."

Julie crossed her arms beneath her breasts and glared. "You think this is funny?"

"Imagining the look on his face?" His full sensual lips lifted with humor as he nodded. "Yeah, kind of."

"Well, it wasn't funny. You had no right to do that. We were on a date."

"I know."

"If you knew that, then why would you pay for our dinner? Didn't you think about how it would make Carlos feel to have another guy pay for his date's meal?"

Dante stood straight. He placed a hand on the doorjamb and leaned in close. "I didn't give a damn and still don't care what Carlos thinks or feels. You should have been there with me. Not him."

If she were a violent person, she would have slapped the smirk right off his handsome face. "I'm not going out with you. I don't want to go out with you."

Dante grinned. "Yes, you do." He turned and strolled into the house.

"Where are you going?" she shouted after his retreating back.

He looked over his shoulder. "Inside." He continued walking.

"I don't want to come inside. I don't want to be here at all."

He spun around but didn't come back to the door. "Yes, you do. If you didn't want to be here, you and Carlos would've been thankful to enjoy a nice meal on my dime. He would have taken you back to your hotel, where, after an awkward 'can I come in for coffee' conversation, you would have either sent him home or invited him inside. Based on the looks you threw my way over dinner, I think you would've sent him home. But on the off chance that you did invite him in, you would have forgotten any indignation over my paying for the meal and had a mediocre first-date kiss. Instead you dropped him and rushed to see me." He rested his hands on his chest. "Why? To pretend as if you're angry? When you're really here because you wanted to see me."

Julie scoffed. "You're conceited and delusional."

"Conceited, yes, delusional, no. Now quit hiding behind your excuse that you can't mix business and pleasure or some trumped-up anger over me making sure Carlos has no doubt that he's got some serious competition."

Julie's body went rigid. She stomped over the threshold and was in his face a second later. "Let's get a few things straight. The reason Carlos and I didn't have the 'come in for coffee conversation' is because I don't invite a guy up on the first date. If he makes it to three or more, then we'll see. For your information, our first kiss was hardly mediocre despite your attempt to butt in on the night."

A dark scowl replaced his smug look. While her goodnight kiss with Carlos was nothing more than a quick peck and a hug, it had been nice enough to describe as more than mediocre, especially to get the triumphant gleam out of Dante's eyes.

"As for me hiding behind an excuse that I can't mix business and pleasure—" she took a step closer, leaning her head back to stare into his eyes "—it's not because I can't. It's because I don't. Proving that I deserve the jobs I get is hard enough without adding assumptions that I'm only successful because I sleep with womanizers like you in order to land projects. So, whether or not you've decided to be *serious competition* with Carlos or not, just remember I'm not some helpless rabbit you can lure into a trap. I've avoided wolves much deadlier than you. You won't catch me unless I want to get caught."

She slid her foot back to step away. His hand shot out and latched on to her waist. Dante closed the scant distance between them and pressed his solid body against hers. "Don't stand so close if you don't want to get caught."

Desire coated every nuance of his voice. The air around them shifted, crackling and sparking with the anger, annoyance and attraction simmering between them. The line between anger and desire was thin, and when his long fingers flexed against her waist, the line snapped. He infuriated her. The audacity of him paying for the meal, declaring himself competition, insisting that being zapped by the electric current between them was inevitable. Yet she couldn't listen to the faint voice that said to pull away. Sucking in a breath, she didn't smell cologne. The clean smell of masculine soap and the intoxicating heat of his body made her mouth water. Her nipples tightened. Heat settled heavily between her thighs.

"Now that I've got you," he said, his tenor lowering to a seductive bass, "what are you going to do?"

Julie swallowed. "Depends on what your intentions are."

"I intend to get the truth out of you." His hand, strong and sure, slid from her waist to her back. She didn't think he could pull her closer, but he did, and the rock-hard proof of his arousal grew between them.

She wanted to turn, walk away and call him a fool. She licked her lips, and slowly drew the lower one between her teeth. His eyes heated, and his lids lowered. She wanted to kiss him more.

Embracing his face with her hands, Julie pulled him down to do just that. Briefly she realized he'd proved her a liar—she'd initiated the kiss. A second later, the pleasure of his lips against hers blew away all other thought. A low groan rumbled through his chest, and his strong arms wrapped around her midsection, squeezing her tight. His tongue traced her lower lip, and she quickly opened her mouth, gliding hers over his in slow, erotic strokes. One of her arms wrapped around his neck; her other hand brushed the stubble on his strong jaw.

The heat between her legs ached for release. Her heart pumped against her ribs. She imagined peeling his clothes off and dragging him up the stairs. She imagined kissing every inch of his perfect body and spending the night moaning his name in ecstasy or having him right here, hot and fast, in the foyer fully clothed. The how and the why didn't matter as long as Dante was pressed hard and deep inside her.

Never had her body yearned for a man as much as it did right now. A yearning so strong that she didn't care about anything other than his lean hips between her legs, which could lead to rash decisions that would hurt her and her career, and add fuel to the rumors of her success.

She broke the kiss but didn't jump out of his arms. A moment later, Dante's eyes opened slowly, the dark irises dazed and burning with the same longing chewing on her insides. She wanted him but not tonight, not when she was going on need alone. Her rule was to never sleep with a guy unless she fully understood what she was getting into, even more so, when sleeping with a guy like Dante could hinder, not help, her reputation. The club opening successfully was the most important thing.

Dante's nostrils flared with heavy breaths, and he watched her with deep, hungry eyes. Her body shuddered. She had to get out of there before she said screw it and screwed him.

"Now that you've caught me," she said, hoping he didn't notice the needy trembling of her voice, "how will you keep me?"

His brows drew together. She lifted on her toes and pressed a kiss to the side of his lips. "Good night, Dante."

Pulling out of his inviting arms was torture. Every agonizing brush of her skin against his as she did so made her want to wrap her arms around him, kiss him again, taste his skin and feel his body on hers.

Not tonight. Not without thinking about this and being sure. Use your head, not your heart.

He let her go and looked just as dazed as she felt. She walked to the door with what she hoped was a confident stroll that masked her wobbly knees. If he guessed how difficult walking away from him was for her and pulled her back into his arms, she'd say to hell with thinking this thing through and drag Dante upstairs directly to his bedroom.

Chapter 8

Dante's ringing cell phone interrupted his repeated attempts to work on the song he was writing for S.A.F. Normally, when he was in his music studio, surrounded by the various instruments his parents insisted he learn to play and gazing at the platinum and gold records hanging on the walls, inspiration struck. But today wasn't a normal day. He'd kissed Julie the day before. No, Julie had kissed the hell out of him, then walked away.

He picked up his cell phone from the corner of the upright piano. He usually didn't bring the phone in here with him, but he'd expected a phone call from his sexy developer. Raymond's number was on the screen.

Swallowing disappointment, Dante answered. "Raymond, what's up?"

"Man, you missed one hell of an after-party last night. What happened?"

Dante could taste Julie's sweet lips and nearly groaned. "Something came up."

Raymond laughed. "I bet it did. Hey, are you busy?"

"Working on a new song." Or he would be if his brain would stop reliving the memory of Julie's curves pressed against him.

"Is this for the solo album you're putting out? Your own music?"

"Not for me but for S.A.F. I'm meeting with them at the studio later today."

The reason Dante chose Malibu for his nightclub instead of LA was the small following S.A.F. already had in the area. Launching S.A.F. in their hometown was the best way to ensure they came out of the gate strong.

"If you're writing the music, then I know it's going to be hot. Look, I called to ask a favor."

"What kind of favor?"

"Nothing big. Since you've already helped Julie pick the contractor, can you handle overseeing the rest of the opening for the next few weeks?"

Dante frowned and put down the pencil he'd been using to erase the last few notes of music he'd put to paper. "Why? Do you want out?"

"No, I just got an offer to perform in London. It's some type of music festival, and while I'm there, my agent said I could work on being a guest judge for this talent show they've got on television. After the concert tour, this will be a good way to keep my music out there. I know I promised to help you open this place."

Dante stood and walked across the room to stand before the window. The view of the solid, long-lasting profile of the mountains from this side of the house inspired him more than the changing tides of the ocean did.

"I understand. You're still building your career. I'd be going, too, if I were in your position. Besides, you've already helped out by recommending Julie. She seems to know what she's doing."

Both with the club and with keeping him guessing. He still couldn't believe she'd walked away without a backward glance. Were his skills slipping? Any other woman would have dragged him upstairs after a kiss like that.

"I told you she would. Julie is the other part of the favor. I hate leaving her out here. I know I just asked you to keep your distance, but do you mind showing her a good time while I'm gone?"

Would he mind? Dante almost laughed at the idea that he would have a problem spending more time with Julie. "The question is will *you* mind?"

"I told you how I felt about Julie, and I trust you."

A microscopic sliver of guilt whispered in Dante's head for the barest of seconds. Along with the idea that maybe he should confess to Raymond that he'd kissed Julie the night before and planned to kiss her a lot more before this project was finished. Even in those barest of seconds, he knew he wouldn't. Dante couldn't shake the feeling that if Raymond really wanted a future with Julie, he'd be paying a lot more attention to her now.

"Have you talked to Julie yet? Maybe Carlos and her hit things off, and she wants you out of town."

"I called her before calling you to let her know. She was upset that I wasn't going to be here but said she understood. Plus, I'm not worried about Carlos. She said the date was fun but that she didn't think they'd be going out again."

Dante grinned and leaned against the windowsill. "She give a reason why?"

"She was vague about why, but that's Julie. She doesn't need a good reason to drop a guy. That's why I know she's waiting for me."

Dante grunted and shook his head, thankful that Raymond wouldn't see his disbelieving expression. "I'll invite her to some parties while she's here, introduce her to some people."

"Cool. I'll call and check on progress when I can."

Dante could hear the goodbye coming, but he spoke up quickly. "You going alone?"

"I'm taking the singer from the club last night. We had a good time, and I'd like to keep it going."

With that, the sliver of guilt vanished completely. "You do that."

They said goodbye, then got off the phone. Dante checked his watch and swore. His choreographer was coming over in an hour, and he'd wasted the entire morning daydreaming about Julie. He couldn't remember ever doing that, not even in his teens. He'd had women throwing themselves at him like rice at a wedding since he had hit puberty.

Dante did an internal calculation of how long he'd practice the new routine for his next music video. If he cut the session back an hour, he'd have time to get to the studio an hour earlier. Hopefully, it would give him just enough time to set up a late dinner with Julie and see for himself just how "upset" she was about Raymond leaving. He would pull out all the stops to impress her tonight. He was Dante Wilson, and women loved him. He was sure that after tonight, if there were any lingering embers smoldering from their kiss, he was going to set them on fire.

* * *

"So how are things going in sunny California?" Evette's excited voice came through Julie's cell phone.

Julie sat back in the chair at the desk in her hotel suite. "Things are going great. They agreed to bring Dominant Development on as a full partner."

"As if there was any doubt."

No need to mention that she didn't give Dante and Raymond much of a choice. She'd come in as if she already had the job. Luckily, Dante was impressed with the contractors she'd chosen.

"Today I'm meeting with the city to make sure I know everything they'll need when I apply for permits. I know we're good zoning-wise, but I'm not sure about what we'll need for the building renovations."

"Is Sheila coming to the meeting?" Evette asked, referring to the contractor they'd hired. Dante had insisted on hiring Sheila over Orlando. They both had good reputations, but Julie was a little concerned with the way Sheila avoided sharing how she always came in under budget on her projects. Julie called her references, and no one had anything bad to say about Sheila's work, so Julie pushed aside her concerns and went with Dante's decision.

"Yep, she's dealt with the people at the city before and knows what they'll ask for. Dante already has an architect handling the redesign of the building, so he's coming, as well. I have no fears things won't go as planned."

"Or as close to plans. Wait until construction starts— that's when things get dicey."

Julie nodded. "Ain't that the truth."

"So how are other things?" Evette's voice was filled with expectancy.

"Things like what?"

"Oh, come on. Every time we talk it's only about work, I can't stand it anymore. Tell me about Dante. What's he like? Is he as sexy in person as he looks on television? What about his voice? Is it as smooth as it sounds on his songs? Does he smell good?"

Julie chuckled. "Smell good?"

"Yes, you can tell a lot about a man by the way he smells."

If Julie went by smell alone, Dante was delicious, filling and addictive. If she were describing food using those words she'd know she would need to be careful about overindulging. After last night's kiss, Julie was on the verge of binging on her craving for Dante.

"He smells all right, I guess. He is nice and eager to get the club opened. He helped pick Sheila."

"He's not one of those micromanagers, is he? Sticking his nose in every aspect of the project?"

"I don't think so. He let me ask most of the questions and handle the meetings. He only chimed in when he needed clarification. I think we'll be okay."

"Good, but I do hope you'll get to have some fun while you're there."

"I'm here for a job. Not to have fun." *Or an affair with a superstar.* "How are things back home?"

They chatted about the two projects they'd started before Julie came to California, and Evette's success with interviewing some new people. After promising to send Julie the names and interview notes before the end of the day, they got off the phone. Julie glanced at her watch; she had two hours until the meeting with the city. She jumped up from the desk and pulled the belt of her silver satin robe tight. She'd already picked out the suit she would wear today and showered before working. All that was left was to eat something quick, dress and get down to city hall.

Someone knocked on the door just as she picked up the phone to order from room service. She pulled the robe tighter and went to the door. She glanced through the peephole and saw Dante. Tiny pinpricks of heat spread up her chest, neck and cheeks. Really—she was blushing, and he couldn't even see her.

The night before she'd considered everything that would have happened if she hadn't walked away, contemplated all the outcomes that could result if she slept with him and concluded that keeping their relationship professional was for the best.

Taking a deep breath, she opened the door. "Can I help you?"

Dante's gaze traveled from the tips of her manicured toes up to her face, so hot and thorough that she might as well have left the robe on the floor. She stood cement still with her arms crossed over her breasts and her chin lifted, hiding how much his gaze affected her, when she really wanted to squirm under his appreciative appraisal.

"Go out with me tonight?"

The request to go out with him wasn't unexpected. She had kissed him pretty thoroughly the night before. A date would give her the chance to talk with him about the project more. All his expected and unoriginal attempts to get her to sleep with him would annoy her enough that finding reasons to stay out of his bed would be easier.

"Where?"

Dante stepped forward and placed his hand on the door. "At this sushi place I like. We'll have time to talk."

"What do we need to discuss?"

"The kiss last night. My plans to keep you now that I've caught you."

The words stirred up the desire she was trying to suppress. She took a step back but couldn't escape the heat of his body or how great he smelled. "I took you for a catch-and-throw type of guy, especially since I'm only in town for a short while."

"You're in town long enough." He reached forward and took one of the ends of the belt that held her robe closed in his hand. His fingers slid across the silky material. "I'm fine with holding on to you while you're here."

He didn't pull on the material, but she was suddenly very aware that she was nearly naked beneath the robe. A simple tug would loosen the knot and the sides would fall open, exposing Dante to her in nothing but a lacy sky blue bra and matching panties. Would he trace the edges of the lace with his fingertips? Would his hands slide across her naked waist to pull her against his firm body? Her breasts felt heavy, and her nipples tightened to sensitive points. The shots of heat beneath her skin took aim and fired at the junction between her thighs.

Think about what he said, Julie. "I'm fine with holding on to you while you're here." He'd already put her in the quick-and-easy-sex category. She didn't do the quick-and-easy-sex thing, especially with men she worked with. She couldn't afford to get caught up in him.

"About that kiss. I was angr—"

His hand snaked around her waist. He pulled her against him and dropped his head to kiss her, taking full advantage of the fact that she was midsentence and that her lips were already parted. All her considerations, contemplations and conclusions crashed into a pile at her feet. Soft, feminine moans surrounded them, and Julie accepted that the man had her purring like a kitten in less than a second. He kissed her softly and thoroughly, her body sliding against his thanks to the slippery material of her robe. Her hands clenched his strong arms, and she shifted her torso just enough that the aching peaks of her breasts brushed his chest. Dante's hands tightened on her waist, his hips pressed forward until the length of his desire pushed against her midsection.

He lifted his head. "Don't say no yet." There was a sexy, confident lift to his full lips, but underneath the swagger, she heard the plea. He really wanted her to say yes. Long fingers flexed on her lower back, and he took in her cleavage, revealed by the gaping opening of her robe. "I'll pick you up at nine."

Refusing to go on one date now seemed juvenile and fearful. She wasn't afraid of Dante—afraid of her body's reaction maybe, but not of him. "Nine it is."

He lowered his head, but Julie quickly stepped out of his reach. He smirked and raised a brow but didn't push. "I'll see you tonight." He softly hit the inside of the door with the side of his hand, then turned and left.

Julie shut the door and leaned heavily against the cool wood. She'd definitely lost this round. Big-time. She knew the rules to the game he was playing. Dante wanted to conquer the walls protecting her panties, not her heart. She was here to do a job, strengthen her business and not add to the rumors trying to cling to her reputation. She'd best remember that and get her head back on what was best for her long-term, not consider a short-term affair with a man who, without purpose, could divide and conquer both walls.

Chapter 9

As much as Dante looked forward to going out with Julie that night, he had to drag himself away from the studio with S.A.F. They'd made good progress putting music to the song he'd written and then started working on other music. If his date was with any other woman he would have canceled, but the memory of Julie in that sexy silver robe and the sweet sounds she'd made when he kissed her had him throwing up deuces to the guys in just enough time so he wouldn't be late picking her up.

When she met him in her hotel's lobby, he wished he'd left the studio earlier. She wore a sleeveless cream jumpsuit. The low V in the front provided a teasing glimpse of her cleavage, and the loose pants draped nicely over her curves. A gold belt cinched her waist, and red heels gave her height. For a second, he could do nothing but stare. Her amber eyes sparkled, and her sensual lips rose in a smile that made his cock twitch and his chest swell.

"You look beautiful," he said when she reached him.

"Thank you. You don't look half bad yourself."

He ran a hand down the front of his outfit: white jacket, black dress shirt, fitted black pants, set off by a black-and-white-checked handkerchief in the pocket.

"I aim to please." He held out his arm for her. She slipped her hand into the crook of his elbow and smiled at him. He felt a dead-on sensation that Julie, on his arm, going out with him, was right—like she belonged next to him and no one else.

Dante shook the thought away. Whatever happened with him and Julie would be temporary. He was nowhere near ready for anything more than a few weeks of fun. Despite her passionate response to his kiss, the way she held a part of herself back told him that she was a woman looking for forever. She wasn't quick to fall, which meant he'd have to be careful when they slept together. He wanted her, but he didn't want to hurt her.

He led her out to his mocha-black Mercedes AMG CLS coupe and opened the door for her.

"I hope you like sushi," he said after getting in on his side.

"I do."

He put the car in gear and slipped into traffic toward Arata, the sushi bar and restaurant named after the Japanese chef who had become a celebrity after a string of successful cooking shows. Dante had hoped to get to know her a little better on the drive, but she guided the conversation with updates on her meetings with the city that day. He was impressed by how much she'd gotten clarified concerning the permits required.

She turned toward him in her seat. "The architect you hired already has the renovation plans drawn up. It's just getting them finalized and submitted to the city for review. If all goes well, we'll have the plans submitted in a week or so, and then we just wait for the city to approve. Once that's done, construction will begin."

He briefly took his eyes off the road to glance at her. "That soon?"

"Yep."

"Dang, you are good."

She laughed. "I wish I could take all the credit, but if your architect hadn't already been on the ball, and Sheila hadn't known as much as she does about the city's permitting process, things would have taken a lot longer. I don't have all the contacts I need out here to maneuver things as quickly."

"And here I thought you were a miracle worker," he teased.

"I am, but I also know my limitations."

He pulled up to the front of the restaurant and Julie's brows rose. "Arata," Julie said. "When I called I couldn't get a reservation until a month out."

She put her hand on the door, and he stilled her with a hand on her knee. "I called up Mr. Arata himself."

She didn't seem as impressed with that as he'd expected, but she did smile. "That's nice."

"I'll get your door." He got out and waved for the valet to wait so that he could open the door for Julie.

"Welcome back, Mr. Wilson," the valet said, taking the keys from Dante. "I hope you and your date enjoy your evening."

"Thank you, Marcel," he said to the man and turned to Julie.

"You're on a first-name basis with the valet," she said as they walked to the door. "Do you come here often?"

"It's one of my favorite places." His favorite first-date place because getting a reservation was so hard that most of his dates were awestruck by his ability to get them in on a moment's notice.

"I read about this place before coming out. They're supposed to have the best sushi in the area."

"Well, I'm glad that I'm able to bring you here," he said with a grin.

She clasped her hands and bounced her shoulders. He wasn't sure if her excitement was for the food or being with him; either way, he was doing well so far. They entered the restaurant, and the hostess, Mika, looked up at them. *Ah, damn, I forgot about her.* He'd slept with Mika right before the concert tour. Her dark eyes widened, and a sexy grin crossed her face.

"Dante, it's so good to see you again," Mika said in a low and sensual voice. "I wondered how long it would be before you came in now that your tour is over."

Dante chuckled uneasily. "Mika, I didn't know you worked on Fridays."

She shrugged. "When I heard we had a special guest coming tonight, I agreed to help out. We've got your table ready."

Julie looked up at Dante with a cocked brow. "Your table?"

"One of my favorite spots," he said.

Mika moved around the hostess stand. She wore the same tight black dress and obscenely high heels that made him invite her to his house for the party before the tour. "And we love that you come here," Mika purred. "All of us." Her voice dripped with meaning.

Julie looked between them, and understanding flashed in her amber eyes. He swallowed a groan. He'd had fun with a few of the waitresses there, as well. There weren't many hostesses or waitresses in this town that he hadn't invited to a party, bought a drink for or flirted with. Maybe he should have driven her to LA instead. More restaurants to choose from with a smaller likelihood he'd dallied with the beautiful waitstaff.

"All of them," Julie said with that knowing smile of hers.

He tried to shrug off Mika's comment. "I tip well."

"Yeah, I'm sure."

They followed Mika to his table in the back, sheltered from view of the other patrons and next to floor-to-ceiling windows that provided a perfect romantic view of the ocean. He waved at a few other celebrities, politicians and businesspeople he recognized. Instead of being impressed by his contacts, Julie's knowing grin only grew as a few waitresses stopped what they were doing to greet him with blushing cheeks and inviting smiles.

"You must tip very well," Julie said once they were seated. "The waitresses love you."

"Overly warm greetings come with the territory of being a celebrity."

"Yeah, sure," she said with a twinkle in her eye before looking at the menu.

"Good evening, Dante," a woman said.

Dante looked up at their waitress and cringed. "Hello, Katie." Of course he'd get Katie.

"I'll be serving you tonight. Don't hesitate to let me know if you need…anything." Her lips curved up seductively.

Julie looked up from the menu and shot a questioning

glance at Katie. Dante shifted in his seat and pretended he hadn't heard the invitation in Katie's voice. He once again second-guessed himself for bringing Julie here. Historically for him, when other women showed interest, the woman he was currently with clung harder. He should have realized that when confronted with his conquests, Julie would pull away.

"Thank you, Katie. We'd like a bottle of—"

"The Fallen Angel sake?" Katie finished. "I've already instructed the bar for you. Would you also like to start with the lobster seviche?"

Julie chuckled and studied her menu. Dante nodded at Katie. "That will be fine."

Were his moves that apparent, that predictable? Well, it wasn't as if he had to try very hard to be imaginative. Most of the time, asking the woman out was enough; bringing her here was just part of the pizzazz of going out with Dante Wilson.

Do you realize how shallow that sounds?

He pushed the thought aside along with the shake in confidence that being Dante Wilson wasn't enough to impress Julie. He hadn't had to try to impress a woman… ever.

Katie made a move to turn. "You know what," Julie said, stopping her. "I'd like to start with the sashimi salad. I don't particularly care for seviche."

She gave Katie a tight smile, then looked back at her menu.

"Oh," Katie said. "Of course. I'll be right back with that."

Dante looked to Julie and decided changing the subject was best. "Are you enjoying your time in Malibu so far?"

She didn't look up from the menu. "Tell me, Dante—

have you slept with every woman in this restaurant or just the hostess and our waitress?"

"Excuse me?"

"I think the question was pretty clear."

"You know what—they don't matter." He reached across the table and pulled her menu away. He took her hands in his. "All that matters is being here with you tonight. I don't want to spend my evening with anyone else."

Some of the skepticism in her eyes diminished, but she still pulled her hands away and rested them in her lap. Damn, he needed to get this date back on track. His cell phone chimed in his pocket.

Julie glanced around. "Did you hear that?"

"Just my cell. That's the sound when I get a text. I'll ignore. I'm more interested in learning more about you."

"Okay, what would you like to know?"

"What made you start your business?" His cell chimed again.

She lifted her brows as if asking if he was going to look, but he ignored it again.

"I couldn't work for Nexon-Jones anymore."

Dante leaned back and regarded her. Nexon-Jones was *the* name in nightclub development. His family worked with them, and he knew the salaries of their top people were well over six figures. "Why not? They've got a great reputation."

"I *was* moving up in the business and could have easily seen myself being there forever. I loved it."

"What happened?"

"We were on the line to open a club in Las Vegas. I really wanted to manage the project because everyone knew that whoever handled the opening of the Vegas club was a shoo-in for a new venue in Japan. My boss approached me about doing a job in New York, and when I brought up the Vegas club, he said he wanted me specifically on the New York club and that landing it was crucial. If I did, I'd be in charge of the Japanese club."

"That doesn't sound like a reason to leave."

"I could only secure the project because the property owner indicated that he'd like to spend some *private* time with me before deciding to sell."

Dante's hand clenched into a fist. "He wanted you to sleep with the owner just to get the property?"

"Pretty much. When I went to HR, they didn't believe me. Neither did his partner, or at least they said they didn't believe me. I think the man just controls the HR department. So I left and took Evette with me. She's my business partner."

There wasn't a hint of bitterness in her voice; he imagined that walking away from such a successful career had to have been difficult. "That takes guts."

"Starting my own business?"

"No, going to human resources. I'm familiar with Nexon-Jones, and I know the culture. It's a definite boys' club. To take your accusations to HR was brave, doing so means the next woman he tries that with will have the history of your accusation to stand on."

"I hope so. I knew nothing would really happen, but if he did that to me, then he'd do it to someone else." Dante's phone chimed again. Julie glanced toward his jacket pocket. "You probably need to check that."

He agreed and pulled out his phone. There were several messages from the guys in S.A.F. They were still in the studio working on the music they'd started, and apparently they were having a major breakthrough on some new music.

"Damn."

"Something wrong?" Julie asked.

He looked up from his phone. "No. Not really. I was in the studio before coming here, and the group I'm working with, the ones I want to headline at the club when it's open, are still there. They've got a new track they want me to hear."

Katie came back with the sake, appetizer and Julie's salad. She grinned at Dante. "Are you ready for me to serve you?"

"Actually, can you give us another minute?" he said shortly.

Katie blinked rapidly, looked between him and Julie, then nodded. "Um, sure, whatever you want."

When she walked away, he looked over at Julie, then glanced around at the restaurant. It was only popular because a celebrity chef owned it, and celebrities like Dante frequented the place to see and be seen. Everything about it was created to impress. The long waiting list, beautiful waitresses and overpriced food that barely covered the plate. All for show but showing nothing, not good enough to really impress Julie. She'd walked away from a position that would have taken her far in order to preserve her values. Despite the sparks between them, she would easily walk away from him for the same reasons.

He met her eye. "You want to get out of here?"

She dropped the menu and nodded. "Yes."

"Good, because I have someplace I'd like to show you."

Chapter 10

Julie expected Dante to take her back to his place or some other fancy location that he would try to astound her with, so when he pulled up in front of an old two-story brick building, she gave him a questioning look.

"What's this?" she asked.

"It's where I make my kind of music." He got out of the car and jogged around to let her out.

"It looks abandoned."

"The first floor is. The second holds a studio."

He grasped her hand, his grip warm and steady, then eagerly led her inside. There was a small open foyer that may have once been a reception area. The dim lights and the lack of a chair or computer behind the dusty desk made her doubt that the foyer was still used. They crossed the scratched wooden floors to an elevator. The wheels creaked and groaned after Dante pressed the up button.

"You make music here?"

"Yep." That was all she got before he ushered her onto the elevator and pressed the second button. The sounds of creaking and groaning seemed much more ominous when she was actually inside the elevator. When the doors opened again, the muffled sound of music greeted them.

The lights were on, but it was still not brilliantly bright. He led her past a few offices on the left and stopped before a door on the right—the source of the music. Dante opened the door to what Julie could see was a music studio. One guy sat in the control room, where she and Dante had entered. Behind the glass, two men played a melodic and upbeat song on violins, another was on drums and a fourth stood behind a turntable playing what sounded like hip-hop that blended with the violins and drums.

The guy at the controls turned and grinned when he saw Dante. He clicked something and spoke into a microphone.

"Guys, Dante's back." The music stopped, and they all turned to Dante.

"Dante, you came back," one of the violinists said after they filed into the control room. He had dark brown skin, a faded haircut and stylish dark glasses that framed beautiful hazel eyes.

"You guys said you were making good music," Dante said. "I thought I'd come and show Julie what I do in my spare time."

All eyes zeroed in on Julie. The musicians all appeared relaxed and comfortable in jeans and T-shirts. She felt overdressed and very on the spot in her jumpsuit. She lifted one hand and waved.

"Hey."

The other violinist, with the same brown skin and

eyes but no glasses and a wild curly afro, put down his instrument and held out his hand.

He smiled, revealing even white teeth. "Hello, Julie," he said.

Dante wrapped a hand around her shoulder. "Guys, this is Julie Dominick. The developer extraordinaire overseeing the opening of my new club. Julie, this is Terrance." He indicated the man who'd come over and shaken her hand. "Tommy." He pointed to the other guy with the glasses. "They are the lead musicians for S.A.F., short for Strings A Flame. This is the rest of the group. Joey." The drummer raised his hand. "Lem." The guy on the turntable gave her a head nod. "And Bobby." He indicated the man who handled the controls.

"It's nice to meet all of you," she said. "S.A.F.—are you a new group?"

Terrance shook his head. "We've been playing together for five years and do shows locally. Dante is trying to take us mainstream."

She glanced at Dante. "Really?"

"Well, since they won't officially let me be a member, I have to promise fame and fortune for them to let me play with them."

She laughed along with the rest of the group.

"Seriously, this is who I've been telling you about. They'll be the entertainment act at my club. I'm introducing them to my fans, and at the same time, I plan to release my first album with them. My own music," he said with excitement in his voice.

"Your music? I'm pretty sure I've listened to your music since I was fourteen."

His arm around her shoulder tightened for a second. "You've heard the mainstream music that my family specializes in. This is what I hear when I'm writing music. Come on, guys—let's show Julie what I'm talking about."

He pointed to a beat-up old leather couch along the wall, and Julie walked over and sat. Dante slapped Bobby on the shoulder before going into the studio. "Let's start with the song we worked on earlier. Then we can get into the music you all put together after I left."

Julie sat on the edge of the couch and watched. After the first few bars, she knew she loved the music. Tommy and Terrance played a catchy melody while Dante accompanied them on the piano. Lem added a bass beat that Joey complemented with the drums. Before long, Julie was nodding her head and swaying. It was a fusion of classical, jazz and hip-hop.

When they finished, Dante glanced at her over the top of the piano. His gaze darted from her to the piano. Was he nervous?

She clapped. "That was fantastic. I've never heard that before."

Dante's shoulders relaxed. He finally met her gaze with pride and excitement in his eyes. He had been anxious about her response.

Terrance drummed his fingers on the back of his violin. "Wait until you hear this. Dante, listen to what we came up with and tell us what you think. We're missing something."

Terrance positioned the violin beneath his chin and counted out the beat. The rest of the group started an upbeat song punctuated with a rhythm from the drums that had her once again swaying in her seat. Dante listened, then joined in on the piano.

"No, it needs vocals," he said after they finished. His

brows drew together; then he snapped. "Let me free-style to it."

They started again. This time, when they reached the chorus, Dante came in with vocals. Julie couldn't believe he'd freestyled right then and there.

Julie became engrossed watching them work on the music, confer together and then play again making various changes. She didn't have an artistic bone in her body but appreciated those who could make something beautiful just from the imagination. She noticed a shift in Dante the more they worked. He was less flashy, less the *I am Dante Wilson—idolize me*. He was serious about this music, jerking his clothes and rubbing the back of his neck when something wasn't working, and clapping his hands and talking excitedly when things did work.

This was the real him. The Dante who'd taken her to dinner and paid for her date with Carlos was the superstar used to getting what he wanted. This was the musician. The guy struggling to bring life to his creation. A man who cared little about his stardom when other members of the group challenged him on an idea.

This Dante impressed her, which was surprising, since she hadn't been impressed by a celebrity in years.

She wasn't sure how long they worked. It was long enough for Julie to kick off her shoes and tuck her feet under her on the couch. Watching Dante be so passionate about his music worked against her reasons not to give in to the sparks between them. His intensity, hunger and fire for what he was doing blazed in his every movement. What would having his creative talents focused on her be like? Warmth spread from her midsection, and she squirmed on the couch.

They finished a song, and Dante jumped up from

the piano stool, his smile bright and eager. He'd lost the coat, and his shirtsleeves were rolled up. Every move he made was fluid—a testament to the great dancer he was. The muscles in his arms, back and shoulders flexed and tightened. Julie pictured him shirtless, moving with the same sensual grace as they made love with his shoulders bunching, arms flexing, hips pumping.

The studio door burst open. Julie snapped out of her daydream but couldn't ignore the slick evidence of exactly what she'd been dreaming about between her legs. A woman with clear brown skin, long black hair and dark eyes entered. She glanced around the room, smiled at Julie, then turned back to the guys.

Terrance put down his violin and hurried out of the studio to her. "Esha, what are you doing here?" Pleasure filled his voice.

Esha lifted on her toes and kissed him. "You're late, so I thought I'd come by and see how things were going." She turned to Julie.

Dante came to Julie's side. "Esha, this is Julie."

Esha raised a brow. "You're bringing dates to the studio now?" She looked at Julie and grinned. "You must be special."

Julie returned her smile. "That's what I keep trying to tell him."

"Well, one thing you should know is that when these guys start working, it's hard to tear them away." She looked to Terrance. "Have you eaten yet?"

Terrance looked guilty. "I meant to eat."

Julie's stomach growled loud enough for everyone in the room to look her way. She pressed a hand to her stomach, and heat rose to her face. She'd lost her appetite after seeing all of Dante's conquests at the restaurant, and she'd honestly forgotten about food in her eagerness to watch Dante play.

Dante squeezed her shoulder. "I'll order something. There are take-out menus in the office next door. Any requests?"

The guys called out various things from pizza to Chinese. Dante looked to her. "I'll figure something out. Come with me."

He held out his hand, and she took it. They left the studio to go into the office across the hall. He went to a desk, opened the top left drawer and pulled out several menus.

"Sorry I didn't feed you," he said. "I got caught up in the music."

"I knew you were talented, but that was great."

He looked up from the menus. "Thank you. I want to go mainstream with it, but everyone thinks it'll fail."

"Everyone thought I was crazy for leaving Nexon-Jones, but here I am. Opening a nightclub with one of the world's biggest superstars."

"Point taken." He slowly flipped through the menus, then looked up again. "How did you know it would work out? Leaving your job and striking out?"

She shrugged. "I didn't know. All I knew was that if I didn't try, I'd hate myself. I could've easily gone to another firm, but I would still be at the mercy of another person. Before I chose that route, I had to see if my dream could support me."

"I worry about my career. One bad album, one wrong move, and the people hate you. Being a success is all I know."

"Being a success takes risks to be appreciated. Easy success means you take it for granted and don't know how to handle things if your success goes away."

He gave her his sexy smile, dropped the menus and came around the desk. "Is that why you're making me earn my time with you?"

"Partly. I just like to weigh options and know what I'm stepping into. I've been blindsided in relationships before. I stick to certain rules to avoid being played again."

He frowned. "What kind of rules?"

"Nothing important." She didn't want to think of all the rules that would support her walking out of this room and forgetting the route her mind had taken just a few minutes before.

He leaned close. "Am I playing by your rules?"

"At the start of the night, you were running the game plan I fully expected."

He took another step closer. His cologne seemed stronger, more intense, but she knew the heat from his body and the fire in his eyes had her acutely aware of everything about him.

"Was I?"

She nodded. "Yes, but then you brought me here. I wasn't expecting to see…you." She closed the distance between them and reached up to place a hand on his face. "I wouldn't mind getting to know you. I shouldn't— doing so breaks too many rules. I should have moved on by now."

He wrapped his arm around her waist. "Well, if you're breaking rules for me, I might as well go all in."

He kissed her long, slow and deep. Julie's hands wrapped around his neck while one of her legs snaked around his. She couldn't get close enough. She was hot, inside and out. On fire for Dante and in no mood to ignore how she felt. Strong hands gripped her and lifted as Julie's legs wrapped around his waist. He spun, never breaking the kiss, and sat her on the desk. Her hands were at the front of his shirt, pulling and tugging to get the buttons open. Dante gripped her hips, then slid his hands down her thighs. Why in the world hadn't she worn a skirt? She wanted to feel his hands on her skin.

She got the buttons free and slowly pushed the material aside. He pulled back, his nostrils flared and his lips parted with heavy breaths. The low lights in the office played with the hills and valleys of his sculpted chest and stomach and gleamed off the platinum chain around his neck. Julie ran her fingers over his chest. The muscles jumped, and she pulled her lower lip between her teeth. Feeling daring, she pinched one of his flat nipples. Dante's eyes narrowed. He groaned, grabbed the back of her head and kissed her again.

She met his fever with her own. Her tongue sliding across his, hands gripping his body, hips pressing forward. Dante cupped her breast, and Julie pushed into his palm. He toyed with the hardened tip, tendrils of pleasure flowing with each pull. Her fingers stopped their exploration of his naked chest and lowered to cup his arousal.

Dante pumped his hips forward. "You want that?" he asked, his voice deep and primal.

"I want you," she said against his lips.

The sound he made—a mixture of excitement, need and urgency—made her heart race. He found the zipper on the side of her jumpsuit and tugged the small device down. Julie pushed one sleeve off her shoulder.

The door opened. "Whoa, hey, my bad!" She heard Terrance's voice, followed by the quick snap of the door closing.

Julie and Dante froze. The interruption took all of ten seconds but was just the douse Julie needed. Dante pulled back. His eyes were bright with desire, his body tense and his arousal hard—hard and still in her hand. Julie jerked her hand away. She sucked in air and tried to think. She could not have sex with him on a desk in some unnamed studio.

Oh, a named studio would be better?

Julie closed her eyes and shook her head. "We should order food."

She opened her eyes. Dante's were closed. Slowly, he backed away, took a deep breath and then looked at her. She lost her breath, so common around him, even more so when he looked like he wanted to push her back on the desk, make her chant his name and speak in tongues.

"Okay," he said softly.

Julie nodded and slid forward on the desk. He stopped her before she got off and leaned in to kiss her gently. "Three times you've kissed me, Julie. I'll be up all night dreaming about the fourth."

Chapter 11

Dante was in the middle of his Thursday morning session with his choreographer when his cell phone rang. Annoyed by the interruption, he considered ignoring the call. The idea that the caller may be Julie sent him to the phone.

"Let me check that," he said to Armando. Wiping his face with a towel, he crossed the room to his cell. His dad's number was on the screen.

"What are you doing?" Otis asked after Dante answered the phone.

"I'm in the middle of practicing a new routine."

"Why do you sound so winded?"

Dante took a sip from the bottle of water he had sitting on the floor next to where his phone had been. "I'm not winded." He took a deep breath. "That's like admitting the moves I made ten years ago are harder now."

Otis laughed. "That's the damn problem with old age. Everything starts creaking and popping, but you don't have anything to worry about. You've got at least another ten years before your body really starts to rebel."

"That's why I keep working out now. I want to make that a lot more than ten years."

When he was a kid and his parents first insisted he learn tap, jazz and hip-hop dance, he'd hated it and thought dancing was for girls. Later he appreciated the lessons. Dancing boosted his star appeal, and he'd learned quickly how much women loved a man who could dance.

"That's what I'm talking about. We've always got to look to the future to ensure W. M. Records has staying power, which brings me to the reason for calling. Antwan will be out your way this weekend. We're close to getting him to sign, but he still wants to do a collaboration with you on his first album. I want you to get with him next weekend. Go to the studio, and see what you can come up with."

Dante gritted his teeth and squeezed the bottle in his hand. "Dad, I told you. I'm working on my own project right now. I'll be in the studio with Strings A Flame this weekend."

Otis's disgusted grunt came through the phone. "Those classical guys. Dante, you're better than that."

"They're not classical guys. Just because they play the violin doesn't mean they can't put together some really hot music."

"Look, son, hip-hop and Mozart don't go together. You've always been a strong R&B and pop star, and I think this collaboration with Antwan will strengthen your appeal to the hip-hop crowd, as well."

"I'm already strong in that market. I don't need to fully

cross over. I don't mind the occasional collaboration with a rap artist, but I'm not a rapper."

"I know that. None of us are. Your sister made sure of that," Otis said bitterly. "But you know what I told you about last year's profits. We need to get ahead of where the music's trending. Right now the trend is music that Antwan is putting out. You're coming strong after the concert tour. Follow up that success with a bang by collaborating with one of the biggest names in rap instead of playing with two fiddlers on music that won't go anywhere."

He had no words to refute his dad's argument. Dante was making headway on his own project, and he wasn't ready to give up his work. "You have to at least hear the music before you toss it out."

"Your mom dragged me to enough symphonies in my life to know that I don't like it."

"But this isn't symphonic music. This is fusion—"

"I don't like fusion. Why does everyone think they need to mix stuff up all the time?"

Dante rubbed his temple with his free hand. Didn't his dad realize that mixing hip-hop and R&B was a form of fusion?

"You need to give it a try. If I were mixing jazz or the blues into my music, you'd be okay."

"Because that's music that gets people moving, music that inspires emotions and makes you want to dance. The only thing a violin can do is make you want to sleep."

"Then why did you insist I learn to play the instrument?"

"Because being successful takes more than just singing. I've always encouraged you and your sister to be multitalented. Singing, dancing and creating songs that people want to party to are your strong points. I won't have you wasting your talents on music that won't go anywhere."

Dante's head hurt, and he wanted to pound his fist into the wall. Arguing with Otis was useless. Not once had his dad tried to even hear the music Dante wanted to put together. He was always brushing it off as boring or not sellable.

He'd have to do this album on his own. W. M. Records wouldn't support it. He made a mental note to call his lawyer, who thankfully wasn't paid for by Otis and was loyal to only Dante. He'd check his contract and make sure he'd be okay to put out the music himself when the time came.

"I spoke with your sister," Otis said easily, as if he hadn't just dismissed his son's dream. "She's thinking of putting out some new music. I'm trying to get a good songwriter, and we've got the publicity department working on her rebranding. Repairing a career once it's broken takes a lot of work."

Correcting his sister's career mistake was going to take a lot of rebranding and publicity. Images of losing his status, scorn and ridicule, and becoming a laughingstock of an industry that had embraced him since he was a kid, flashed through his mind. Success meant nothing if you didn't struggle for it. Julie's philosophy sounded well and good when he was in the studio, pumped up on the music they created. What if Otis was right, and the music he was making with S.A.F. was unsuccessful and scorned?

"Tell Antwan to give me a call when he's in town," Dante said. He thought about how he could work in a few sessions with Antwan along with S.A.F. It would be difficult but doable.

"Good. I will." His dad's smug voice came through.

Dante bristled, feeling like he'd just caved. "I may even have a party on Saturday."

"Where?"

"My place. I'll also invite a few musicians—make it kind of an impromptu jam session. We'll see if Antwan and I can come up with something good for that." And he'd invite S.A.F. and test out the songs they'd put together.

"Excellent. I'd try to skip out on this trip to New York to come out and see that, but your mom is looking forward to seeing her brother."

"That's no problem. Just make it out in time for the club opening."

"When will that be?"

"A few months out, but things are coming fast. The permits are already applied for."

He talked to his dad for a few more minutes about the club. Otis didn't have a problem with Dante opening his own place. Mostly because he probably didn't believe it would be a place for Dante to showcase the classical–hip-hop fusion music he loved and would be another venue for W.M. artists. Dante couldn't deny the fear of failure. His dad's years of experience in the music industry was a cold, hard truth that he really didn't want to face, but he also couldn't give in completely. He'd throw the party and invite a few music bloggers and other celebrities. He'd kept his music to himself for too long. Time to introduce some of his fans to what he ultimately wanted to do.

Chapter 12

Unlike her previous visit to Dante's home when she'd wanted to choke him for ruining her date with Carlos, this time Julie didn't care about Carlos, or anyone else. She looked forward to seeing Dante. She hadn't seen him much during the day over the past few weeks. She'd had too many meetings with the architect and contractor, preparing the plans for submittal to the city along with her constant contact with Evette on their other projects to have enough time to see him. He had called a few times and asked her to come down to the studio and listen to him and S.A.F. in the evenings. She'd gone and left before she found herself on the desk with him again.

Valet attendants handled the parking, but Julie didn't have to worry about that because Dante had sent a car to pick her up. A pleasant surprise that she also knew was his way of making sure she came to the party. It would also control, to some extent, when she left. He needn't worry. After seeing the less flashy side of Dante, and the more she realized he was afraid of what people would think about his music, she'd relaxed her guard.

Julie arrived well after the party was scheduled to start, not wanting to appear too eager to see him, and she wasn't surprised by the crush of people in his place. If the pool party she'd stumbled into was a last-minute thing, she expected that something planned would be elaborate. There were celebrities, hired security and waitstaff. The appetizers could have been served at a five-star restaurant instead of what was ultimately a house party.

Outside was just as dazzling. A stage was set up next to the pool, which was a brilliant blue, thanks to the lights that brightened the water. She couldn't hear the ocean over the music, sounds of laughter and constant popping of champagne bottles, but she could smell the salty air on the warm breeze.

"Hey, Julie." Esha's voice came from her left.

Julie turned and smiled at Esha, who had her arm around Terrance's waist. Julie was used to attending functions alone, but a wave of relief rushed through her from seeing someone she knew in the sea of Hollywood elite.

"Familiar faces, finally," Julie said.

Esha nodded. "I'm glad you made it. Dante was starting to worry that you wouldn't come."

Julie turned her head and toyed with her dangling gold earring to hide her delighted grin from those words. "I was just running late."

Terrance held a beer in his hand and gestured toward the stage. "Now that you're here, he'll be ready to start the show."

"Show?"

"He wants to perform the song we've been working on but didn't want to do it until you were here."

More happiness bubbled up inside Julie. This time she didn't turn away. "Where is he? I'll let him know I'm here."

Terrance pointed to the other side of the pool. "Right over there."

Julie turned in the direction Terrance indicated. Dante stood talking to another guy whose back faced her. Dante wore distressed styled jeans that probably cost enough to feed a family of four for a month, and a black V-neck shirt. He looked casual and sexy. He looked up as if sensing her gaze. Awareness jolted down her spine when their eyes met. He stopped talking and grinned at her.

If she'd known he'd greet her arrival with that smile, she would have gotten here an hour earlier.

She started in his direction. He met her halfway. "Julie, you made it." Relief filled his voice. He took her hands in his.

"Of course, why wouldn't I?"

"I don't know—you always surprise me."

"Well, I couldn't miss your debut."

Dante chuckled as his thumbs brushed the backs of her hands. "I've been performing since I was thirteen. This is hardly a debut."

"It's the debut of your new music. That's a big deal."

He nodded, glanced around and shifted from foot to foot. "Yeah. It is."

Julie tilted her head to the side. "Hey, are you okay?"

"Of course. Why wouldn't I be?" His voice held all the bravado that she expected from Dante Wilson, the superstar, but underneath there was something else.

"You're afraid."

He scoffed. "Hardly." He released her hands. Julie reached out to grip his arm, which was hard and tense.

"It's okay to admit it. You put everything into this music. Now you're letting the world see a piece of you that they've never seen before. If you weren't a little bit afraid, I'd think you were heartless," she said softly.

The tension left Dante's arm. The corner of his mouth lifted, and he met her eyes. "I'm far from heartless. If I were, I wouldn't feel so mixed up over you."

Warmth spread up Julie's face, and her breathing stuttered. He didn't mean that, couldn't mean the words. While she wanted to try to guess his angle, guess what his ulterior motive was, she couldn't. Not when he gazed at her with such sincerity, when he seemed just as baffled by the feelings stirred up when they were together.

"Well, well, well, if it isn't Julie Dominick," a male voice said.

Julie's gaze swung to the left. *Antwan?* Her stomach tightened. Her palms got slick with sweat. What the hell was he doing here? She'd seen him only twice since the opening of his nightclub—the night when the three other women he'd been sleeping with showed up. Julie's body went ice-cold. She was over Antwan and avoided guys like him. Or she had until flexing her rules and getting closer to Dante.

Don't just stand here like an idiot.

"Antwan," she said with a short head nod.

Antwan was cute, but his swagger and confidence made him downright irresistible. He wore a pair of dark jeans and a shirt along with a red plaid button-up over the ensemble and a gaudy platinum-and-diamond chain.

"Julie," he said in a slick voice that held too many memories she'd like to forget. "I didn't know you were out here." His tattooed hand rubbed his chin. Julie thought he'd added more. God, to think she'd once pressed that hand to her heart. It made her stomach lurch.

"I'm partnering with Dante and Raymond on a new nightclub."

Dante looked between the two. "You know each other."

Julie nodded. "I helped Antwan open a nightclub in Atlanta."

"That's right. I remember Raymond said something about that."

Antwan shifted and regarded Julie with an affection that she knew was all for show. "Julie and I used to date."

"A long, long time ago," she said.

Dante pointed at Julie, then Antwan, and frowned. "You two dated?"

Well, at least she could rule out that Dante and Antwan had shared secrets about her. "Like I said, years ago." She regarded Antwan. "What brings you to Malibu?"

Antwan nodded toward Dante. "We're working on an album together."

Julie turned to Dante. "Really?"

"We're thinking about it. Antwan's considering signing with my family's label, and it's only natural we'd consider a collaboration."

"What about your music?"

Antwan laughed. "It will be his music. He'll write the song—I'll do the rap. In fact, Dante and I are going to perform tonight. Give a little test run of what we can do together."

Julie turned back to Dante. "Terrance said you were doing another song."

Dante nodded. "We are after I indulge Antwan. Why

don't you grab a drink and sit close to the stage? I want you to see both and tell me what you think."

He sounded as if her opinion was important to him, which started a fluttery feeling in her stomach. "Sure."

"Good seeing you, Julie," Antwan said. He ogled every one of her assets highlighted by her sleeveless cranberry-colored minidress, lingering on her thighs and cleavage. His gaze was both familiar and unwanted. "I really hope we can catch up while I'm in town."

Julie barely refrained from rolling her eyes; she did, however, give him an uninterested smirk. "Don't count on it."

Antwan snickered. "Why? You hooking up with Dante now, or is Raymond still sniffing around, keeping other men away?"

Anger shot up Julie's spine. Her eyes narrowed, and she prepared to tell Antwan just where to go when a tall beauty that Julie recognized as a model hurried over and threw her arms around Dante's shoulders.

"Thank you for inviting me," she said in a sexy purr and kissed his cheek.

Dante's lips curved into a tight smile that didn't reach his eyes as he pulled the model's arms from around him. "Alicia, hey, when did you get here?"

"Just now. And guess what?" She turned and used her finger to tell another equally tall and beautiful woman to come over. "I brought my sister. Maybe we can re-live Vegas." The sister came over and plastered herself on Dante's other side, putting a matching lipstick print on that cheek.

"I'm down for that," the sister said in an equally enticing voice.

Antwan howled with bawdy laughter. "Damn, Dante, you party like that?"

As the girls laughed, Dante glanced at Julie. Julie took a step back. The rose-colored glasses that she'd seen Dante through crashed to the ground. No matter what she thought she'd seen in him over the past few weeks, this was the real him—a partying playboy who would probably treat her just as casually as Antwan had.

"You guys have fun. I'm going to get a drink." She turned her back on the disgusting display and hurried to the bar.

Carlos sat on the edge of the bar. He raised his hand in a friendly wave when they made eye contact. She hadn't talked to him since their date. There were no sparks there, but for now, she was happy to have a conversation with a guy without the sparks and flutters that caused her to make dumb decisions.

Carlos pushed out the stool next to him, and she gladly accepted. "Thanks."

"I was hoping you'd be here tonight," he said.

"Why is that?"

"I enjoyed our first date." She raised a brow, and he held up a hand. "The ending was different, but before that, it was very nice." He leaned over, placed his hand over hers and squeezed.

"I had a good time, too." She pulled her hand, but his tightened.

"Maybe we'll get together again sometime. Unless Dante won your affections."

Julie refused to look back at Dante and the wonder twins clinging to his side. "Does it look like Dante has won my affections? We work together. That's all."

Carlos let go of her hand. "Good to know. How about

tonight's our do over? And we end things the way I'd hoped we would have the first time?"

"How did you want things to end?"

He waved at the bartender, pointed at his drink, then held up two fingers. "I'll just say a lot differently than they did."

The music lowered, and the crowd cheered. Julie swiveled toward the stage where Dante and Antwan were.

Antwan took the microphone. "As some of y'all know, I'm considering moving over to W. M. Records. When that happens, you'll get a lot more of what you're about to experience. Let's do this."

The DJ cranked up the music, and Dante's smooth tenor started the song. Julie had to admit, Dante's vocals and Antwan's rapping was hot. The crowd loved them together. Any song they put out would be a surefire hit. Would he really give up a chance for another almost guaranteed hit to make an album with S.A.F.?

They finished, and, of course, the partygoers went wild and begged for more. Dante grinned, his brow glistening with sweat from his exertion.

"Hold up, hold up," he said to the crowd. "I've got something else I want you all to hear." Terrance, Tommy and the rest of the group came up onstage. "This is something new that I'm trying. Tell me what you think."

Julie was a ball of nerves. Her heart pounded, and her stomach twisted as if she were the one debuting new music. Dante looked across the space directly at her. His eyes filled with the same nervousness that fluttered in her stomach. She lifted her glass to him in salute. Dante raised his chin, then started the music.

Instead of watching him, Julie gauged the reaction of the people at the party. There were looks of confusion when the violins started, but there was also curiosity. When the drums and bass picked up the beat, the confusion gave way to enthusiasm. Before long, the rest of the partygoers were bobbing their heads and moving to the music. When they finished the song, the crowd was on their feet, clapping and cheering.

Julie put her drink down and clapped with them, a huge smile on her face. If Dante needed a boost to tell him this was what he should be doing, then he'd gotten just that. He glanced at her, his grin so big and triumphant that her heart stuttered in her chest. She turned to get her drink off the bar to raise to him.

Her hand bumped against Carlos's. She turned, frowning, as he pulled his hand away from her glass. His smile was apologetic. "Sorry, I was trying to move the glass out of the way."

"Was it in your way?"

He shook his head. "No, the bartender was wiping things down."

She glanced at the bartender, who was wiping the bar but was not near them. Still, he could have been right behind her when Carlos tried to move her glass.

"No harm, no foul," she said.

She took the glass, then turned back to Dante and raised it. His joy from earlier was gone. He scowled at her, then turned his glower on Carlos. He couldn't possibly be upset that she was sitting with Carlos. If anything, *he* deserved the angry stare after he'd had two supermodel sisters offer up their favors to him so blatantly. Here she was, once again, getting caught up into thinking there was more to him than she'd originally expected just because his music moved her.

She took a sip from her drink and turned back to Carlos. "How did you enjoy the music?"

Carlos looked from her glass to her. "I liked it okay, but it's nothing like the music we played on tour. I think they should just stick to that."

"Really?"

"Just my opinion. But, hey, who knows what catches on and what doesn't? I wish him well." He picked up his drink and held it out to her. "A toast to his success."

Julie touched her glass to his. "To his success," she said, taking another sip. She glanced at the stage. One of the model sisters had jumped up and was trying to plaster herself against Dante. Dante still glared at Julie. Heat spread up her cheeks. *God, I'm ridiculous. Blushing, again, just because he's looking at me.*

Julie downed her drink. Time to go before she became even more wrapped up in the crazy feelings he evoked in her.

She smiled at Carlos. "I think I'm going to call it a night."

He pouted, odd for a grown man. "That sounds like a goodbye. I thought we were making tonight our do over."

"I'll have to take a rain check on that. I'm really not in the mood for partying." Or watching Dante scowl at her when she talked to another man while simultaneously having a supermodel trying to jump his bones on stage.

"Let me at least walk you to the door."

"There's really no need."

"I don't mind." He gave her a cute smile. "Maybe I'll convince you to let me drive you home."

"I'll let you walk me to the door, but driving me home isn't necessary." She stood.

"You said that about walking you to the door, but you

changed your mind." His voice carried too much confidence that she would let him take her home. Too bad for him; she wasn't in the mood for any guy to try to sweet-talk his way into her pants.

She couldn't bear to look back at Dante and see him probably fawning over the two models. Instead she waved at Esha and headed to the door.

"You really should let me drive you home," Carlos said. "You've been drinking."

Julie's lip twisted. "Only two. Besides, Dante sent a driver, so I'm good either way."

"Are you sure?"

"Positive." Her footing slipped on the way into the house. The lights danced, and her vision went blurry. "What the…"

Carlos quickly wrapped an arm around her waist to steady her. "Are you okay? You drank a lot. I couldn't let you drive home like this."

His voice was raised. The sound made her head throb. She pressed a hand to her temple. The people, lights and furnishings all spun like a merry-go-round. Her stomach churned. She hadn't drank enough for this to happen.

"I'm…okay."

"No, you're not. I'll make sure you get home, okay?"

He sounded way too eager. Carlos pressed her closer to him, his hand resting on the side of her breast, his thumb caressing her through her dress. The churning in Julie's stomach intensified.

"What did you put in my drink?" Her voice slurred.

He leaned close to her ear. "Just something to make you a little friendly. Don't worry—you won't remember anything tomorrow." His hot breath blew in her ear.

A tremble of fear and disgust racked her body. *No.*

This could not be happening. "No!" She tried to yell, but again her voice came out sluggish and slow.

"Yes," he said in a louder voice. "You can't drive like this. I insist." He dragged her to the door, and she was too sick to stop him.

The room spun faster; then the weight of Carlos's body was gone. Julie slumped against the wall. Loud, angry male voices rang out to her left. Her head felt as heavy as a bowling ball, but she managed to drag it up. Dante was in Carlos's face. In slow motion, she watched Dante's arm pull back, then forward. His fist landed on the side of Carlos's face. Julie's eyes would have widened if they didn't feel like thick velvet curtains.

The room continued to spin, and the edges of her vision blackened. Her stomach pitched and rolled. Saliva filled her mouth. She was going to be sick. She slid down the wall. Strong arms swooped her up. No, too fast. She sucked in a breath. *Dante.* She'd recognize his scent anywhere. Her heart rate slowed. For a second, she felt safe, before throwing up the drink and everything else she'd had that night.

Chapter 13

What happened last night?

The words hit Julie's brain before a splitting head-ache took hold. She squinted her eyes even though her room was dark and slowly rose to a seated position. Her mouth felt like dirty cotton and tasted worse than that. Pushing back the plush covers, she eased her legs over the side of a bed.

Two blinks later, her vision cleared and several things became apparent at once. (A) She was not in her hotel room; (B) she was naked except for a sleeveless T-shirt; (C) the shirt did not belong to her.

Running her fingers through her short hair, she looked around the room. There was a humongous bed covered in rich, royal blue sheets, dark masculine furnishings, a colossal flat-screen television along one wall hooked up to a gaming system, platinum records on another. The last wall was nothing but floor-to-ceiling windows dimmed to an opaque that she was sure turned clear with a push of a button to provide a view of the ocean. Even without the decor, she would have known she was in Dante's bedroom. The sheets smelled like him, seductive and inviting, and after spending the night in his bed, she smelled like him.

A bottle of water and ibuprofen were next to each other on the nightstand with a note that read, "You'll need this."

"What did I do?" she murmured to herself. She grabbed both and downed three pills and half the bottle of water. She paused to take a physical check of herself. She didn't feel like she'd spent the night having sex. She just felt hungover. The inside of her elbow was sore. She glanced down at the Band-Aid there. When she pulled it off there was no sign of an injury. Add that to the list of mysteries. Her stomach growled, and she was hungry.

She stood quickly. Her stomach rolled; her head spun. She took a deep breath and both cleared. *Okay, maybe too much to drink.* She glanced around the room. No sign of her clothes. If she'd come to bed with Dante after drinking too much, she would expect to see her clothes strewn over the floor in a haphazard attempt to get them off.

Where in the world is Dante?

She went into what she guessed was the bathroom and sighed with relief at the sight of the enormous gray marble shower and bathtub. The time to worry about what she'd done the night before could wait. She stripped off the shirt and got into the large shower. While she washed away the grogginess, she tried to remember how she'd ended up in his bed. Antwan had been there. Dante was thoroughly enjoying the sexy sisters eager to please him. Shouldn't they be in his bed? She dropped the soap.

. For the life of her, she hoped her inhibitions hadn't dropped that much the night before!

Picking up the soap, she finished her shower. No matter how hard she pushed her brain, the only thing she remembered was sitting at the bar, saluting Dante after his performance and then having a brief conversation with Carlos. Hadn't she told him she was leaving? If so, why was she here?

Only one way to know. Find Dante.

She got out of the shower. Thankfully, there was a toothbrush still in the package inside one of the multitude of drawers surrounding the sink. She wrapped a towel around herself and searched for her clothes. When she still couldn't find them, Julie said to hell with it and went into Dante's closet. The closet was the size of a mini-boutique and set up like one, too. There were cushioned stools, a wall of various loafers and sneakers and all of Dante's clothes lined up neatly on racks behind glass doors. She opted for a black T-shirt and, since his pants would be too long, a pair of starched white boxers.

"If we slept together, then I might as well get over feeling guilty for wearing his clothes."

Julie left his bedroom and stopped. Half a dozen people were upstairs cleaning up the mess from the previous night. The movement of so many people was a surprise compared with the absolute silence in Dante's bedroom. She gave them tight nods, then hurried downstairs, where another half dozen were cleaning. A woman sweeping up broken glass at the foot of the stairs glanced up at Julie and smiled.

Julie cleared her throat and tugged on the bottom of the T-shirt, which covered the boxers. Great, she had to do the walk of shame in front of the entire cleaning crew. "Is Dante around?"

The woman shook her head. "You must be Julie. Dante had to go out for an appointment, but he asked that you stick around until he gets back. He wants to make sure you're okay."

Why wouldn't she be okay? *Maybe because you woke up in his bed and don't know how you got there.* Exactly why she wouldn't leave until she found out the hows and whys of last night.

"Thank you," she said to the lady as she made her way to the kitchen.

Sunlight streamed through the large windows and gleamed brightly off the white marble countertops. Julie almost felt bad for pulling out items to make a sandwich in the middle of the cleaning efforts, but her growling stomach couldn't be ignored. She quickly put together a sandwich, then searched for someplace to hide until Dante returned, someplace other than his bedroom.

The only room where there wasn't any cleaning going on was in his home theater. Setting her food on one of the plush seats, which was more like a couch than anything, Julie searched for something to watch in the media tower next to the large screen.

"Musicals," she said with delight. As a fan of classic movie musicals, she was pleasantly surprised by his choices. She slipped in one of her favorites, *Singin' in the Rain.* After another five minutes of figuring out the blasted player and sound system, Julie settled in.

She was almost halfway through the movie, at the scene where Gene Kelley did his famous dance routine in the rain, when the door to the theater opened and Dante walked in. She took one look at him and gasped. His right eye was blackened and his jaw was bruised. Julie jumped up from her seat and rushed over.

"What happened?" She placed her hands on his cheeks and turned his head to get a better look. "Who hit you?"

He took her hands in his and lowered them, concern filling his eyes. "Forget about me—how are you? Do you need me to call a doctor?"

Julie frowned. "Doctor? For what? You're the one with the black eye."

"You don't remember what happened?"

"Did I do that to you?"

The concern in his face gave way to a small grin. "I think you did want to hit me at one point last night, but you didn't do this."

"Then who did?"

Dante's nostrils flared. His hands clenched hers almost painfully. "Carlos."

Julie twisted her hands until his grip loosened, but he didn't let her go. "Carlos? Why?"

"He didn't like it when I stopped him from taking you away from the party. I thought I saw him slip something into your drink, but I couldn't be sure from where I was on the stage. When you walked to the door and stumbled, I knew I wasn't mistaken. He was practically dragging you to the door, pretending as if you were drunk and as if he was being a Good Samaritan by driving you home."

Julie's headache and sick stomach had settled after the ibuprofen and food, but a nauseating feeling twisted her midsection. They'd been talking, and his hand had moved her glass. She'd thought that was weird…then she could barely remember going to the door.

Her eyes rose to Dante. "He drugged me?" Anger hardened her voice. "I'm going to kill him."

"He's already been taken care of." Her brows rose, and he shook his head. "No one killed him, but between me, S.A.F. and Antwan, he got the shit beat out of him before we called the police. I had to meet with my publicist this morning to handle damage control. I'd invited several reporters and music bloggers to the party to hear my new music. Carlos's stunt, and the subsequent fight, obviously overshadowed everything at the party."

"I'm so sorry."

"Don't be. What happened wasn't your fault, and I don't regret the fallout." He brushed her short bangs to the side and ran his fingers down her face. The tenderness in his eyes started a yearning deep in her chest.

"How did I end up nearly naked in your bed?"

Dante dropped his hands and grimaced. "You were falling, so I picked you up. I think too fast because you threw up."

Julie pressed her face into her hands. "Eww!"

"Tell me about it," he said with a laugh. "I took you to my room. Esha cleaned you up and put you to bed. She sat with you while the doctor checked you out. He drew your blood. The police will need to test it for the drug to have a case against Carlos."

She touched her arm where the Band-Aid had been. Mystery solved. "You called a doctor?"

"I wanted to make sure you were okay. My doctor lives nearby. If I would have shown up at the hospital with you it would have been a media circus. After I threw everybody out and dealt with the police, I came up and watched you all night."

Julie lowered her hands to stare at him. "You stayed with me all night? Why?"

"I was pretty sure whatever he gave you would just

knock you out, but I didn't want you to get sick again and no one be there."

He said the words as if fighting for her honor, calling a doctor and keeping vigil at her bedside was the most natural thing. Briefly she considered a life where Dante was the man who always looked out for her, protected her and stayed beside her all night. She liked the idea.

"Thank you," she said softly.

Sex was always her choice and never entered into lightly. Before taking any guy to bed, she weighed all the consequences. After being played for a fool, she'd taken control of her dating life, her heart, her emotions and her body. In the blink of an eye, Carlos had almost stolen that from her—a blow she wasn't sure how she would have recovered from.

Trembles racked her body, tears burned her eyes and thoughts of what could have happened carved their way in vivid and bitter detail through her brain. Blinking rapidly to stop herself from crying about what might have been, Julie met Dante's eyes. "Thank you so much." Her voice cracked.

Dante cupped her face in his hands, his thumbs brushing her cheeks. Concern filled his dark eyes again, and she saw some of the same fear she felt. If he hadn't seen what Carlos had done…if he hadn't followed her to the door…

"Julie, I had no idea what he was capable of. He almost…" His hands on her face tensed, and his eyes burned with focus. "If he would have hurt you, I would have killed him. I won't let anyone hurt you."

Maybe it was the fierce intensity in his eyes, the protectiveness in his voice or the fact that he'd been her own personal superhero the night before, but Julie wanted nothing more than to have Dante's body against hers. No analyzing the consequences, no thoughts of tomorrow or what any of this meant. Just the ability to do something *she* wanted to do.

She lifted onto her toes and pressed her lips against his. He froze, but she didn't have time for hesitation and skated her tongue across his lower lip. Strong arms clasped her tight, pulling her against his body. Dante's lips parted, and he kissed her hard. *That is more like it.* Julie pulled on the front of his T-shirt, bringing him closer. Her hips twisted and pushed forward, sliding against his quickly hardening erection, leaving no doubt about what she wanted.

Dante stepped forward, and she walked backward until her back hit the lowered screen. The lights from the movie flashed across them. The sound of music, the ballet scene, intermingled with the sounds of their heavy breaths and Julie's soft moans. Dante kept one hand on the side of her face, fingers deep in her hair, while the other skimmed down her body, leaving a trail of heat behind the touch. His deft fingers found the opening in the boxers she'd borrowed. Slipping inside, he brushed slowly back and forth across the outer folds of her core.

Sparks of heat trembled through her. Slick desire pooled where his fingers caressed. Julie sucked in a breath, and her head fell back. Firm lips kissed her cheeks, down to the side of her neck, then possessively suckled on the sensitive skin. Her legs spread, and his fingers skimmed across the sensitive bud at her center, then pulled back.

"Dante." His name on her lips was an urgent plea for more.

"Julie," he answered, sounding just as needy.

Dante grabbed the bottom of her T-shirt and lifted. Julie's arms rose so he could completely remove it and toss the shirt to the floor. He quickly pushed down her boxers. When she stood before him, covered only by the flashing lights from the movie, a sinful smile curved his lips—one that promised pleasure, seduction and decadence. Julie unbuttoned his jeans, then pushed the rough material and his white boxers past his waist. Her gaze fixed on his long, hard erection.

Dante's fingers wrapped around his length. "Julie." His voice was low, deep, possessive.

He cupped the back of her head and kissed her again with all the demand and need that had coated his voice. Julie's hand lowered to push his aside and wrapped her fingers around his shaft, caressing him with firm but gentle strokes. Dante groaned and pressed her against the screen. His kiss was deeper, more erotic.

This was what she wanted. This is what she'd wanted from the second her eyes met his over the piano—him, hot and hard against her. The fact that someone had dared try to steal her choice the night before made every kiss with Dante more precious and every caress that much more exquisite. He was *her* choice. For the moment he belonged only to her, and even though he could easily snatch her heart if she wasn't careful, right now she wanted to give him everything she could.

Dante pulled away to retrieve a condom from his pants with quick, jerky movements. Before Julie could open her mouth and beg him to hurry, his body was back on hers. Gripping her thighs, he hoisted her up and pressed her back against the screen. Julie's legs wrapped around his trim waist. The hard length of his cock pulsed against her slippery center. His mouth plundered hers, branding her and wiping away any thoughts of another. Maybe indefinitely. Dante lifted her higher and lowered his head, slipping one puckered nipple into the welcoming warmth of his mouth.

"Dante," she begged, pushing her chest forward.

He suckled her deeply and moved his hips back and forth in short, steady strokes that ran the length of his cock against the swollen nub of her sex. Tension built as her hips gyrated, and her body was drenched with need. Julie gripped his head at her breast. Her breaths came faster, harder.

Oh, God, I'm going to come.

"I want you to come," Dante replied.

Had she said that aloud? The thought was fleeting because Dante lifted his head from her breast as his hips continued their grinding in pleasurable torture. Panting his name, she gripped his shoulders and moaned louder as the pressure built higher. He kissed her, then dropped a hand to position himself at her opening. Julie shifted lower, and the tip of him slid inside. With a deep, guttural groan, Dante pushed forward, filling her completely.

Chapter 14

"So, why all the musicals?"

Dante looked away from the bunch of grapes he'd been feeding Julie. They lounged on one of the couches in the theater. Julie's head rested in his lap, and his hand gently traced across her flat stomach. *The Wiz* played on the big screen. There was a spread of fruit, cheese, crackers and juice before them. After having the most mind-blowing sexual experience of his life, he'd wanted to take her upstairs and make love to her again and again. But he wasn't sure how she really felt after the ordeal of the night before. What happened earlier had been spontaneous. He wanted to take the time to make sure she was okay, then take her upstairs and get her to make those sexy noises while he was buried deep inside her.

"Inspiration," he said, plucking a green grape from the bunch and popping the firm fruit into his mouth.

"Inspiration how?"

"Most musicals have great dance sequences. I study the dance, and then I try to master the moves myself."

"Really?" She shifted away from the screen and onto her back to look him directly in his eyes. "I thought you were more of a hip-hop dancer."

"I am, but my parents wanted me to know about all forms of dance. At first I didn't get their reasoning, but now I realize that understanding all the fundamentals is what made me better."

"Is that the same with music? You play a lot of instruments."

Her hand absently caressed his forearm. Dante liked her like this—soft, open, sexy, her eyes unguarded, her smile lazy and relaxed. Even more so, he liked the way he felt with a warm and happy Julie after he'd wiped away the fear and anger that had clouded her gaze. He'd always thrilled at the chase and celebrated the victory, but this feeling was different. He'd protected his woman and wanted to keep on protecting her.

She pinched his arm. "I asked about the instruments," she said.

"*Dominance* and *excellence* are two words as reverent as prayers in my family. With a legacy like we have, and in order to maintain our level of success, there's no room for half steps. Knowing how to play the piano isn't good enough. You have to also understand drums, strings, wind and brass. I can play the violin, saxophone and trumpet."

He didn't say it as if bragging, but there was some pride in his voice.

"Sounds like your childhood was spent in music and dance lessons. Did you ever have fun?"

He smirked and ran his hand across her short, silky hair. "Honestly, not much. Not until I had my first hit and went on my first tour at thirteen. That's when the fun kicked in. I was a kid, and the world loved me, my music and my family. I still had a rigorous schedule, but my dad loosened the strings enough to let me enjoy myself."

"Loosened the strings…yikes."

He chuckled and nodded. Then his smile drifted away. Many times he had resented the constant pressure to be great at everything until the perks of being successful kicked in. Dante would admit that he was spoiled, pampered in a way that other celebrities wouldn't understand because his family had been successful for generations. He'd never regretted or resented that part of his life until last night. He'd never thought much about the people he surrounded himself with, but someone in his group had almost hurt Julie. Time to take strong inventory of who he invited into his circle.

"I guess if they hadn't pushed me so hard, I wouldn't be where I am today," he said, setting aside his thoughts. "Right now I'm ready to do something that I really want to do. Why have an appreciation for all this music and not try something different?"

"Why the collaboration with Antwan?"

He stopped stroking her hair. Dozens of questions about her previous relationship with the rapper ran through his head. He damn sure didn't want all the details, but for the life of him, he couldn't picture how they got together. Julie didn't seem like the type to fall for a player like that.

A player like me.

Dante cleared his throat and ran his fingers through her hair again. "My dad is pushing that. W. M. Records needs a boost. We've had declining sales the past two years. Not enough to do major damage but enough for people to smell blood in the water. If I work with Antwan and get him to sign with us, it'll go a long way to keeping the stars we've got and signing new ones."

"But it'll also make working with S.A.F. harder."

He nodded. "Yeah. Choosing between my dream and my family's legacy is next to impossible. I want to do both—sign S.A.F. to our label and bring something new to the company. My dad's against it."

She was silent for several seconds. "Doing something different from what you've always done can be difficult. You almost feel as if you're going against yourself."

"You understand the feeling?"

She nodded and resettled in his lap. "I do. When I was younger I was so spontaneous. I didn't always think through all the consequences of my actions. Just listened to my gut instinct and went with that."

"Most kids are like that."

"True, but for some people, going with your first instinct can lead to trouble. For me, things always seemed to work out. That was my compass, to trust myself and to know that I could be secure in my decisions. Now I analyze everything. I wonder about the repercussions and weigh the pros and cons."

"That can be smart, especially when starting a new business."

"It's not just business—it's every aspect of my life." She frowned, frustration filling her voice. "I scrutinize everything in my personal life, every step that I take, just so I don't end up blindsided."

She turned her head to stare at the screen. Dante doubted she paid attention to the movie.

"Were you that way with Antwan?"

She blinked, looked at him, scoffed and sat up. "Why would you say that?"

He wanted to pull her back against him. "He broke your heart."

She shrugged, but the stiffness in her back proved the move wasn't indifferent. "We just weren't on the same page in our...relationship. If you'd call it that. I thought we were exclusive, and I was wrong. Guess I shouldn't have been so quick to believe a guy as famous and popular as him really meant it when he said that I was his heart, and that I was the only one for him. Even worse, I assumed that him saying, 'I want you to have my baby,' meant he wanted to marry me."

She jerked a grape off the vine and tossed the fruit in her mouth.

"Julie."

She held up a hand. "Don't. I've heard it all. 'He shouldn't have said that if he didn't mean it' or 'You're not dumb for thinking you were special to him.' Because regardless of any of the excuses, I should have paid attention to the signs. I brushed off the flirting women, numbers in his pocket and rumors of him sleeping around as part of the hassle that came with dating a celebrity. When we were together, he gave me all of his attention, but when we weren't together, he didn't reach out to me, didn't even act as if he missed me. After I realized I was one of many, and was devastated, Raymond was my only friend to be straight with me. He let me know exactly how I'd been played and how to notice the signs in other relationships. Now I strive to be clear about the expectations before going into any relationship."

Dante clenched his teeth to keep from swearing. His

toe tapped against the floor while he weighed his words. He couldn't make any excuse for Antwan—hell, he *was* Antwan. He'd said and done the same things over his life as a celebrity, with the exception of the baby comment. He had whispered promises of more in the middle of sex—promises that later bit him in the ass but were quickly forgiven and forgotten.

No wonder Julie had originally pushed him away. She'd seen in him the same type of guy who'd broken her heart, no matter what she said. After last night, all Dante wanted to do was protect her heart, cherish her, but what could he possibly do to make her believe that?

"What are your expectations for us?" he finally asked.

She turned to watch him, and as he stared into her amber eyes, his heart played wildly in his chest. The smallest beat of hope that she'd felt the same connection he had when they'd made love earlier accompanied the rhythm.

"We're mixing business and pleasure...against our better judgment."

The beat died. "What if my better judgment says mixing business and pleasure with you is the right thing to do? That not being with you goes against everything in me? That something tells me this is worth exploring?"

Her lips parted. The tip of her tongue darted out across her full bottom lip. Her eyes softened for a second before her lips lifted in a teasing grin, and she shook her head.

"It's just the afterglow from earlier. We're both hyped up from last night." She popped some grapes in her mouth, then looked at him. "Don't worry—I know this isn't going to last long. Right?"

Wrong. So very wrong. He wanted this to last. But could it really? He was in California; she was in Georgia. He toured, lived his life on the road and got more numbers, naked groupies snuck into hotel rooms and invitations than Antwan could imagine. Before meeting Julie, he wasn't ready to settle down. He'd had a threesome just a few weeks ago. Now, after one time with her, he couldn't imagine spending his nights without Julie by his side.

Would she believe him? Did *he* believe himself? This type of stuff, the feeling of completeness, didn't happen after one round of sex. Could it?

He wasn't sure if he could answer the question. Not right now. For once he needed some time to think over what he expected from a relationship.

"You're right, just a little fun. Do you want to see me do the dance from one of the movies?" he asked, needing to change the subject before he blurted out his thoughts— thoughts she'd probably scorn.

What looked like disappointment flashed briefly in her eyes before she grinned. "Any one I call out, you can do?"

"I promise."

She bit her lower lip and pulled her brows together, thinking. "Hmm. I'll go with the famous sequence from *Singin' in the Rain.*"

"Really? Why that?"

"Because I'm in love with Gene Kelly and his thighs. If you pull it off—" she leaned close and ran her hand up his leg, squeezing his thigh "—I might let you get in between my thighs again."

His cock went from soft and sated to half rigid and ready. Thoughts of the future could wait until tomorrow. Today he wanted Julie back in his arms. Taking her hand in his, he lifted her from the seat. "Deal."

Chapter 15

Three days later, the only thing Dante could think of was Julie. She hadn't spent the night and had chosen to go back to her hotel room after the doctor checked her out to verify she was okay and they'd made love twice more. He'd asked her to stay. When she'd insisted on leaving, he'd almost begged.

Thank God I have some pride.

Dante Wilson did not beg. He should be glad that she hadn't called in the past three days or hadn't gotten needy after they slept together. Instead he was irritated and had picked up his phone to call her too many times, only to put the thing down. He needed some distance. He would not be the dope that fell in love with a woman who guarded her heart like a navy SEAL, analyzed every move he made like a computer software program and dissected his every word as if they were a middle school science project.

"Hey, Dante, you made the blogs," Terrance said from where he sat on one of the sofas in the studio. They were the only two there. The rest of S.A.F. was not expected to show up until later that afternoon.

Dante looked up from the sheet of music he was supposed to be reading instead of wondering about his *feelings*.

"What are you talking about?"

Terrance stood and crossed the room. He gave his cell phone to Dante. "I checked out the blogs from the people at your party the other night. Instead of talking about our music, they're talking about the fight. How you and Antwan beat up the guy who drugged Julie."

"What?" He scanned the words on the screen. A few lines in, and he cursed. The blogger, Gary Mo, had gotten the gist of what happened and filled in the rest for entertainment value.

He read aloud. "Promising real estate developer Julie Dominick hit it big after opening a nightclub for her former lover Antwan and is now cozying up to Dante Wilson while helping him open a nightclub in partnership with her longtime friend and suspected lover Raymond. Sources say the fight actually started earlier in the night when Dante and Antwan were both vying for her attention. The stunt pulled by a drummer in Dante's circle sparked the animosity brewing between the two. Hopefully, Dante and Antwan won't let—" Dante gritted his teeth and took a deep breath "—*a piece of tail* ruin a collaboration that the music world is pining for."

He gripped the phone, and his arm flexed with the need to throw the damn thing. If this had been a blogger with a small following, Dante wouldn't care. But Gary not only had a popular site about what was new in music, he also had a side job as the music correspondent for a weekend news show on a popular entertainment channel.

Dante glared up at Terrance. "This is ridiculous. He's calling what happened to Julie a *stunt*? This completely ignores the statement my publicist put out and creates a problem that isn't there."

"I know," Terrance said with a disgusted look.

"Are all of the bloggers we invited posting this?"

Terrance shook his head. "Not like this. A few talk about the music and the people there, but they do, eventually, go into the fight. That's the highlight of every story. This is the first one I read that went into Julie's history with Antwan."

"Anyone reading this will think I'm working with her because I'm sleeping with her and not because she was the best person for the job."

Dante's shoulders bunched, and he slapped the phone back into Terrance's waiting hands, guessing his friend knew he was close to smashing it. Julie's voice was filled with pride and determination whenever she talked about why she started her own firm. The reasons for her success were the exact opposite of what Gary implied.

Dante jumped up and dug into his pocket for his cell. "I'm going to call him and tell him he's out of line."

Terrance held out his hands. "Hold up—I wouldn't do that." When Dante glared, Terrance shrugged. "Calling him will only stir the flames. You know Gary. He likes to be the first person on anything new. If you call him, he's going to take what he said to be the truth, and before you know it, the story is not just on his site but being broadcast on *Hollywood News*. The best thing to do is let this story die down. Julie is okay. Carlos got his ass kicked, was arrested and, between you and Antwan blackballing him, will never work with anyone good again. Besides, some of the bloggers had good things to say about our music."

"I don't feel right leaving things like this. Julie is the victim here, and instead of pointing that out, he's painting her as someone who has to sleep her way to the top."

"Dante, half of what's reported on a celebrity's life is a lie. You and I both know that. Julie is a big girl, and she's been around this business long enough to know how things work. She probably doesn't want any more attention brought up about this anyway. Just leave it alone."

Terrance slipped his phone into his back pocket. "I'm going to grab some lunch. Think about that while I'm gone."

Dante nodded and watched Terrance leave. He knew what Terrance said made sense. There'd been so many rumors and mistruths reported about him in the news that he spent most of his time laughing at the stories journalists came up with. This shouldn't be any different. If anything, the potential tension between him and Antwan would probably lead to more buzz about a collaboration between them.

Dante pulled out his phone and checked the sites of the other people he'd invited to the party. As Terrance said, almost all of them had good things to say about the music, but the biggest chunk of coverage was given to his song with Antwan. He wasn't surprised, but he was still disappointed. Anything he and Antwan did together would be hot. People would buy the music and flock to a concert. His career would continue to rise. W. M. Records would get the boost it needed, and other artists would sign. Though there were no negative comments about him and S.A.F., there also weren't any gushing words telling people to anticipate a new and different sound.

Intermingled with everything he read was some version of the same assumptions about him, Julie, Antwan and even Raymond. None as blatant as the one Gary wrote, thankfully. If he called Gary to get the story straight, the guy would gleefully report that Dante called him to try to shut the story down and stifle his freedom of the press, bringing more attention to his relationship with Julie. Even though she had his thoughts scattered like notes in the wind, currently the extent of their relationship was exactly what Gary reported. They'd slept together, nothing more. The thought nagged him, going against the need to protect Julie from further harm.

The best thing to do is let this story die down.

Terrance's words made his instincts rebel, but his brain held firm. He had to go with Terrance's advice to ensure this entire situation blew over. For the first time in his life, Dante didn't like what came with being a celebrity.

Julie pretended to check emails on her phone while the building inspector went through the latest renovations for Dante's nightclub. Sheila accompanied the inspector on the walk-through. From what Julie could overhear, she answered all of the inspector's questions with no problems. Still, Julie's stomach fluttered. Sheila hadn't given Julie much doubt in hiring her as the contractor for this job, and she had confidence things would go well. She needed this inspection on the electrical system to pass so they could move forward.

When the inspector and Sheila came to the front of the

building, Julie slid the phone into the pocket of her suit and looked expectantly from one to the other.

"So, how did things go?" Julie asked.

Sheila didn't look at Julie. Dread landed in Julie's stomach with a heavy thud. She turned to the inspector and raised her brows.

The inspector pursed his lips before checking his notes. "You haven't sprinkled the building. You can't cover up the ceiling until that's in."

Julie's eyes widened, and she turned to Sheila. "There's no way we would have not sprinkled the building."

The inspector shook his head. "I checked, and there are no sprinklers."

"That wasn't on the plans," her contractor said.

Julie frowned. "On the plans or not, I think we should have known to install sprinklers."

"If it's not on the plans, I don't put it in. Take that up with the architect," Sheila said.

Julie ground her teeth to keep from swearing. "Did you know we would need sprinklers?"

Sheila lifted a shoulder. "I thought we might, but since it wasn't on the plans…"

Julie pressed her lips together and raised a hand. "You decided not to say anything." She would take this up with the architect, but she couldn't believe Sheila would let them get this far without saying something.

The inspector grunted. Julie turned narrowed eyes on him. "Is there anything else?"

"That's the main thing. Everything else is minor. Normally, I'd be surprised that you didn't notice they weren't installing sprinklers, but I guess I can understand why you might overlook that."

Julie's head cocked to the side and she crossed her arms. "Really, why?"

"Well." The guy chuckled. "You know," he said as he looked back at his notes.

"No. I don't know," Julie said. "Maybe you can explain why your plan reviewer didn't notice that before approving the plans." Julie didn't like to play the blame game, but if he was going to fill his voice with judgment about her capabilities, she would do the same.

The smirk disappeared from the inspector's face. "All I'm saying is the building needs sprinklers installed. If you're thinking about calling downtown to complain and get my boss to override this, save your breath. I'm calling to let him know, and I'm not signing off until I see sprinklers installed."

Julie's shoulders straightened. "I'm not calling downtown to complain. I follow the building codes on all my projects."

The guy grunted as if he didn't believe her. He tore off a carbon copy of his inspection and held it out to Julie. "Call me when the sprinklers are in." He looked to the contractor. "And don't think about closing up that ceiling beforehand. I'll get you to tear it out to prove you installed the system."

Sheila bucked up. "Do you know who's behind this project?"

"A celebrity is behind every project in this town," the inspector said. "That doesn't mean I'm cutting corners." He glanced at Julie. "No matter how *close* you are to Dante Wilson."

Julie glared. "My professional relationship with Dante has nothing to do with how well I do this job. We'll get the sprinklers installed."

The inspector's doubtful gaze flicked over Julie. He grunted, then turned and stomped out the door. His look annoyed her more than the issue with the sprinklers. She'd spent one day in Dante's arms, one day that no one should know about. Well, there was the cleaning crew. How many of the stories about celebrities originated with their staff? For all she knew, everyone knew that she'd spent the day having sex with Dante, annoying building inspectors included.

Julie swung back to Sheila. "Seriously? You didn't think to bring up that we needed to install sprinklers?"

"It's a renovation. I didn't think the code called for it. Besides, do you know how much money that'll cost?"

"I don't care. Do you know how many people will die if a fire breaks out and we don't have sprinklers? What type of scandal that will put on Dante's name?"

Sheila raised her hands. "Fine. I'm on it."

Julie gritted her teeth to keep from strangling the woman. She ignored the headache that started after the inspector left and focused on figuring out her next step. She wanted to put the entire blame on Sheila and the architect, but honestly, she hadn't paid nearly enough attention to the project, thanks to her preoccupation with Dante. First, the trips to his studio, followed by sleeping with him over the weekend.

She didn't regret sleeping with Dante, not really. After what almost happened with Carlos, she'd needed to, but something inside her heart had shifted when they'd made love. The mixture of hero worship for him beating the crap out of Carlos and lust from a fantastic day of sex put her very close to losing her heart. She needed space. Time to stop being distracted by Dante's dream and focus on hers before she got more looks like the inspector had given her.

Julie spent the rest of the afternoon going over the last few inspection reports and was surprised to find that this wasn't the first mention of the sprinklers. She also noted other instances where the inspector pointed out other small ways that Sheila had tried to get over on certain code requirements. By the time Julie left for the day, she'd fired Sheila and called Orlando to see if he could complete the job. He'd taken another project but would be able to send one of his crews to work for her in a few weeks.

Even though she needed to keep as much distance between her and Dante as possible, she went to his studio at the end of the day. She hated to report that she'd let something so major go unnoticed, but she didn't back away from admitting when she messed up. He needed to know Sheila was out and Orlando was taking over.

She entered the studio to find Dante and S.A.F. working on new music. The melodic sound of his voice combined with their music soothed her ragged emotions. They finished the song, and Dante immediately turned to her. The smile on his face seemed forced compared with the easy grin he'd worn while they practiced. He lifted his chin in a quick acknowledgment of her presence and looked away.

A dull pain spread through her gut. *You're right, just a little fun*—his words, and his agreement to what she had said. She couldn't feel hurt because he didn't seem happy to see her. He'd sampled the girl; the novelty had worn off.

"Let's take a few minutes, guys," he said and came over to her. "Hey, what are you doing here?"

The question hurt. He'd never asked before—further proof he hadn't been moved by what happened between them. "Is there somewhere we can talk?"

"Sure, let's go next door." He pulled her out of the room and led her into the office across the hall. Her gaze drifted to the desk. Her mind visualized what they would have looked like the last time they were in that room together, when he'd sat her on top, kissed her and made her body yearn for more.

Tearing her eyes from the desk, she looked to Dante. He didn't meet her gaze. He sat on the edge of the desk, his brows drawn together and a pensive look on his face. It was the look of a guy who didn't want to have the weird, where-do-we-go-from-here conversation after sex. He probably thought she'd brought him in here to have a heart-to-heart about what had happened the other day.

Julie straightened her shoulders and tried to give him an I'm-cool smile. *Never act weird the day after sex. Keep things the way they were before.* Rules she'd strictly followed to prevent a guy from thinking she was getting attached.

"Look, don't get weird about what happened the other day," she said. "We both know that was just us blowing off some steam from the attraction that brewed from the moment we met. It's no big deal. We got what we wanted, and now we can work together like professionals."

Dante's pensive expression changed. His brows drew together and his eyes narrowed. Crossing his arms, he leaned forward. "I wasn't going to get weird about what happened. Why would you think I am?"

"You're avoiding eye contact, asking why I'm here. I just want to talk to you about the nightclub. Not, you know, rehash what happened. I've already moved on."

His mouth had opened before Julie finished speaking, but it snapped shut with her last remark. He took a deep breath. "You've moved on?"

"Of course. Haven't you?"

Dante scratched his chin, then ran a hand over his head. "Yeah. It's not like something magical happened."

She couldn't tell by his tone if he was mocking her or was upset. Regardless, it caused a knot in her chest. "Right. I just want you to know that I'm not expecting more."

He nodded as a line formed between his brows. "Neither was I."

They stared at each other. The silence grew to an awkward pause. Frustration and anger clenched her midsection. Did he have to sound so blasé about the entire thing?

"What did you want to talk about?" The frown on his face cleared, and he uncrossed his arms to rest his hands on the desk.

"I fired Sheila and hired Orlando today. She cut corners and was trying to get by without meeting all the codes. We almost got in trouble today with the building inspector, but I made it clear that things will be back on track. I'd hoped by the end of the week, but Orlando can't take over the job immediately."

"You did all that without talking to me first?"

"Did you want to keep a crappy contractor on the job?"

"What happened?"

"They haven't installed sprinklers. Sheila says it's because the architect didn't put them on the plans. I don't know how they were approved without that, but it really doesn't matter. We need them and can't move forward until they're installed."

"How much will this delay the opening?"

"Orlando won't be able to start for another three weeks. I know I made a big decision without talking to you or Ray, but I didn't trust Sheila to finish the job without additional issues."

He nodded, then shrugged. "It sounds like you've got things handled."

"Are you upset?"

He shook his head. "I have no doubt about your abilities. If you think firing Sheila is for the best then I'll trust you." He frowned and rubbed his temples. "Three-week delay. I guess I can live with that."

"I'll see if Orlando knows someone who can at least get the sprinklers installed before he takes over."

Dante nodded. "Do that. Maybe it'll keep us on time. Is that all you wanted to talk about?"

He sounded like he expected her to say something else. There was plenty more she wanted to say. Why did he so readily agree that the other day meant nothing? Had he really not felt something magical between them? *God, don't be silly, Julie.* The guy slept with supermodel twins regularly. Of course, an afternoon of sex with her wouldn't be life changing.

"That's it. Was there something you wanted to talk to me about?" She hoped he didn't notice the expectancy in her voice.

"Actually, there is. I thought you would have read the blog post by now."

"What blog post?"

He pulled out his phone, and, after a few swipes of the screen, he handed it to her. "This one."

Julie scanned the blog. Her muscles tightened with each word. No wonder the inspector doubted her competency. He didn't expect her to know a thing about getting the club opened correctly as long as she got publicity and the chance to warm Dante Wilson's bed.

Her head snapped up. "Are you going to correct them?"

"I've already released my statement about what happened. This is a really bad twisting of events for entertainment value. Regardless of what I say, reporters and bloggers will choose their own angle. I'm not going to say anything else."

"What? Why not?"

"Because fighting with Gary about his article will cause more harm than good. Coming to your defense will make it look like something's going on between us and support their accusations."

Something was going on between them, but she refused to say that. "So you're going to let them think that I'm only here because I'm sleeping with you."

"We both know that's not true. Once you get the club opened, everyone will see that you did a great job and that it had nothing to do with our…situation."

Situation? "Fine. Do what you want." She spun on her heel and marched to the door.

Her hand touched the knob, and Dante's hand slammed into the door, preventing her from opening it. "Julie."

She took a deep breath, but instead of calming her frayed nerves, she breathed in Dante's masculine cologne. Her mind swam with memories of being wrapped up in nothing but his arms, his scent. Awareness buzzed in her midsection. "What?"

"It's killing me to not say anything."

"I'm sure it is, Dante."

He pressed closer, the heat of his body burning into her skin. "Julie, I'm furious about the way he glossed over what happened to you. Staying quiet will let this blow over faster."

She turned and faced him. He stood so close to her that her head fell back to meet his eye. "So you can get back to focusing on your music."

"No, so we don't have the media combing through your past and trying to find further justification to malign your character. I won't have them dragging your name through the mud and victim blaming you when Carlos is the one who should be ripped to shreds. Letting these rumors fade into the sunset is the best way to keep your name out of the media's spotlight. He's going to jail for what he did. And I've already taken steps to make sure Carlos never works in this business again when he's released. This is my fault. All of it, starting with trusting Carlos."

His voice vibrated with frustration and anger. Her shoulders slowly relaxed. Dante was right; another statement from him would look like he was trying too hard to justify partnering with her and would only backfire. Thanks to his decision to call the police and his doctor, if convicted, Carlos could go to jail for at least ten years. By the time the club opened, this would be a distant story in Hollywood's fleeting memory. When the club was successful, regardless of the rumors, it would go a long way to show she could handle opening larger projects.

"I don't like it, but I get it. This isn't your fault. Not really."

"I still feel terrible. I don't want to give anyone else reason to make light of what happened." He brought his hand up to the side of her face. "You're too special for that."

Her lips parted, and a soft sigh escaped her. Her heart

turned mushy for him all over again. Julie shifted so that his hand fell away.

"So, I guess I can't touch you now?" His smile was easy, but his voice was tight.

Julie wished the door was open so she could step back or that Dante would move away and she could escape the seductive cocoon of his presence.

"Dante, my reputation as a developer is the most important thing to me. After I left Nexon-Jones, rumors started that I had to sleep with clients to get where I am, add to that the disaster of my relationship with Antwan after opening his nightclub, and automatically people doubt my ability to grow so fast so quickly on my own merits. This job was supposed to help Dominant Development, not hurt it."

"Don't use your business and the assumptions of other people as a reason to ignore what we both feel."

"Not hard to ignore something that isn't magical, right?" she threw back.

"What the hell am I supposed to say, Julie? You come in here claiming to have moved on. You haven't reached out to me since walking out of my place, then tell me not to get weird. Am I really supposed to admit that not only did the other day mean something to me, but that I want a whole lot more of you?"

Julie's mouth opened and closed, one hand pressed into her stomach, the other pushed against the door behind her. Words wouldn't come.

"Don't say we can't or we shouldn't be together because of the chance of rumors. Everything that I do causes rumors. That's a weak excuse."

Her eyes snapped to his. "No, it is not."

"Yes, it is, especially when you're using it as a barrier

to ignore what's happening between us. I never took you for a coward, Julie."

Her chin lifted. "I'm not a coward."

"Then don't run from me now."

Dante lowered his head. His warm lips brushed hers before pushing forward, demanding more. Her lips parted, and her hands cupped his face, drawing him closer. Dante's hard body molded to hers. The kiss, deep, challenging, stealing her breath and her thoughts, tore through her instincts to do exactly what he accused her of trying to do—run far and fast before she was trapped and wouldn't be able to protect her heart.

Dante lifted her leg, settling his hips better between her thighs, and thrust his growing erection into her. Moaning low and deep, Julie's hips rolled forward.

A strong hand pulled her blouse from her pants, then slid up her side to cup her breast. His thumb rubbed her turgid nipple. "Don't run from this, Julie." His voice was a dark, husky whisper.

Julie popped open the button of his pants and jerked down the zipper. "Who's running?"

Dante's sexy grin sent thrills through her body. He kissed her again, and Julie gave in to the pleasure. Tomorrow she'd figure out her next move. Tonight she was no one's coward.

Chapter 16

Then she ran.

For the next few weeks, Julie made herself unavailable to Dante, except on her terms. She may not be a coward, but she also wasn't stupid. Her body wanted Dante, but her heart wanted in on the deal. She had to use her mind and be strategic about things. This meant focusing on getting the club opened during the day, not going to the studio every night, not coming over when he called and only having sex with him on her schedule once per week.

The only reason she'd come to his house in the middle of a weekday today was because he'd said he needed to discuss the opening. With her renewed efforts to personally double-check the work of the sprinkler installer Orlando had recommended, they were almost back on schedule, and she needed to give Dante an update. Though she didn't push away the thought that the invite could just be his way of trying to get her in his company. Dante hadn't shown signs of noticing how she was subtly handling their hookups, and if he did notice, he didn't seem to care.

Her hand hovered over the bell, but the sound of a car pulling up in the long drive behind her caught her attention. Turning, she watched Raymond park his black Ferrari next to her rental. He got out, and her smile widened.

"When did you get back?"

Raymond hurried over; his black pants and white T-shirt looked wrinkled while his gold chain flashed in the California sun. When he reached her, he pulled her into a hug. "I just got off the plane. Dante had told me you were coming over here when I couldn't reach you on the phone." After releasing her, he pulled back and scanned her from head to toe. "Are you okay?"

"Yeah, I'm fine. You're right on time. Dante wants to talk to me about the upcoming opening, and I need to give him an update on the progress of the club." She turned and rang the bell.

"Apparently so," Raymond said in a weird tone of voice.

The door opened before Julie could ask what was up with that. The same housekeeper who'd greeted her when she'd woken up in Dante's bed and wandered downstairs answered.

"Come on in," she said. "Dante received a call after buzzing you through the gate. He asked that you wait by the pool. I'll bring out some refreshments."

Julie smiled. "Thank you."

Instead of sitting by the pool, they moved to one of the seating areas in the garden that overlooked the sparkling blue waters of the Pacific. Raymond sat next to Julie on the couch they shared, his arm resting behind her. He watched her intently, searching for something.

Julie shifted in the chair to face him. "What's wrong, Ray?"

He ran his hand over his precisely faded haircut. "Did someone really drug you?"

Julie winced; thinking that Raymond wouldn't have heard the story in another country was crazy. He followed the entertainment sites and blogs more than anyone. Even though Dante ignoring the accusations had prevented the story from blowing up, the entertainment shows had reported on the fight after.

"Yes, but nothing happened. Dante saw what he did and stopped things from getting out of hand."

Raymond rubbed his eyes. "A fight is getting out of hand." He dropped his hand. "Damn, Julie, I should have been here."

"Why? What would have changed if you were in town?"

"I would have been with you. Everyone there would have known you are my girl, and no one would have dared mess with you."

Julie held up a hand. "Whoa, wait a minute. What do you mean, your girl?"

"Come on, Julie—we both know you're my girl."

"I'm your friend, Raymond. You're one of my best friends, but that's all."

Raymond's face turned serious. "You know there's more to us than that." He dropped a hand to clasp one of hers. His palms were sweaty. "We're meant to be together."

Julie's heart jumped into her throat. "Where's this coming from, Ray?"

"I haven't forgotten the promise we made. That when we were ready, when the time was right, if we were still single, we'd be together."

"Ray, that was a promise made when I was crying and heartbroken. I never meant to hold you to it."

"Maybe you didn't, but I took it seriously." He brought her hand to his chest. "You know how I felt about you then. I still feel the same now. Julie, you're the one."

Julie stood up in a rush. She turned to the ocean and shook her head. "I'm not *the one*. Not for you."

Raymond came up behind her. "Yes, you are, and I'm the one for you. I can protect you and make sure no one ever hurts you."

Julie turned to Raymond. "Ray, you're a great friend, and I appreciate the fact that you're always there for me and that you always look out for me. I'm here with the job of a lifetime because of you. I treasure your friendship, but that's all I want. Nothing more."

"We'd be good together." He reached to rub her cheek.

Julie leaned away. "No, we wouldn't."

"How do you know that?"

"Because you taught me too well about the way men think. You're upset about what happened to me, that you weren't here for your homegirl, and thinking that means we should be together. When we both know that anything romantic between us wouldn't work. It didn't work then and wouldn't work now. You're really not ready to settle down, and I don't want to settle with you."

Raymond's face turned hard. "But you're ready to settle down with Dante?"

"No, where's that coming from?"

"There's nothing going on with you?"

She wouldn't lie to her friend. "We hooked up a few times, but there's nothing else. I know that this is just sex and not romance."

"Julie, what did I tell you? When you tell a guy that

you're not looking for a relationship and are only interested in sex, then that's what the guy hears. He's not going to change his mind or suddenly fall for you."

The truthful words were a dagger in her heart. A dagger she hid behind a smile blanketed in confidence she didn't feel. "I know that."

"You deserve better than that. If I'm not ready, then I know he's not. He's not the guy who turns away the groupies on the road. If anything, he indulges in them. He's lived a life where fame, money and women all come easily."

"I know."

"Do you? Because you deserve so much more than that, Julie," Raymond said earnestly. He brushed her cheek with his hand. "You're better than just another number he can add to the long list of conquests."

Julie squared her shoulders. "Don't worry, Raymond. I'm handling the situation. You think I don't know this thing going on between me and Dante is nothing? I've been very deliberate about keeping my emotions out of things. He's a hookup, nothing more."

Her voice came out sure and confident, when inside she knew she was a liar. If she didn't have to work so hard to control this situation, then she could say every word and mean them. Seeing his love of music, his drive to try something new, even his fear of the unknown, had slowly started the process of etching his name in her heart. She feared she'd have a hard time erasing it.

"Good," Raymond said. "I don't want to see you hurt again. I love you, Julie."

Julie smiled and kissed Ray's cheek. "I love you, too, Ray." The sound of a throat clearing interrupted them.

Julie swiveled toward the sound. Dante smiled, but the look he threw her and Raymond was ice-cold.

Chapter 17

"Sorry for keeping you waiting—my dad was on the phone." Dante had no idea how he kept his voice so cool when boiling-hot jealousy coursed through him.

Julie's wide eyes glanced from him to Raymond and back to Dante. He'd heard most of their conversation, including her refusal of Raymond, and he knew her declaration of love for Raymond wasn't in a romantic sense. That didn't stop the jealousy he felt after seeing her kiss Raymond's cheek and hearing her flippantly call Dante nothing more than a hookup.

"Is everything okay?" Julie asked. Her voice was calm despite the uncertainty in her eyes.

"Yeah, things are all good." Dante strolled around the couch over to her and Raymond. "Raymond, I'm glad you're back in town."

Raymond lifted his chin. "Oh, really?"

"Yes. I was telling my dad about the plans for the nightclub, and he wants to come check out the progress. He's coming with my mom and sister next week. I'm thinking of making it a small dinner party, and I want you to come so that they can hear your thoughts. Maybe if they hear that you're interested in offering different types of music, they won't think I'm so crazy."

Raymond chuckled. "You're not crazy. I think people will flock there despite the music. You're Dante Wilson— you can have whatever you want, whenever you want."

Dante would have normally been okay with that description, but after hearing the way Raymond described him to Julie, he wondered if Raymond was using the words as another veiled warning for Julie to stay away from Dante.

"That doesn't mean I'm capricious about what or who I go for." He looked directly at Julie.

She lifted her chin as the uncertainty in her eyes turned to a mocking disbelief. He could imagine the doubts going through her mind. He didn't have much room to stand on if she were to call bull. He knew she'd pulled back in their relationship. Her actions had him standing on a sea of uncertainty. He wanted to demand that she tell him where they stood, insist that she admit her feelings and do exactly what he hated when women tried to do the same to him. He didn't need to, though, because apparently her feelings were locked safely behind those walls she put up.

Raymond shifted from foot to foot, drawing Dante's attention. "What day next week are you doing this?"

Dante forced his attention back to his parents coming to town. "They'll be here at the end of the week. I'm thinking dinner on Friday night."

"I'll be here."

Dante looked to Julie. "And you?"

"You want me to come?"

"Of course. You're our partner in this project and know more about what's happening with the renovation than I do. Knowing my dad, he'll have questions on that."

She nodded. "Sure, if you want me to be here, then I'll be here."

He wanted her there, not because she worked with him, but because, out of everyone, he knew she was the one who truly believed in his venture. Tightness filled his chest; Dante rubbed the spot. He was actually hurt by her easily tossing him aside.

Raymond's phone rang. "I need to take this." Raymond answered the phone and strolled away.

Dante crossed to Julie. "So I mean nothing to you?"

Julie turned toward the ocean. "We both knew what we were getting into."

"You're running again."

She spun to him and crossed her arms. The wind played with the ends of her bangs, and despite her angry posture, he thought she was beautiful in the tight cream-colored dress. "I'm not running—I'm being honest. Don't play games with me."

"Why do you insist this has to be a game? That I don't want more from you?"

"Then tell me what you envision for our future, Dante. Me moving to California? You moving to Georgia? You deciding that you're ready for a serious long-distance relationship? The agreement that we don't sleep with other people, and then me believing that you'll walk away when another set of eager women are waiting in your hotel room after a concert?"

"I'm not that bad, Julie."

"Aren't you? We won't work. Let's just call this what it was and move on. Don't get caught up in the moment. It's only fleeting."

"I want you to be my girl."

"That's the thing, Dante. I'm a woman, not a girl. I may open nightclubs, but I don't spend my weekends in them. I want a house and kids. I want to sit on the couch watching television and have date nights at the movies. I want a guy who works from nine to five who comes home and kisses me on the cheek, then tells me about his day at the office. Not a guy who calls from his tour bus while his entourage is partying in the background. Tell me you want that, and then we can talk."

He didn't. Not the version she spouted off. "I don't." Her jaw clenched, and pain flashed in her bright amber eyes before she looked away. "But you don't either."

Her gaze whipped back to his. "Excuse me?"

"That life you described doesn't protect you from heartache. I'm not Antwan. I'm not going to make promises I can't keep or say things I don't mean. Do I want to marry you? Hell, I don't know. I don't know if I ever really want to get married. Kids—I can't even imagine. Right now, all I want is you in my life. I don't know how we'd work out, and I can't promise you we will. But that doesn't mean I'm afraid to try. When you're ready to stop making excuses, come and get me."

He turned on his heels and walked away.

Chapter 18

I want you to be my girl.

Julie's stomach fluttered and her knees wobbled. She tried hiding both by smiling at the housekeeper who opened the door to let her into Dante's home.

Those words had floated around Julie's head since he'd uttered them the week before. Each time her heart celebrated, her brain slapped the silly organ into submission. She'd been someone's *girl* before. Played the role of ignoring whispers of infidelity, putting up with the phone calls and the groupies. She wouldn't do that again.

As she followed the housekeeper, Julie stiffened her resolve. She did want a future with a guy who wasn't a part of this life. She would be happy with a house in the suburbs, date nights on the couch and talks of what happened at the office. Dante wasn't into that. Impromptu pool parties, concerts at his home on the weekend and wild parties in Vegas—that was his life.

She entered the spacious living area, and immediately her gaze searched for Dante. He stood across the room talking to his father. She'd recognize Otis Wilson anywhere. He was a superstar in his own right. Otis's blue suit was tailored perfectly to show off a body that nearly rivaled his son's despite the twenty-plus year difference in age. There were a few wisps of gray in his short, curly dark hair.

"Julie," Raymond said from her left.

Dante looked her way. Their gazes locked, and in that second, her heart skipped a beat. Tearing her gaze from Dante, she looked at Raymond. "Hey, Raymond."

"Guess who's coming tonight?" Excitement filled Raymond's voice.

"Who?" she asked, very aware that Dante and his father were crossing the room to them.

"The Roberson family."

Julie's eyes widened. "*The* Robersons?" Raymond nodded, and Julie's brain struggled to process the information. The Roberson family's legacy in music was almost as big as the Wilsons'. Julie loved their music and couldn't suppress her own wave of excitement.

Dante and his father made it to her side. "Julie," Dante said. "This is my father, Otis Wilson."

Julie smiled and held out her hand. Otis's dark gaze sized her up quickly, but she couldn't read his opinion after the quick examination.

"It's a pleasure to meet you, Mr. Wilson," Julie said. Holding back her starstruck grin was difficult.

"The pleasure is all mine, Ms. Dominick. Dante's

told me about the hard work you've put into opening our nightclub."

Julie glanced quickly at Dante, whose jaw hardened into a hard line. "I didn't realize you had an interest."

"I have an interest in every venture taken by my family. The Wilson name and legacy is the most important thing to me. I can't ignore anything that may hurt either."

His voice was smooth but underlined with steel. This nightclub was Dante's way to try his hand at building his own dream, his own legacy. She'd forgotten Dante said his father didn't support his plans. From the tone of Otis's voice, Julie guessed he had other ideas for the place. The thought disturbed her far more than it should.

"You know my wife and daughter, no doubt."

Otis turned to Vivica and Star, who had risen from the couch. They crossed the room looking like music royalty. Vivica's short, stylish hair was a deep russet color that complemented her light eyes and the deep red scooped-neck shirt she'd paired with black pants. Dante's sister, Star, wore a blue-and-white dress that clung to her curves while her jet-black hair hung to the middle of her back.

"Again, it's an honor to meet you both." She glanced to Star. "I've listened to your music and loved it for years."

Star gave a sincere smile and shook Julie's hand. "I'm glad you enjoyed it."

Otis turned to Julie. "What did you think of her last album?"

Star stiffened, and Otis watched Julie closely. Julie was well aware that her last album had been a flop that resulted in Star being ridiculed from those in and out of the industry.

"It was different," Julie said.

Otis smirked. "A nice way of saying the album was terrible. I told her not to do it."

"Actually, I liked the song on there about not being the guy's doormat," Julie said. "That was my favorite. I admire people who try something different. So many are afraid to leave the status quo."

"I appreciate that," Star said.

Vivica smiled at Julie. "How are things coming with the nightclub?"

"Very well. We had a few challenges but were able to get things back on track."

Raymond rubbed Julie's back. "Julie always handles her business."

Dante's eyes zeroed in on the movement, and Julie fought hard not to step away from Raymond.

"Does she now?" Otis said, his eyes also on the hand still at Julie's lower back. "How long have you two known each other?"

"Six or seven years," Raymond said. "Julie and I have been good friends since college."

"Raymond's like a brother to me." She looked to Dante but couldn't read much in his expression.

"And Julie's my heart," Raymond said.

Before she could reply, the rest of the guests arrived. Otis and Vivica were all bright smiles and hugs when the Robersons arrived. Julie's own lips spread with her excitement, which was short-lived when their daughter, Missy, came into the room. The five-foot-nine-inch pop singer was gorgeous: golden-brown skin, long blond hair and a body that was nothing but curves. A grown man's fantasy in a might-as-well-be-Velcro black dress that clung so good.

"Dante," Missy said in a throaty purr. Dante smiled and kissed the woman's cheek.

Julie's stomach soured. Dante and Missy had been music's most famous couple about four years ago. You couldn't turn on the television or open a magazine without seeing the two together.

Raymond moaned softly next to Julie. "She is so sexy."

Julie cut her eyes at Raymond. "And here I thought I was your heart."

Raymond grinned at Julie. "You had your chance to nab me the other day."

"How easily you move on," she said, teasing.

"You are my heart, Julie. Just because we agreed not to be in a relationship, it doesn't change the fact that I care about you. You're my oldest and closest female friend. You'll always be in my heart. No matter who you end up with."

"Raymond, sometimes I forget that beneath that playboy exterior of yours is the good guy who helped me mend my broken heart."

Raymond's devilish smile returned. "You're my girl, Julie. Remember that when I try to go home with Missy tonight."

Julie laughed and pushed Raymond's shoulder. When she glanced back, Dante was watching the two of them. His eyes were guarded. The welcoming smile he'd had when Missy came in was gone.

Dante cleared his throat and glanced away. "Now that everyone is here, we can eat."

Missy put her hand in Dante's. Julie wanted to slap Missy's hands out of Dante's.

"Looks like my chances are slim," Raymond said.

"Not surprising. I overheard Otis telling Dante he should get back with Missy. He says it'll be good for business."

"Did he agree?"

"He didn't disagree," Raymond said.

Julie swallowed hard. Lifting her chin, she pushed away the hurt. This was for the best.

She zeroed in on Dante and Missy. Dante looked at her briefly, then turned to lead Missy into the dining area. *You pushed him away. Men like Dante don't sulk.*

"We should go," Julie said, dismissing the thought. Raymond nodded and put his hand on her lower back again to escort her to the dining room.

Jealousy seared through Dante's gut like battery acid, preventing him from enjoying the meal. He felt like he was in some crazy parallel universe. Julie on Raymond's arm, laughing with him like they were…well, old friends. Him, entertaining Missy after his dad mentioned, after the fact, that he'd invited the Robersons to dinner. In a heartbeat, he and Julie had gone from lovers to this distant business-friendly relationship.

"Dante," Otis said. "Despite the fight, I heard good things about the song you did at your party."

Dante snapped his mind out of the clouds and focused on his father. "I'll admit that even I was surprised at how much they liked my collaboration with S.A.F. I'm sure an album with them will be hot."

Otis scowled. "I'm not talking about that. I mean your collaboration with Antwan."

Missy ran her fingers over Dante's arm. "It's hot, Dante, just like you."

Dante gripped the fork in his hand. "I'm not going to do the album with Antwan."

Otis leaned back in his chair. "Yes, you are. We've already started promoting the upcoming collaboration. You need to do everything you can to keep the momentum going." He looked meaningfully between Dante and Missy.

Dante knew the meaning behind that look, and understood the reason the Robersons and Missy were at dinner. An album with Antwan combined with a reunion between Dante and Missy would mean the federal government couldn't print money fast enough to keep up with the sales.

Dante glanced at Julie, but she studied her food. He wondered if seeing him with Missy caused the same battery-acid corrosion of her insides that he felt when he thought of her with Raymond.

"I'm not interested in owning the charts. I'm ready to do my own thing, including the nightclub."

"Don't you care anything about our family's legacy?" Otis vented.

Dante looked back at his father. "You know that I do."

"Building and holding a legacy takes planning. You've got to lay the groundwork. One year—hell, six months without proving that you belong at the top is enough time to make others forget your contribution to the music industry."

Vivica leaned forward. "Your father is right, Dante. After your sister's last album, we need to do whatever it takes to remind people that the Wilson legacy is still strong."

Star flinched but didn't disagree. Dante hated to see how she just took her parents using her failed album as putting them on the cusp of ruin.

"People love a comeback," Dante said. "When Star

puts out new music, then they'll love her, and no one will care about that one album."

Star smirked. "That's not true, Dante, and you know it. They'll move on, but they'll never forget. We need a big splash to remind people why W. M. Records is at the top. I agree with Dad—you should do the album with Antwan."

Dante looked to Missy. "What do you think?"

The smile on her beautiful face made most men lose their ability to speak. "I support you in everything you do, Dante." Her hand rubbed his arm, and she lowered her eyes prettily. "But I do agree with your family. I know your little project is important, and you can still dabble in that after doing the song with Antwan." She lifted her eyes and dropped her hand to his knee. "Then we can collaborate again. I miss working with you."

Her tone implied that she missed a lot more than a musical collaboration. Dante shifted until her hand fell away from his knee. He glanced again at Julie, but this time, she was studying the art on the wall. He'd think she didn't care if her jaw wasn't clenched so tight. Hope blossomed in his chest. She was jealous, and if she were jealous, that meant she had to care.

"That's nice, Missy, but I want someone who'll support me, my new music and my plans. Not just encourage me to do the same thing over and over."

Star grunted. "Dante, don't be crazy. You saw how the press obliterated me after this last album."

Dante turned to his sister. "That's because you were insincere. You were trying to be something you're not, and people saw that."

"Wouldn't you be doing the same with this album?"

Julie made a noise, and everyone looked her way. She

glanced around the table, then met Dante's eyes. "No, he wouldn't. I've heard the music and seen him perform with S.A.F. Dante's really into this sound—you can hear it, feel his intensity with every note. It's not the same as his other music. It's more real. More him."

A swirl of emotion Dante was too unfamiliar with to name rose in his chest. That's why he wanted her.

Otis grunted. "That's a nice sentiment, Ms. Dominick, but sentiment isn't what sells music."

"I'd disagree," Julie said. "Music speaks to people. A song can make you laugh, cry, fall in love. Music is nothing but a mixture of various sentiments, and that's what makes you love an artist. If their music pulls at something deep inside of you, you never forget. When you hear the same emotions you're struggling with in one of their songs, it becomes your favorite."

Otis raised his chin and regarded Julie for several seconds. "I can't disagree with you on that."

"Then would you agree that if Dante does music with Antwan, even though he doesn't want to, people may notice the disconnection?"

Otis's eyes narrowed. "Well said, Ms. Dominick."

"Julie," she said, raising her chin.

Otis watched her for a second, then turned back to Dante. "Did I tell you that I saw Octavia Quinn in New York last week?" Otis said, referring to another music producer.

Dante let his dad change the subject. For Otis to do so meant he needed to consider Julie's point. The argument with Otis wasn't over, but Julie had given him another weapon in the war. Dante glanced at her and gave her a thankful smile. Her quick argument had probably done more to make his case than anything he could have ever said to his own father. Otis loved his kids, but he also was used to running their lives, especially when it came to music.

Missy shifted at his side, and placed her hand on his knee again. Julie turned to talk to Raymond, and in that beat, the connection was gone.

Chapter 19

"I appreciate the way you stood up for my son in there," Otis said as they left the dining room and walked into the sitting room. He stopped her at the door. "You must really care about him."

"Caring has nothing to do with it. Like I said to Star, I admire those who are willing to go after their dreams."

Otis nodded. "I work with Nexon-Jones, and I know why you really left."

"What is it that you think you know?"

"That you brought up a complaint against the owner after he offered you a project if you were willing to sleep with the client."

"A project isn't worth my self-respect."

"Because of that, I don't believe the rumors that you're out here because there's something going on between you and Dante. I need you to remember that you are his business partner only. While I appreciate your willingness to step in and offer your support, at the end of the day, Dante always does what's right for the family. He'll make the album with Antwan, and he'll get back together with Missy. Both are good for business, despite any sentiments that may temporarily distract him."

The words had their desired effect. She was just a temporary person in Dante's life. Her small amount of support while she was out here would not change a lifetime of choices. People didn't change unless they wanted to, and Dante had given no real signs that he wanted to change his lifestyle. He just accused her of not being truthful about what she wanted.

"I'm very aware of that. I'm here to get the nightclub opened. Whatever happens after that is up to Dante."

She nodded at Otis and walked farther into the room. Dante watched her from where he stood with Missy. The beautiful singer talked, but he didn't appear to be listening. There was something different in his eyes as he watched her. Something she wanted to believe was an emotion deeper than lust. But she knew the rules. She'd stood up for him, and now he was grateful.

She was ready to go back to her hotel room and try not to think about how her unavailability left plenty of room for Missy to snuggle up in his bed. She walked over to Dante and Missy. "I'm going to leave now. Thank you for inviting me to dinner."

Dante frowned. "Are you sure?"

"Yes, it's been a long week, and I'm tired."

Raymond came over. "Julie, you're leaving. I can give you a ride back to your hotel."

Julie shook her head. "No need, I drove."

"Before you go, do you have a few minutes? I want to talk to you about the opening," Dante said.

She'd given him an update yesterday and was about to refuse when Missy shifted closer to Dante and stared at him with barely disguised lust. *Looks like Raymond's hopes are dashed.*

"Sure, let's talk," Julie said.

"We can talk in my office." He stepped away from Missy. "Just give us a few minutes."

"Hurry back," Missy said.

Julie followed Dante out of the sitting room and into his office down the hall, a room with gleaming modern furniture, a high-end computer and posters of his album covers on the wall, including the one with him in nothing but a pair of boxers. The album was titled *Sex*, and it was released when she was nineteen. She'd drooled over that picture too many times that year.

Julie didn't go far into the room and stood right inside the door. Dante pushed the door closed and leaned his hand against the wood. He watched her, his dark eyes swimming with what made her want to be his girl.

"What did you want to know?" She took a step backward.

"That was an excuse to get you in here. Thank you for what you said at dinner."

Julie shrugged. "I'm nothing if not honest."

"That you are. Even though you've been to the studio and listened to us play, I hadn't realized you felt that way about my music."

He leaned forward and stared at her.

"I love your music. The music you're making is beautiful, vibrant and full of everything that makes you who you are."

"I put everything I have into my music." He crossed his arms and leaned on the door. "Sometimes I think about the arguments my dad makes. I don't want to do the same mainstream stuff everyone else is doing, but I don't know what to do if I fail."

"They are right. Your song with Antwan is hot, so you still have some spark for what you've been doing."

"That's because I love music. Early in my career, everything was new. I didn't care much as long as I got the next hit, owned the charts—" he met her eye "—landed the girls. Now it's not so much about that. I still care about my brand, but I've fallen in love with the actual creativity of my job again. Now that I've rediscovered my love of creating something, I don't know if I can give it up."

He sounded so conflicted, as if he had already accepted that he would have to give up his dream. As someone who understood how hard fighting for success could be, she reached out and cupped his face in her hands. Dante blinked and focused his dark eyes on her. "Then don't give up."

The smile he gave her was small, sad. "It's easier to believe I can do this when you're around. When you leave, it'll be the status quo again."

"You started this before I ever came into your life. You'll finish when I'm gone."

She pulled her hand back. His shot out to gently grab her wrist. He pulled her against him. Julie pressed her palm to his hard chest. The heavy beat of his heart tapped against her palm, every vibration resonating through her body.

"I meant what I said the other day. Don't talk about leaving as if it were nothing." His hand gripped her waist, holding her closer until the heat of his body seeped into her bones.

"I never said leaving you would be easy."

Dante shifted forward, his chest brushing the hardening tips of her breasts. His warm hand released her wrist to brush against her jaw. Julie's heart thudded, pumping blood through her in quick spurts.

"No rules, no games, just the truth. You don't like me saying I want you to be my girl, fine—I won't say that. But I do want you, Julie. You can argue all day about wanting some quiet life with some quiet guy who's squeaky-clean, but that won't satisfy you."

"How do you know that?"

"Because there is fire and fight in you. You'd eat a guy like that up, then spit him out in no time. You need a guy who isn't going to back down when you toe the line and won't let you use excuses to talk yourself out of going for what you want."

"Maybe so, but that doesn't mean you're the right guy."

"Maybe I'm not. I can't say for sure that I'm your forever guy, but I know one thing—if we don't try to make this work, we'll both regret it."

"You won't have time to regret it. Raymond overheard your dad saying he wants you and Missy back together. Otis repeated the same thing to me."

"My dad said that to you?"

"Yes. See, you've already got your rebound set up. I'm moving aside with no drama. You're free to be with Missy."

She tried to step away, but his grip tightened on her waist. He pulled her forward, his eyes flashing with desire. "I'm not begging Missy to be with me right now, am

I? No games, no rules, just honesty. Tell me right now, Julie, that you don't want to give this a try."

She shook her head and looked away. "I don't want to—"

He cut her off with a kiss. The lie she was about to tell was forgotten, no longer important because his lips were on hers. No matter how hard she tried to control her cravings for this man the second their lips touched nothing else mattered. Her hands clenched his shirt and pulled him closer. His head tilted, and the soft sweep of his tongue against her lips was his sensual demand for more. Julie quickly parted her lips. Her arms lifted to wrap around his neck.

Only a kiss. That's all she was going for. His hand on her waist moved to grip her ass and pulled her farther into his body. No way could she walk out that door without more.

Dante's strong arm lifted her. Their bodies moved before he set her down on the top of the table next to the door. Vaguely, she thought about the room full of people next door, how easily they could get caught and why they should stop. Then his hands were on her breasts. His fingers rubbing and squeezing the heavy flesh, toying with her aching nipples. Julie jerked up his shirt and ran her hands over the hard planes of his stomach. Between slitted lids she watched him in the dim lights. She watched the play of his muscles beneath his shirt, the fire burning in his dark eyes and the urgency of his movements. He wanted her, and in that second, she wished for forever.

"Dante," she whispered his name.

His head rose, and he brushed his fingers through her short hair. "Julie." His voice was low, deep, possessive.

Long fingers pushed her skirt up and slipped into the side of her panties.

Eyes rolling upward, Julie's head fell back, her legs widened. Pulling her head forward with the hand that was in her hair, Dante claimed her mouth with another searing kiss. Julie unbuttoned his pants, freeing him from his briefs. Her fingers wrapped around the hard length before slowly sidling down to gently cup the heavy sac beneath.

Stepping back only to push down his pants and pull out a condom, Dante slid on the protection, then came back to kiss her. One hand pushed her panties to the side. He positioned himself at her opening, then thrust forward.

"Mmm, Dante, yes," she moaned. Her leg wrapped around his waist.

He gripped her waist with one hand; the other cupped her face. He kissed her slowly, thoroughly, while his body pushed in and out. His entire body tensed, humming with the same pleasure that had Julie panting and moaning. He broke the kiss to suck on her neck. Inhaling deeply, he groaned. "Damn, Julie."

Hips pumping harder, Dante broke her walls. All the emotions she didn't want him to expose tumbled around inside her. She was screwed, so royally screwed for falling for a guy like him. A guy that made her want to try to make something work and trusted that they could. Her body shattered in waves of pleasure. Her leg squeezed him tighter, and her vision blurred.

Dante's rhythm slowed, then stopped. The world came back into focus. He lifted his head, the triumph in his eyes unmistakable. His hand squeezed her thigh. "Be my lady, Julie. Say you'll be mine."

Her body froze. The words were different, but the situation and the tone all the same—words asking for a for-ever that came right after sex. *Never trust what was said during sex*, another rule she followed. Words of love and promises of forever could always be blamed on throes of pleasure, and when brought up later, considered unfair. She'd say yes and think she and Dante could work, only to find him back to his old arrogant ways in no time.

She pushed Dante away and jumped off the table. When he reached for her, she pulled away.

"Julie, what's wrong?"

She kept her back to him while she fixed her skirt. "I've got to go." He reached for her again, but she opened the door and escaped.

Chapter 20

"I had sex with him, on a table, with his parents in the next room."

A heavy sigh came through Julie's cell phone after her confession. Julie pictured Evette cringing on the other end.

"You didn't?"

"I did, which is why I need to go ice queen and leave him alone. I don't think straight when I'm with him."

"Sometimes you don't want to think straight."

Julie snorted and stared out of her hotel window at the mountains in the distance. "Not thinking straight gets you in trouble."

"But sometimes it can lead to a lifetime of happiness."

Julie rolled her eyes because Evette wasn't there to see it. "Who do you know that's had a lifetime of happiness with a guy like Dante? First I was a challenge and didn't just fall into his bed. Now that I have, I'm an interesting conquest, but that's it."

Be my lady, Julie. Say you'll be mine.

Dante's words rang through her head. But words spoken after sex, on a table, with his family one wall over, were not words that made a strong foundation for a relationship.

"Can you, for once, stop analyzing everything a man does in a relationship and just go with things?" Evette asked.

"This has nothing to do with my rules." So what if not trusting words spoken during sex was one of her biggest rules?

"It has everything to do with them. You're probably reciting them in your head right now."

Damn Evette and her insightfulness. "Maybe I should recite them constantly. From the moment I got here, I've ignored my rules and got involved with Dante. I need to finish this project and get the hell out of California."

"Look, I can't say whether or not Dante is the right guy for you. He is a big party guy and is linked to a lot of different women, but—"

"How can you possibly have a but?"

"But," Evette said, enunciating the *t*, "knowing that you've gone against your normally rigid stance, I think you have some feelings going on for the guy. And," Evette said in a hurry, as if she could sense Julie opening her mouth to argue, "for him to ask you to try to make things work between you makes me believe there's more going on than raging libidos and a need for a conquest."

"Maybe, but that also doesn't mean the lifetime of happiness you referred to. Before I lost my mind and slept with him on a table—"

"With his parents in the next room."

Julie groaned. "Before all that, he was laughing with his beautiful ex-girlfriend, who stuck to him better than pantyhose in the summer. His dad wants them back together to boost his career, and there's a good possibility he's going to be working with Antwan."

"Good possibility isn't definite fact. He screwed you on a table, not his beautiful ex-girlfriend. Points to Julie."

Julie thought about the intense pleasure from that incident and twisted her thighs together. "Who knows what he did after I left."

"If you would've stayed, he probably would've screwed you on another table, then the bed, maybe even the pool."

"Evette, stop!" Julie jumped up from the chair. Her mind and body going into sexual overdrive with all the possibilities. "None of that matters. He's just like Antwan, and I'm not going down that road again. He's not the guy for me."

"Then who is the quote-unquote guy for you, Julie?" Evette asked with exasperation.

"Huh?"

"Who's this dream guy you're waiting on? You are hit on by more men than anyone I know. Most women would love to have the guys you repeatedly shoot down ask them on a date. You keep saying you're waiting for someone outside of the business, but even when you meet a guy like that, you never trust him enough to let him get close. I'm not telling you to ride off into the sunset with Dante, but you need to take a long, hard look at yourself and what you really want. Because for someone who says they eventually want a relationship, you're too mistrusting to ever get there."

Evette's words stung. That was the way with the truth.

Julie ran her hand over her face and sighed. "I just don't want to get hurt."

"I know. Antwan broke your heart. Raymond wanted to be the next guy, but he was too busy sleeping with anything with two X chromosomes. A lot of the men we meet are just trying to play games, but that's life. You and every other woman out there are dealing with the same thing. Eventually, you have to stop using not wanting to get hurt as an excuse to throw away a chance at love or just accept that you're old and bitter."

"I'm not bitter."

"I can get a thesaurus and look up another word for it, but the meaning's the same."

Julie wasn't ready to cave in just yet. "You heard about the fight—there are already rumors that I got this job because I'm sleeping with Dante. If I openly date him, then what? More proof that my big projects are because I'm involved with the men."

"It doesn't matter if you never sleep with a client, people will always make their own judgments. Next excuse?"

"Once this project is done, I'm back in Atlanta, and he's still here trying to decide if he should hook up with his ex."

"Okay, that's kind of a good one," Evette admitted. "But not good enough to not even try. There was a chance Dominant Development would fail, but you still gave it a try. Stop being afraid, and admit that you're really into Dante."

"Fine. I am." Julie stomped her foot. Frustration and fear bubbled in her stomach. "I can't let myself hope that he feels the same. I can't go with my feelings and get caught up in thinking that this will be a real relationship only to end up exactly where I was years ago, heartbroken, when he tells me I've become one of many. So, yes, there's more going on. Yes, I feel like I'm falling in love with him. Yes, I want to give this a try, but for my own self-preservation, I'm keeping my focus on opening this club and leaving without him ever knowing how I feel."

Julie sucked in several ragged breaths. Her heart pounded. Evette didn't immediately answer. Guess that was the way of things when someone, normally so put together, had an outburst over the telephone. A rush of words that proved just how scared Julie was.

"Oh, Julie." Evette's voice had the sympathetic and comforting tone of a mother about to give heartwarming advice to a forlorn teenager.

Julie didn't want to hear it. Evette hadn't been humiliated and broken the way Julie had when Antwan laughed at her in front of a club full of people.

"I've got to go. I'll call you tomorrow." Julie ended the call before Evette could finish.

Chapter 21

Dante burst into the studio. His mind still reeled over how easily Julie ran away the night before. He'd never, *ever*, put himself out there like that. He'd asked—no, practically begged for a woman to admit that she had feelings for him. That wasn't what Dante Wilson did. He was supposed to be in control of his own life, his own destiny. Now he was fluttering in the wind. He was caught up in a relationship Julie didn't want while simultaneously being forced to make an album he didn't want.

"What's wrong with you?" Terrance asked. He and Tommy stood next to the piano reviewing music.

"Too many people in my head trying to tell me what to do," Dante answered.

"The album with Antwan?" Tommy asked.

Dante nodded, not willing to admit the feelings he had for Julie also contributed to his foul mood.

"My dinner with my family last night was supposed to persuade them that opening this nightclub and doing my own thing to promote Strings A Flame and our music is what I should be doing next. Instead, they invite Missy, have already started promoting this new album and, based on the latest blog by our friend Gary—" Dante pulled out his cell and waved it "—Missy and her family having dinner at my house last night marks the beginning of us getting back together."

He slammed the cell on the top of the piano. Rubbing his eyes with the heels of his hands, Dante clenched his teeth to keep from yelling his frustration.

Terrance frowned and leaned one arm on the piano. "Wasn't Julie there? How did she take things?"

Dante dropped his hands and smirked at Terrance. "Remarkably calm. She basically told me to move on, and that I'm free to pursue whatever I want with Missy."

Right before making love to him and joining his heart with hers. Even if she didn't realize that.

"I don't believe that," Terrance said.

"You didn't see the impassive look in her eye when she said it." Or feel the pain in Dante's chest that resulted afterward.

"Julie was here in the studio cheering you on. I see the way she looks at you. That woman is crazy about you."

"Well, she's not crazy about being crazy about me. She doesn't want a relationship with me. She wants to go back to Atlanta, and find some guy outside of the music industry to settle down with. Some guy who won't have groupies throwing panties at him after a show or twin supermodels offering threesomes at parties."

Tommy chuckled. "That is your life."

"That was my life before Julie. It wouldn't be my life if I had Julie."

"Did you tell her that?" Terrance asked.

Dante looked at Terrance and shrugged. "I did, but she doesn't believe me. She won't say it, but I know she's comparing me to Antwan."

Tommy scowled. "Why?"

"Because they dated once, and he treated her like he treats most women." Dante's voice filled with disgust. Mostly for himself—he'd treated women the same. Beautiful conquests with little regard to what happened when he was ready to move on.

Tommy and Terrance flinched. "He may make good music," Tommy said. "But he's not the person I'd recommend as the example for what it's like to date a musician."

"Tommy's right, Dante," Terrance said. "You've got to show her that you're serious."

"How can I show her that when she's not even willing to give me the chance to prove myself?"

"By not giving up and doing something she wouldn't expect from a guy who was only interested in having a little fun."

Dante sat on the piano stool and ran a hand over his face. He thought about what he'd done the night before and chuckled.

"What?" Terrance asked.

"I wrote a song about her. I haven't done that in years—written a song about a particular woman. Last night, I couldn't get the feelings out of my head until finally I grabbed a notebook and started writing."

Tommy held out his hand. "Let us see."

"It's no good. Just some feelings running in my head. Nothing that needs to see the light of day."

Tommy didn't drop his hand. "Words written with feeling always deserve to see the light of day."

Terrance nodded. "He's right, Dante. Let us hear the lyrics."

Dante looked at the two brothers. Heat burned across his neck and cheeks. They'd think he was crazy or that he was crazy in love. He never should have said anything about writing the music. Damn sure shouldn't have spent the night writing a song about a woman who'd turned him down more than any other woman he'd ever met.

He glared at Tommy's outstretched hand, then met his expectant look. They were musicians; they wouldn't laugh. Hopefully.

Sighing heavily, Dante pulled out the notebook in his backpack and slapped bound pages into Tommy's hand. Terrance scooted next to his brother and took a look. For several tense seconds, Dante watched as they read over the words that had thrummed through his mind the night before.

"Have you thought of the beat to go with it?" Terrance asked.

"Not quite. I'm hearing something, but it's not coming clear," Dante answered.

"Tell us what you're thinking—let's see what we can do."

Dante raised a brow. "Are you sure? This really isn't for production."

Terrance slapped the back of Dante's head. "Play the damn beat."

Dante rubbed the back of his head and glared at Terrance, who didn't look the least bit regretful.

"Fine," Dante gritted out. He swung around on the piano stool. Running his fingers along the cool keys, he took a deep breath, then strummed out the start of a melody that hovered at the back of his mind.

Terrance nodded, listening to the music. He picked up his violin and began to play, adding to Dante's piano melody. Tommy headed to the drums instead of picking up his own violin. He tapped out a beat, and instantly Dante could hear the song coming together.

For the next hour, they worked on the song. When the rest of the group came in, Dante gave them the pieces of the melody they'd worked out and continued to practice. By the end of the set, the words that hovered in Dante's mind were transferred from the notebook to the pages of several sheets of music. A rough draft, to say the least, but very close to being the finished product.

His cell phone rang after they ran through the song again. It was Otis. "Hold up, guys, I need to take this call."

He answered the phone on his way out and to the office next door.

"I'm calling to see if you're available for dinner with the Robersons again tonight. I think it'll be good to get reservations at Arata where you and Missy can be seen together."

Dante gritted his teeth to keep from cursing Otis out. "No. I'm not going to Arata with the Robersons. I'm not doing the same old songs I've always done, and I damn sure am not getting back together with Missy."

"Are you raising your voice at me?"

"Depends, are you trying to run my life?"

"No one is trying to run your life."

"Then stop thinking that the work I'm doing with S.A.F. is some little project. Stop stomping on my dream to do something different. Stop stepping to the woman

I'm trying to be with and telling her that I belong with someone else. I'm a grown man. I'm not the thirteen-year-old who first started in this business. When I want your advice, I'll ask for it."

There was a long pause. "You're too big for my input now, huh?"

"I'll always value your opinion when I ask for it."

"You don't care about W. M. Records? Getting with Missy and the collaboration with Antwan are all a part of the plan to help revive sales." Otis's voice seethed with frustration and disbelief.

Dante did care. How could he not care for the company that was so much a part of his success? He also cared for his dreams. He couldn't let those go.

"*If* Antwan signs I'll consider a collaboration for his album. That's it."

"Will your mom and I at least see you for breakfast before we leave town tomorrow?" The anger had drained from Otis's voice.

"Yes."

"Good." Otis sighed. "I hope I didn't ruin things with Ms. Dominick."

"Nothing I can't fix." He hoped at least.

They ended the call. Dante felt as if a huge weight was lifted from him as he entered the studio again. Otis didn't say it, but Dante had won the battle.

The guys were all settled around the room. Tommy played the music they'd put together on his violin. Esha and Terrance were on the sofa. Their arms were entwined, and they looked as if there was nowhere else in the world they'd rather be. Longing hit Dante hard. That's what he wanted with Julie. For her to be wrapped in his arms, smiling, happy, content in their relationship.

Tommy stopped playing and looked at Dante. "All good?"

Dante nodded. "All good."

"Alright. Now, what are you going to do with this?" He held up the pages that held the lyrics.

"I'm going to release it," Dante said.

Terrance's head tilted to the side. "You want to get your family's company to release it?"

Dante shook his head. "No. I'm going to release it. Or better yet, S.A.F. will. Independently, without giving my dad or the rest of the suits at his company the opportunity to strip the song of what it truly is. Then we'll put out the rest of our music. Just in time for the opening of the club."

Terrance and the rest of the group brightened with excitement. Exhilaration rushed through Dante's veins. He would step out on his own and pray to God he didn't fall on his face. This was what he really wanted to do. This song, this music, was just as hot as anything else he'd done. He had enough of a fan base to know they'd love it. He hadn't been in the music business for seventeen years and learned nothing.

The only way to convince Otis of that was to do it on his own. If Otis came to Dante later and asked for him and S.A.F. to produce their music for the company, he'd leave that to the group to consider. Though he'd much prefer to keep doing their music on their own. Dante had more than enough clout in the music industry to get his music promoted without the machine behind his father.

"Dante, are you sure we can do this?" Terrance asked. "The club opens in a few weeks. That means we need all of our music ready."

"Our music is ready. I've been delaying putting it out because I've let my dad's offer linger in my mind too long." Terrance nodded, and Dante knew that even though they supported his decision either way, his hesitation was holding them back. "Let's show people what Strings A Flame is about."

Chapter 22

Julie looked around the finished space of the club and smiled. Dark wood and leather furniture, muted gold accents. Across from the stage was a two-sided bar that would serve patrons inside and those sitting outside overlooking the ocean. The place had a warm, welcoming feel. She turned to smile at the building inspector. "Are we good for the CO?"

The inspector wrote something on his inspection form before looking up to meet Julie's eye. None of the same doubt or resentment he'd harbored after the fiasco with the sprinklers was there. Julie knew he'd never admit it, but she'd impressed him with her efforts to turn this project around.

"I'll have the certificate of occupancy ready for you this afternoon. You can open up this weekend with no problems."

Julie's smile broadened, and she held out her hand to shake his. "I'll be there to pick it up before five."

He shook her hand and gave her a hesitant smile before walking out. Julie did a quick spin on her toes before stopping and grinning. She'd done it. She'd opened a nightclub with one of the music industry's biggest stars, in a city she'd never worked in before, only a week behind schedule and slightly above budget. The sprinkler thing had ended up costing them more, but thankfully Dante and Ray hadn't balked at the excess cost. She was just glad that was the only snafu of the entire process.

The opening party for the club the next evening was already one of the most anticipated events in the city. Julie planned to attend. As the developer, she wouldn't dare not be there to see the fruits of her efforts in full effect. She wouldn't stay long. She doubted Dante would even notice if she came or left. After she'd pushed him away, their relationship had been distant. Not that she blamed him. No man she knew would chase after a woman who'd pushed him away the second after they had sex. She'd made her position clear, and he'd respected it. She should be overjoyed, not nearly heartbroken by the thought.

She left the finishing touches to the workers in the nightclub and went back to her hotel. On the ride to the hotel, she called Dante to tell him they were good for tomorrow, but her call went unanswered.

"Dante, it's Julie. I want you to know that I'll pick up the CO for the building this afternoon. Everything is set for the opening tomorrow. If you have any questions, give me a call. I'll be at my hotel."

Her voice was cool, formal. None of the inner turmoil she felt after turning him away showed through. Her biggest rule—never show the other party your hand. Right now, her hand was full of broken hearts. She never should have crossed the line. Now she was in love with a man she couldn't be with. Not truly.

After she ended the call, the commercial on the radio ended, and the announcer spoke.

"And we're back with Dante Wilson here in the studio. Dante tell us about this new nightclub you're opening."

Julie's foot nearly slipped on the gas. She sat forward and twisted the volume knob up until Dante's voice filled the car.

"It's not your typical spot," Dante said. "I want to showcase my music there."

"Your music? Haven't we heard your music for nearly twenty years?"

"You've heard a version of my music, but this is the music that I really want to do. It's a fusion of hip-hop, rhythm and blues, jazz and classical. Throw in some lyrics that speak to what I'm feeling, and you've got a new sound."

"A new sound. After what happened with your sister last year, I'm surprised you're venturing into new territory."

"I'm not here to talk about Star or what she did. I'm only here to promote my music. You've got to do what's in your heart. For most of my career, I did that, but working on this new album with this group has given me a new sense of purpose in my music. The club will showcase them and other artists in the future. For those who don't want to just follow the crowd and are willing to find their own flow, my spot is the place to be."

Julie grinned, knowing that his words were a challenge. No one liked to consider themselves part of the status quo. By promising something different, he would pique the interest of everyone in the vicinity.

"All right, then let's hear some of this new music. Tell me about this song I'm about to play."

"It's something new. Something that was rolling around in my head, and I had to get the words out. I think anyone who's ever fallen in love unexpectedly will relate."

"What do you know about unexpected love?" The announcer's voice dripped with curiosity.

"I know that just when you think things are going great as they are, the perfect person can walk into your life and show you all the things you never knew you wanted. The song is called 'Turned Tables' because I had a woman do that to me. I didn't want or expect to fall, but I did."

"Can I ask who?"

Dante chuckled, and tingles spread across Julie's body. "You can ask, but I won't tell."

The announcer laughed. "Fine, but you know now everyone is going to be anxious to find out who turned the tables on you. You heard it here first. Dante Wilson has fallen in love, and this song is for that lucky woman who landed this sexy man."

Julie's heart and mind raced. She barely heard the first bars of the music or the words to the song. He'd fallen in love? With who? Her? Julie shook her head. That was crazy. They'd barely spoken the past few weeks. He couldn't mean her. He'd never said anything about love. She'd made sure to hide any indication that her feelings were going in that direction.

Don't be silly, Julie. Of course he's not talking about you.

She shook her head again. For once, she didn't want to listen to the voice of reason in her head, to the voice that said to never hope. The voice that was turning her into the bitter woman Evette accused her of being.

Getting out of her head, Julie listened to the words of the song, hoping to get an idea of who he could be talking about.

You turned the tables on me
Snatched my heart and threw it away
You turned the tables on me
Grabbed my love and said no way

I never wanted love
Never wanted to be that guy
But you came into my life
Snuck into my mind
Then turned the tables and snatched my heart away

Julie's heart pounded; her palms sweated. His voice oozed with love and pain. Had she hurt him? No, ending things was for the best. He was considering his dad's deal and would be working with Antwan if he accepted. He had Missy and twin supermodels to fall back on. But this guy, the guy singing, didn't sound like someone waiting on supermodel twins or superstar ex-girlfriends to fill the void.

Without realizing it, Julie had driven to her hotel. The valet attendant watched her through the driver's window, a friendly smile on his face. He probably thought she was crazy. Maybe she was for wanting the song to be about her. Julie got out of the car and handed over the keys. She stood outside in the sunshine, thinking. For the first time in a long time, she felt like her logic concerning relationships may be flawed.

Chapter 23

Julie entered the nightclub at ten the next night. Outside a line trailed past the door with people waiting to get in. Inside people crowded the bar and filled every table. The dim lights reflected off the dark wood and leather furniture. The second floor was reserved for VIPs, and with the best views of the stage, it was crowded with other musicians and celebrities.

Julie wanted to squeal with delight. This had to be the best club she'd opened yet. Thanks to the partnership with Dante and Raymond, she was sure it would be around for years to come. Maybe she and Dante would be together just as long. She wasn't going to push him away anymore. Not if he wrote the song for her.

And if he still wants you. Her stomach fluttered. That was a big *if.*

"Julie." Esha's voice came from the crowd.

Pushing away the doubt, Julie scanned the crowd until she spotted Esha at the bar. Julie wove through the crowd to her side.

"Don't get up," Julie said before Esha could stand. She leaned in to hug her. "Opening night is a hit, huh?"

"To say the least. This is fantastic. But I'm still nervous."

"About the performance?"

Esha's head bobbed up and down, her bright eyes wide. "Yes. Everyone seems to be okay with the music, but the performance will really show what's up."

Julie recognized that the music playing in the background was the fusion sound similar to what S.A.F. played. The bobbing heads and swaying bodies meant so far no one hated the music.

"Don't worry," Julie said. "S.A.F. makes great music. I know people will love it."

"You're just saying that because you need your new nightclub to be a hit."

Julie laughed. "True, but I also want S.A.F. to be successful. I love the music. It deserves to be heard by many."

Esha leaned back against the bar and grinned. "I see why Dante likes you so much. You really do care about what he's doing."

The nervous fluttering in Julie's stomach increased in rhythm. She hadn't called Dante after hearing his song on the radio. Fear of rejection was hard to overcome, and she didn't want him to laugh at her over the phone. Not that getting laughed at in person was any better, but at least face-to-face she could gauge his reaction when he saw her. Would there be elation, desire, the same hope dancing in her, or indifference, disgust, anger? His reaction would set the tone for how she proceeded.

"I am into what he's doing. I just wonder if he's into me as much as I'm into him." Saying the words out loud was kind of freeing.

"You heard the song. I know he is."

"We don't know the song is for me."

"Who else could it be about?"

Missy! the ever-pessimistic voice of reason shouted in her head. She would be optimistic about this. She wanted Dante. She had no clue how or if they could make a relationship work, but if he'd written the song about his feelings for her, she was willing to try.

"Have you seen him?"

Esha shook her head. "Not since earlier. They're about to start the show, so I'm not sure. We can check backstage."

Esha stood, and Julie followed her through the crowd to the back, where they flashed their backstage passes to the security guards. Julie's stomach twisted and fluttered the entire time. She was going to go with her instinct and trust her feelings for Dante. She only hoped she was right for going against all the rules that guarded her heart.

They found Dante and the rest of S.A.F. backstage. Julie's gaze landed on Dante, and she couldn't breathe. Missy stood before him, her arms wrapped around his shoulders. His hands were on her waist. Julie's heart, her hope, shattered into a million jagged pieces. What kind of a fool was she for thinking he'd written a song about her?

Maybe she made a sound. Maybe he felt the sharpness of her gaze. Maybe he just needed a break from staring at the dazzle that was Missy, but Dante looked directly at her. He didn't scramble to pull away from Missy. Instead he slowly slid his arms from around her waist and lowered his head to say something to her. Missy glanced over her shoulder at Julie; she cocked a brow before nodding and stepping aside.

Dante crossed the room to her. Even when her hope for them was broken, she couldn't deny he was devastatingly handsome with a dark shirt, fashionably worn jeans, maroon jacket and platinum chain. He took her breath away, made her body heat with remembrance.

He stopped in front of her. His dark gaze slid over her from head to toe. "You came." He sounded normal, not excited, nervous or even happy.

"Of course I came. I always come to the opening of my new nightclubs."

His head tilted. "Is that the only reason you're here?"

"What other reason do I have to be here?" Admitting the reason she really came now, after seeing him and Missy so close, made her cheeks burn.

His jaw clenched, and he ran a hand over his chin. "I'd hoped…" He trailed off.

"You and Missy look comfortable."

"Missy came to congratulate me and wish me well. She hugged me."

"It looked like a lot more than a hug." God, did she have to sound so jealous? She cleared her throat, looked away and then crossed her arms.

"It wasn't anything more than that. Why do you always have to try to find the bad in things?" He sounded disgusted.

Her heart hurt even more. Her defenses went up. "Because it's hard to trust the good you want to see."

"Do you really want to see the good?"

Before she could answer, Terrance came over. "Dante, it's time to start the show."

Dante frowned but nodded. He turned back to Julie. "We'll finish this conversation later."

He watched her for several more seconds before turning to join Terrance. Julie went back out to join the rest of the crowd. Surrounded by people, she felt alone and silly. She pulled out her phone and texted Raymond. He should be here.

Almost there.

He texted back. Relief swept through her. At least if he was there, he would distract her for a while before he found someone to go home with.

Dante and S.A.F. came onto the stage, and the crowd cheered. Dante grabbed the microphone. "Are you ready to hear my music?"

A series of cheers and "yeahs" vibrated through the air.

"All right, let's do this." He turned to the group. "This is Strings A Flame, also known as S.A.F., and we're ready to show you what we can do."

Dante sat at the piano. The melody was slow, sensual notes hovering in the air. Then came Terrance and Tommy with their violins, and, finally, the drums and the turntables adding the hip-hop flare. The crowd got into the music—clapping, cheering and dancing. Song after song, the ones with Dante on vocals and the ones without, were all received by the crowd with growing enthusiasm.

Julie was so proud to see that the place she'd helped develop had such a fantastic start and how much the crowd responded to Dante's music. No matter what, she knew there would be a place for him in the industry. They went into one of their more upbeat dance numbers. Julie temporarily forgot her shattered dreams as she smiled and danced with the crowd. Then Missy jumped onstage and proceeded to twist and gyrate against Dante, which drove the crowd into further hysterics. Camera phones came out and people cheered them on.

The pain and humiliation from before slapped Julie's midsection. She spun away from the stage. The song ended. The clapping and cheering grew louder. Glancing over her shoulder, she caught Missy onstage, planting a kiss on Dante's lips. The pain in Julie's chest wouldn't have been worse if the crowd had danced on her heart. Squeezing her eyes shut, she swiveled and hurried to the exit. She was just at the door when the notes of the song she'd heard the other day started.

"This last song is dedicated to the woman who stole my heart," Dante said.

Julie froze, her hand on the door.

"One guess who that is." Missy's voice rang through the club.

The crowd cheered. No, the pain could get worse. Without looking back, Julie pushed out into the warm night.

Chapter 24

Dante snatched the microphone from Missy, but it was already too late. Julie was out the door. He glanced at Missy, at the excited crowd chanting for him to sing. His hand squeezed the microphone.

She'd turned him down, several times. She overanalyzed things. She'd automatically assumed the worst earlier. He should let her go. His chest tightened.

Turning, he made eye contact with Terrance and Tommy. They both smiled and nodded toward the door. Dante dropped the microphone and jumped off the stage.

He pushed through the crowd, ignoring the questions and sending up a quick prayer that bailing out on his first performance here didn't completely ruin his nightclub.

"I think Dante's going for the girl he really wants." Terrance's voice rang through the microphone.

Dante glanced back at his friend onstage and gave him the thumbs-up.

"Go get her," Terrance said.

Dante turned and ran from the club. He hoped to catch Julie. She couldn't have gotten her car from valet that quickly.

Outside he was greeted by a flash of cameras that temporarily blinded him. Dante held up his hands and glanced around. Raymond stood next to his Ferrari at the front of the valet line, frowning toward the driver's seat where Julie sat. She slammed the door closed. Raymond sighed and shook his head. A second later, the car jerked away from the curb. *Julie!*

Dante ran toward Raymond. "Julie, stop!" he yelled toward Julie's direction.

Raymond turned toward him as his car kept going. "What are you doing out here?"

Dante pointed toward the retreating vehicle. "Trying to catch Julie."

"She doesn't want to be caught. She said you and Missy were back together."

"I'm not with Missy. I'm not thinking about Missy. Didn't she know that damn song was about her?"

Raymond frowned. "It is?"

"Yes, and despite her efforts to keep pushing me away, I saw the look on her face before she ran out. She's just as crazy about me as I am about her. I want to be with her."

Raymond took a deep breath. "She's going back to her hotel. Have the valet bring your car round and go get her."

Dante briefly considered Raymond's change of heart, but he honestly didn't have time to really get into that. He turned to the valets, knowing that no matter how fast they moved, the time would pass slowly.

"Just treat her right, Dante," Raymond said.

Dante turned and looked at Raymond as if he'd lost his mind. "Of course I'll treat her right. I love her."

The surprise on Raymond's face was comical. The feeling of admitting his feelings for Julie was exhilarating. He loved Julie.

A white BMW pulled up. Dante grinned and ran to the driver's side. After wrenching the door open, he practically jerked his sister out.

"Hey, Dante, what's going on?" Star squealed, scowling at him.

"No time, I need your car. Mine's in valet." He jumped in and put the car in gear. Ignoring the flash of the cameras, stunned looks and Star's screams for an explanation, Dante tore away from the curb.

Julie parked in front of the hotel. A young valet attendant strolled to her door, but she made no move to get out. Her entire body felt numb, startled into shock with the realization that she'd once again been humiliated and heartbroken by a guy at the opening night of one of her clubs. What else should she have expected? Of course he would move on after she pushed him away.

The attendant bent over to peer into her window. She couldn't sit there forever. Smiling weakly, she opened the door. He mumbled something about the night being good, and she wanted to tell the kid to get lost. She just wanted to go in, pack and go home. The club was open, and her part was done. Evette could handle the follow-up. Julie couldn't bear to talk to Dante again.

Tires squealed behind her. Julie spun just as a white BMW swung into the hotel parking area and jumped onto the curb in a haphazard park. Julie hopped back even though the car was far from hitting her.

"What the hell is wrong with you?" she yelled. She was ready to lash out at someone, and the crazy driver seemed like the perfect person.

The door opened, and Dante jumped out. Julie gasped, the hand over her racing heart fell to her side. "Dante?" Her voice was filled with all the longing that she'd denied herself. "What are you doing here?"

He stomped over to her. "Why did you run away?"

She frowned and shook her head. "What?"

"Why did you run away?" He towered above her, snatching her breath away and infusing her with the heat of his body. "If you don't care about me. If you really want me to do whatever I choose, and you don't want to give us a chance, then why did you run out of the club tonight?"

"Because...you and Missy. She said the song was for her."

"Don't be crazy, Julie. The song isn't about her."

"It's not?"

He shook his head. "Julie, who else would the song be about but you? I was happily single. I was enjoying my life, thinking I'd never *ever* want to be with just one woman. Now I'm completely uninterested in another chance with Missy and can't think of anyone but you. I need to know if what you told Raymond is true. That you really don't feel anything for me and this thing between us was just a hookup. Because if that's the case, I'll turn around and go back to the concert." He pointed in the direction he'd come. "It'll hurt like hell, but I'll find a way to forget you."

Julie shook her head. "No. I don't want you to forget me." The words were out before she'd thought about them.

He didn't smile, just took a deep breath and stared at her with dark, wary eyes. "Then what do you want?"

Go hard or go home. She couldn't deny her feelings anymore. "I want you. Even though I know we may not be able to make this work."

The tension left his body, and warm hands lifted to cup her face. "We'll figure things out."

"I don't want you to feel like you're in a relationship that you can't really commit to."

"I can and I want to commit to you. I love you, Julie."

Joy, warmth and desire filled her heart. She smiled so hard her cheeks hurt. "I love you, too." No negative voice of reason made her feel crazy for admitting her feelings.

Dante pulled her into his arms. His firm lips pressed against hers, and she opened her mouth so he could deepen the kiss. The weight of years of fear from the results of trusting her heart with a man lifted from her shoulders. She wanted Dante, no games, no rules. The only rule that mattered was the one that said she was doing the right thing.

Chapter 25

Julie lounged on one of the chairs next to Dante's infinity pool, soaking up sun and drinking a margarita with Esha. Dante was having another one of the pool parties he was able to throw together within thirty minutes. Something that still boggled Julie's mind.

"Do you think he's really coming?" Esha said, grinning behind her glass.

Julie nodded. "In the ten months that I've dated Dante, he hasn't disappointed me yet. I believe him when he says he's coming."

Esha shifted on the chair. "I know that Dante knows him but to actually meet the guy in person…" Esha placed the frosted glass against her forehead. "I might faint."

Julie chuckled. "Better not let Terrance see that."

"Terrance knows that Irvin Freeman is my weakness. I would throw myself at him like a horny teenager if I didn't love Terrance, and if Irvin wasn't in love with that nurse he met."

"Well, good thing you love Terrance."

"You're awfully calm. Aren't you the least bit interested in throwing yourself at him?"

"No. I'm not." She sipped her margarita.

Julie was excited to meet the movie star, Irvin Freeman. The guy was one of Hollywood's biggest leading men—the fantasy of women everywhere, even more so now since he'd met a small-town nurse during a promotional weekend the year before, fallen in love with her and given up his career in front of the camera to be with her. Or so the stories went. Excitement wasn't enough to make her want to look at any guy other than Dante.

"Oh, my God," Esha exclaimed and gripped Julie's arm. "There they are."

Julie looked in the direction Esha stared at. Dante walked out onto the patio with a tall, handsome guy and a cute woman with an open smile. Julie instantly recognized them from the newspaper articles. Hollywood's current *it* couple were garnering a lot of attention from the other people at the party, but Julie only had eyes for Dante. His chest bare, a pair of red shorts sitting low on his hips and the sun shining down on all his sculpted perfection sent heat to her midsection.

She never would have thought she'd be so happy. When he'd asked her to stay on the West Coast after the club opened, she'd agreed. Surprisingly, Evette had encouraged her, even though Julie worried her friend would feel neglected. Julie was already working on another nightclub in LA while Evette oversaw redeeming Dominant Development's name by opening a new place in Miami. They were a two-office operation now. Julie could barely believe it herself.

Dante strolled over with Irvin and his girlfriend, Faith. Esha gushed, and Julie did her own blushing. Irvin didn't tempt her away from Dante, but she had to admit his smile up close was something to behold.

"Told you I know him," Dante said after Irvin and Faith left to change into their bathing suits. He'd promised to introduce her to the movie star after Julie got excited when Irvin earned a nomination for best director.

They sat on the edge of the pool with their feet in the water. Raymond played water polo with the rest of S.A.F.

"Yes, you did. So what do I owe you again?" she asked.

"Hmm, I'll have to think up something that involves you with a minimal amount of clothes."

Julie laughed and leaned into his side. "I don't consider that losing."

He wrapped an arm around her and pulled her in for a kiss. "Neither do I." He sighed and stared at the group in the pool. "So I got a call from my dad today."

"Really? What's up?"

"He wants to sign S.A.F. to the label. The success of the nightclub proved to him that I knew what I was talking about."

"That's great, Dante."

He shrugged. "We're not taking the deal."

Her eyes widened. "You're not?"

"No. I put the offer to the rest of the group, and they all decided we want to remain independent."

"How did your dad take the news?"

"I haven't told him yet. I'm good with the decision. I'll still make music for the label and do a few collaborations like the one I did after they signed Antwan. I can't let W.M. go completely. It's my family legacy, but I want to keep this part of my music separate. I'm happy with the choice."

"I'm proud of you."

He grinned, then kissed her temple. "I heard more good news today, too."

Julie sipped from her glass and laughed when Raymond was hit in the head by the volleyball. "What else?"

"Irvin let it slip that he's going to propose to Faith. I think at the award show later this year."

Julie's eyes widened; her attention swung back to Dante. "That's fantastic. They are such a fairy-tale ending."

"Yeah, I can see that, but it kinda got me thinking that I want us to have our own fairy-tale ending."

"Oh, really?" she asked with a raised brow.

He reached into the pocket of his shorts. "Really." He pulled out his hand and held it up for Julie. A brilliant diamond ring sparkled on his pinkie.

Julie couldn't breathe. Her eyes jerked from the ring to his face. "Are you serious?"

"Yes. I know this is soon, but I also know what I feel. I love you, Julie. I've spent the past seventeen years chasing tail and having meaningless relationships."

"So not the time for that reminder."

"What I mean is, I know what's out there, and I don't want what's out there. I want you. Forever. We'll split our time between here and Atlanta. We'll make things work. I'd just rather make things work with my wife. Not my girl or my lady. Will you marry me?"

No voice of doubt. No pessimism. Just joy and the thought of spending her life with the man she loved. "Yes!"

He kissed her, pulled back to put the ring on her finger, then kissed her again. "I'm going to love you for the rest of my life, Julie. That's one rule I'll never break."

* * * * *

**IF YOU ENJOYED THIS BOOK
WE THINK YOU WILL ALSO LOVE**

**HARLEQUIN
DESIRE**

*Luxury, scandal, desire—welcome to
the lives of the American elite.*

Be transported to the worlds of oil barons, family dynasties,
moguls and celebrities. Get ready for juicy plot twists,
delicious sensuality and intriguing scandal.

6 NEW BOOKS AVAILABLE EVERY MONTH!

*Alaskan senator Jessup Outlaw needs an escape...
and he finds just what he needs on his Napa Valley
vacation: actress Paige Novak. What starts as a fling
soon gets serious, but a familiar face from Paige's past
may ruin everything...*

Read on for a sneak peek of
What Happens on Vacation…
by New York Times *bestselling author Brenda Jackson.*

"Hey, aren't you going to join me?" Paige asked, pushing
wet hair back from her face and treading water in the
center of the pool. "Swimming is on my list of fun things.
We might as well kick things off with a bang."

Bang? Why had she said that? Lust immediately took
over his senses. Desire beyond madness consumed him.
He was determined that by the time they parted ways at
the end of the month their sexual needs, wants and desires
would be fulfilled and under control.

Quickly removing his shirt, Jess's hands went to his
zipper, inched it down and slid the pants, along with his
briefs, down his legs. He knew Paige was watching him
and he was glad that he was the man she wanted.

"Come here, Paige."

She smiled and shook her head. "If you want me, Jess,
you have to come and get me." She then swam to the far
end of the pool, away from him.

Oh, so now she wanted to play hard to get? He had no problem going after her. Maybe now was a good time to tell her that not only had he been captain of his dog sled team, but he'd also been captain of his college swim team.

He glided through the water like an Olympic swimmer going after the gold, and it didn't take long to reach her. When she saw him getting close, she laughed and swam to the other side. Without missing a stroke or losing speed, he did a freestyle flip turn and reached out and caught her by the ankles. The capture was swift and the minute he touched her, more desire rammed through him to the point where water couldn't cool him down.

"I got you," he said, pulling her toward him and swimming with her in his arms to the edge of the pool.

When they reached the shallow end, he allowed her to stand, and the minute her feet touched the bottom she circled her arms around his neck. "No, Jess, I got you and I'm ready for you." Then she leaned in and took his mouth.

Don't miss what happens next in...
What Happens on Vacation...
by Brenda Jackson, the next book in her
Westmoreland Legacy: The Outlaws series!

Available March 2022 wherever
Harlequin Desire books and ebooks are sold.

Harlequin.com

Love Harlequin romance?

DISCOVER.

Be the first to find out about promotions,
news and exclusive content!

f Facebook.com/HarlequinBooks

🐦 Twitter.com/HarlequinBooks

📷 Instagram.com/HarlequinBooks

📌 Pinterest.com/HarlequinBooks

You Tube YouTube.com/HarlequinBooks

ReaderService.com

EXPLORE.

Sign up for the Harlequin e-newsletter and
download a free book from any series at
TryHarlequin.com

CONNECT.

Join our Harlequin community to
share your thoughts and connect
with other romance readers!
Facebook.com/groups/HarlequinConnection